DASH and DINGO

IN SEARCH OF THE TASMANIAN TIGER

CATT FORD
AND
SEAN KENNEDY

Published by
Dreamspinner Press
4760 Preston Road
Suite 244-149
Frisco, TX 75034
http://www.dreamspinnerpress.com/

Dash and Dingo

Cover Art by Paul Richmond paulrichmondstudio.com

ISBN: 978-1-61581-066-6

Printed in the United States of America
First Edition
September, 2009

eBook edition available
eBook ISBN: 978-1-61581-067-3

To all those who dream of adventure
and believe in the impossible,
even when the evidence
speaks to the contrary.

When the stars threw down their spears,
And watered heaven with their tears,
Did he smile his work to see?
Did he who made the Lamb make thee?

Tyger! Tyger! burning bright
In the forests of the night,
What immortal hand or eye
Dare frame thy fearful symmetry?

—William Blake

AUTHORS' NOTE

ONE of the problems of writing something set in a time different from your own is that you have to pay attention to and reflect the sensibilities of that period. This includes the use of certain terms that have become "loaded" since then. In the case of *Dash and Dingo*, we have used the word "Aborigine" and other derogatory terms to refer to the native people as it was in Australia's past. In contemporary society many indigenous people of Australia find the word offensive as it is linked to colonization and the injustices that were inflicted upon them, the ramifications of which are still found today. Although Henry and Dingo display attitudes that may have been revolutionary for the time, although they were not alone in them, they still would have been unaware of the future weight of the word.

The last known thylacine, which died in the Beaumaris Zoo in Hobart in 1936, was known as Benjamin. Despite the name, however, there are many conflicting reports as to the proper sex of the tiger. We had to choose one for the purposes of our story, and we have elected to make Benjamin female.

—C.F. and S.K.

PROLOGUE

"DINGO! NO!"

The wall of water was upon them so quickly that Henry barely had time to jump clear with Dingo's pack. The compression of the walls of rock upstream released just as the river reached their clearing, making the water surge past them at breakneck speed.

Dingo made a snatch for the heavy bag, overbalanced, and fell into the angry river, disappearing into the yellowish dirty foam.

"You fucking thrillseeker," Henry growled. He took off his glasses and folded the temple pieces, hanging them carefully on a branch of a nearby tree before he threw himself into the racing water without hesitation, kicking strongly for where he saw the blur of Dingo's sandy head bobbing.

It took only seconds for the water to swallow him up as well.

1. IN WHICH WE ARE INTRODUCED TO HENRY, OR 'DASH' AS HE IS SOON TO BE KNOWN BY SOME

THE light falling across the pile of books and loose papers on his desk suddenly made Henry Percival-Smythe aware that it was far later in the morning than he thought it was. He frowned and almost knocked over the cup of tea that Hill had brought in for him what seemed like only moments before—but one sip of the now ice-cold contents of the cup proved that it must have been hours ago.

He made a face at the excessive tannin that now sat in the cup where fresh tea once had been. Henry removed his glasses and rubbed at the bridge of his nose. He gave the glasses a good wipe, so he could return to reading the documents spread out before him. But first he rang for Hill and requested a new pot of tea. Hill was duly unimpressed with the fact that the previous pot had gone to waste, but Henry didn't notice as he had already returned to the small packet of photographs that had been wedged inside a field journal.

It was a magnificent creature. It was also the strangest, almost unimaginable, creature that you could have ever seen. And it had Henry enthralled.

"Are you looking at those again, sir?"

Henry almost jumped; he was so surprised by Hill's sudden reappearance at his side. The manservant to the department carefully made some room on Henry's desk where he could place the tray bearing the teapot, milk and sugar jugs, cup, and strainer.

"It's the thylacine, Hill."

Hill gave the pictures a cursory glance and then turned back to the more important subject of his own sphere. "Would you like me to pour for you, sir?"

"Please, Hill." Henry pulled out one of the larger photographs and tried to coax some interest from the other man. "Of course, it's also commonly known as the Tasmanian Tiger or the Tasmanian Wolf. But they're misnomers, of course. It is actually a marsupial."

"One or two sugars?"

"One, please. It's perhaps the strangest animal to come out of Australia, and that's saying something because *all* of their animals are unique and bizarre."

"Lemon or milk?"

"Milk," Henry sighed. As usual, it was an uphill battle to try and get anybody interested in his own private obsession. "It's a sad story, Hill. The thylacine has been hunted until now it stands on the edge of extinction. Besides a few disputed local sightings, the only place you can really see one alive now is in a handful of zoos around the world."

"Here you go, sir." Hill pointedly handed him the cup, so Henry was forced to recognize its existence. "Anything else?"

Henry shook his head despondently, and Hill nodded before leaving the room.

The photographs captivated him again, and Henry laid the cup of tea aside without having taken a sip.

There was something about the tiger's outlandish appearance that charmed Henry and made it truly beautiful in his eyes. Sadly, the last thylacine in captivity in a London zoo had died in 1931, before he had formed his obsession. Henry had only seen black and white photographs and jerky film footage of it, but he knew the tiger to have a caramel-colored coat with distinctive dark brown stripes that wrapped around its back and a tail as stiff as a broomstick which usually jutted out at an angle from its body. It could also be mistaken for a strange dog until it opened its most enthralling feature: the mouth. The gaping jaws opened like that of an alligator; some of the photos Henry owned of it yawning could still send a shiver through him. The thylacine was a miracle.

And he had come across its existence purely by accident. It hadn't been that long after he had come to work in the archives section for Ealing College, a job that he had only managed to obtain because of strings his father had pulled. Henry hated nepotism, but he wanted this job so badly he didn't care in this instance. Why work for the public library system or the archives of some Fleet Street broker when you could work as a junior level researcher and archivist in the world of academia at a small but prestigious college?

The oblong cardboard box addressed to his section hadn't seemed that out of the ordinary when it was first brought to him. It sat on his desk for a couple of hours before he finally got around to it, using his pocketknife to cut the twine that held it together. A pungent smell emanated from it, and he wrinkled his nose unhappily. But when he pulled the cover off, he saw for the first time the glorious pelt of the thylacine, along with the first photographs that would become part of his collection.

His collection. Of course, it wasn't his and he had no claim to it. But he had come to think of it as his and his alone. What he hadn't expected were the tears that came to his eyes as he ran his hand over the fur while reading the notes that came with the pelt. The photos gave the animal a face, the fur gave it a sense of realism, and the fact that it was merely a pelt made the tragedy of the thylacine hit him with full force. With great sadness he cataloged the specimen and found himself returning day after day to gaze upon it. Then he began the research.

That had been two years ago. It was now beyond an obsession. Henry's tea had grown cold again as he excitedly pored over the new mail that had been handed to him that morning by Hill. It was the letter addressed to him which had come from Tyenna, Tasmania, that made his blood sing with joy and fear.

December 30th, 1934

Mr. Percival-Smythe,

I enclose for you some recent documents following a rash of sightings of the thylacine in the area of Maydena. It has been quite some time since the thylacine was seen around here, but lately we are getting a wave of them reported by reliable witnesses. This may be just what you're looking for. A friend of mine is on his way to speak with your superiors to try and give weight to our claims and support you in launching a personal investigation. His name is Jack Chambers, and they, as well as yourself, may find him… a little rough around the edges. But he is the man you are looking for, and you will get what you need with him. He will probably arrive not that long after you receive this, and he will be bringing further evidence with him. I hope this means that we will see you soon in our country and we may begin to undo the damage that has been done by both of our governments.

Respectfully,

Gordon Austin

Henry wasn't too happy about this strange Australian about to turn up at the college to try to lay claim to his own personal project, but he trusted Gordon. Henry had been in correspondence with him ever since he had first seen the pelt, and Gordon had supplied him with more pieces for his collection. The thylacine had become a popular exhibit, although most of the people who gawked at it seemed to see it as some sort of monster rather than the creature of beauty and mystery it truly was.

So now it was time to pull out the big guns. Henry quickly swept up his papers and stuffed them into his satchel. He slung it around his shoulder and ran out the door with it bumping against his hip. Professors and students alike turned in his hurried wake to wonder what he was doing, showing such disregard for social order in the very halls where dignity reigned.

The sunlight that had previously made him aware of the passing hours had disappeared; it was now raining heavily as he ran through the courtyard that would take him to the main administration building. He was instantly soaked through, even in the brief time it took him to get from one end to the other. He burst through the outer door of Jonathon Larwood's office, all decorum absent, dripping wet and panting.

Diana Winton, Larwood's personal secretary, ran a cool gaze over him. He shivered under her scrutiny.

"You're wet," she observed matter-of-factly.

"It's raining," he said, feeling rather stupid.

"I take it you got the message I sent you?"

Henry frowned. "No. You sent me a message?"

"Oh, honestly!" she said disapprovingly. "Nobody ever picks up the telephone in your department."

"I never even heard it."

"Was that meant to surprise me?" She stood up and moved from behind her desk to a small closet built into the wall, her high heels clacking on the tiles he was dripping on. Diana held a towel out to Henry in her manicured hand, her marcelled hair and red-lipsticked mouth a direct rebuke to his disheveled appearance. "You can't go in to see him like that."

"See him?"

Diana shook her head. "I just don't know what to make of you sometimes, Mr. Percival-Smythe."

"I've told you to call me Henry."

"And I've told you that wouldn't be professional, Mr. Percival-Smythe." She gave him an aloof smile. "Now, dry yourself off. Mr. Larwood is speaking with someone at the moment, but he'll want you in there presently."

Henry began rubbing his hair dry. "Who's in there with him?"

Diana sat back down behind her desk. "Well, I can't tell you that. But oh…." She trailed off with a strangely dreamy smile on her face.

"Oh?" Henry repeated.

"He's a foreigner. From the colonies."

"American?" It had been a long time since America was their colony, but regarding them as such was a particular amusement of the British.

"Australian. His accent would strip the paper off the walls, but he is very charming." There was that smile again. "Very, very charming."

Henry felt an odd pang of jealousy, even though he had never been interested in Diana that way.

"Really?" And then the realization struck him. "Australian, you said?"

"Yes, Mr. Percival-Smythe."

"His name wasn't Jack Chambers, was it?"

"If it was, that wasn't how he introduced himself."

"Oh." Henry was relieved. It meant he still had time to try and win Larwood over to his side before Chambers could show up to try and take it all away from him.

"May I get you a cup of tea while you wait?"

He nodded. "Please."

Henry was enjoying his first hot cuppa of the day when Larwood stuck his head out of his office and noticed Henry. "Ah, Miss Winton, I was just coming out to ask you if you had heard from young Henry."

Henry winced internally. He hated being called that; it was a result of having practically grown up in the college due to his father's philanthropic endeavors with the faculty.

"As you can see, he's here," Diana replied, sipping her tea.

"Quite," Larwood said. "Would you make another pot of tea, please? Henry, come through."

Henry smiled at Diana, and she gave a slightly unprofessional roll of her eyes in return. He left his empty teacup with her and followed Larwood into his office. The dark walnut paneling made the interior seem even darker than the wintry day outside, as much as the bankers' lamps tried to rebel against it. Henry could make out a dark form slumped comfortably into one of the chairs before Larwood's desk, with one muscular leg swinging over the arm.

"I have a visitor here," Larwood said. "Mr. Chambers, this is Henry Percival-Smythe."

The dark shadow stood and moved into the light. "Christ, Larwood, I told you, Mr. Chambers is my dad."

Larwood appeared slightly flustered. "Erm, yes. Henry, this is Mr.... uh, *Dingo*. Mr. Dingo Chambers."

The oddly named man could now be fully seen in the meager light from the window. "You almost got it there, mate. Dingo Chambers."

"Dingo" was like a fictional character out of an Edgar Rice Burroughs novel. Tall, broad-shouldered, and bronzed, he was an Antipodean Adonis, and Henry found himself catching his breath. His sand-colored hair was strangely tousled, and Henry immediately found himself searching the chair the man had just vacated; his deduction proved correct, for a hat was propped against the leg. Henry looked back over to the man Diana had dubbed "the foreigner" who was looking back at him with unabashed interest. Henry realized Dingo's nose was slightly squashed, as if it had been broken and set unevenly, although it only served to give his face character, especially when partnered with the crooked smile beneath it.

"Give us your handle again, mate. I didn't catch it," Dingo said around his thick accent.

Henry looked at him in confusion. "Handle?"

"Your moniker, mate. What's your name?"

"Oh, of course." Henry offered his hand. "Henry Percival-Smythe."

"Jesus, that's a mouthful," Dingo replied. But as he said it, his gaze passed over the crotch of Henry's trousers and an almost lascivious smirk spread across his face.

Henry froze. Was that meant to be some sort of double entendre? He looked to Larwood for support; the other man seemed oblivious, and rather in awe of Dingo himself, although it could have been fear of what this strange native from the distant colonies might do next more than anything else.

As if he hadn't done a thing to unnerve the other man, Dingo continued. "I'll just call you Dash, okay?"

"But that's not my name," Henry said, realizing with each passing second he sounded even more stereotypically prissy and British than before.

"What, do you think my parents christened me Dingo?" The man in question tipped back his head and laughed heartily.

Henry eyed him suspiciously. "Quite frankly, it wouldn't surprise me."

"For heaven's sake, Henry," Larwood finally spoke up. "You heard me introduce him as Jack Chambers."

"I've been Dingo longer than I've been Jack," Dingo said abruptly.

"Well, no doubt you two have a lot to discuss," Larwood said hopefully. "Why don't you take Mr.... er... Dingo, to your office, Henry?"

"Professor Larwood, I was hoping to—" Henry started.

"Right, that we do." Dingo scooped his hat from the floor and clapped it onto his head. He grabbed Larwood's hand and pumped it heartily. "Thanks for the nice welcome, mate, and I've no doubt we'll be meeting again as soon as Dash here and I finalize our plans."

"Wait, we can't just—" Henry protested.

"Sure we can," Dingo said cheerfully. He grabbed Henry's bicep and dragged him to the door. "We should get to know each other better. We'll be spending a lot time together, and it's a trial to be out in the bush with a man you can't get on with."

Henry looked back pleadingly at Larwood over his shoulder, and the older man shrugged philosophically, but a tiny smile played over his lips. Henry imagined that Larwood was thinking *"rather you than me"* as Henry was hauled from the room, feeling Dingo's fingers squeeze his arm as if assessing how much muscle he had.

In the anteroom, Dingo released him to smirk engagingly at Diana, saying, "Thanks for the cuppa earlier, Miss Winton. Warms a man's bones on these nippy days."

"Diana, please call me Diana," the usually unapproachable Miss Winton purred, practically melting under the sun of Dingo's smile.

"The name of a goddess too," Dingo said admiringly. "Huntress of the moon. You've got the look of her. Saw a statue once, in Rome."

Henry seethed as Diana's slender figure seemed to shiver with delight at the broad compliments, although he wasn't certain what ticked him off more, her reaction or Dingo's easy confidence in his own powers of attraction.

"Will we be seeing you again, Mr. Chambers?" Diana tried to seem nonchalant as she asked.

Dingo winked at her. "Try and keep me away. Although Dash here," he clapped Henry on the back, nearly sending him staggering awkwardly toward the door, "and I have a lot to discuss about our expedition."

Thrilled, Diana's eyes opened wide. "Where are you going?"

Leaning closer, Dingo confided, "Deep into the wilds of Tasmania. It's a dangerous country, full of snakes, spiders, and wild animals. And the Aborigines; a savage lot they are. We may never be seen alive again."

"You—and *Henry*?" Diana emitted a dainty trill of laughter.

Henry glared at her, clutching his satchel under his arm. What was so funny about the thought of him in Australia? *Not* that he'd agreed to go *anywhere* with this crazy colonist, and as soon as he got him alone, he would tell him so. And of course, he didn't much like the sound of those spiders.

"Why, don't you think Dash has what it takes?" Dingo turned to glance at Henry and something about his laughing face made Henry want to hit him. And he wasn't a violent man.

"Why do you keep calling him Dash?" Diana leaned her chin on her hand, prepared to be enthralled with Dingo's answer.

"Why, it's that fine, fancy, double-barreled last name of his, isn't it?" Dingo laughed. "Percival *Dash* Smythe. Too much to mouth over every time. We Aussies like to cut to the meat of things."

"Dash." Diana giggled when she said it, but her gaze was newly speculative when she looked at Henry.

Dingo turned to hoist a well-worn bag to his shoulder from where it leaned against the wall and hooked his arm through Henry's. "Come on then, Dash. You're wasting this pretty lady's time, standing here flirting with her."

"Me?" Henry sputtered. "I haven't said a word—"

"Bit shy with the ladies, is our Dash," Dingo confided to Diana. She giggled again and wiggled in her chair as if she could barely contain her delight. Of course, Diana wiggling was merely the motion of shifting in her chair once or twice. But for Diana, it was practically akin to standing and breaking into a wild, bohemian Charleston.

Once in the hallway, Henry tried to pull his arm free, but Dingo was a bit sturdier than he and didn't let go so easily. "Where the fuck—"

"Blimey! You do have a mouth on you after all," Dingo said admiringly, and Henry was embarrassed to feel a flush of gratification at the praise. "Tell me, got a bottle in your office?"

"A…a bottle… of what?"

"Grog, mate. Booze. I need to wash the flavor of that tea from my mouth. It's a fretful taste, Dash."

"My name isn't Dash, and I don't have a bottle," Henry disclaimed, although he actually did have a little nip stashed away in a certain locked drawer.

"I guess it's the local for us then, Dash."

Henry succeeded in freeing his arm at last. "I'm not going anywhere with you, not the pub nor Australia. This is *my* project, and I'm doing it on my own."

"Right you are, and I'm going with you." Dingo grinned. "Call yourself the head of the expedition if you like, but you'd play hob without me. Think you've only got to stroll up to Tassie's home and knock on the door? 'Come on in, Dash, and have a cuppa', they'll say, right before they have you for their tea."

"Of course I don't think that," Henry sputtered. "For one thing, the thylacines do *not* eat people. But surely—"

"Don't call me Shirley, call me Dingo," the other man urged. "And are you *certain* they don't? Anyhoo, if you've any humanity in you, show me to the nearest pub. I'm dry as a desert."

"Fine, I'll show you where it is, but I'm not coming in with you," Henry said with a sinking feeling that Dingo wouldn't hesitate to drag him inside by main force. He opened the door and stepped out into the pouring rain for his second soaking of the day.

2. IN WHICH MORE IS DISCOVERED ABOUT DINGO

AN HOUR and several pints later, Henry was both fascinated and furious with Dingo.

"So you Brits come to Australia with your hounds, and it stands to reason that a few of them run off into the bush. I mean, you already did it to us with the rabbits, didn't you? A few years later and feral dogs are roaming the countryside, terrorizing wildlife and livestock alike, and everyone blames poor Tassie. So it's really your fault the thylacine are so rare, and by rights you ought to do something about it."

"I know all that, not that I'm taking personal responsibility for the dogs," Henry retorted. "And I *was* planning to do something about it, I just want it clear that if the college funds this expedition, *I* will be in charge."

"What are you planning to do?" Dingo challenged before commenting, "Good ale, but warm."

Henry ignored this sally. "The zoo in Hobart has the last known remaining thylacine. If we were able to find a small pocket, even a family, or at least a male and female, then we could bring them all back to London to start a breeding program—"

"And why London?" Dingo interjected. "Why not keep them in their own land?"

"The London Zoo has one of the most scientific and prestigious reputations in the world." Henry tried to be as tactful as possible. "No offense, but even Gordon Austin has said that your zoos cannot measure up, as they are slightly primitive—"

"Primitive?" Dingo bristled.

"You know what I mean," Henry said quickly. "And if you are as committed to the survival of the tigers as I am, then you have to admit the zoo here is more capable—"

As if not wanting to have to admit to anything that cast aspersions on his homeland, Dingo changed the subject, attracting attention in the noisy pub with his hoot of glee. "And you're planning to just slip a leash over Tassie's head and say 'heel' and expect him to follow along behind you all meek and mild. Dash, you *are* a one."

How was Dingo so successful at making him feel incompetent, Henry wondered, when they'd only known each other a few hours? "If Tassie's as smart as you say, why not? A few days training, a little positive reinforcement… I shouldn't wonder if Tassie, as you call him, wasn't eating out of your hand by the end of the trip."

"Tearing my hand off, more like." Dingo chuckled. "Have you seen those razor-sharp teeth in that crocodile mouth of theirs?"

"Not personally." Henry took a deep breath. "Have you?"

Suddenly Dingo looked remote, as if he were reliving a distant and unspeakable sight. "Yeah."

"Alive?" Henry shivered, his objections to Dingo's brash personality and habit of sweeping all before him melting away.

Dingo glanced both ways with a secretive look. "I should swear you to silence, Dash."

"Why?"

"There are some who want the tiger to die out, understand? They don't take kindly to tales of sightings, and they don't want a male to reach a zoo. Alive, anyway." Dingo raised his glass and drained it, licking the foam from his mouth.

Henry watched absently as the pink tongue traced over the well-cut lips. "They would try to stop us?"

Dingo smiled at Henry's use of the word "us," seemingly binding them into a unit on this adventure. "If we tell everyone what we're going into the bush for, yes."

"Then what are we going to say?"

"That we're going after diamonds," Dingo whispered. He leaned back with a broad grin. "They'll just think we're crazy and pay us no attention."

"There are no diamonds in Australia," Henry said.

"There are, but not many, like South Africa," Dingo said. He yawned suddenly. "Sorry. Been a long day. Maybe I should find a room."

"You can stay here," Henry said in a preoccupied voice. "It's close by the college, and it's a pretty decent inn."

"Meet me here for breakfast, and we'll discuss our approach with old Lardarse," Dingo invited.

"Larwood," Henry corrected automatically.

Dingo rolled his eyes. "Don't have much of a sense of humor, do you, Dash?"

The mischievous grin that spread over Henry's face made Dingo think perhaps he may have underestimated the other man.

"I've as much of one as I'm going to need," Henry said. "By the way, how much of what you say can I actually believe?"

"What do you mean?" Dingo asked.

"Those fearsome Aborigines you were telling Miss Winton about."

"Miss Winton?"

"Diana. Lardar—Larwood's secretary."

Dingo smiled at the memory of her. "Ahh, Diana." His face then fell, and he had the grace to look a bit embarrassed. "Well, perhaps I like to embroider somewhat. Working in this business, you have to build yourself up a bit, you know?"

"Really?" Henry asked drily.

"Admit it," Dingo said cheekily. "You were a bit nervous when I mentioned them, weren't you?"

"I might have been if I hadn't done my research on Tasmania and found out that its last full-blooded Aborigine died there in 1878," Henry said smugly. "Plus, I don't really think there's that much to fear from them. They're only human after all, the same as us."

Dingo's tongue made a brief appearance at the corner of his mouth as he looked at Henry thoughtfully. "Not much seems to get past you, does it, Dash?"

"Henry," the other man reminded him. "And no, it doesn't."

Dingo grinned unabashedly. "That's what I like."

WITH a shiver, Henry tossed his keys into the Indian brass bowl he kept on the stand near the door. He couldn't wait to get out of his damp clothes and turn on the gas fire. The warm amber glow from the fireplace and the lamps made his flat feel cozy and snug compared to the grey drizzle outside.

Ordinarily, Henry was a stickler for hanging up his clothes immediately when he took them off, particularly when they were damp, but tonight he let them crumple on the floor in his eagerness. He walked naked across his bedroom to the small wardrobe where he had amassed his travel gear; all the items he thought he would need for the projected journey to Australia.

He had taken great pains to acquire the trousers, boots, and khaki shirt, all used and previously worn, not wanting to appear ludicrous in a crisp new outfit. The shirt had belonged to his older brother James IV, who had been on safari to Africa and couldn't stop talking about it. The rest Henry had hunted out in second-hand shops and local bazaars. He'd even purchased a bush hat at the church jumble sale once, when his mother pressured him to help her bring her boxes down.

It had felt like some sort of fantasy treasure hunt while he was putting all the items by, but the flutter of excitement in his stomach as he donned the clothing now made it seem as if his dream was going to become a thrilling reality at last—even if it only seemed so because Dingo had intervened on his behalf. He didn't want to be beholden to the other man, but there was a part of him that was grateful nonetheless.

He went into the lounge to peer at himself in the mirror that hung over the fireplace, turning up the collar on his shirt. Henry donned the hat and pulled it well down over his eyes, admiring how the brim was turned down on one side while it curled rakishly up on the other.

"Dash," he mused. The name sounded as foreign as Dingo's and just as improbable.

He pushed his glasses up his nose. The hat made them tend to slide down a bit.

"Dash Percival-Smythe. Dash Smythe. Dash Smith."

As if he could hear Dingo's boisterous laughter, Henry frowned at his reflection and took off the hat. "Damn. It'll never work."

Deflated, he took off his expedition wardrobe and hurried into pajamas and his dressing gown. His feet were cold. He put his slippers on and went into the kitchen to make himself a nice cup of tea before sitting in front of the fire with his feet on the fender.

"Dash and Dingo," he muttered. "No, he would insist on coming first; it'd have to be Dingo and Dash."

Next to the bluff, breezy colonial with his broad muscular shoulders and golden skin, Henry thought he looked pale, skinny, and bookish. And rather silly in his carefully chosen bush gear.

"It's still *my* expedition," he growled, "no matter how charming he is."

Rather appalled at the trend of his own thoughts, Henry rinsed out the cup, turned off the fire and lamps, and retired to sink into a somewhat uneasy slumber, dreaming of Dingo and the Tasmanian Tiger, both showing all their copious, dazzling teeth as they laughed at him.

"STRIKE the trip to the zoo, Dash. It isn't going to happen," Dingo said, his jaws moving as he munched his bacon.

"But I've got to see a thylacine alive, haven't I? If I'm going to be able to identify one in the wild," Henry countered.

"It's not bloody likely that if you saw one you'd mistake it for, oh, say a sheep," Dingo chuckled. "If we pay a visit to old Benjamin, the game would be up. Everyone who goes tiger hunting stops off there first; so it's no go."

"Fine, perhaps you've a point." Henry fumed. He wanted to see the last known thylacine, which had been given the rather incongruous name of Benjamin, before the term of its natural life came to an end. "We travel by tramp steamer. I figure it'll take approximately twenty-eight days to get to Tasmania—"

Dingo shook his head vehemently. "Nah, mate. We'll hop a plane. I've got this friend who flies the mail from here to Hobart, and we'll be there in four days. And it's free, can't beat that."

Henry tried not to look too defeated while Dingo appeared to be a little smug. Even though he was oversetting all of his plans, Henry had to admit he could see the value in the offer of free travel; it would make his proposition all the more appealing to Larwood. However, he wasn't prepared to let Dingo march off with all the honors in this battle of wills.

"Dingo, just remember, Larwood is an academic. He will respond more favorably to a well-reasoned argument that lays out the advantages to this institution, in terms of money, publicity, and a profitable arrangement with the London zoo, should our quest prove successful."

"Damned if you English don't know how to speak the language," Dingo observed. "If I read you right, Lardarse is a dull old dog, and you're aiming to play into that. I say we hit him where he lives."

"And where, according to you, does he live?" Henry snarled.

"It's all about selling a dream, Dash. We've got to get him so excited, he won't even know he's saying yes while he's agreeing to our terms."

There it was again. We. Us. *Our*. Henry could see how people got swept up on the tide of Dingo's enthusiasm. He almost did himself but remembered the glazed look of Diana's eyes and swore to himself that he wouldn't look as besotted. Even Larwood seemed in awe of the man.

"Well?" Dingo asked.

Henry realized he had been lost in his own thoughts and may have even been staring at Dingo while doing so. He pushed his glasses back up his nose hurriedly and tried to look as blank as possible. "Yes."

"Did you even hear what I said?"

"Of course I did." Henry checked his watch and was relieved to see that it was almost nine. "I have to go. One of the geology classes is coming in for a tour, and I have to show them our igneous collection."

"No wonder you're itching to get out to see Tassie, if that's what you have to do all day." Dingo said this pleasantly, but it still stung Henry.

"I happen to like my job," Henry replied, bristling slightly.

"Of course you do," Dingo said. "But—"

"But nothing." Henry got to his feet, mustering up as much dignity as he could. "Enjoy the rest of your breakfast, Mr. Chambers. I will schedule a meeting with Mr. Larwood and present our case to him."

Dingo nodded. "Hey, Dash, if I offended you—"

"You didn't," Henry said stiffly, although his meaning was more than apparent to the other man. "I'll let you know the results of the meeting."

"On your bike, then," Dingo said, by way of goodbye.

Henry wasn't exactly sure what that meant, but he felt he would lose face if he had to ask, so he nodded and left one bemused Australian in his wake.

HENRY burned with the fire of indignation all morning as he led a small group of bored students around the geology department's archives. He ended up being snippy with the class, taking out the anger he felt against Dingo upon them. When their time together was finally up, both sides were relieved.

He wasn't sure why Dingo's easy dismissal of his work affected him so much. The truth was that he *was* slightly bored with it all. Much the same as the morning's students had been. It was the thylacine that had awakened this need for something new within him.

So he decided to go and pay a visit to his thylacine collection, the old friend that always gave him a sense of peace despite its inherent sadness.

But when he got there, he realized he wouldn't be alone.

Dingo sat at the large table, the pelt of the thylacine spread out before him.

"What are you doing?" Henry asked brusquely.

Dingo jumped slightly, which made Henry happy. It was good to know that the man could be startled occasionally. "Dash," he said softly.

That was another surprising thing. That he *could* speak softly and the strine of his voice faded so much when he did so. It took Henry aback for a moment, and Dingo continued to stare at him.

Henry finally found his tongue again. "This is a *priceless* collection. How did you get in here, anyway?"

Dingo grinned, and it seemed like he was back to his normal self as well. "Through the door, Dash."

"You need a key." Henry moved around him; it was a tight fit to get between him and the table, and Dingo stood to let him squeeze past. They bumped chests, and he was surprised by the amount of warmth that poured off Dingo—as if he were composed of the bright sun of his homeland itself.

"I've never met a lock I couldn't charm." Dingo tipped slightly, and his chest brushed against Henry's once more.

Flustered, Henry swayed away from him and began to gently pack up the pelt. "So you're admitting you broke in here."

Dingo gave him that disarming smile again. "Ah, yeah, mate. I just did."

"And you think that is acceptable?"

"Well, I knew if I asked you, you'd let me."

"You're presuming too much. How did you find the pelt, anyway?"

Tiring of the interrogation, Dingo sat back down. "I can read a catalog, you know."

"Oh," Henry said, deflated. "Of course."

"Yeah, of course."

Knowing that he had overstepped the bounds of propriety, Henry was at a loss on how to proceed. He stared down at the pelt and tenderly stroked the caramel fur. For a second, he caught a fleeting glimpse of how it would look in the wild, wrapped around a living, breathing, sentient creature. It would be just a flash against the lush green of the Tasmanian rainforest, gone so fast you would wonder if it were just a dream… or your heart wanting you to see something so badly it would pull it out of the realms of imagination to make it real for you.

"This isn't just a thing to you," Dingo said, breaking his reverie.

Henry blinked, collected himself, and met the other man's gaze. "No," he replied simply.

"I came in here to touch base," Dingo told him. "I'm still battling with myself, wondering if this is the right thing to do. But when I saw that pelt and thought that in a few years' time this could be all that's left of the poor buggers… we have to do whatever we can. Even if it means coming here—one last chance. It's probably all they've got."

Henry nodded.

"I like that you give a shit," Dingo said. "That's why I already met with Lardarse and told him you were going with me, no arguments."

"You saw him without me?" Henry protested.

"Do you ever listen to a bloody word I say?" Dingo asked.

Confused, Henry pressed the lid back onto the pelt box. "And what did he say?"

"Well, he was as mad as a cut snake, said I had no right to boss him around. But in the end, he knew I had him by the balls."

Henry looked at him agape.

"Not literally." Dingo scowled. "Get a grip, Dash!"

"But what does that all mean?"

"That you're coming to Tassie, of course. I always get my way."

Speechless, Henry did the thing he least expected to do, and before he could even think of the possible ramifications. He threw himself into Dingo's arms and hugged him enthusiastically.

"I'm going to Tassie!" he cried. "I mean, Tasmania."

He felt the warm breath of Dingo's chuckle against his cheek, and he came back down to earth when he realized the position he was in. He pulled away and instantly regretted it. Dingo stared at him with faint amusement.

"Er, sorry," Henry said hastily.

"No worries," Dingo replied. "You know, Dash, if I knew you felt that way about me, I would have had all this sorted out on the first day I got here."

"It's a British custom," Henry lied, regaining his usual haughty demeanor. "I'm sure when I get to Australia I must allow for the cultural differences there."

There was a tiny little smirk playing upon Dingo's lips. "Custom, huh?"

Henry pushed his glasses up. "Yes. When one gets excited by something, one becomes… a little exuberant."

"Okay. I have to get back to the pub and start making arrangements, get in touch with Deano and find out when he's flying. I'll call you later."

"Sure," Henry said, still trying to collect himself.

He didn't get a chance, as he was suddenly enveloped in Dingo's strong arms when the man hugged him. The slight beard on his cheek grazed against Henry's clean-shaven one, and Henry felt as if he had suddenly been marked.

"Custom, right?" Dingo asked, with a devilish glint in his eye. "I'm excited, you see. Exuberant."

Henry nodded, the burn from Dingo's cheek finding new skin.

Dingo let him go and picked up his hat from the table, setting it firmly upon his head. "Tooroo, then, Dash."

Henry nodded, and when Dingo closed the door behind him, he pressed his hand against his warmed cheek. He couldn't help but feel the other man had seen right through his act, but somehow he didn't mind. Which was practically akin to him breaking out and joining Diana in the Charleston.

3. HENRY'S SENSE OF ADVENTURE IS NOT SHARED BY ALL

"WHAT is this I hear about you going on some madcap expedition to the colonies?"

Henry grimaced and took a sip from his cup of tea to steady himself. "How did you hear about that, sir?"

James Percival-Smythe III delicately tapped the ash from the end of his cheroot and stared at his son. "Do you think that there is anything you do at that college that doesn't come to my attention?"

"Professor Larwood told you," Henry said flatly.

"He's concerned about you."

"Why?"

"He thinks you've come under the spell of this mad Australian with the absurd name."

"Dingo."

His father snorted to himself, as if his worst fears were confirmed.

"Is that why you invited me over here tonight?" Henry asked.

"No." James III twirled his cigar ostentatiously between his fingertips. "Your mother thought it had been far too long since you had come to dinner."

"I've been busy," Henry said feebly.

"Cataloging? I had no idea it was such an absorbing activity." His father's tone dripped heavily with disapproval.

"You'd be surprised, sir."

"I don't know why you're wasting your time as file clerk in some basement. My name alone would have obtained a higher-level entry position at the college for you."

It was a story Henry had heard often, and he always had to give the same stock answer in reply. "That wasn't the way I wanted to do it, sir, and you know that. I wanted to make it on my own name."

"You still needed *mine*, even to get that menial job," his father reminded him.

As if Henry could ever forget.

His father sighed. "And how long will that take you?"

"That's why this trip is so important to me. It's how I can make a name for myself."

"Your mother thinks it will more likely get you killed."

"I doubt it," Henry said, trying not to choke on the heavy fumes coming from his father's cigar.

His father's disappointment rolled over him in waves. "Go in and see your mother before dinner is served. I'm sure she'll want to have one last look at you before you go off to your death."

Henry nodded and gladly fled.

AFTER a long and mostly silent dinner, Henry decided that he would rather go back to his department than his small flat.

He switched on only the small banker's lamp on his desk and sat in its comforting glow. He sighed heavily and rubbed his temples.

Then the door to the office crashed open, the knob practically gouging a hole in the wall opposite. Henry jumped but relaxed again when he saw it was Dingo.

"Haroo," Dingo called out, as if he were storming the palace gates.

Henry looked up and frowned. "Pardon?"

"Haroo," Dingo repeated, making himself comfortable in the chair opposite.

"And that means?"

As if he were talking to an imbecile, Dingo drawled, "Hello…."

"Why don't you just say 'hello' then?" Henry asked irritably.

"Well, *hello* to you, sunshine," Dingo said dismissively, reaching for the pot in front of Henry and grimacing at the contents as he opened the lid. "Any chance you can call for coffee?"

"Hill's off for the evening," Henry told him.

"And you don't know how to make a cuppa?"

Sighing heavily, Henry stood and shuffled over to the small burner behind him and began readying a pot of coffee.

"Is it too much for you, mate?" Dingo asked. "Should I try coming in again and seeing if you're in a better mood?"

Before Henry could reply, Dingo was out the door. There came a knock at it.

"I know it's you," Henry said curtly.

"Evening," Dingo said with a tip of his hat.

"What are you doing here?" Henry asked.

"Well, that's no better, is it? *Good evening, my good sir*." Dingo bowed exaggeratedly, clutching his hat to his chest. He then turned to his left and addressed the empty air. "*Hello there, Dash*." He jumped back to his original position; it was dizzying to watch. "*Toodle pip, what what, Dingo*?"

"Good evening, Dingo," Henry snarled, getting the message. "But what are you doing here?"

Dingo eased himself into the chair opposite him. "Looking for you, of course."

"How did you know I would be here?"

Dingo grinned. "Where else would you be?"

"I could be plenty of places!" Henry protested.

"Yeah?" Dingo asked. "Where would you be, then?"

Flummoxed, Henry fell back on the required social graces. "Coffee's ready."

"Nah, don't feel like it now. Scratch it," Dingo ordered. "What grog have you got in your drawer?"

Henry had to resist throwing the contents of the pot at the other man, but he knew Dingo was only trying to get a rise out of him. "Grog?"

"The good stuff, mate. Don't play dumb."

Reluctantly, Henry leaned across his desk and slid open his bottom drawer, extracting the small silver flask within. "Whiskey?" he offered.

"Sure. Got any ice?"

Henry looked at him blankly. "Are you trying to be funny? You're in England."

Dingo grimaced. "I guess I'll have it straight, then."

Henry couldn't be sure, but as he reached behind him for two glasses he thought he heard Dingo mutter, "Bloody Poms."

Dingo watched him pour, and Henry slid a glass over to him. "Mind if I propose a toast, Dash?"

Wearily, Henry said, "*Henry*. And go ahead."

"Thanks, Dash. Anyhoo, here's to the tiger and our journey beginning on Thursday."

Henry almost spilled his glass. "Pardon?"

Dingo regarded him cheekily over the rim of his glass. "I booked our flight. Thursday. Eight in the morning."

"But—"

"Don't get cold feet on me now, mate. It's all arranged."

"How?"

"I *told* you, I have a mate in Imperial Airways. They're only running the mail at the minute, although they're going to start taking passengers soon. So we're stowaways, really. Hobos of the air!" He downed his whiskey triumphantly.

"And how long will it take us to get to Australia?"

"About ten days."

"Ten! You said four!"

"Aha! So you *do* listen. Well, it all depends. Better than the month on the boat, mate."

Henry nodded somberly. "Yes, you're right."

"You don't sound too sure about that."

Henry collected himself and attempted to sound cheerier. "No, I'm sure."

"You look down in the mouth about something. Come on, spill it."

Henry couldn't help but be swayed by the astonishing depth of compassion in the other man's eyes. "Do you like your father, Dingo?"

Dingo looked surprised, as if it were a question with a foregone conclusion. "Yeah, of course. Why?"

Henry cleared his throat uncomfortably and shook his head. "No reason. Would you like another drink?"

Once again, a question with a foregone conclusion. Dingo pushed his glass back over the desk and watched Henry top his drink off. He decided to bite the bullet. "Do you not like your dad, then?"

Henry's eyes widened, and he downed his fresh drink in one gulp. "That's rather presumptuous."

"You were the one who brought it up."

"It's… complicated."

"He's pretty high up here, isn't he? I remember Lardarse mentioning it at some point."

Henry considered having another drink but decided against it. "He's more well-known and regarded for his financial contributions than his academic ones."

"Ah, gotcha. Completely different to you, then."

Henry colored. "I'm not known for my academic contributions, Dingo."

Dingo shrugged. "I've a feeling you will be, one day."

Henry couldn't look at the other man, too afraid he would give something of himself away.

"Can I give you a bit of advice, Dash?"

Henry didn't correct him on his name this time. "I believe you would give it to me anyway, even if I did refuse."

"See, you're getting to know me already." Dingo grinned.

"What do you advise?" Henry wasn't too sure he would like it, whatever it was.

"Don't treat what we're doing like it's some way to prove yourself to your old man. Chances are you're never going to get what you want from him," Dingo said in all seriousness. "You had the purest of motives before. Think of the tiger. That's all."

It took Henry a moment to give a small nod in response.

"So, are you in it for the tiger?" Dingo asked.

"Yes," Henry said with complete honesty. "It's always been for the tiger." He didn't need to close his eyes to see that shrunken pelt before him, without shape and rightfully belonging on a living, breathing creature that deserved the opportunity to survive and thrive.

"Good," Dingo said, satisfied. "I'll be off, then. See you Thursday."

As Dingo got to his feet, Henry tried not to let the disappointment sound in his voice. "I won't see you before Thursday?"

"Have things to do, places to go, people to meet, matey," Dingo said off-handedly. "You going to miss me?"

Henry tried to answer, but confusion and the inability to form a coherent sentence got in the way.

"Don't worry, we'll be in each other's pockets so much soon enough that you'll be sick to death of the sight of me," Dingo said with a laugh.

Henry was starting to think the opposite but replied, "Yes. Most likely."

"Don't get up," Dingo said, while Henry remained seated. "I'll see myself out."

Remiss of his manners because he was still fighting the turbulence aroused in him by Dingo's casual ways, Henry leaped to his feet. "Oh, sorry."

"I said I'll see myself out, and I'll take a rain check on the hug."

Henry sat down with a heavy thud, his stomach even more twisted by Dingo's recall of what had happened between them only the day before.

"But I'll expect it next time," Dingo said with a wink. He slapped his hat back on his head and sauntered out the door, leaving a speechless Henry behind him.

4. HENRY DISCOVERS THAT MODERN TRAVEL IS NOT ALL IT IS CRACKED UP TO BE

FROM Croydon to Paris and then a series of quick stops that included Rome, Athens, Cairo, Delhi, and Rangoon, it took a number of days flying in the little tin can high above the ocean for Henry and Dingo to reach Bangkok. During that time, Henry barely saw Dingo—part of the reason he had been able to arrange for their flight was by agreeing to co-pilot. He and his friend Major Dean Franklin were taking turns flying, and when one flew the other slept. Henry was already nervous enough about being amongst the clouds and so far from Mother Earth that he was too apprehensive to sit with Dingo in the cockpit and risk distracting him from keeping them in the air.

At first, he had been surprised when Dingo had told him that he would also be flying the plane, although looking back Henry knew he really shouldn't have been. It was Dingo, after all. Henry hadn't known him for that long at all, but it seemed he was capable of anything.

It was when this thought crossed his mind that Henry realized he was acting as if he had a school-boy crush. And he should know all about that; after all, he had suffered the indignity of going to an all-boys boarding school for eight years.

It was just after some fumbling experiences in university, he had put all that behind him. And not only with men. The world of academia seemed so safe to him, where he could hide himself away at Ealing College and not have to worry about being swayed by others. It helped being where he was, as he was largely ignored and left to do his own job.

But Dingo could be his undoing, if Henry let him. The man was flirtatious, but it appeared to be his nature and not anything one could take seriously. Henry knew better than to take things at face value—once again, boarding school had taught him that. It was one of the reasons he was so reticent now.

Bangkok was their midway-point, and it had been decided that they would have a rest stop there. At the airport they were abandoned by Dean, who disappeared before Henry was even aware of his absence. Dingo stumbled down the small set of stairs from the plane to the tarmac, where Henry waited for him. He yawned, closed up the door, and smiled tiredly at Henry.

"Where did Major Franklin go?" Henry asked.

Dingo gave a small laugh. "Bangkok isn't just our rest stop. Deano has a friend here."

"I take it you mean a friend of… the friendly variety?" Henry asked tactfully.

"If you mean a girlfriend, yeah. He has a few."

"A girl in every port?" Henry said with a slight blush.

"Not yet. But that's his goal." Dingo slung his bag back over his shoulder and gestured for Henry to start following him.

"Do you…" Henry cleared his throat nervously, "do you have a girl in every port?"

Dingo tilted his head to look at him with a clouded expression upon his face. "No. I don't."

Henry felt relieved at this answer, although Dingo's inscrutable look troubled him more than he liked to acknowledge to himself.

Dingo's face cleared, and he was back to his usual jovial self. "What, were you worried I was going to abandon you here and leave you to fend for yourself?"

"No," Henry said quickly. "I didn't think you would do that."

Dingo seemed satisfied. "Good. Now let's get to the hotel. I need a bath."

IF HENRY had thought it was hot when he first got off the plane, it was even worse by the time they got to the hotel. The humidity was something he had never experienced before; his shirt was plastered to his back, and as he sat in the cab pools of sweat formed behind his knees. Beside him, Dingo looked much the same as he ever did; he was obviously used to the extremities of the heat. Henry fanned himself with his notebook, and Dingo laughed at him.

"Are you hot, then?"

"Can't you feel it?" Henry asked in exasperation.

Dingo shrugged. "Feels like home. Perfect Aussie weather."

"So this is what I have to look forward to?" Henry asked him.

"A bath'll do you a world of good."

It was the second time Dingo had mentioned a bath, and Henry felt like the temperature inside the cab had risen exponentially. "I think you may be right."

"Well, you're not sharing with me. Get your own."

"I wasn't suggesting—" Henry spluttered and stopped when he saw the smile on the other man's face. "You have to stop doing that."

"But it's fun," Dingo protested.

Henry was relieved when the cab pulled up outside the hotel and he could be distracted by checking in and receiving their keys. He was glad to be off the streets, which were even more crowded than those he was used to in London. Dingo had arranged for adjoining rooms on the second floor, and they said their goodbyes at their respective doors after getting off the elevator.

"Have a drink before dinner later?" Dingo asked.

Henry nodded. "Enjoy your bath."

Dingo grinned. "I will."

Henry entered his room and shut the door behind him. He could hear the thud of Dingo's door doing the same, and he closed his eyes briefly. It was a bad idea, as his mind exploded with the image of Dingo peeling off his clothes and padding naked into the bathroom. He had no idea what the man looked like naked, but his imagination had no problem volunteering to fill in the details. Henry groaned, knowing that it would have to be a cold bath, for reasons other than the temperature.

AS HE lay in the bath, however, with the temperature quickly going from pleasantly cool to uncomfortably lukewarm in mere minutes, his imagination could not be quelled. Knowing that Dingo was probably mere inches away from him and separated only by a wall, he couldn't help but think of Dingo lying naked in his own bath. He foolishly wondered if Dingo could be thinking of him and felt himself growing hard, even with the water.

This was getting ridiculous. He had to take care of this if he wanted to get through the evening without going crazy. He took himself in hand and tried not to think of Dingo. It was impossible. As he slowly stroked himself, he imagined that it was no longer his hand doing the act, but another—Dingo's. This only made him speed up, wanting to find release. He bit his lip to hold in his cry as he came.

He sagged back against the curve of the tub, and now that the urge was satisfied he realized he still felt unfulfilled and a little embarrassed by the fact that he was acting like an oversexed adolescent unable to control himself.

He stretched his leg out and maneuvered the tap with his toes so that a fresh supply of water would allow the bath to grow cold again.

HENRY'S eyes flew open, and he looked around in confusion before remembering where he was.

He had been stupid enough to fall asleep in the bath—he was lucky he hadn't drowned. Feeling a bit shaky, he pulled himself out of the water and dried off. Despite the heat he dressed in fresh clothes and stood in the middle of his room, staring at the door that joined with Dingo's room. He must have missed that when he first came in, he had been so desperate to feel clean again.

Should he knock, or would Dingo be asleep? He checked the time and decided it was close enough to dinner to take the chance. He moved slowly toward the door but faltered as he stood before it, his hand raised and ready to knock. Sighing, he rested his palm against the warm wood for a moment before giving a short, sharp rap upon it.

The door flew open before he had even finished knocking, and Henry's eyes widened as he became aware that Dingo stood before him in a state of disarray.

"Sorry," he stammered. "I'll let you get dressed."

Dingo raised his hand dismissively. "It's too hot at the moment. Come in for a drink."

Henry didn't know where to look without it being conspicuous. Dingo wore only a towel, which seemed to be defying gravity as it hung loosely upon his hips, teasing the possibility that it could fall away at any second. *Why were his lips suddenly dry?* Henry could feel them crack as he gave a low assent to Dingo's question.

Dingo turned and walked back into his room, the towel suggestively giving shape to his cheeks as the material shifted over them.

"Hot enough for you?" Dingo asked as he rummaged in the bathroom.

Once again, Henry couldn't tell if that was meant to be a double entendre, so he made a grunt that could be taken for agreement.

"If you're drinking my beer, you're going to have to talk to me," Dingo said, handing him a frosted bottle.

Henry looked down at the bottle in surprise. "It's cold."

Dingo gestured toward the sink. "I sent for ice."

Henry practically shoved him aside to see. Sure enough, the small sink was brimming with ice. Henry moaned with appreciation and grabbed a handful. He sat on the chair near the decking and rubbed it around his neck.

Dingo laughed. "Enjoy it while you can. It won't last long in this temp."

Holding the rapidly melting handful of ice against his neck, Henry looked around him for a glass for his beer. At that moment Dingo drank directly from the bottle, and Henry felt decidedly prissy for not doing the same. With Dingo watching him, Henry relished the first taste of the cold beer. No wonder Dingo had been disgusted by the warm beer served by the pubs back home; in this weather, this was the only way to drink it, and it seemed to have a clearer, crisper taste when cooled.

"That'll get a dog up ya," Dingo said appreciatively.

Not knowing what that meant, Henry nodded as if he understood perfectly. "Yes. Quite."

Not fooled, Dingo laughed. He stretched his feet out upon the bed, and the fold of the towel fell away to expose a muscular thigh. Henry gulped down even more beer, as if it could chase away the thoughts coming to mind, even as his gaze tracked up the line of Dingo's leg, taking in the curly golden hair that glinted against his tanned skin. The towel cast a shadow where his inner thigh curved toward his pelvis, hinting at what lay beneath. Henry wanted nothing more than to snatch away the towel and—

Gasping, Henry turned and plunged toward the window, peering out between the slats of the blinds, holding his bottle to his forehead. It was still rather cool, and the condensation that dripped from the bottle felt good against his heated skin. He willed himself to stop thinking about the nearly naked man sprawled on the bed behind him and at least pretend to take an interest in his new surroundings.

Despite the heat and heaviness between his legs, Henry forced himself to concentrate on the city outside their hotel. The sky was not yet black, just the rich blue of dusk that contrasted so well with the yellows, pinks, and reds of the insistent neon signs. He was surprised at the mix of traditional Siamese architecture, with the upturned corners and sweeping rooflines decorated with knobs and ceramic figures of dogs, right alongside copies of traditional French buildings with mansard roofs, mingled with the sleek silhouettes of spare modernist office blocks towering at least six stories high.

Having never been outside England except for a brief visit to Paris, Henry was unprepared for the cosmopolitan atmosphere of Bangkok. And all of the automobiles! In his imagination, he'd pictured rickshaws, of which there were indeed plenty, weaving in and out of the cars with a reckless disregard that made him resolve not to be caught in one, although if Dingo sensed his reluctance, Henry had not a doubt that he would insist on their taking one.

Damnation! He couldn't seem to get Dingo off his mind, and the knowledge that the other man was lolling virtually naked upon the bed behind him didn't help Henry at all. Especially the way the towel clung to Dingo, outlining suggestive shapes in certain places—Henry quickly took a swig of his beer, grimacing now that it was nearly warm.

"So, what do you think?"

"Beautiful," Henry muttered, and then he flushed in embarrassment. He could feel heat roll over his entire body, breaking into a sweat when he realized Dingo had come up behind him.

"What's that? I didn't quite catch?"

Irritated, Henry turned, bumping his elbow into Dingo's ribs, the other man stood so close. "I said it's exotic!" Henry said, embarrassed again that his own discomfort had made him practically shout the words. He heaved a sigh of relief to see that Dingo had put on his trousers and presumably his underpants as well.... Of course, he had no business thinking about Dingo's underpants. Golden hair followed a line from Dingo's navel to spread over his broad chest. Henry licked his lips at the sight of the dusky nipples peeking from the light covering of fur and abruptly turned to face the window again.

What was Dingo going on about now?

"Exotic to you maybe, but the Siamese call it home," Dingo said with a laugh.

"I'm hungry," Henry announced. Then he cringed, considering the trend of his thoughts and the uncanny way Dingo seemed to be able to read his mind.

"I could use a bite and some more beer," Dingo agreed.

He turned away to find a clean shirt, much to Henry's relief. Taking care of himself in the bath earlier seemed to have made no impression on his unruly organ at all; he was uncomfortably half-hard in his trousers.

"So what'll it be? English pub food? French? Indian? Siamese?"

"Siamese," Henry answered. "I've never had that."

"I like your style," Dingo said, reaching for Henry's hand and pumping it. "Tonight you are going to experience a meal the likes you've never seen in England."

Henry had become a bit more used to Dingo's… touching habits and braced himself just in time. "A willingness to try foreign cuisine is hardly a mark of character," he said.

"You're going to love it," Dingo assured him. "Love it." He clapped his hat on his head and held the door open for Henry.

"What's the food like?"

"Ever eaten spicy squid?" Dingo countered with a grin. "Goat? Or wait, I know, coal-fired tarantula. You'd like that, I expect, especially when the hairs are singed off—"

"I'll pass on that and the dog as well," Henry said firmly. "I'm rather interested in trying the squid though, and yes, I have had goat."

Dingo seemed disappointed. "Well, once you've had goat, you know not to try it again. Right then, let's go." Dingo's fingers bit into Henry's shoulder, and he was swept from the room without being given a chance to close the door that led to his. "Leave it all to me, Dash, me boy."

Adventurously, Henry decided against wearing his hat, feeling that the Siamese could hardly expect it of him, not knowing him. For the first time he realized that he was out of England at last, far from the traditions and expectations of his narrow circle, in a place where people didn't know him at all. He could reinvent himself, so to speak.

He walked beside Dingo when they emerged onto the crowded sidewalk, enjoying the coolness of the night air stirring his hair. Dingo hadn't bothered with a jacket, and Henry was beginning to think that his rolled-up shirtsleeves were the way to go as he eyed the way the hard sinew rippled in Dingo's bare forearms... He took off his jacket, sighing in relief as the air cooled his damp shirt, and slung the jacket over his shoulder, feeling rather jaunty and devil-may-care.

It filled him with exhilaration to be walking freely with Dingo on the sidewalk in another country far from home. For a moment he forgot all about Tassie and why he was even here in Bangkok. Street vendors pressed close around them as they walked, offering goods and food of every description. Henry was impressed when Dingo smilingly refused them in some pidgin argot of English and what sounded like Siamese. Apparently he hadn't been kidding about the spiders; one vendor seemed to specialize in roasted bugs of all sizes and description.

"Where are we going?" Henry shouted to be heard over the cacophony of street noises.

"Little place I know. I think you'll like it," Dingo said over his shoulder. "Stay close. Wouldn't want to lose you."

"Don't worry," Henry murmured under his breath. "I don't want to lose you either." It suddenly struck him that despite the struggles he was having hiding his urges, he quite liked Dingo in some ways. He hadn't had a friend since graduating from university, at least not one he felt close to the way he was beginning to feel with Dingo. Or *allow* himself to feel with Dingo, even if it was verging on dangerous territory.

Dingo plunged down a side street, where there were fewer automobiles and no street vendors. Henry relaxed while walking on the less crowded sidewalk, able to stride along beside Dingo now, rather than trailing him through the blur of people.

"Do you come here often?"

Dingo gave him one of those knowing, amused glances from under his lashes. "Is that a come-on line, or do you want the story of my life?"

"How long a story is it?" Henry retorted.

"Longer than we've got time for in one night, but maybe I'll be able to catch you up on the trip." Dingo turned into an open doorway, holding out an arm to guide Henry inside ahead of him. "Here we are."

"Dingo!"

Henry looked up to see a wizened Siamese man who appeared to be about eighty, standing behind a glass display case that doubled as a counter.

His face was creased in a huge smile, exposing a missing tooth, and he held both hands up in salute. It seemed to be a family establishment, as his wife, two younger men, and one pretty girl emulated him, holding up their arms and crying out the greeting. "Dingo!"

"Phraya, you old dog!" Dingo raised his arms as well. "*Quam sook T die pop coon!*"

Henry wondered if he ought to join in this orgy of salutation. And also found himself wondering just how accurate Dingo's grasp of the language was, although at this point nothing he learned about Dingo would surprise him.

"You come, bring friend," Phraya said, still beaming and pointing to Henry.

"My friend, Dash," Dingo explained, drawing Henry forward.

Henry ducked his head and gave Phraya a shy smile.

"Dash!" Phraya exclaimed raising his hands in the air once again. His family aped his behavior, crying out, "Dash!"

Henry grinned and raised his own hands in the air. "Phraya!"

Dingo stared at him with his mouth open, as if he couldn't believe this was his staid Henry. But Henry was feeling rather Dash-like at the moment, laughing when he thought of his father's disapproving reaction if he could have seen him now. The thought of becoming *Dash* was an intoxicating one. Especially if it meant he would remain in Dingo's world.

"Sit! Sit! I fix you!" Phraya gestured at an open table.

"Thank you," Dingo said. "Bring us a beer, *Sway*!"

"Is that her name?" Henry asked.

"Her name is Maew," Dingo said. "I'm calling her beautiful, I hope."

"Better watch out, or she'll fall in love with you," Henry said, watching how the girl giggled and smiled as she brought two cold bottles to the table, unloading them from a tray with a curtsey. He was pleased to see a look of dismay come over Dingo's face.

"Cripes, I never thought of that," Dingo muttered. He toned down his smile from the heat of the sun to a gentle simmer, but Henry thought anyone might still fall for the man. "*Khurp*, thank you."

"*Khurp* is thank you?"

"Yeah," Dingo answered. "Eat is *Gin*. Drink, *Durn*, and when you need the toilet, *Hung Nam.* That's all you really need to know. Most of them speak a little English."

"Well, you can't go wrong either way saying *Gin*," Henry quipped.

Dingo stared at him for a moment before breaking into a loud guffaw. "Damn me! I never thought of that! You're quick."

"I try." Henry grinned and took a long drink of the cold beer. It was hot in the little restaurant, but the crisp taste of the chilled beer was just as satisfying as the first one in the hotel room. "So what did you order?"

Dingo looked a bit uncomfortable. "I don't actually know. I just come here, and Phraya makes up a platter for me. I've never asked what anything was. I feel certain I'd rather not know."

"So, the tarantulas?" Henry teased.

"I hate to say this, but they're actually quite tasty, if you can get past the idea," Dingo said thoughtfully. "And the legs. But Phraya doesn't do them here. Apparently they're better fresh out of the ground."

"Damn," Henry said, pretending to be disappointed, although he was secretly glad he wouldn't be expanding his gastronomic horizons quite that far. "How did you meet Phraya?"

"Just walked in here one day. The most amazing smell was coming out the door, and I was hungry." Dingo shrugged. "How does one meet anyone?"

"I guess it depends what circles one moves in," Henry said thoughtfully. He leaned back to allow Maew to set down a platter of something that was completely unrecognizable, although it smelled rather appetizing. "*Khurp.*"

Maew smiled and nodded, before backing away with a bow.

Henry picked up the chopsticks and dug them into the pile on the platter, lifting whatever it was to his mouth, which was instantly filled with a spicy, savory flavor of something garlicky. It was some kind of vegetable, still a bit crunchy as he chewed.

"You know how to use chopsticks?" Dingo said, as if amazed by Henry's prowess with them.

"I *have* eaten in Chinese restaurants, you know," Henry said with a grin. "This is quite tasty."

"Hope it's not goat," Dingo muttered as he selected a piece.

Henry wondered what kind of experience Dingo had had with goat, but didn't bother to inform him that the dish consisted of vegetables in a spicy sauce.

"Not goat," Dingo said in a tone of satisfaction.

While the two men ate, Maew came to the table with two bowls of sticky rice, indicating that the vegetables should be eaten with them.

Henry identified a hint of basil, but the subtle flavors of unknown spices escaped him. He decided that he liked it anyway, and the beer complemented the food perfectly. His usual limit was two, but he was already on his fourth, although he was sure he wasn't getting drunk. It was still warm enough that he felt he was sweating out the alcohol almost immediately.

"What's our next stop, and when do we leave?" Henry asked.

"Prachuab, another stop in Siam. Then on to Malaysia," Dingo answered. "Why? Are you in a hurry to leave?"

Henry gave a sigh of contentment as Maew brought a dish that he recognized as shrimp with some unidentifiable vegetables. "I've never traveled before, overseas I mean, bar going to Paris once with my parents and brother on a school holiday."

"You definitely have to get out more, Dash." Dingo grinned as he watched Henry lift a shrimp to his mouth, almost as if he were gloating over something, perhaps Henry's lack of travel experience.

Instantly Henry's mouth was on fire, and he gasped in pain, breaking into a sweat. He continued to chew the shrimp, rather than spitting it out, and swallowed, which left a burning trail down his throat. He could feel heat flare in his stomach and grabbed for his beer.

"*Lao kao!*" Dingo shouted, looking very amused. "I should have warned you, the shrimp are a tinge on the hot side."

"Thank you," Henry replied in a hoarse whisper. "The warning's a little late, though."

"I didn't want to ruin your experience of it," Dingo said virtuously.

"It *was* delicious, if unexpected," Henry admitted. He grabbed for the glass of clear liquid that Maew placed on the table before him.

Dingo raised his glass as well. "Bottoms up."

Henry would have choked over the choice of words, but he was still in the process of lifting what he supposed was water to his lips, drinking hastily to wash away the last of the hot chilis and the visions brought to mind by

Dingo's toast, only to realize he was drinking some sort of alcohol with an herbal taste that had to be at least fifty proof. He put the glass down, sputtering and coughing whilst glaring at Dingo, who apparently found his performance quite hilarious.

His voice completely out of commission at this point, Henry croaked, "You could have warned me!"

"But it's so much more fun this way," Dingo said with a smirk. "Besides, I'm right with you." He lifted his glass and took a sip.

"*Durn!*" Henry whispered in Maew's direction.

"Bring us some water, *nam,*" Dingo said. "You'll need water as a chaser."

"I'm not going to keep drinking that," Henry squeaked as his voice began to return.

"You don't want to offend Phraya, do you? This is his homemade brew. He doesn't give it to just anyone; you should be flattered that he brought it out for you on your first time," Dingo remonstrated. "He didn't give me any until my second visit."

Henry glared at Dingo. "Do you always get people to do whatever you want?"

"If only," Dingo muttered. Then he grinned. "Come on, be a sport. How often in your lifetime are you going to be in Bangkok? Besides, the herbs in the hooch are a kind of natural hangover antidote. No matter how drunk you get, you won't feel a thing tomorrow."

"I don't think I can feel a thing *now,*" Henry warbled, his voice climbing at least an octave. With Dingo looking so deliciously edible, he wasn't at all sure that getting drunk with him would be a good idea, but a certain recklessness was growing within him. "What the hell." He raised the glass of alcohol and took another swig. "It's better than I thought," he said appreciatively.

"Keep them coming, *Sway*!" Dingo shouted. He laughed as Henry aimed his chopsticks for another shrimp.

5. HIDDEN DESIRES IN THE DEAD OF NIGHT

DINGO hummed to himself as he staggered into the hotel, unsteady from all the *lao kao* he'd drunk and from Henry's weight bearing him down. On the last leg of their return journey to the hotel, Henry's feet had stopped moving, and he would have fallen if not for Dingo's grip around his waist and his arm draped over Dingo's shoulder.

Dingo nodded to the uniformed boy who ran the elevator and managed to maneuver both himself and Henry inside with a minimum of bruising. "Two," he said, and the boy nodded, beaming at him and closing the cage with a metallic clash.

Dingo propped Henry's insensible form up against the wall of the elevator, feeling his knees give as the elevator started its journey upward. He swayed against Henry's body when the elevator came to rest on their floor. "Got a bit of muscle under those natty suits, don't you, Dash," he muttered admiringly. "Dash! You awake?"

When Henry let out a snore, Dingo grinned and said, "Guess not." He stooped to allow Henry to fall over his shoulder, grunting as he pressed upward with his burden. "*Khurp.*"

"You are most welcome, sir," the elevator boy answered in perfect, if accented, English.

Dingo wandered down the hall, eventually finding his room after squinting blearily at the numbers. He leaned forward to rest Henry's weight against the wall and free a hand to fumble for his key, interrupting himself to pat the tempting rounded flesh of Henry's bum, upturned over his shoulder. "Tasty, verrry tasty," he slurred.

After only four tries, he finally got the key into the lock and eventually even remembered to turn it. Pushing off the wall, Henry's weight caused him to enter the room somewhat precipitously, and he staggered unsteadily toward the bed, where he allowed Henry to roll off his shoulder and bounce onto the mattress.

"Gotta get me keys," Dingo reminded himself, and he made his way back to the door, hanging onto a bureau for support along the way. He extracted his key after only a minor struggle and shut the door, sliding the bolt across. "Hot," he muttered. He dropped his hat on the floor, missing putting it onto the bureau on the way back, and stripped off his shirt, letting it fall where it might. He bent to remove his shoes and fell forward, catching himself on his hands. "Better sit down. The ocean is rough tonight. Don't want to get seasick."

Sitting on the floor, he laboriously removed his shoes and socks, unbuckled his belt and pushed at his trousers, somewhat bemused that he couldn't get them past his arse. "Oh well." He stood up and took a step, tripping as his trousers fell to his ankles. "Oh, that's where they are," he said, observing his trousers hobbling him. With exaggerated movements, he carefully lifted each foot one at a time, stepping out of them.

"Dash is probably hot too," he reminded himself. He moved toward the bed with the most humane of intentions. "This is only to help Dash. He'll thank me for it. In the morning. Yes, he will."

With shaking hands, Dingo unbuttoned Henry's shirt. He hesitated to touch the smooth, toned chest, even though he wanted to. Henry was built like a swimmer, long and lean, in direct opposition to his own more tightly knit build. Dingo wanted nothing more than to caress the creamy skin, perhaps take a taste of the innocent looking pink nipples so temptingly displayed, but he had an inchoate sense that it would not be the honorable thing to do, although he couldn't exactly remember why that might be.

"Gotta make him comfortable. Depending on me," Dingo told himself. He managed to wrestle Henry out of his shirt without spilling him off the bed. Shoes and socks were easy, and Dingo only jumped once when the shoe he'd tossed over his shoulder smacked against the wall. "Oops."

Trousers went without a hitch, and Dingo was pleased with himself. "Getting the hang of this," he murmured as he undid the fly and grasped the waistband. He braced himself and yanked, pulling the trousers out from under Henry like a tablecloth from under the dishes. "That's more like," he whispered.

A light sheen of sweat made Henry's skin gleam in the faint starlight that lit the room, but Dingo bent to peer into Henry's face. He removed Henry's glasses, folding them carefully and placing them on the nightstand. "Beautiful," he murmured.

Henry wasn't conventionally handsome; his nose was a little bony but his cheekbones were high, his jaw beautifully sculpted. Thick dark lashes swept over his cheeks, and his lips were parted as he breathed in slowly. He looked younger when he wasn't guarding his expression so carefully, and Dingo liked what he saw.

He reached out to cup Henry's cheek, surprised and gratified when Henry turned his face into his hand, rubbing his cheek against Dingo's palm and smiling a little. Carefully, Dingo let his fingers trace the line of Henry's jaw, over his Adam's apple down, to the little dip at the base of his throat. It felt vulnerable and soft under his thumb as he rubbed a tiny circle there.

Dingo gasped, wondering if touching a man in such a simple way had ever moved him this much. "There's something about you, Dash…." He reached up to ruffle the other man's hair, liking the silky feeling of the straight locks slipping over his fingers. Very unlike his own coarser strands.

Realizing he mustn't go any further, Dingo forced himself to step away from the bed, suddenly feeling much more sober. The very idea was dangerous, but he wondered what Dash would do if he woke up to find them curled together in the same bed. "Probably give him a heart attack and then that's it for poor old Tassie," Dingo said, grinning at his own fantasy.

He looked around, seeing for the first time that they were in *his* room with Henry asleep on *his* bed. At least he hadn't given Henry time to bolt the door between their rooms before they left for dinner, he thought, and he chuckled as he weaved his way into Henry's room.

He might not be able to have the thrill of sleeping with Henry in his arms, but at least he could still have the amusement of Henry's horrified face in the morning, when he figured out he had slept in Dingo's room. Resolving to wake early so he could be having a shower when Henry woke, Dingo fell across the bed in the other room and fell asleep almost instantly.

HENRY smiled before he opened his eyes and stretched luxuriously. The sounds from the street below reminded him that he was in Bangkok, and he felt rested, alert, and ready for anything.

He opened his eyes to the unfamiliar room, watching a tiny beam of sunlight dance over the wall where it had slipped through the blinds. He turned onto his side, thinking of breakfast, a large pot of tea, and a shower, although not in that order. He could feel the remnants of yesterday's sweat dried on his body, which reminded him of the bath the night before. His hand wandered lower, and he stroked himself lazily as his gaze wandered over the room.

Spotting a pile of clothing crumpled on the floor, Henry frowned. Those trousers did not belong to him. And the hat was definitely *not* his; in fact, he remembered quite clearly that he hadn't worn a hat the night before.

His erection forgotten, he sat up abruptly, staring around the room, hoping that he hadn't done anything he might regret in his drunkenness of the night before. In fact, his last clear memory was in the restaurant with the wizened Siamese cook who kept sending dish after dish to their table.

And then it hit him. He was in Dingo's room, in Dingo's bed.

"Bloody hell," he muttered, clenching his cheeks, hoping that nothing… untoward had happened. He didn't feel sore. In fact, he was still wearing his boxers. He clutched the waistband as if they alone guarded his virtue.

He peered around. He seemed to be alone in the room. No sounds echoed from the bathroom. So if he was here in Dingo's room, where was Dingo?

Cautiously he got out of bed, his attention drawn by the adjoining door standing open. Peering cautiously around it, he chuckled silently at the sight of Dingo on *his* bed, still in *his* boxers, snoring heavily.

Relieved beyond measure that he hadn't betrayed himself, Henry reflected that he didn't even know if Dingo was *that way*, despite his effusive physicality, that it would never do to become entangled with a man one was traveling with, particularly as he needed Dingo's help to complete his mission.

Henry decided he needed a shower. A cold one, and immediately. But then, he would need fresh boxers. Faced with this dilemma, it seemed there was only one solution; he would tiptoe into Dingo's, or rather *his* own room, secure the underpants and retreat to Dingo's room for a shower.

The spirit of adventure that seemed to be growing with every day he spent away from England gave his foray almost an illicit thrill as he creeped into the darkened room, successfully capturing the object of clothing and retreating back into Dingo's room.

Once in the bathroom, the decision of whether to bolt the door seemed insurmountable. If Dingo woke up and realized where he was, wouldn't he wish to return to his own room to wash and shave? It therefore seemed impolite to lock Dingo out of his own room. In the end, Henry opted to close the bathroom door, but not lock it, and to hurry in the shower, so as not to be caught off guard.

The cold water felt good streaming over his sticky skin, and regretfully Henry wondered if he could manage to fit a swim in during this layover. Most probably not, but he hoped perhaps at some point that he would have a chance to swim in the waters of Tasmania. He had read that the beaches of Australia were some of the most beautiful in the world, and with such a reputation as that he couldn't resist the opportunity if it arose. He scrubbed himself well and stepped out, drying off before wrapping the towel around his waist.

Because the shower had been a cold one, the mirror hadn't fogged over, and he was able to shave straightaway, deriving a tiny thrill out of using Dingo's shaving mug and razor. He donned his boxers and hung up the damp towel neatly, feeling a sense of triumph that he'd gotten away with it.

When he opened the bathroom door, Dingo's snores assured him that the man was still asleep. Henry picked up the phone and ordered an English breakfast for two to be delivered to Dingo's room, opting for the exotic sounding Siamese tea they offered rather than Indian.

Then he went into his own room to rouse the other man. "Dingo! Time to rise and shine," Henry barked loudly.

He chuckled when Dingo jerked on the bed and grabbed a pillow, dragging it over his head. "Don't shout," came the muffled plea from under the pillow.

Pulling the pillow out of Dingo's grasp, Henry shouted, "What was that? Didn't quite hear you."

"Lord help me," Dingo groaned, prying his eyes open to glare blearily at Henry. "Don't you have a hangover?"

"No, never have. Besides, you promised me that filthy stuff you made me drink last night had magical herbal powers and it seems to have worked. For me, at least."

Henry's laugh seemed heartless to Dingo, and he stared at him reproachfully. "If I'd known I was traveling with a bloody sadist, I'd have…."

"You'd have what?" Henry asked, his smile fading.

"Nothing," Dingo said hastily, sitting up. He grabbed his head as the movement made his head start to pound. "What did I drink last night that you didn't?"

"We were drinking the same thing, only you had more than I did," Henry said. "Want an aspirin?"

"Coffee," Dingo moaned. "Then aspirin, then ice, and then maybe a gun, so you can put me out of my misery."

"I'll add it to our order," Henry said, crossing to the telephone. He felt a bit self-conscious, clad only in his boxers, but figured that two could play at this game. After all, yesterday Dingo had worn only a towel after his bath, and men who didn't like other men apparently weren't self-conscious about what they were or were not wearing, and suddenly it all seemed too confusing, keeping track of what "normal" men did or didn't do before other men. The hell with it. "Room two sixteen, I'd like to add a pot of coffee to our order. Cream, yes, and sugar."

"What did you order for us?" Dingo asked curiously.

"English breakfast, buttered muffins, bacon, eggs…." Henry paused, grinning maliciously as Dingo turned a delicate shade of green. "I hope you're hungry."

"I need a shower," Dingo announced. He got out of bed and headed for his own room.

Henry was glad to see he was a bit unsteady on his feet. After all, Dingo couldn't have everything all his own way. "Take my towel. I used yours," he said, going into this bathroom to get it. He tossed it at Dingo, who caught it with both hands against his chest.

"Thanks," Dingo muttered, looking surprised. He paused for a moment, taking an appraising glance up and down Henry's body.

Henry could feel the flush start on his face and spread down his neck and chest, wondering why he felt so exposed. "Your shower?"

"Right," Dingo said, and he turned and marched into his own room, closing the door firmly behind him.

"Score one for Dash," Henry murmured and smiled.

AFTER an uneasy breakfast, they took a taxi back to the airport where Henry was left to himself as Dean and Dingo conferred on flight plans, fueling, and schedules while stowing the new batch of mail and parcels they'd picked up. Henry had the distinct impression that Dingo was trying to avoid him, which was a new one on him, but it left him feeling lonely and like a bit of an interloper.

Dean and Dingo disappeared into the cockpit, leaving Henry to make a nest for himself amongst the mailbags in the back. He'd found it was the most comfortable way of traveling, as there were no seats in the body of the plane, nor were there windows, so he couldn't pass the time by looking out unless he wanted to hold his body in a crouching position and peer past the two pilots' shoulders.

It robbed him of the wonder of actually flying to be shut away from the action in the dark. The feeling of movement and the noise battered his senses into a somnolent state, from which he would periodically jerk awake if he heard a sound or the plane lost altitude in one of those sickening drops. Dingo had explained that it happened sometimes, but that it didn't follow that they were going to fall out of the air.

"If the engines cut out, *that's* when it's time to worry, although worry will buy you nothing," Dingo had said with a laugh. "Donning a parachute makes more sense, but don't bother unless I tell you."

Henry had wanted to ask, "What if you're incapacitated? Do I use my best judgment or go down with the airplane?" But he hadn't wanted to appear pansy to Dingo. Not pansy, precisely, but Dingo seemed to have no fear, laughing gleefully whenever the plane did take a dip.

After Prachaub, quick stops in Singapore, Batavia, Bima, and Koepang put them within reach of Australia. Darwin was Henry's first taste of Australia, and the hour that they spent there was disappointing and one that he hoped wouldn't be representative of the entire trip. A desert airfield in the middle of nothing made him realize how big and empty this newfound land was and why the British still sneeringly referred to it as "the Colonies." The next few stops assuaged his fears, as they proved that Australia truly was a land of many temperate zones and landscapes. Finally they landed in Melbourne, where Henry climbed stiffly from the plane, clutching his duffle bag while he shook hands with Dean, the pilot, thanking him for the lift.

"No worries!" Dean said. He turned to Dingo, and the two men shook hands before giving each other a rough hug, clapping each other's back. "Tooroo, Dingo! Any time you want to fly with me, give me the word. Can always use a co."

"On your bike, then," Dingo said with a big smile. "Who knows, we may need to give old Dash a lift back to England."

"When will that be then?" Dean asked.

"Yes, Mr. Chambers. What *is* your schedule?"

Henry turned to gaze at the owner of the new voice, surprised at how he took an instant dislike to the man it oozed from.

He had black hair, smoothed back sleekly from his forehead, shiny with oil, small blue eyes, a long nose, and a disagreeable pursed look to his mouth, even though he was smiling. He ignored Henry, boring into Dingo with his beady eyes.

"Clarence, you shouldn't have!" Dingo said with an insolent grin. "You met the aeroplane to welcome me back to my homeland. And here I could have sworn you didn't like me!"

Dean clapped his hand on Dingo's shoulder. "Dingo did me a favor, Mr. Hodges. I lost my co-pilot in England, and he crewed for me on the way back."

"I didn't come to the airport to *meet* you," Hodges said icily. "I happen to be here on government business and caught sight of you, and—"

"And you couldn't wait to say hello! I'm touched, I tell you, touched." Dingo grabbed Hodges's hand in a crushing grip and pumped vigorously.

Henry tried to hide the smirk that curved his lips when Hodges darted an angry glance at him.

"Who's your friend?" Hodges inquired as he wrested his hand away from Dingo and wiggled his fingers to return the feeling to them.

"This is my cousin, Dash, over on a visit to meet my folks, his auntie and uncle," Dingo declared, stepping closer to put his arm across Henry's shoulders. "Long lost, like."

"Dash Chambers?" Hodges inquired, holding out his hand so that Henry could take it.

Henry opened his mouth, but Dingo forestalled him. "That's it; that's just it. Dash Chambers, cousin to Dingo, Baz, and Johnno."

Wondering who all these people might be, Henry shook hands, amused when Hodges tried to put the crush on *his* hand. He tightened his grip, maintaining his expression of innocence as Hodges began to squint in pain and tried to withdraw his hand.

"Pleased to meet you!" Henry boomed, mimicking Dingo's accent with a varying degree of accuracy that made the other man stare. "Dingo here's told me all about you."

"He has?" Hodges asked uneasily, wringing his fingers once again. "What brings you to Australia then, Mr. Chambers? I could have sworn you were here at the behest of Gordon Austin."

Henry froze at the mention of Gordon's name and the realization that Hodges knew exactly who he was. He had no idea who this Hodges was or how he was involved in all of this, but when he met Dingo's eyes, they were brimming with mischief. Whatever was going on here, it was best to play by Dingo's rules for the moment. A crazy idea came to him, so farfetched it seemed perfectly logical to be accredited to Dingo. "Don't tell anyone then, but…" he paused thrillingly before whispering, "diamonds."

Hodges immediately assumed a bored and condescending air and said, "Rather. Well, you'll have your work cut out. Tell me, Mr. Chambers, have you any interest in the native wildlife?"

He knows, Henry thought. *I don't know what to do.*

Luckily Dingo came to the rescue. "What, like kangaroos?"

"Nothing that common," Hodges said disdainfully.

"What, you want to play a round of *Animal, Vegetable, Mineral*, Clarence? Dash here can tell you anything you want to know about rock. Igneous, sedimentary, or metamorphic. Name your poison!"

"What would you say diamonds are then, Mr. Chambers?" Hodges asked with his eyes narrowed.

"They could be said to be all three," Henry answered glibly. "When an organic compound becomes a fossil, it falls into the sedimentary category, when pressure and heat are applied it becomes metamorphic as in coal, and depending on the amount of pressure and heat, a diamond would then fall within the igneous classification."

Hodges looked somewhat taken aback; Dingo was impressed, while Dean was merely watchful. "Uh, right, that's—I see you know your stuff. Pleased to make your acquaintance."

"The pleasure's all his," Dingo assured the man. "Smart boy, I told you. He's been to college."

"Your parents must be proud," Hodges said inanely, glancing at his watch. "I'm late for an appointment. You'll forgive me…."

"You must come for tea and say hello to me old dad, sometime!" Dingo bawled after the retreating figure. "He'd like to see you again."

Hodges looked at Dingo with barely concealed distaste before he hurried to a car parked beside the wooden tower, got into it, and drove away, leaving a cloud of dust in his wake.

"What was that all about?" Henry asked.

Ignoring his question, Dingo demanded, "Was all that folderol about diamonds true?"

"Haven't a clue. I made it all up," Henry admitted. He grinned as the other two men broke into surprised laughter. "One of the advantages of a college education, learning to bullshit."

"That and a fancy ten-dollar vocabulary." Dean chuckled. "Well, Dash, it's been a pleasure. Call on me for a lift any time." He shook hands with Henry, who wondered at this mark of respect from a man who'd all but ignored his presence for the entire trip, relaying his commands through Dingo.

Dean turned to confer with the man who'd descended from the tower and approached them with a dolly for moving the mailbags.

Dingo picked up his own bag and led the way toward the tower. Henry hurried after him, repeating his question. "So what was that all about? Who was that man?"

Dingo gave him a sidelong grin. "You're in the wars now, mate. Clarence Hodges works for the government, but he's got his own agenda. And I'm well-known as being one who wants Tassie left well alone. He keeps an eye on me. I'm not quite sure what he suspects me of, but he keeps tabs on my comings and goings."

Henry pondered for a moment. "He knew about Gordon Austin. That means he'll find out who I am, if he doesn't already know."

"And what will he find out, then? You were giving some sort of rock tour that day I talked to Lardarse, right? So he'll think you're a rock-hound."

Henry didn't see how it could be that simple, and he wondered why Dingo was missing what seemed obvious to a blind man. "And what'll he think about you lying about my name?"

"Nothing. He knows not to believe a word out of my mouth," Dingo said dismissively. "I like pulling his leg. It's—"

"Fun, I know," Henry finished for him. "Where are we going now?"

"Home. Like I said. You have to meet your long lost auntie and uncle," Dingo said, linking his arm with Henry's. "Think Lardarse will let out what you're here for?"

Henry smiled without amusement. "Stiff upper lip and all that. The British do not announce their intentions, only their victories. If I were to fail and he'd puffed off the expedition everywhere, well, not to be borne, eh? No, Lardarse will more likely tell everyone I've gone on holiday."

"Lending credence to *our* story that you're here to meet the family," Dingo said. "And here's your cousin, then, my brother Baz."

Henry withdrew his arm from Dingo's in a hurry, flushing red when he saw an older, mellower version of Dingo standing beside a battered truck. It didn't help that he still felt uneasy about Hodges. The man seemed to see right through their lies, and Henry didn't like the fact that Dingo was brushing Hodges off so easily. There had to be more of a story to it all.

"Haroo!" Baz cried out.

"Haroo to you!" Dingo echoed.

Henry watched, bemused as they executed some secret ritual comprised of a peculiar handshake and a stiff little dance that stirred the dust at their feet.

"And this must be Dash," Baz said, extending his hand to Henry.

"Er, Baz?"

"That's the name, *cousin*." Baz couldn't have known the whole story of what Henry's sudden claim to family involvement, but he took it all in his stride. "Throw your bag in the back, and let's hit the road." Baz turned and climbed in, opening the passenger door and sliding through to the driver's seat.

Henry hung back for a moment but felt Dingo's hands, warm on his upper arms as he was propelled toward the truck.

"Short for Barry," Dingo explained. "Come on, then. You take the hump."

Henry wondered how the hell one got from Barry to Baz; he also wondered what a hump was and then found out as Dingo climbed in beside him and he was pressed between two sandy-haired, muscled Chambers men, both of whom instantly spread their legs wide, encroaching into his territory and snapping his own legs together by force.

Dingo draped one arm out the window and the other over Henry's shoulders. "So you don't impede Baz's driving. He needs all the help he can get."

Henry jumped when Dingo hit the side of the truck with his open palm. "Hit it, Baz!"

"Righto!" Baz said and put the truck in gear.

6. HENRY'S FIRST HOURS IN THE COLONIES

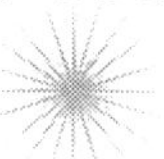

ENGLAND'S influence was obvious in the names of the suburbs they passed through. Ascot Vale, Essendon, Brunswick… Henry wouldn't have been surprised if they had also come across Westminster and Bath. The suburbs seemed familiar and yet alien at the same time. It was like a parallel universe of his homeland, except it had been baked in an oven and left out in the sun to bleach.

Dingo and Baz chatted amiably between themselves, catching up on everything Dingo had missed in the six weeks he had been away from home. Henry tried to listen in but was distracted by all the new sights that passed in front of him. Dingo's arm was still hanging casually behind his neck, and Henry unconsciously leaned into it, using it as a headrest. When he became aware of what he was doing, Henry wished that Dingo would stroke the hot skin of his neck.

One suburb had bled into another, but this one seemed to be different. The houses weren't as uniform; they had more character and the architecture was varied. The people he could see out and about on the streets weren't so consistently Anglo-Saxon either, Mediterranean hues of skin marched along with Orthodox Jews, and Henry craned his neck to watch them pass with interest.

"Where are we?" he asked.

"Carlton," Dingo replied, grinning at the obvious delight Henry was displaying. "Also known as home sweet home."

"Yeah." Baz snorted. "For slackers who still live with their folks."

Dingo whacked the back of his head. "I'm hardly ever at home long enough to justify getting my own place." He leaned in to Henry. "And this coming from a guy who only moved out last year."

"Yeah, because I got married."

"Oh?" Dingo teased. "Not because you were wanting to be footloose and fancy-free?"

"You'll get hitched one day too," Baz replied laconically.

Dingo's face darkened momentarily. "That ain't gonna happen."

Baz laughed. "There's no woman who can tie him down, Dash. He's just too much man for a woman to handle." He yelped when Dingo cuffed him around the ear, and they almost swerved off the road.

"Watch it, you dick!" Dingo scowled. "Keep your eyes on the road."

Baz only laughed like a loon again, amused by himself.

Henry swallowed heavily, glad they were still alive and not killed by the oncoming traffic. But Baz's words still stung. "Really?" He risked looking back at Dingo, who still held the remnants of a scowl upon his face.

"They all love him, though," Baz continued.

"Can it," Dingo growled.

Henry still didn't know Dingo well enough to second-guess his moods, but the man looked dangerous at the moment. Baz blithely ignored it, secure in the history of sibling camaraderie and conflict.

"He hates it when we discuss his personal life."

"Look, there's the Melbourne Cemetery," Dingo said desperately, to take the spotlight off himself.

Immediately interested, Henry peered past Baz's profile to peer at the large city of the dead on his right. He gave a slight whistle. "It's enormous."

"That's what my wife said, and she should know," Baz said, amusing himself.

Double entendres obviously run in the family, Henry thought as he heard Dingo snickering on his left.

"Biggest cemetery in Melbourne," Dingo said, turning on the voice of the tour-guide once he had composed himself. "Used to be closer in to the city, but they moved the headstones farther out to start a new one up here."

"Moved the *headstones*?" Henry asked pointedly.

"Yep, the bodies are still there," Dingo said cheerily.

"Doesn't anybody care?"

Baz snorted. "They're dead, aren't they? How can they complain?"

Henry was horrified. "But it's a basic tenet of our society to respect the dead. Leaving the bodies behind but pretending to show respect by moving the headstones is just morally bankrupt."

"You're dealing with a historian here, Baz," Dingo said, as if that explained everything.

Which apparently it did, to Baz. "Ah."

"I suppose being a plunderer, you quickly lose respect for the dead," Henry said snottily.

"Who's a plunderer?" Baz demanded.

"Dash," Dingo warned, and Henry couldn't help but heed the tone.

"Is he calling our dad a plunderer?" Baz asked, his voice rising.

"I think he was actually insulting me," Dingo drawled.

"Oh," Baz relaxed behind the wheel again. "That's okay, then."

Henry turned to Dingo. "I wasn't—"

"I'm not a plunderer," Dingo said softly.

"Oh, you two are going to work perfectly together." Baz laughed. "A regular Burke and Wills."

Dingo groaned, and Henry felt confused all over again as he still hadn't recovered from the shame he felt at apparently insulting the man.

"Who?" Henry asked.

"Australian explorers," Baz explained. "They died trying to map the north."

"Oh," Henry said, crestfallen. "That's not exactly a cheery analogy."

"*Comrades in great achievement, and comrades in death,*" Dingo mused.

"Pardon?" Henry asked.

"That's what's written on their tomb." Dingo grinned.

"You're just as bad as your brother," Henry murmured unhappily.

"That's what they say," Baz said, shifting slightly in his seat. "Almost home."

Henry felt Dingo sit up, more alert. There was a genuine smile on his face; he was happy to be home and see his family again. Henry wondered if there had ever been a period in his life when he had worn the same expression in respect to his own homestead. As bad as boarding school had been, the prospect of returning home in the hols had never seemed that much more attractive.

"I still can't believe Dingo found somebody as crazy as himself to tag along on this expedition," Baz muttered.

"You don't understand, Baz," Dingo said tiredly and simply, a reaction to an oft-repeated argument.

"Nah, I guess I don't. That's why Dad's so glad you've taken on after him."

"Your father knows about the thylacine?" Henry asked Dingo, dumbfounded.

"Knows about it?" Baz exclaimed. "He's a bloody expert! What, you didn't tell him, Jack?"

Dingo glowered at the use of his real name. "I thought Dad would be the best to talk about it."

Baz directed the car to pull up outside a two-story Victorian terrace house. It didn't look as stately as some of the others on Faraday Street, but it looked comfortable and lived-in. Henry liked it immediately, his mood in no way dampened by the bickering of the brothers he was sandwiched between.

"So your new friend doesn't know that our grandfather was one of the biggest bounty hunters of the thylacine in his day?" Baz asked, incredulous.

Henry was too shocked to speak; all he could do was turn to Dingo with wide eyes and an open mouth.

"Thanks, Barry," Dingo said dryly.

"Well," Baz said, clearly uncomfortable. "I'll meet you blokes inside. It looks like you need to have a chat."

"Thanks, Barry," Dingo repeated in the same tone of voice.

Baz gave both of the other men a quick look and then hightailed it into the safety of his parents' house.

"Dash—" Dingo began.

"That's not my name," Henry reminded him, feeling childish but still resisting the nickname as if it gave Dingo some right to claim him. For this moment, anyway. He was too angry.

"Henry, then," Dingo said, and it sounded strange coming from him.

"Why didn't you tell me?" Henry asked plaintively.

"Because it's got nothing to do with me," Dingo said, frowning.

"Of course it has something to do with you!" Henry interjected. "Your grandfather contributed to the massacre of the thylacines!"

"And that's why my father and I are trying to save them now," Dingo said, staring at his feet, still unable to look Henry in the eyes.

"That's commendable, but you still should have told me. Why didn't you?"

"I thought, well, I thought that maybe you wouldn't have come if you knew."

Henry sighed.

"Would you have?" Dingo asked.

Henry paused to consider.

"See?"

Henry took a deep breath. "If I hadn't gotten to know you, maybe not. Perhaps I wouldn't have trusted you. But I heard how you spoke about the thylacine. You can't fake that."

"But maybe if I'd told you straight away, you wouldn't have given me the chance to show you how I cared about Tassie," Dingo pointed out.

Henry opened his mouth to object but remembered his first reactions toward Dingo's abrupt appearance in his life and closed it.

"There you go," Dingo said sadly.

"Maybe. Maybe not." Henry shrugged. "But we're here now, aren't we?"

"You'll find out the whole, sorry tale soon enough."

"But it won't change the fact that we're the new Burke and Wills," Henry said, trying to get a smile out of him. "Hopefully without the death part, though."

Dingo rewarded him with a smile. "Yeah."

There was a sharp rap at Dingo's window, and both men jumped. Dingo rolled it down, and an older man stuck his head in and peered at them.

"So, have you two kissed and made up yet?" he demanded.

"Dash," Dingo said. "This is my old man."

IT TURNED out that "old man" and "old lady" were genuine terms of affection by Australian youths for their parents, even though it sounded slightly disrespectful to Henry. He was instantly accepted as a member of the family, such was the Chamberses' effusive welcome. Maybe he could take up that disguise of long-lost cousin without being unmasked as a fraud after all. Henry was interested to see that Dingo and his brother Baz took after their dad, with his sandy hair and square jaw, but while he and Baz shared hazel eyes, Dingo had his mother's clear blue ones.

"It's a pleasure to meet you, Mr. and Mrs. Chambers," Henry said, shaking their hands stiffly.

Apparently Dingo's dad was as tactile as his son. Henry was crushed against his chest and fought for air as the older man bellowed, "None of that Mr. stuff, call me Hank, mate."

"Uh, okay… Hank," Henry replied, confused even further, the name sounding foreign on his tongue. He was then passed on to Dingo's mother as if it were a do-si-do at a local town hall.

"And you may call me Helen." The beaming woman seemed to share Dingo's wide grin as well. She was tall, with long grey hair and a beautiful, if wrinkled, face.

It seemed *really* disrespectful to address an older woman and maternal figure informally by her first name, but Henry quickly decided that when he was in Rome he should do as the Romans did and nodded.

It was at this point that Henry discovered Dingo's father also shared his name; Mrs. Chambers called him Henry while asking if he wanted a cup of tea. Henry looked at Dingo, wondering what else had been kept from him, although the coincidence of a shared name was in no way as huge as the revelation attached to Dingo's grandfather.

Baz said his goodbyes, saying that he had to get home to the "little lady," obviously his wife, Henry decided. Baz looked disappointed, however, to be missing out on the family welcome upon the return of his little brother and his new friend.

"Come over for dinner tomorrow night," his mother suggested. "And bring Margot."

Baz agreed eagerly. "Margot will want to say hello to Dingo. And meet Dash."

"Not the family reunion," Dingo groaned.

"Don't be so ungrateful," his mother chided. "Your brothers will want to see you properly after you being off gallivanting in old Blighty."

"I wasn't gallivanting," Dingo protested, and Henry smiled at seeing him put in his place.

"Henry, dear," Helen said.

"Yes?" both Henry and Hank replied.

"Oh, sorry, I was talking to my husband," Helen said, and Henry colored. Now it was Dingo's turn to laugh. It turned out that Hank was called Henry only, and they *meant* only, by his wife. "Henry, do you want to show the boys through to your study, and I'll prepare the meat for dinner?"

"Sure, love," Hank said warmly. "Lead the way, son."

Dingo nodded, and he gestured to Henry to follow him. They made their way down a dark hall that led outside to a bright, overgrown backyard. Henry followed Dingo, maneuvering around a large pit with a tin cover over it, wondering briefly what it could be.

Hank's study was actually a weatherboard shed that leaned slightly to the left. Henry was amused, standing back and admiring the architecture as Hank fiddled with the lock that hung from the latch on the door.

Hank pushed the door open. "Come into the office, Dash."

Henry sighed mentally; it seemed that Dingo's nickname for him was contagious. Maybe he would just have to accept it, as it would certainly make life easier if he spent any amount of time with the Chambers family. He stepped into the shed, which was dim despite the large window. The window was encrusted with dirt and looked as if it hadn't seen a clean in decades.

Hank noticed where he was looking and said gruffly, "To keep people from spying."

Henry was about to ask what on earth could possibly be so secretive that people had to be discouraged from peeping through the window when Hank swatted at the bare hanging bulb above his shoulder, and Henry found himself face-to-face with a thylacine!

He jumped back before his brain told his body it was obviously an excellent example of taxidermy, but his heart still pounded. Breathing deeply to try and calm his pulse, he circled around the tiger as Hank and Dingo watched him with interest. Henry reached out and rubbed the pelt, which felt exactly the same way as his specimen back at the college did; but this one was draped artfully over a wire frame and mimicked the true shape of the animal. He marveled at the way the back sloped down to the stiff tail, which looked exactly as they did in the photographs he pored over, unlike the flattened piece of fur that he unrolled from its nest of protective paper in the archives section.

Finally looking up, still trying to imagine the thylacine alive and how it would move, the sounds it would make, how the eyes would glisten with life rather than dully stare past him because they were made of glass, Henry could see that the walls were covered with photographs and newspaper clippings. Many of the photos were ones he hadn't seen before, and he immediately coveted them for his own collection, hoping that he would be able to obtain copies before he left Australia for good.

Quite a few photos showed the same handsome man over and over again, and in some of them a young boy also appeared. The man was obviously a hunter, and his prey lay supine at his feet. A lifeless thylacine, spread out and looking like the pelt Henry knew so well back in England. While the man looked proud and confident, the young boy scowled and looked as if he would rather be anywhere but there.

"That's you," Henry said to Hank, pointing out the boy in the photograph.

Hank nodded. "You got me."

Henry turned to Dingo. "So that must be your grandfather."

Dingo nodded. "That's the old bastard, all right."

Henry knew from his tone of voice that there was no affection contained within "old bastard" like there was with "old lady" or "old man."

"Jack!" Hank said sharply, and Dingo jumped at the sound of his father using his real name. Hank softened when he saw the look on his son's face and said softly, "He may have been an old bastard, but he's still your granddad."

"How often did you go on the… hunt?" Henry asked hesitantly.

Hank closed his eyes momentarily and then opened them again. "Too many times."

"What were the tigers like?"

Hank smiled. "They're miracles, Dash. This land is full of the strangest creatures, and every one of them is extraordinary. There are no other animals like them on the face of the earth, as far as we know. That's why it's a crime that the Tassie government tried to wipe them out."

"Tell him about what it was like when you were a kid," Dingo prodded him. His eyes shone with excitement and eagerness to hear the tale again himself, even though Henry knew he had probably heard it countless times before.

"Yes," Henry breathed. "Please do."

His hand trailing gently along the flank of the stuffed thylacine, Hank's mouth grew bitter. "They were always shy, but they got used to us enough that pretty soon at night they would come around. I used to leave them food sometimes, when there was food enough to be left. You could see their eyes glint in the night, and the snuffling noise they made as they ate. If I took a lamp, sometimes I could see their caramel fur move against the brush, their stripes standing out as clear as day. They would cry out to each other—"

Forgetting his usual sense of decorum, Henry interrupted excitedly. "What did they sound like?"

Hank threw back his head and barked a short series of noises—*yip yip yip*—that made Dingo smile affectionately and fascinated Henry.

"I thought they would have sounded more fierce," Henry said in wonder.

"That's the tragedy of the tiger," Dingo told him. "They weren't fierce at all. They were scapegoats for the common dog, brought over by the shipful by the British, and many of them becoming wild."

"They had trouble competing against the feral dogs for food. The dogs are far more aggressive," Hank said.

"Tell Dash about that farm near you where the family had a thylacine as a pet," Dingo urged.

"The Digbys, when my father was a boy. He said they kept a thylacine as a watchdog. It would play with the kids and slept in the house. If you caught one young, as a cub, you could tame them," Hank said sadly.

"How fascinating!" Henry exclaimed. "I never heard that. And despite witnessing that, your father still had no qualms about trapping them?"

"The bounty offered for a thylacine, alive or dead, was too much for him to resist. Especially seeing that our farm failed miserably year after year," Hank said, emotion straining his voice. "I helped my father massacre the tigers in our area. I may not have lifted a gun to do so, but it was my years of making them feel safe on our land that made them so easy for my father to find."

"You were just a kid, Dad," Dingo said comfortingly. "There was nothing you could have done."

Hank shrugged. "Over the years the numbers of them dwindled," he continued, for Henry's benefit. "I moved off the farm as soon as I was old enough. Helen and I married, had our kids."

"When did you move to Melbourne?" Henry asked.

"When I was six," Dingo said.

"Did your grandfather ever take you on a hunt?" Henry asked, dreading the answer. He knew if it was in the affirmative, he shouldn't hold it against Dingo, who would have only been a child. But he didn't want it to mar the respect he was developing for him.

Dingo shook his head. "There was little to hunt by then. The thylacines grew too wary of humans and made sure to stay far away. By then, to kill them, you had to truly hunt them."

"I wouldn't have let any of the boys go anyway," Hank said firmly.

"Our farm failed as well," Dingo said. "That's why we moved."

Henry looked at Hank with awe. "But your obsession survived."

"The same obsession you obviously have." Hank nodded. "It was Gordon who told me about you in the first place."

"You know Gordon Austin?" Henry asked.

"Dad taught him everything he knows about the tiger," Dingo said proudly, and Hank hushed him with an amused glint in his eye.

"Then you know a lot," Henry said with admiration. "Gordon taught me much about the thylacine."

"Even though he's now living in Sydney, he takes an active interest in the survival of the tiger." Hank nodded. "Anyway, he told us about your plans, and that's what got Dingo involved."

Henry looked at Dingo, who was scratching his cheek absentmindedly as if he wanted to downplay everything. "Oh?"

Hank nodded. "Dingo wrote to me from England before you two arrived, telling me all about you and the work you had been doing in England. That's why I knew you could be trusted, Dash. I've had problems before…." He faltered.

"With other people?" Henry asked.

Hank stared at the floor, his mouth tight. "People who wanted to exploit my knowledge so they could find the tiger more easily."

Suddenly the earlier confrontation at the airport made more sense to Henry. "That Hodges fellow."

"He's no *fellow*," Hank said darkly. "Don't underestimate him."

"We saw him at the airport!" Henry exclaimed.

Hank turned on his son. "You couldn't bloody well tell me before this?"

Dingo scratched at his chin, looking slightly ashamed. "Yeah, it slipped my mind. I would've remembered soon enough, though."

"If Hodges is sniffing around, it's a bad sign," Hank said. "You boys are going to have to be careful out there."

"I'm *always* careful," Dingo assured him.

"You're going to have to be *extra* careful," Hank admonished him. "I mean it, Jack."

There it was again. Henry could tell that Dingo's real name was always used when a point was meant to be driven home. And Dingo knew that as well, because he laid a hand upon his father's shoulder and said with full meaning, "We will."

"And you'll have to look after Dash here," Hank reminded him. "That boy doesn't know what he's getting into, so you have to make sure he'll be okay."

"I'll guard him with my life," Dingo promised. "Do you trust me, Dash?"

Henry didn't even have to think about it. "Yes," he replied immediately.

Dingo smiled at him, and Henry once more felt that warm feeling begin in his stomach. He tried to will it away, knowing it would only complicate things. But he couldn't look away. And Dingo held his gaze.

Henry didn't know how long they would have stood like that, staring at each other, but Helen appeared at the door, and their contact was broken.

"Meat's ready," she announced. "Time for you to do some work, Henry."

"What would you like me to do?" Henry asked politely.

Helen pointed at her husband. "*That* Henry. You're a guest, Dash. Your job is to relax."

Henry colored, and Dingo clapped him on the shoulder to lead him out of the shed, his touch burning through the material of Henry's shirt and searing the skin beneath.

7. GETTING TO KNOW THE CHAMBERSES; AND, CONFUSING SIGNALS

THE giant pit in the backyard was what Dingo called a "barbecue." Hank lifted the lid that covered it, and there was a small hand-made grill that sat within it. Dingo collected a small pile of wood and started stuffing it beneath the grill, interspersed with sheets of newspaper. He pulled a box of matches from his back pocket, and Henry tried not to observe how the material pulled over his buttocks and molded to them like a second skin for a few seconds. Soon Dingo had a perfectly contained fire roaring, and Henry was glad of it, for now that the sun was going down a cold wind had started up.

Dingo noticed him shivering. "That's Melbourne for you." He laughed. "Four bloody seasons in a day. That wind comes right up from the Antarctic, and it goes right through you."

Henry didn't want to look too prissy by getting into his jacket, but he moved closer to the fire.

Dingo handed him a beer. "That'll warm you up."

It certainly helped. The alcohol warmed his veins, heating him from within. Henry watched Hank as he laid steaks and sausages across the grill. There was also a cast-iron tray that Helen had filled with potatoes, onions, and mushrooms. Henry's mouth was watering already.

Dingo leaned over the food and poured a liberal amount of beer over the meat, which spat merrily at its strange marinade. Dingo laughed at Henry's perplexed expression. "Tenderizes the meat," he explained, and Henry just decided to accept it.

And when they ate, the meat *was* the tenderest Henry had ever tasted. Who would have thought beer had such magical properties? Once food began to fill his belly, for Helen had also provided a tangy potato salad and fresh homemade bread cut into thick slabs and spread indulgently with butter, Henry felt unaccountably tired watching Hank, Helen, and Dingo laugh and reminisce beside the barbecue pit. But that wasn't the end, for after they made a toast to "Dash" and his first Aussie barbecue, Helen produced a banana pudding the likes of which Henry had never tasted before.

"Dingo, dear, Dash can't keep his eyes open," Helen said. "For pity's sake, take him up to bed."

For some unaccountable reason, Dingo's father seemed to find this amusing, but Henry couldn't for the life of him decipher why.

"You boys will bunk together," Helen continued. "I've aired the sheets and opened the windows."

"I'm not sleepy," Henry mumbled, although his eyes felt heavy and he'd brought his head up with a jerk several times when he nodded off.

"Ah, Dash, come on. I'll take you up and show you where everything is," Dingo said. "It's been a long day, and we haven't seen a proper bed in almost a week."

"Don't worry, son," Hank said, meaning Henry, not his own son. "You can't be off to the wilds of Tasmania tomorrow anyway. Take the time to get some rest because you may be on the run once you get—"

"Henry, dear," Helen said warningly.

"Yes?" Both Henry and Hank answered at once, Henry in confusion and Hank with amusement.

"Henry, dear, you won't mind if I call you Dash, I'm sure," Helen announced. "It'll make everything so much easier, especially tomorrow when both the other boys will be here."

"Of course," Henry mumbled. He startled when he felt Dingo's hand on his arm, pulling him to his feet. He gave an awkward little bow. "Good night, uh, Helen and Hank. It's so good of you to have me."

"It's not them what's having you, Dash, I'm putting you up in my room," Dingo said with a grin. He put his arm around Henry's shoulder. "Your bag is already up there. Up you go then."

Henry was too tired to protest. He stumbled along, almost grateful for the warmth and support of Dingo's arm but uneasy about sharing a room with the man. However, it was likely he could turn to face whatever wall was closest to the bed they put him in and pretty much keep his eyes off Dingo, if not his thoughts.

With the ease of long familiarity, Dingo didn't turn on the downstairs light as he led Henry up the dark stairs.

"The loo is here," Dingo said as he flicked on the light.

The bathroom was small, all the fixtures white, but excruciatingly clean.

"Mum's put out the blue towel for you," Dingo said, pointing it out. "My room's this way."

He led Henry across the hall and turned on the light. Despite the sporting trophies, books, photographs, and models that crammed the shelves, all Henry could take notice of was the bed.

The only bed.

That he was apparently going to have to share with Dingo.

"I can't—we can't—" Henry sputtered.

Dingo gave his shoulders a squeeze. Henry thought he looked unaccountably pleased, his mouth stretched in a wide smile that showed all his gleaming teeth.

"No worries, Dash. I won't be testing your virtue… too much," Dingo teased.

"But I—"

"Look, you can't sleep on the couch; you've been on those mailbags for the past few days. Get some proper rest, Henry. I'll be up later," Dingo said, looking away from Henry, who was relieved because he was afraid that the emotion he felt at Dingo's saying his real name so gently would show on his face. Dingo moved to the door. "Sleep well."

"Which side do you—"

The mischievous smile spread over Dingo's face once more. "I sleep in the middle. Usually. But then, I usually sleep alone." With that Dingo left the room.

Henry stood there for a moment, feeling doomed. There was no way he could sleep in the same bed as Dingo without betraying himself. He imagined being sent home to England in disgrace, his mission a failure and Dingo finding another companion to travel to Tasmania with. Then he yawned. Suddenly he felt so tired that even going to the bathroom to brush his teeth, let alone going to Tasmania, seemed to be an insurmountable expedition.

Methodically he removed his clothing down to his boxers. He hadn't brought pajamas, knowing it was summer in Australia and that most likely he wouldn't be needing them in the bush. Now he would have given anything for the security of pajamas to act as a barrier between him and Dingo. He trudged into the bathroom, making quick work of washing and brushing.

Once in Dingo's room, Henry wanted to explore, but he was too tired. Resolving to try to remember to ask what the trophies were for in the morning, he turned out the light and was soon fast asleep, securely tucked into the left side of the bed with one of the throw pillows lying by his side.

STRUGGLING out of the throes of sleep, Henry felt unaccountably warm. His waking brain tried to make sense of it; the sun coming through the window was hot and bright, even for the early hour, and the slight breeze coming through the window was also balmy. But that wasn't accounting for everything. There was heat against his back, and it felt like a band of burning iron was lying across his chest. Henry looked down and realized he was tightly snuggled into Dingo's tanned arms. He tried to ease away cautiously, even though he felt quite delirious with delight to rest against that firm chest. He also couldn't resist running his hand along the muscle of Dingo's arm, his palm being tickled by the blond hairs beneath it.

He felt Dingo move behind him and dropped his hand away immediately. Out of the corner of his eye, he saw Dingo lean over and his eyes widen with confusion.

Henry opened his mouth to hurry into explanations and apologies, but he was forestalled by Dingo pulling away with a jerk.

"Dibs on the bathroom," Dingo said, and then he was gone.

And that was that.

Henry lay in the bed, not knowing what to do. He could hear water being run in the bathroom, and downstairs it sounded like Helen and Hank were starting to get breakfast ready. He threw on some trousers and a light shirt; it was already so warm he decided to pad down to the kitchen in his bare feet, where he was greeted by the smell of brewing tea and what was obviously a pot of coffee for Dingo and his anti-tea bias.

"Morning, Dash," Hank said cheerfully as he started breaking eggs into a large bowl. "Sleep well?"

"Yes, thank you," Henry replied, trying to look more cheerful than he actually felt.

"Did my great lunk of a son wake you up when he finally stumbled into bed?"

Henry shook his head. *But I definitely was awake when he left it.* He managed to croak out, "Finally?"

"He was going over plans with me until the wee hours of the morning."

"Oh." Henry felt slighted that he wasn't apparently part of this, especially seeing as he was the one actually accompanying Dingo on his travels.

"You're not a morning person, are you?" Hank asked, sizing him up.

Henry realized he wasn't doing a very good job at being a genial guest. "Oh, sorry."

"Are you one of those who need a pot of tea before they can get going?" Hank pushed a cup and saucer before him and headed over to the stove to oblige him.

"I guess so," Henry said, glad for the excuse.

"Just like Dingo." Hank laughed. "Except he can't stand the stuff. Coffee, for him."

"I've noticed." Despite his melancholy, he smiled faintly.

Hank studied him for a moment. "Are you… getting along with Dingo?"

"Getting along?" Henry asked in confusion.

Hank took the pot of tea off the stove and began pouring into his cup. "You know, do you like him?"

"Yes," Henry said falteringly. "He's very easy to… get along with."

"He's a charmer, all right." Hank laughed. "Do you like milk or lemon?"

"Do you have lemon?"

"Have a tree full of them!" Hank disappeared for a few seconds while Henry added sugar to his tea, coming back with a healthy specimen with a fragrance that Henry could smell even before it was cut. Hank sliced it deftly and presented it to his guest. "I'm glad. He doesn't have many friends, you know."

Henry found this hard to believe. "Dingo?"

"Oh, he's got plenty of *acquaintances*. He can talk with anybody, but he hasn't got many *close* friends. I can tell he thinks of you as one."

"How so?" Henry asked, interested.

"He's just so bloody comfortable around you."

He wasn't ten minutes ago, Henry thought. "He seems comfortable around anybody he meets."

"There are differences." Hank shrugged. "You'll probably notice the longer you know him."

At the moment, Henry didn't feel like that would be much longer. He watched the slice of lemon bob upon the surface of his tea and took his first sip.

DINGO'S mood, however, was much changed after breakfast. It seemed any discomfort he felt after waking up had been completely obliterated from his memory, because after he helped Helen wash the dishes, he announced grandly that he was taking Henry to see the sights of Melbourne.

"I reckon that means you're taking my car." Hank frowned.

"That's all right, isn't it, Dad?"

"I guess so."

Surprisingly, Henry found himself speaking up. "If you don't mind, I'd rather go by public transport. I always find that's the best way to explore a city. And to study the people more."

"Looks like my car is mine again," Hank said happily.

"Dad *hates* people borrowing his car," Dingo explained to Henry.

"Not everybody, just you," Hank needled his son. "You're too heavy with the clutch."

"A car needs to be ridden hard every now and again." Dingo smirked. "Just like the person driving it."

Helen struck her errant son with the tea towel. The wet end of it was extremely effective as a whip, and Dingo yelped as it cracked soundly across his arm. "Get out of here, you dirty boy," she said without venom.

Dingo winked at Henry and made a dash out of the room.

"Honestly," Helen sighed. "I don't know what to do with those boys sometimes."

It was an affectionate tone, however. Henry gave her a quick smile, but his mind was already replaying the wink that Dingo gave him and what it meant in context with his ribald remark. He didn't understand the man and his mixed signals; Henry's hopes were raised many a time and destroyed just as quickly in the next moment. He didn't know how he was going to survive the rest of his time in Australia.

8. A MELBOURNE ADVENTURE, WITH A CAMEO BY THE VILLAIN HODGES

"OH, THE light rail," Henry enthused, his face beaming in the warm sunlight pouring through the open window. "This is the way to travel!"

"It's just a tram, Dash," Dingo said, trying not to laugh at his friend's eagerness as the electric vehicle noisily trundled down the track in the middle of the street. They passed beneath an electric node, and a shower of sparks flew past their window as the connector bow made contact. "You do have them in London, remember?"

Henry waved his hand dismissively. "But this is an *Australian* tram. It's new and exciting." He turned his face upward into the sun; *that* was certainly something you didn't experience that often on a London tram.

They got off on Lygon Street and searched for authentic Italian coffees. Henry could close his eyes and pretend he was in Italy as immigrants from that country spoke quickly and furiously in their own tongue above the sound of the espresso machines. Over coffee he wrote Gordon a quick note letting him know that he had arrived safely and was now in the care of Dingo, and then he ran out to post it in a box. From there they jumped on another tram and headed into the city, where Henry marveled at the architecture that in parts seemed so much like London. He especially admired the recently completed Manchester Unity Building just across from the Melbourne Town Hall, which seemed to touch the sky with its Gothic spires. A postcard of it was procured from a street-side newsstand, and Henry surreptitiously stuck it into his journal, which he had thus far managed to keep hidden from Dingo.

A beer was had at Young and Jacksons, a pub a few doors down that had an air of notoriety for its scandalous exhibition of Jules Joseph Lefebvre's nude portrait *Chloe*. Henry flushed upon first viewing the mysterious woman exposed for all to see, and Dingo laughed at him. Her head was slightly turned, as if awaiting her lover to come and ravish her.

"She's… quite pretty," Henry mumbled, as Dingo seemed to be awaiting some reaction from him.

"She also killed herself," Dingo replied matter-of-factly. "She ground matchsticks into a powder, added gin, and drunk the whole thing."

"That's tragic," Henry said, noting that the painting had now taken on a rather morose light.

"That's what love does to you." Dingo shrugged, downing the rest of his beer. "Onward, ho!"

Henry didn't even get to question him about his cryptic statement as they burst back out into the sunlight and fresh air, a sweet relief from the cramped and smoke-filled conditions of the pub. Dingo quickly led him past the ornate façade of Flinders Street Station, where the many clocks hanging above the entrance informed Henry it was only just past eleven in the morning. Had he truly been drinking beer at this time of day? These Australians apparently never wasted a moment of time.

They hopped on board another tram, this time their destination was the beachside suburb of St Kilda. "Worst bloody football team in the league," Dingo sneered, and Henry pretended that he understood what he was talking about.

St Kilda Beach was a bit of a disappointment after all Henry had read about Australian beaches. The sand felt like crushed egg shells and was more grit than sand. Too much like an English beach. Dingo told him that the best beaches were found further down south and on the west coast nineteen hundred miles across the border. Despite the heat of the day, neither decided to go for a dip, and instead they bought ice cream from a local store in order to cool down.

Henry was surprised by how much he felt *alive* in Melbourne. He loved London, but there was something to the character of this strange city—how foreign, and yet how familiar, it seemed! He felt comfortable here, although that could have had a lot to do with the man walking by his side. Dingo seemed to have the ability to put him at ease like no other person ever had. Although they were really only at the beginning of their adventure, Henry didn't even want to think about what would happen once he had to return to England. He was already feeling that he couldn't go back to that cloistered, sheltered life he had been resigned to back home, not when a new world had been opened up for him.

Dingo suddenly took him by the arm, and Henry protested when the creamy remains of his chocolate ice went flying into the sand.

"Down here," Dingo instructed, steering him toward an underground pedestrian walkway that led from the beach to the main road.

"What are you doing?" Henry asked.

"I swear I just saw Hodges following us," Dingo said shortly.

"That man from the airport?"

"One and the same."

"But what is he doing here?"

"Are you not listening to me, Dash? As I said, he's *following* us."

"But why?"

"Just keeping dibs on us, probably trying to figure out when we're setting off for Tassie."

Henry felt that if they were being followed, seeking refuge in a small tunnel with only one possible exit was probably not the wisest thing. But he felt it prudent not to bring this up with Dingo and at least trust that the man had some alternative course of action.

"When I say so," Dingo muttered, still gripping Henry's elbow, "run."

Henry didn't like the sound of that but readied himself.

Dingo looked back behind them. Henry did so as well but couldn't make anything out. There were a few other people using the tunnel from both directions, but they were little more than silhouettes due to the fact that the sunlight behind them rendered them so.

"Run!" Dingo commanded.

Henry took off without a second thought; there was really only one direction he could go. He could hear and sense Dingo behind him, their footfalls echoing heavily in the confined space. Henry collided with someone walking in the opposite direction and called out his apologies but felt Dingo shove him in the back to keep him moving.

They burst out back into the light, and Henry felt dizzy at the sudden sensory overload. Dingo grabbed him once more by the elbow, and Henry ran blindly. His eyes gradually adjusted again, and he became aware that they were racing for a tram that was just closing its doors.

Dingo banged upon the door, and the driver opened up for him. Both men jumped on, and the doors immediately closed behind them. The tram shuddered and accelerated away from the stop just as Hodges banged upon the doors to try and get on. This time, the driver ignored it as they were already in motion.

"That was close," Henry said as they showed their tickets to the inspector.

"It's not over yet," Dingo said, pointing out the window to where Hodges was trotting resolutely a short distance behind the tram. "He'll catch up at the next stop."

Henry didn't even understand why they were running from Hodges; it hadn't seemed like Dingo had been scared of him before. Then he realized that Dingo was enjoying this and was treating it like a game. All to get the better of the other man and keep him four steps behind whatever Dingo's plan was.

There was a huge grin playing upon Dingo's lips as he looked up at the tram tracks ahead. "Come on."

Henry followed him up the aisle to where the second set of doors sat in the middle of the tram. As was the nature of trams, there were doors on both sides with one set disabled, depending upon which side of the tracks the passengers would enter and exit.

"What are you doing?" Henry asked, already knowing he wasn't going to like the answer.

"We're getting off."

Henry assumed that he didn't mean the traditional way. That would be far too tame for Dingo. The tram was beginning to slow as it reached the next stop, and Hodges was going to make it. As the tram rattled to a stop, Henry pushed the doors open and peered down the track.

"When I tell you to, jump. Grab the left handle, and I'll grab the right," Dingo instructed.

Henry saw a tram coming toward them from the opposite direction and realized what Dingo wanted them to do. "You have to be joking!"

"Nope," Dingo said maddeningly.

"This is stupid!" Henry cried. "He knows where we're going to end up at the end of the day! At your parents' house! Why bother?"

Dingo shrugged. "Because it'll piss him off."

Henry knew this was mad, but Dingo was determined to do it. And even though he didn't feel threatened by Hodges one bit as nobody else seemed to take him that seriously, Henry still didn't want to remain on the tram and have to talk to him or even acknowledge his presence.

"Ready?" Dingo asked.

"No!"

"I thought you said you trusted me?"

"I didn't know it would involve stupid stunts like this!"

"Live a little, Dash! One.... two...."

Hodges, panting, clambered up the steps to the doors at the opposite end of the tram and immediately began searching for them. Henry could see the glint in his eyes as Hodges spotted his quarry in the middle of the vehicle.

"Three!" Dingo bellowed.

As the tram shuddered past them, the two men leaped through the air in the incredibly narrow space between the two vehicles. Henry immediately grabbed the door handle on the left, which was the only thing keeping him balanced on the small inch of foot space available on the closed door. Dingo, however, was not so lucky. His feet skidded out from under him, and he was left hanging on the right side handle. He kicked his feet up so they would stay off the rapidly moving ground below them and scrambled up to find his footing. Henry reached out with his right hand and steadied him as he found sure ground to support himself. Dingo threw him an appreciative look and then whooped with delight as he turned back to see Hodges's irate face pressed against the window on the other tram, disappearing in the distance.

"What now?" Henry yelled above the sound of the wind and the machinery.

"We go home," Dingo said, using his left hand to pry open the door. The two men fell into the tram, landing awkwardly against the stairs. They lay there for a moment, stunned, and then began to laugh at the fact that they had actually survived the crazy thing they had just done.

"I told you to trust me," Dingo panted, patting Henry's shoulder.

"I must be crazier than you are," Henry replied.

Dingo's hand rested upon his shoulder, and the man was staring at him intensely. Henry didn't know what to say, but the tram began slowing, and the jerk caused them both to fall back against the stairs again. Dingo's hand fell away as he reached for the rail to support himself.

A conductor was racing down the aisle toward them at the same time the driver's door banged open, and the furious-looking driver came barreling down the aisle from the other direction. "What the hell are you two pork chops playing at?"

"You could have been killed!" yelled the conductor. "Bloody idiots!"

Mortified at this public spectacle, Henry staggered to his feet and stood behind Dingo.

However, the driver's face changed at the sight of Henry's companion. "Dingo!" He turned to the conductor. "It's okay, I know them. Well, this fool at least."

"Rick, mate, how are you?" Dingo leaned in and pumped the other man's hand furiously as the conductor made his way back to his stool and continued glowering at them.

"Do you know everybody in this bloody city?" Henry asked irritably, not liking the level of familiarity between the two men.

"We're old friends," Dingo said smoothly. "Good thing we landed on your tram, huh, Ricky?"

Ricky jerked his head and winked, grinning broadly. "I'm sure you have friends wherever you land, right, Dingo?"

The two men continued to talk to each other as Dingo accompanied the driver back to his squab, and Henry moved away to take a seat, retrieve his handkerchief from his pocket, and mop his brow. The adrenaline that had been pumping through his veins had rapidly subsided, and he was now left with a strange feeling akin to jealousy.

Henry knew he had to stop feeling this way, but he couldn't help it. He stared out the window and longed for their quick return to Carlton.

9. HENRY FINDS EVEN MORE CHAMBERSES TO CONTEND WITH

THE roar emanating from the front yard alerted Henry to the fact that Dingo's brothers had converged on the old family manse, although he would have thought that two men and their wives weren't capable of making such a din. Of course, Dingo *was* down there to greet them, along with his dad.

"Dash! Get yer bloomin' arse down here!" Dingo bawled from the foot of the stairs. "We'll be out back!"

Henry grinned as he tossed his book aside, speculating that the quiet was finished for the night. He didn't realize how right he was as he made his way down the stairs.

Helen greeted him in the kitchen, where she was piling great slabs of raw meat onto a tray. "Dash, dear, go right on out there. And please bring this out to Henry." She smiled at him as she hefted the tray and thrust it into his hands.

He gasped, almost dropping it in surprise at the weight. Helen handled it as if it were a featherweight, whereas it must have been at least twenty pounds.

"Off with you then, Dash. The children will be getting hungry," Helen said with a doting smile.

Somehow Henry knew the smile was for her grandchildren and not for him. While Helen turned back to her preparations, Henry nudged the screened door open with his hip, wincing at the cacophony that struck his ears.

Shrieks of gleeful joy echoed from where Dingo was walking, albeit with great difficulty as he had a little carbon copy of himself clinging to each leg. Henry marveled at how much the boys bore the family resemblance, as if they had sprung from one of the brother's loins fully formed, with no assistance from a woman.

Dingo was growling, Baz was howling with laughter at something his father had said, and another man, his face bearing the inimitable Chambers stamp, was shouting something at the boys who held Dingo captive. Henry deduced that he must be Johnno. Two young women were conversing excitedly, their voices shrill to be heard over the noise.

To Henry, used to the quiet decorum of his own family gatherings, it felt as if the yard were crowded with people, all of them yelling and laughing at once. For a man used to reserved politeness, it was mayhem, and yet Henry felt more at home than he'd ever been with his own parents and brother.

Dutifully he made his way to the older Henry and yelled into his ear, "Helen sent this out for you!"

"Righto then, Dash. Set 'er down round about there," Hank answered, pointing vaguely at the rock ring that now encircled a briskly snapping fire. "Coals aren't ready yet. Women know nothing about roasting meat outdoors. Lost without a stove, they are."

"You must be Dash. Johnno here. Pleased to meet you." Johnno waited for Henry to set his burden down and pumped his hand vigorously. "My boys, Jack and Baz," he said, waving a hand toward Dingo and his riders.

"Isn't it confusing to name them after your brothers?" Henry asked.

"Why, who *else* would I name them after?" Johnno roared with laughter. "Besides, Dingo never answers to Jack unless dad is reading him the riot act, and we don't live near enough Baz for it to matter three days out of seven. Watch this." He turned his head, put his hands to his mouth, and yelled, "Baz, on the double!"

Henry snickered as Johnno's son and brother both blithely ignored his summons.

"See? Don't make any difference," Johnno said proudly. "They're all a proper bunch of varmints. Won't get tamed down 'til some woman catches hold of them."

Henry winced slightly at the thought, even while noticing the two young women eyeing him with interest. "I should go and introduce myself—"

"Lori Lou! Margot! This here's Dingo's mate, Dash!"

Henry almost covered his ears when Johnno began to bellow out the introductions, but Dingo's brother had a firm hold on his nearest arm.

"Lori Lou's my ball and chain. Margot's Baz's," Johnno explained.

Henry wondered if Lori Lou could *really* be her name but was too polite to ask. He would find out later through Dingo that because she came from an area in the Victorian countryside known for its wild ways, she'd had the nickname bestowed upon her.

"My, he's a good-looking fellow, isn't he?" Margot giggled.

"If you like them skinny," Lori Lou said. She slid her hand into the crook of her husband's arm, squeezing his bicep. "I like a bit of meat on a boy."

"Well, but you're not taking him home when you've got Johnno then, are you?" Margot insisted. "I'm just speaking hypothetically in any case, seeing as he belongs to Dingo."

Blushing furiously, Henry stammered, "Your boys are very, uh, spirited, Mrs. Chambers."

Lori Lou joined her husband in laughter. "Well, they'd have to be, don't they? They're Chamberses. If I'd given birth to a quiet bookish sort, Johnno'd think I'd played him false, wouldn't you, honey?" She smiled up at her husband, who grinned back.

"Right you are, love. No insult intended, Dash," he added hastily, as if just remembering that Henry was pale, skinny, and wore glasses, sure signs of bookishness, if there were any.

"None taken," Henry said, amused. "Some of us are doomed to the bookish pursuits."

"It's the glasses," Margot agreed, nodding wisely. "Hard to play cricket in specs."

"Actually," Henry started, beginning to puff himself up a bit. After all, he had played all through college, and rather well, too, although not on the house team. But his panegyric about his own athletic prowess was cut short when Dingo, burdened by his nephews, barreled into him, knocking him off his feet. At once, Henry found himself rolling in the rough grass, gasping when Dingo's weight pressed him into the earth only to roll off, leaving him the prisoner of two small boys.

"Grab him, Baz!" Jack cried shrilly, attaching himself to Henry's right arm and using his full weight to pin it to the ground.

Baz Jr. didn't answer, being busy with trying to sit on both of Henry's long legs at once.

Dingo laughed from where he was sitting in the grass. "Looks like *Gulliver's Travels* for you, Dash! Cheerio!"

"Hey, you can't leave me here, a prisoner of these ruthless—" Henry gasped as Jack kneed him accidentally in the solar plexus. "Oh, you two are so going to regret this. Don't you even wait to be introduced to people before you take them prisoner?"

"Yo ho ho, we're going to stew you in Grandpa's giant pot and eat you!" Baz Jr. screamed.

"Savage cannibals, eh? You can't eat me, not if I eat you first!" Henry shook himself free, gently tumbling the boys onto the grass and got to his feet. Both boys hurled themselves at him, but he caught them round their waists and lifted one under each arm, letting out a yelp of triumph. "Where's that pot? I've got dinner right here."

Dingo was still sitting on the grass, laughing fit to kill himself. "Dash, I never thought you had it in you," he cried unhelpfully.

"Point me to the nearest cage. I've got to keep these two prisoner while I sharpen my knife," Henry said threateningly. He grinned at the delighted squeals from the two boys, who wriggled in his arms trying to get free, even though it was all he could do to hold them.

"Toss me the big one, and I'll show you where we pen them up 'til we cook them," Dingo said.

It wasn't much of a toss, but when Dingo's hands were supporting Jack, Henry shifted his weight to transfer the boy. "Lead the way, Dingo." Henry shifted young Baz up onto his shoulders while Dingo raised Jack with seemingly little effort, slinging him crosswise over his own shoulders.

"Dad, look what we've caught for you to barbecue for dinner," Dingo said, heading for Hank.

Hank played right along, poking a finger into the tummy of his giggling grandson. "These are nice juicy ones. And the fire's almost ready."

"Grandpa, it's me!" Jack shrieked. "You can't eat me!"

"Why, they talk too! Where did you find such a fine specimen?" Johnno said.

"Dad, no, it's us!" Baz Jr. cried out.

"And they're pretending to know us too," Johnno said admiringly. "Clever ruse!"

"All right, then, that's enough," Helen said calmly, much to Henry's relief.

Even though he'd started it, he'd had no idea how to finish the charade. Helen gave him a warm smile, and, from the twinkle in her eye, he suspected that she had realized his dilemma and had taken mercy on him.

"I'll take them," Lori Lou said, holding out her arms.

Henry admired the way she was able to heft both of them on her hips, although both boys slid down and ran away from her as soon as they could.

"Whew," Dingo said, slinging his arm across Henry's shoulders. "Got nephews?"

"One," Henry admitted.

"He must love you. You're good with kids."

Thinking of certain illicit fishing expeditions he had enjoyed with his nephew as his brother James deemed it a sport below people of their status and better left to gamekeepers, Henry's face creased in a secret smile. "Perhaps."

"Meat's ready, boys," Hank called out.

Dingo clapped Henry on the back. "Let's eat."

HENRY enjoyed watching the Chambers family members as they ate. The noise continued unabated, and he wondered that the neighbors seemed to accept it with equanimity as none of them appeared to complain. The two boys were so excited to see their uncle Dingo that they barely let him eat and didn't eat much themselves, amusing themselves by howling in his ears like dingos whenever he took a bite.

It amused Henry to see that Lori Lou and Margot seemed to be able to put away almost as much beer as their husbands. Everyone drank, but no one got noticeably drunker, as nobody sat still for any appreciable length of time.

When the fire died down to embers, Helen brought out a flashlight and shone it upward on her face, giving herself a lugubriously spooky look. She started telling a ghost story, and at a critical juncture, handed the light to her son Johnno, who took up the tale with relish.

Henry deduced that this was for the benefit of Johnno's sons. They listened with wide eyes and open mouths, gradually abandoning Dingo and creeping closer to their mother.

By the time the flashlight reached Hank, the boys were fighting to stay awake, and accordingly Hank let his voice grow lower and lower until they were asleep.

"Better take them up to bed, John," Helen said.

"Right, mum."

Johnno picked up Jack, while Lori Lou lifted Baz Jr. "We'll see you lot in the morning. Thanks for playing with the boys, Dash."

Henry felt a little glow at Johnno's praise. Dingo bumped his shoulder gently and smiled at him.

After Johnno and his family went upstairs, the group around the embers grew quieter, Helen nestled in Hank's arm, and Margot pressed up against Baz for warmth.

Self-consciously, Henry drew a little way away from Dingo, feeling the odd man out in this familial gathering for the first time that evening.

HENRY awakened in what must have been the early hours of the morning. The room was bathed in a chalky, blue-ish moonlight, throwing everything into a muted relief; it was also blessedly silent of Dingo's snores.

Because Dingo was also awake and staring right at him.

"Is everything all right?" Henry asked hesitantly.

Dingo didn't say anything; he merely nodded.

Henry grew puzzled as Dingo pulled down the blankets that covered them. Clad only in his boxers, Dingo then rolled over onto his side and slowly inched them down over his hips. Henry couldn't withhold his breath and gasped as he first sighted the cleft between Dingo's buttocks. The boxers continued coming down, and with his back still turned to the other man, Dingo casually reached down and threw them free of his body.

Henry wanted nothing more than to turn Dingo around and gaze at him fully, but he could only watch fascinated as Dingo ran his hand over his own arse, stirring the light golden hairs upon the cheeks. Henry could feel his cock straining against his own boxers, a small damp spot already forming from his own excitement.

He sighed with desire as Dingo gently parted and lifted one of his arse cheeks, presenting himself as if a gift.

"Dingo…." Henry breathed, as if awaiting verbal permission.

Dingo still didn't say anything but remained in the same position.

Henry couldn't control himself any longer. He sucked on his index finger, slicking it up. He tentatively traced around Dingo's hole, and Dingo withdrew his own hand. It was now all Henry's, to do with whatever he wished. Gently, Henry breached Dingo with his finger, and the other man's back arched. Henry supported his neck with his free hand, his finger exploring further within. He massaged the silky walls, and Dingo moved in closer to him.

"Is that good?" he asked, but Dingo's only response was to try and impale himself further.

Henry withdrew his finger and sucked on it again for further lubrication. This time he was rewarded with the musky taste of Dingo himself, and his cock surged with a further rush of blood. Dingo gave a small grunt as he was thrust into again, this time Henry curved his finger tip slightly and found the nub he was searching for. Dingo was now writhing in front of him, and Henry's cock was begging for release. With a slight sucking sound, he pulled his finger out and offered it to Dingo to suck upon. As he felt Dingo's mouth close over it, Henry groaned and wriggled out of his boxers as best he could. His cock jutted painfully free from the fabric, and his boxers went flying across the room. Henry regretfully pulled his finger out of Dingo's mouth, and with both hands turned Dingo upon his stomach. His delectable bum rose before Henry, and he scaled it as if he were the first explorer to ever do so. His cock brushed against Dingo's cleft, the tip threatening to slip in and begin penetration. Henry dragged himself further up Dingo's back, his balls tightening as they brushed against Dingo's bum. Desperate for friction, Henry ground his cock against one of Dingo's arse cheeks—

—Henry's own groans suddenly woke him up. Panicked, he realized he was lying flush against Dingo's chest. His cock was rock hard, and he was thrusting against Dingo's thigh. Before he even fully realized what he was doing, he thrust a little bit more to the left and hit the full hardness of Dingo's own cock. Now Henry was speeding up, feeling his balls tighten. He moaned with an equal measure of fear and lust; he knew he shouldn't be doing this, but he was too far gone. This was tantamount to taking advantage of Dingo, using him as a means to get off. He almost stopped when Dingo moaned in his sleep, but the other man was now mirroring his thrusts as he strove toward his own climax. Henry stopped and rested his cock against Dingo's, and then he wriggled his hips to grind deeper into the other man as he finally came, spurting into his boxers.

Henry shuddered; his body was slick with sweat, but Dingo continued to jerk his hips, and Henry couldn't help but watch the other man as he was about to come. Dingo's lip curled, his eyes screwed shut in sleep, a low moan emanating from him that caused blood to rush to Henry's cock again. Dingo jabbed Henry's thigh and rested there; Henry felt the warm wetness of come seep through the material, and some of it found a home amongst the hair on his leg.

Fearfully, he waited for Dingo to wake up, but Dingo just smacked his lips contentedly and settled back into a deep sleep. Relieved, Henry continued to lie there, guilt threatening to overcome him as he remembered the sheer wantonness of his dream and felt the sweat and come on him begin to cool. He couldn't help but run his finger along the spot where Dingo's spunk had settled upon his thigh, and he scooped it up and brought it to his lips. It was salty, sweet, and he felt as if he had just drunk up Dingo whole.

He could almost have fallen asleep smiling, if it hadn't been for the fact that he wished Dingo had been awake and wanted him just as badly in return.

WHEN Henry woke again, it was to sunshine and an empty bed. He remembered immediately the events of the previous hours and sat upright, panicked. His boxers were crusty against him, and he flushed as he looked down at his thigh and could make out a slight snail trail of Dingo's dried come.

He had no idea where Dingo was, but the bathroom was free so he immediately bathed, washing the evidence of the night's crimes away.

What if Dingo had seen for himself the state of Henry's shorts when he had woken up? Sure, Dingo's own boxers would also bear fruit, but what would he think? This was unbelievable!

He could only take heart in the fact that he hadn't been awakened by a punch in the face, which was what he deserved.

"Stupid fucking Henry," he murmured disconsolately to himself. "This could ruin everything."

There was no sign of Hank or Helen when he made his way into the kitchen half an hour later. Now he was really feeling paranoid. Henry walked into the backyard, determined that at least a brief respite in the sunlight should do wonders for his mood. As he did so, the door to the outside toilet flew open, and Dingo emerged from within.

Henry flushed as Dingo stretched lazily. He was still only clad in his boxers and nothing else. The fur on his chest gleamed in the sun, and as the muscles on his abdomen contracted, the boxers slipped on his hips and Henry was treated to the sight of a large tuft of hair that gave promise of what lay further beneath the material.

Dingo yawned and scratched at his belly. He finally saw Henry standing across from him.

"Morning," he said affably. "The dunny's free, if you need it."

Henry could barely meet his eyes. "No, I'm fine, thank you." He couldn't look at Dingo, especially in this state of undress, which just made Henry want to revisit what had happened during the night. Except this time, he wanted to see Dingo naked, to see him erect and wanting him….

"Did you sleep well?" Dingo asked.

Henry nodded. "You?"

"Best night's sleep in a long time," Dingo said innocently. "You're not that bad a bedmate, Dash."

Henry had absolutely no idea how to react. "I'm going to make tea," he said finally.

Dingo nodded. "I'm going to get scrubbed up."

Henry watched him walk inside, even more confused than he had been moments before. He had no idea what Dingo was up to, but he had no choice but to play along.

10. FOR THOSE IN PERIL ON THE SEA

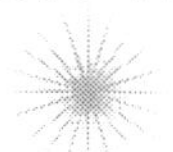

THAT afternoon, Helen and Hank drove Dingo and Henry to the docks of Port Melbourne that were to be their departure ground for Tasmania. They were booked on a ship that had only just recently started taking paying passengers along with cargo. “Friend of a friend helped set it up,” Dingo said airily, only further proving Henry’s belief that the man knew everybody who happened to breathe in the city.

Contrary to the stately and regal names given to ships of the Empire, this ship had the strange and alien name so suited to the country it serviced: the *Taroona*. It was a smaller ship compared to those Henry had seen in his time, but it still towered above them, and its two funnels stretched proudly into the sky. It had only been launched that year; the green paint on the hull still seemed fresh.

“It can carry four hundred and fifty passengers and thirty vehicles,” Helen mused aloud while leafing through the brochure she had picked up on the dock.

“I know it’s no *Titanic*,” Dingo said to Henry almost apologetically, his white teeth flashing in the sun with his smile.

“Let’s hope not, for both our sakes,” Henry replied, and he was gratified by the loud laugh that emanated from his colleague. It appeared that the tension between them, even though it seemed to come all from Henry’s side, had evaporated.

“If you’re brave enough to get on that tin can that flew you across the world, I wouldn’t think you’d have a problem with the *Taroona*,” Hank observed, with a shiver that Henry couldn’t fail to notice.

“No problem,” Henry said more blithely than he felt. “No problem at all.” Truth be told, he was more afraid of being alone with Dingo again. He hoped it would be single beds in their cabin; he did not want a repeat of last night’s somnambulistic performance.

It was very easy to get caught up in the romance of boat travel as they said their goodbyes to friends. Henry was surprised by how quickly he had formed an attachment to the Chambers family, especially Helen and Hank. He was genuinely sad to depart from them and heartened by the fact that he would get to see them again before he had to return to England. He also hoped that wouldn't be the last time.

Especially because that could quite possibly mean it would be the last time he would see Dingo again.

But he didn't want to think about that just now.

"Dash," Hank said suddenly. "Walk with me."

Henry could see Dingo's eyes widen and then narrow with suspicion as he tried to figure out why his father might be pulling Henry aside. But he couldn't do anything about that; he just allowed himself to be led farther down the jetty and edged away from the water by Hank until they were well out of range of Dingo's hearing.

Henry gave a last quick desperate look to Dingo's direction, but he was talking with Helen. Perhaps trying to glean from her what Hank's motives could be for this tête-à-tête.

"Sir, I—" Henry began, but Hank cut him off.

"What have I told you, Dash? No formalities here."

Henry thought that over. "All right. But what is it that you want to talk to me about?"

Hank laughed. "You're no fool, Henry, so stop acting like one."

Those words made Henry's blood run cold. "I'm not sure what you're saying…." He drifted off as Hank raised a skeptical eyebrow at him. He drew himself up further. "Perhaps you should just say what it is you want to say, Hank."

Hank nodded respectfully. "Okay, then." He took a deep breath. "Dingo is different to his brothers. Different in a way that, no offense, you're also different."

Henry didn't feel his blood could get any colder. "I'm not sure what you mean," he said, his tone brittle.

"Don't try and lead me on a merry dance, Dash. I know the steps, because I love my son, and I have seen them in him. Now, it doesn't make a lick of difference to me, his mum, or his brothers. The only people it seems to bother are those whose business it doesn't concern anyway. We just want him to have the happiness we have found."

Henry cleared his throat and was able to croak out, "And what does that have to do with me?"

"Just that we've all taken a shine to you, Dash. But Dingo means everything to us, and we don't want to see him hurt. We just want you to do the right thing by him."

Henry opened his mouth to speak but was forestalled by a loud screech from one of the funnels of the *Taroona.*

"Time to board." Hank said. "Are you ready?" He turned to rejoin his family before Henry could even answer.

Henry wanted to yell after Hank that no, he wasn't ready. In fact, he was even more confused than he had been before. Was Hank saying that Dingo was… *like* Henry? A queer? It seemed unfathomable that a man like Dingo could be one, at least going by the other people with similar sensibilities that Henry had met. Of course, it could also be said that Henry's own experiences had been rather limited. The more he was beginning to see of the world, the more Henry was beginning to understand that there were a lot of things he knew very little about.

But he knew now, as he thought of his cloistered existence in the basement of Ealing College, that he was glad he had come on this adventure. And right now he didn't even want to think of it ending.

He just wished he could be more clear on the most troublesome aspects of this new adventurous life. Dingo, of course, was the most troublesome. And also the most pleasurable.

For all of Hank's sincerity about wanting to put everything on the line, Henry was now even more confused by the coded statements that he'd made. After all, it was only the other day that Hank had been telling him that Dingo had many acquaintances, but very few true friends. Most probably, he was just alluding back to that, Henry thought with regret. There was no way that *Dingo—*

But there was no time to dwell upon that now.

"Come on, Dash!" Dingo yelled. "We don't want to miss the boat!"

After receiving another crushing last-minute handshake from Hank and a hug from Helen, Henry started up the gangplank. He looked back to see Dingo exuberantly hugging his parents goodbye and giving his mother a resounding kiss on the cheek. He was touched by the other man's open affections and his lack of embarrassment about it. The last time he had seen his parents before he left for Australia, Henry had stiffly shaken his father's hand and gave his mother a quick peck. They would have been astounded and ashamed of him if he had been any more demonstrative.

The confusing emotions welling up within him told Henry that he was much more upset about leaving the Chamberses than he was his own family. How quickly their attachments to each other had formed!

Dingo bounded up the gangplank to join Henry. "Come on, you're holding up the line."

"Me?" Henry spluttered, but Dingo merely tossed him a grin and dragged him to the railing on the passenger deck, where they waved to Hank and Helen below them.

"So," Dingo said casually, although it was apparent to both of them that his interest was anything but. "What did my old man want with you?"

Truthfully, even Henry didn't really even know. And he wasn't sure if he could tell Dingo what he suspected his father had shared with him. "Oh, just to make sure I didn't let you get into any mischief."

Dingo frowned as if he didn't fully believe him. "Dad knows this whole business is based on mischief."

"He's your father," Henry said simply. "He worries about you."

The boat lurched beneath their feet as the gangplanks were lowered and the *Taroona* started to pull away from its moorings. They stood in silence once more as they waved to the Chamberses along with the other passengers who were waving goodbye to their own loved ones.

As the ship headed for the wide blue expanse of the sea, Helen and Hank became mere specks among a mass of indiscriminate shapes. Dingo sighed sadly, like he was heading to another country rather than merely another state.

"Do you get seasick, Dash?" he asked, as if distracting himself.

Henry frowned. He had never been on a boat before. "I'm… I'm not really sure, to tell you the truth."

Dingo whistled. "This is going to be a trial by fire, then."

Henry didn't like the sound of that. "What do you mean?"

"This is one of the roughest seas in the world, mate. Notorious amongst even seasoned sailors."

Henry's grip tightened on the railing, and he stared out at the ocean. The shoreline of Victoria was getting further and further away, and he was now beginning to realize just how empty and limitless the water beneath him truly was. "You mean to say you *knowingly* put us on a dangerous ocean in this *tiny* little piece of tin?"

"Shush, Dash," Dingo said earnestly. "You'll make the womenfolk nervous."

Henry looked around him. All of the other passengers on deck seemed oblivious to his newfound terror as they chatted amongst each other without a care in the world. It was all an adventure to them, it seemed. Or maybe they just didn't know the danger they were in.

They probably also didn't have a tour guide like Dingo to blithely point out just how many ways they could die in this God-forsaken country.

"Are all Australians barking mad?" Henry asked.

Dingo pushed his hat back on his head and sniffed deeply at the salt air with relish. "When your time's up, it's up, Dash. No need to worry about until it happens."

"It doesn't follow that I want to be complacent and invite death to come looking for me either," Henry countered.

Dingo laughed. "The way you're going, Dash, you'll probably have a heart attack before you're forty."

"Thanks very much! If I live that long!"

"Just telling it as I see it," Dingo said, his voice now taking on a distracted tone. He suddenly became alert, like a rabbit sensing a predator. Except this bunny grinned, because it knew it would outwit the fox. "And I see our old friend Hodges is aboard."

Henry peered over Dingo's shoulder to see their supposed nemesis at the other end of the deck. Hodges grinned rakishly and tipped his hat to them.

Dingo moved as if he were going to reply with a totally different gesture that would have been out of place in polite society, but all it took was Henry saying his name gently to make him sigh and lean back against the railing.

"I wonder how he got on board without us seeing him," Dingo growled.

"It wouldn't have been that hard." Henry shrugged. "The passenger list is quite extensive."

"I should have seen him."

Henry stared at the other man, who was glowering with badly disguised anger. "You can't see *everything*, Dingo."

"It's your fault," Dingo fumed.

"*My* fault?" Henry asked in amazement.

"Yes! If you hadn't distracted me—"

"*Distracted* you?" They were playing the echo game again, apparently.

"Yes!"

"So I'm a distraction?"

His guard down, Dingo seemed furious with himself for not being aware of Hodges before the man let his presence be known. Henry wasn't sure what the history was between the two men, but he could only assume Dingo didn't often let Hodges get the upper hand. "I've always managed to dance a step or two ahead of him. Yes, you're always a distraction—" Dingo broke off quickly.

Henry was bewildered, unsure of his meaning. And he hated the way his heart began to race, eagerly hoping that Dingo was talking about something else entirely unrelated to this situation with Hodges. It brought to mind his conversation with Hank and gave him false hope that it could be an indication of the way Dingo really felt about him.

"Anyway," Dingo said, trying to cover up just as quickly. "I'm going to make sure our luggage reached our room."

Henry didn't know whether he should stay or follow him. He stood there, feeling rather stupid, but Dingo turned back to him.

"You coming?"

Henry followed him wordlessly, his heart still beating dangerously. If he could turn back time, he would go right back to the instant the boat whistle blew for boarding and demand that Hank be less obtuse.

Now it all just felt a thousand times worse.

NIGHT had barely fallen when Henry started feeling the effects of seasickness.

He and Dingo had eaten a brief dinner and were trying to walk it off on the deck when Henry felt the first roll of his stomach. It was actually moving in time to the rolling of the deck. The weather was worsening, and large waves were beginning to crash against the side of the boat.

"How are you not sick?" Henry demanded, hanging onto the railing for dear life.

"To tell you the truth, I'm feeling a little crook myself," Dingo admitted. "But it helps getting my mind off it by having to look out for you."

"I don't need looking after," Henry said peevishly, then groaned as the boat lurched underneath them.

Dingo laughed. "I know."

The railing made Henry feel a little more steady on his feet, and he tried not to look down at the boiling sea below them, a form of vertigo he did not need to be introduced to. "Maybe we should get inside," he groaned.

"Fresh air will be better for you," Dingo told him.

Henry felt as if his face were being torn open by the sharp corners of the wind and the salt that whipped into the wounds caused by them. *Yes, refreshing*, he felt like saying in the most sardonic tone he could muster, but he felt that if he opened his mouth again he would only vomit.

The *Taroona* lurched beneath them as if the ocean had suddenly drained away, and Henry distinctly felt the deck drop away from beneath him as the boat sought to find water again. The slap of the hull against the waves and the subsequent jerk that followed did him in, and he leaned over the railing to empty his stomach.

"Ah, Dash," Dingo said sympathetically, laying his hand on the other man's shoulder.

Henry closed his eyes for a brief moment, taking what comfort he could from Dingo's touch. "I'm fine," he said stubbornly, wiping his mouth.

"No, you're not."

"I assure you—" Henry didn't get to finish his sentence as he was leaning over the rail again and trying to bring up whatever was left in his stomach.

This time, Dingo's hand moved down to the small of Henry's back, beginning to rub small, soothing circles. Henry knew it wasn't having any physiological effect upon his illness, but the psychological benefit was great. He leaned into the touch, wanting more even though his body was rebelling against him in every way. But it wasn't for long, as he was retching again.

Now Dingo's hand slipped against Henry's stomach and supported him against his chest. "Just let it go, Dash," he murmured.

The warmth from Dingo's body was agony to Henry; it reminded him of the few awkward sexual fumblings he'd had with other men and provided an all-too-vivid recollection of what had occurred between him and Dingo the other morning. This was all madness. But as his body tried to continue rejecting what was no longer left within him, he didn't dwell upon it.

"I think… that's the last of it," Henry gasped, trying to catch his breath back.

"And I think I should get you into bed," Dingo replied.

With Dingo's arms around him, it was almost possible to believe the man meant it in an entirely different way than Henry was supposed to take it. He sagged against Dingo and then realized what he was doing and straightened up. Armed with some strange bravado borne from being sick and feeling dangerously on the edge, Henry decided to play the double entendre game as well. "Yes, yes, I'd say you're right."

Dingo kept a hand on his arm, but Henry shrugged it off. "I'm okay."

But even that didn't last for long. Once they were back in the cabin and Henry was lying on the single bed that only hours before he had been thankful to see, he began to be sick again even though there was nothing left in his stomach. Dingo dampened a towel and laid it across his forehead; he also managed to scrounge up a small bowl from beneath the basin.

"You're sweating," Dingo said matter-of-factly.

Henry could only groan in reply.

"Don't take this the wrong way," Dingo said, and he began unbuttoning Henry's shirt.

Henry felt feverish, and he thought that all reason was leaving him. He wanted to challenge Dingo's assertion and tell him that it was okay if he wanted it the wrong way, because Henry himself wanted it the wrong way and had been feeling that for quite some time. And that the wrong way was the *right* way. But he could only shiver beneath Dingo's deft touch as he was manipulated out of his shirt.

Dingo covered Henry up with the sheet and said, "I won't be long. I'm just going to see if I can get you something."

"Only one thing—" Henry murmured, too late as he heard the cabin door close.

Henry was aware in some deep recess of his mind that Dingo had left him. The bed he was in remained steady at his back, but the ship was still rolling. Henry gripped the edge of the mattress as hard as he could; the silver bowl on his chest went clattering to the floor.

He phased out again but knew Dingo had returned because he could hear him moving about in the room.

"I know your footsteps," he slurred. He felt safe under the cover of his illness, vaguely remembering that he had started telling Dingo that there was only one thing he wanted, but he had fallen asleep before he could let it be known that he had wanted Dingo's arms around him, holding him until the illness had passed.

But of course, Dingo was oblivious to all that.

"Good," Dingo replied, somewhat amused. Henry watched him as he moved to the small tap and basin, which sat mounted on a cupboard between their beds, and filled a glass of water. From his pocket he removed three small packets of powder given to him by the ship's doctor and tore one open. He watched the powder dissolve in the water and stirred the glass vigorously to make sure it was blended throughout.

Gently, he lifted Henry's head so he could drink more easily. "Drink this," Dingo instructed.

"What is it?" Henry asked.

"Just something to make you feel better."

Henry grumbled, but the words were indistinguishable. However, he drank the water obediently, and hoped that it would settle his stomach rather than give him something new to start throwing up.

Dingo busied himself by folding Henry's clothing and putting them on top of his bag. Henry watched him for a small time, but felt his eyes grew heavy and finally allowed them to close. But when he felt the slight, feathery touch of Dingo's lips against his skin and then brushing over his eyebrow he stirred slightly but could not open his eyes.

I'm dreaming, he thought. *Aren't I?*

But it was nice to hold onto the dream and pretend it was real.

BROW furrowed, Dingo watched Henry anxiously for a few moments, wondering that he had dared to risk that gentle kiss. Henry was still sweating, but he remained still.

Dingo hated himself for feeling his cock swell slightly as he stared at the shirtless man beneath him. He wanted to run his hands over Henry's smooth chest, so different to his own; he wanted to taste that nipple beneath his tongue....

Dingo collected himself, reached down, and removed Henry's glasses. He seemed to be out of it, but Dingo wasn't taking any chances with his lascivious thoughts, so inappropriate regarding the situation, being so easily read on his face if Henry opened his eyes. He folded the glasses neatly and placed them in the basin cupboard that sat between their beds. He then unbuckled Henry's belt and became fixated by the line of hair that ran down from Henry's navel and became a path that was ultimately hidden by his boxers. Dingo couldn't resist letting his fingers trace over the short silky strands before grasping the waist of Henry's trousers and pulling them free.

"Yes, Dingo," Henry breathed.

Dingo's breath caught, but he managed to choke out, "Are you awake, Dash?"

But Henry said nothing more. He was asleep.

"Ah, Dash," Dingo said regretfully. He went to his own bed and swallowed a dose of the powder before rinsing the glass out and putting it back in the cupboard. No need for Henry to know about it, but he was feeling a bit queasy himself. Lying down upon his bunk, he watched Henry's sleeping face until the powder took effect and his vision began to blur. He closed his eyes and snuggled under the blankets, a slight smile upon his face.

IN THE morning, Henry's stomach was feeling more settled, although his thoughts certainly weren't. He rolled over in the narrow bed, expecting to see Dingo lying across from him on the opposite side of the room.

The bed was empty and neatly made. Henry couldn't believe he had slept through Dingo getting up, but he must have because he had vague memories of Dingo returning to the room during the night and preparing for bed.

His legs still felt boneless as he unsteadily planted himself before the small basin and drew water to try and clean himself as best he could. He was looking forward to having a proper bath at whatever hotel they booked themselves into once they arrived in Hobart, but he still felt remarkably fresher once he had changed clothes.

The waves were much smaller than they had been last time he'd seen them. Henry closed their cabin door behind him and took a moment to stare at the ocean roiling beneath the rails as he looked over them. Once he had satisfied himself he wasn't going to be sick, he moved up to the stern of the boat, where he knew he could find a cup of tea.

The small dining area was reasonably crowded. Dingo wasn't anywhere to be seen or even heard, as one could usually hear him before one saw him, so Henry decided to take his cup of tea and his piece of dry toast in hand and return to the passenger decking. Leaning against the railing, he demolished the toast ravenously and wished he had picked up an extra piece. Having made short work of the tea, he decided to go back for seconds but lingered in the fresh air, unsure how he might feel if he went inside. The ocean was beautiful in the sunlight, and he did feel a bit better. Finally he turned around to find Hodges standing well within his personal space.

"Mr. Percival-Smythe," Hodges said courteously, tipping his hat. "I don't believe we've been formally introduced."

Henry was being pressed against the railing, and he wondered in a moment of blind panic if Hodges intended to push him over the edge, if not for the fact that there were too many witnesses around. And then he realized that Hodges had used his real name.

"Excuse me?" he asked stupidly.

"No need to play coy with me." Hodges winked. "I've found out quite a bit about you, *Dash.* Or should I say, *Henry*?"

"Fine, Dash is just a nickname." Henry forced himself to shrug casually, but his heart started racing. *What* had Hodges found out about him? He'd thought he'd been careful enough…. "My real name doesn't mean a thing."

"Does that mean that I can also dismiss your apparent reason for being in Australia?" Hodges asked. "Not that I believed your crazy story about diamonds on the day."

"If you know why I'm here, why bother asking me?"

Henry winced as Hodges pressed closer to him, their chests bumping. "I just want to hear it from you, without your *friend* around."

"If you know so much about me, why should I bother?" Henry countered.

Hodges hesitated and then grinned a gloating grin that anybody named Clarence should never have been able to produce. "You want to play that game? I would be happy to oblige."

Henry was starting to wish he'd kept his mouth shut.

"Henry Percival-Smythe. Son of James Percival-Smythe III. Desperately wanted to follow in his father's footsteps but could never live up to his reputation or his standards. Lives in his shadow and also in that of his brother, James IV. Ended up taking the lowest of all low-level jobs in the archives section of Ealing College in which his father made a name for himself, and only got that job out of sheer nepotism."

To Henry's dismay, Hodges continued to list everything he had fought against for years. Hearing the facts recited so plainly and yet smugly made him feel even more pathetic, but he hadn't been hanging about with Dingo for the past month without learning at least a bit of self-preservation. He remained impassive although he had to wonder just what about his history excited such gleeful contempt from Hodges.

"Became obsessed with the rare Australian marsupial, the thylacine. Tried to rise through the ranks of the archive department but was continually turned down as he trains people who eventually become his supervisors. Comes to the attention of the Chambers family, who take pity on him and invite him along on their current but disastrous foray into saving the Tasmanian Tiger. You're only here because of Jack Chambers and his father. I'm not sure why they would pluck *you,* of all people, from behind a safe fortress of books to go into the jungle."

"I don't know what you're talking about." Henry moved forward, crowding Hodges, expecting him to fall back and let him pass.

"Not so fast." Hodges remained firmly in place and lit a cigarette, taking a long drag of it to draw out the suspense. He blew the smoke slowly and deliberately into Henry's face, grinning as he choked. "I assume you're here because of the correspondence you have been maintaining the past couple of years with Gordon Austin."

"How do you know that?"

"I know quite a lot, Mr. Percival-Smythe. I know your reasons for coming to Tasmania. And you should know, you're not going to succeed. Not as long as I'm dogging Chambers's every move."

"I've had enough of this. Let me pass!" Henry demanded, pushing at the other man.

With the cigarette still in his mouth, Hodges leaned in closer, and before Henry even realized what was going on, his hand was clutching Henry's cock and balls through his trousers, squeezing his member mercilessly.

Henry staggered back against the railing, letting out a guttural moan as his stomach lurched once more in sync with the pain from his groin and lights danced before his eyes. But this was nothing compared to the disastrous fact that his cock betrayed him by hardening slightly, and he knew Hodges was aware of it as his smile became even more feral as he squeezed his fist like an evil heartbeat.

"You don't play terribly rough, do you, Henry?" Hodges asked. "So very civilized. So *British*. I've seen the way you watch Chambers. Do you really think you'll be able to keep up with him out there in wild? If you think Chambers will admire a man like you, you're sadly mistaken. Do you think you have the tenacity for this hopeless trek?"

Humiliated, Henry wanted to pull away or to punch Hodges, just do *something*, but just then Hodges savagely twisted, and Henry was almost brought to his knees. The teacup he was still clutching fell out of his hand and smashed upon the deck. It was only that sound and the possible attention it could attract that made Hodges release him, letting the folds of his trench coat fall away, no longer concealing how he had been molesting the other man.

"I think," Henry wheezed, "you're dreaming, or perhaps it's *you* who wants to go along with Dingo to—"

Henry yelped at a burning sensation against his wrist. He looked back up in shock to see Hodges putting his cigarette back in his mouth and tipping his hat once more with a cruel smile.

"Just a little reminder of this conversation. You're stubborn, Henry. I suspect that's the one thing you've got in common with Chambers." Hodges shrugged and turned to walk away, his coat flapping in the wind.

Hodges was mocking him, Henry realized. But all he could do was stare dumbfounded at the small, raw wound that stung like the heat of a thousand fires amongst the singed hairs on his wrist.

"Sir, are you all right?"

Henry became aware of a deckhand, who stood before him with a small dustpan and broom.

"I'm fine, thank you," Henry managed to reply. "I'm sorry about the cup."

"Happens all the time, sir. Bit of a rough wave, was it? Would you like another cuppa?"

Henry could only shake his head and stumble back toward his cabin as the deckhand began to clear his mess.

He didn't even know how he could explain this whole situation to Dingo, or even if he should. He was humiliated by the two physical assaults upon him and also wounded by the depressing summation of his life so far. And the barbs volleyed at him about Dingo hurt just as badly.

Thankfully their cabin was empty when he entered. But where the hell *was* Dingo?

Henry drew water again in the basin and rested his hand in it. The perfectly round burn seemed even rawer beneath the surface of the water, and Henry rested his forehead against the mirror, still plagued by his thoughts.

11. ALL OUT IN THE OPEN; REVELATIONS AND RECIPROCATIONS

THE door crashed open against the wall, and Dingo demanded, "What the hell happened out there?" He stood with his hands on his hips, glaring at Henry as if it had been he who had cornered Hodges against the railing.

Henry wondered how he even knew, but it must have been the stricken look on his face that confirmed his suspicions as it brought Dingo across the cabin in two strides.

Henry flinched, but before he had time to hide his wrist, Dingo had taken it gently in his hand. Henry braced himself for a barrage of invective, but Dingo just said, "I shouldn't have left you alone like that."

"Where were you?" Henry burst out, sounding a bit more distressed by the abandonment than he'd planned to.

"Don't worry about it," Dingo said tersely. "We need to get you to the ship's doctor."

"No," Henry said stubbornly, and then he smiled, thinking of Hodges's assessment of how he and Dingo were alike. "I'll be fine."

"If you were planning to tell me that burn doesn't hurt, I'm willing to let you try to convince me." Dingo smiled swiftly. "And then you're going to the doctor."

"And tell him what when he asks me how I came by it?"

"Someone stumbled into you when a wave hit." Dingo rolled his eyes in exasperation. "We need to get you some salve. I'm afraid it's going to blister, and you shouldn't take the chance of infection."

"I think I'll live," Henry said, secretly pleased with Dingo's concern. Then he deflated a bit, thinking that Dingo was probably already viewing him as a hindrance and that an infection would render him even more useless.

"No need to give me the stiff upper lip, limey, not when you've already been so sick."

Henry noticed Dingo locking the door to their cabin behind them and remembered he had not when he'd gone to breakfast. "What *were* you doing—"

"Later," Dingo warned him. "Luckily, when Hodges searched our cabin he didn't come upon much other than what I left for him." He tapped his forehead with a finger. "I carry it all up here."

Henry couldn't help it. He had to laugh; the release of tension was such a relief. "What, your clean underwear and socks too?"

"Clean underwear isn't exactly necessary in order to find what we're after." Dingo led the way to the doctor's quarters, having been there the previous night.

The doctor didn't ask for an explanation, nor did he seem interested in how Henry had come by the burn. Henry started to explain, but Dingo nudged him into silence, shaking his head slightly. After the doctor dressed the wound and gave Henry supplies for the several days he would have to tend to it, they left, Dingo leading the way to the bridge.

"We can't go up there," Henry stammered. "The captain—"

"Sure we can," Dingo said. "The captain's my mate."

"*Another* one?" The man apparently even knew people in territorial waters! "Did you go to school with him too?"

"Only met him this morning," Dingo said, and he winked. "Sometimes that's all it takes."

"And why did you—"

"If Hodges tries to make a stink, this way the captain already knows me, see? And he's less likely to buy whatever flotsam or jetsam that Hodges has to peddle. Besides, it's quieter up here. And we'll be able to see if anyone's coming."

Henry followed Dingo up the steep stairs, studiously keeping his eyes off the tempting bum at eye level. If Hodges had already noticed his interest, better not to provide him with more ammunition. A sudden appalling thought struck Henry: what if Hodges sought Dingo out and told him of his suspicions?

"Feeling a bit queasy again, Dash?"

Henry looked up to find Dingo eyeing him uneasily. "Do I look green?"

"A bit."

"I'm fine."

"If you say so." Dingo lifted his hand in greeting to the captain, who remained inside the glassed-in bridge.

Henry could see why; the wind whipped at them savagely, the freezing chill making his wound burn anew by contrast.

"What was Hodges saying to you?" Dingo's eyes narrowed suspiciously, but Henry knew it wasn't him that Dingo feared.

"He found out my real name."

"Well, you expected that. And?"

"He said he knew we weren't going after diamonds." Henry stared as Dingo began to laugh. "What's so funny? I could use a chuckle."

Smugly, Dingo said, "If he found the map I left in our cabin, with cryptic markings on them, signifying diamonds had been found there, he was trying to get you to tell him something different."

"You planted—a false map—" Henry felt dazed that Dingo would have contrived such an intricate red herring. "You *knew* he was going to go through our things?"

"It didn't surprise me to find that he would. I just didn't realize what a dirty scum he really is. To go through another gentleman's things—What have I said to set you off?" Dingo asked, puzzled by Henry's sudden shout of laughter.

Henry shook his head, unable to explain why he found it amusing that *Dingo*, of all people, should have the scruples of a gentleman after all his trickery with Hodges. But those were mere pranks, compared to violating one's sanctuary. "Go on."

"You go on, what did you say to him?"

"I told him Dash was my nickname, and that if he thought he knew so much, *he* should tell *me* what he'd found out."

"Didn't know you had it in you, Dash," Dingo said approvingly. "Or rather, I did, I just didn't know *you* knew."

For the first time that morning, Henry felt proud of himself, but the feeling faded when he recalled what had really happened between him and Hodges. There was no possible way he could confide what had really happened and the extent of the physical assault. The burn was humiliating enough. "He took me by surprise—" he started.

"He must be getting desperate. He's escalating. I'd heard rumors—" A faint look of distaste flitted across Dingo's face. "He's always been ruthless, but he's stayed within the confines of the law until now. I think we'd best be prepared for anything with that one."

"What rumors?"

Dingo gave Henry a sidelong glance. "You don't want to know. Let's just say it's been said his methods are—unsavory."

"So where *were* you while he was questioning me?"

Dingo gave Henry a smug look. "I was searching *his* room."

"Hey! And you're complaining about him doing the same thing!" Henry pointed out.

"Turnabout is fair play, and he started it," Dingo said, his lips a bit grim. "He went into ours after you left it, and I thought there'd never be a safer time to nip into his."

"And what did you find?"

"A photograph," Dingo said. All at once he looked terribly worried. "A blurry photograph. You might have thought it was just the grass casting a shadow, but…." He shook his head as if to clear it.

"Of Tassie," Henry whispered, feeling a shiver pass over his body.

"I'm afraid so. Someone has been passing information to the government, and Hodges is hot on the trail. You know what this means, Dash, don't you?"

A slow smile crept over Henry's lips, and he was glad to see the same glow ignite in Dingo's eyes. "Someone's tracking a *living* thylacine on Tasmania."

"Maybe even more than one. And Hodges knows it."

Both men started as the door of the bridge was flung open. The captain, a bluff man with a red face and fierce ginger moustaches, cried out, "Dingo, I never knew such a fellow for standing about in a gale. Get your arse in here and warm it up!"

"Aye aye, sir!" Dingo said smartly. He gave Henry another wink. "Captain Ahab, this is my friend Dash."

"Dash and Dingo!" The captain laughed immoderately. "You should be a vaudeville team. Can you dance?"

"And sing," Dingo averred as they followed the captain inside.

"That wouldn't surprise me a bit, mate," said the captain affably.

In the small cabin of the bridge, Henry couldn't help himself and asked anyway, "Your name isn't really Ahab, is it, Captain?"

The man laughed so hard it seemed the bridge shook around them. "No, Dash. It's Francis. Although you could say at times this big lumbering lady is the equivalent of my white whale."

His tone of voice suggested that he thought of the *Taroona* as anything but. It was a rare captain indeed who didn't love his ship more than anything. He turned back to the crew and left the two men to find their own entertainment.

"Why are we up here, Dingo?" Henry asked in a low voice as he took the man aside.

"No safer place than the captain's bridge on a boat," Dingo replied with a smile plastered to his face that seemed slightly forced.

"Are you expecting the ship to go down?" Henry asked. "Or are we in danger from something else?"

Dingo pursed his lips, as if he wanted to tell Henry but felt he shouldn't.

Henry continued on, now feeling rather mutinous. "If it is Hodges you're talking about, and he's already searched our cabins, should we really be leaving our belongings unattended for him to do a second look-see?"

Dingo finally relented. "I left him a few more clues so he wouldn't get too suspicious if he does. But the important stuff is on me."

Henry glanced over him; he wasn't carrying a bag. "Where?"

He almost had to drop his gaze when without shame or preamble, Dingo ripped his shirt open. The press studs came apart easily, as if they had been designed especially for this purpose. Nestled amongst the golden hairs of Dingo's chest was a small waterproof pouch with a cord that was knotted around his neck. Dingo reached into the pouch and pulled the cord so that it would open fully. Henry leaned in, so close he could feel the warmth of Dingo's skin emanating toward him. A few more inches and his nose would have been tickled by the hairs on Dingo's chest. Within the pouch were the maps, the notes, and the photographs Henry and Dingo had mulled over so many times to the point they almost didn't need them as they were practically memorized.

"Oh," Henry said stiffly. "I see. Well hidden."

Dingo smirked as he fastened his shirt up again.

Show-off, Henry thought, glowering. But all he said was, "Clues?"

"I left some other… misleading documents for him to find. Hopefully he'll be on his way to the other end of Tassie as soon as we get there. Like Burnie."

Henry was surprised by the flash of anger he felt briefly erupt within him. "Hodges isn't stupid. He's going to be watching us so he can follow us, even if he does take note of the false clues you've made."

Dingo seemed disturbed by Henry's vehement response and even a little upset. "Dash—"

"You have to stop thinking of this as a game. It's not a game, this thing with Hodges. Not anymore."

"It never was," Dingo said grimly, lost in memory for a moment.

Henry watched him, expecting more to the story, but Dingo shook it off. The other man looked at him, seeming at a loss for words. Henry didn't like it; he was used to Dingo being cocky and funny, being everybody's best friend.

"Dingo—"

"He hurt you, and I'm sorry," Dingo said softly.

"It wasn't that bad, really—"

"I know you might think I don't take him seriously. But I do. I just joke around because… well, it's the only way I can treat it. I've seen him do a lot of bad things—"

"Bad things?" Henry breathed, not liking the sound of *that*. The small burn on his wrist throbbed, making him aware once more of its existence.

Dingo only nodded and didn't elaborate. "Sometimes I've had to do bad things to stop him. I was stupid to think he wouldn't go after you, to try and get to me."

"But why would he think using me would get to you?"

Exasperated, Dingo threw his hands in the air. "Because he knows the last thing in the world I would want is for you to get hurt! Dad was right; you shouldn't have come."

For the second time that day, Henry felt assaulted. But this was even worse than Hodges's molestation of him and even more painful than the burn of the cigarette. Dingo's words were a heavier, more painful, brand. And this time against a far more sensitive part of his body, because it was across his heart.

"You don't want me here?" Henry asked, having had to swallow painfully in order to get the words out. "If you think I can't keep up, I don't have to get off the boat; I can go back to Melbourne."

"I didn't say *that*," Dingo began.

"Land ahead!" boomed the captain, and the crew began clapping as another safe journey across the sea came to an end.

Henry turned away from Dingo, glad for the excuse. The far greener land of Tasmania, a marked difference to what he had seen of the rest of Australia, shimmered on the horizon. He could imagine it to be a part of England, if he were so inclined. He could feel Dingo behind him, and he wanted him to say something to defend himself or to take it back, but the other man didn't speak.

"I'm going back to the cabin," Henry said, turning back to face him. "We'll be disembarking soon. We should be packed."

"Dash—"

Henry couldn't give him the chance to say anything else; he had to get out of there *now*. As he got to the door, he heard Dingo speak once more.

"Henry, please—"

Even the use of his real name, spoken so plaintively, couldn't stop him.

Henry pushed his way out through the door and made his way back to their cabin.

HENRY wasn't left to himself for very long; he was only beginning to pack up what few clothes had been left lying about when the door to their cabin opened and Dingo entered.

He didn't try to speak, sensing that Henry wasn't going to put up with any attempts at cajoling him. They worked in silence, packing and tidying up the small cabin together. It didn't take them very long at all.

"How long are you planning on giving me the cold shoulder?" Dingo finally asked.

Henry looked at him fully in the eye for the first time since they had left the bridge. "I don't know; what do you think is an appropriate time?"

"I think time's up," Dingo said brusquely.

Henry shrugged and peered out the porthole. They were still only sliding into port; heaven knew how much longer this ship could take to berth. "If you say so. After all, you're in charge."

"Dammit to hell!" Dingo clenched his fists against his sides. "This is a *partnership*, Dash."

The word burned Henry like no other. He snorted derisively.

"What was that for?" Dingo demanded.

"Nothing."

"It didn't sound like nothing. It sounded like a whole lot of something. What's up your arse?"

Henry's mouth dropped open, and he fumbled for words. What eventually came out sounded stupid even to him. "You used your personal magnetism as a tool to get on the captain's good side!"

Dingo hooted with laughter. "Personal magnetism? Listen to you!" He stopped laughing when he saw Henry's expression.

"You use your personal magnetism to get on *everybody's* side," Henry grumbled.

"I also use it to get on *your* side," Dingo replied in a low tone. "Fat lot of nothing it gets me."

Henry opened his mouth to speak, but Dingo quickly continued.

"Do you stop using your brain out of fairness if you're smarter than your adversary? You have to play the hand you're dealt, Dash."

"You don't know how you—you—*affect* other people," Henry blurted.

There was a moment of silence before Dingo asked, "Do you?" Before it got too uncomfortable once again, he added, "Does anyone? Look, have you finished packing? If you haven't, I can do it for you."

"It's done. And I'm not a cripple, Dingo, it's just a tiny burn," Henry replied shortly, expecting Dingo to take the piss with him. Instead he looked up to find Dingo glancing at him with concern.

"I just hate what Hodges did to you," Dingo said finally.

With their eyes locked together, the burning sensation from his wrist seemed to flow throughout Henry's body, centering on his groin. The way Dingo was staring at him, his eyes like glowing embers, ignited some deeply hidden source of courage in Henry, and damn it all, this time he *would* find out whether—

Without giving himself time to think or to talk himself out of his rash impulse, Henry charged across the cabin and pushed Dingo up against the wall. His first attempt was clumsy, and his kiss landed on the corner of Dingo's mouth, but miraculously Dingo's hands came up, clasping him around the waist, and Dingo was actually helping!

And then Henry melted under the heat of Dingo's warm mouth, lips seeking his, hot tongue thrusting into his mouth, claiming him....

His knees went weak, but Henry pressed himself fully against Dingo, feeling an answering surge and a delicious hardness against his thigh. Grinding mindlessly against Dingo, Henry lost all sense of where they were or what they were doing. Dingo's mouth demanded everything from him; he sucked air urgently through his nose, his mind wanting very much to live to find out how this had happened while his body was on fire with sensation.

From the way Dingo was pressing against him, it seemed that he wanted this too.

"Dash..." Dingo said breathlessly, "I mean, Henry—"

"I like it when you call me Dash."

"Dash—"

"Dingo, just be quiet for once and let me—"

Henry was dizzy with triumph and lust and something else as he reclaimed Dingo's mouth for his own, and then he was just dizzy as with blinding speed, Dingo reversed their positions, using his weight and muscle as a welcome prison, pinning Henry against the wall.

Dingo's eyes were alight with mischief, his lips shining and swollen as he gave a low laugh, but Henry didn't feel as if he was being made fun of. "Well, well, well, Dash, who'd have thought you'd have such a tiger in you?"

Henry felt absurdly proud of himself even as he started to mumble the usual apologies.

Dingo dropped a tiny kiss on his lips to shut him up. "Nothing to be sorry for, Dash."

Henry blundered into incoherent speech. "I never thought—I'm sorry—It's just that—I never—He said he couldn't imagine why you—"

"*Who* said?" Dingo snapped, but he didn't release his hold on Henry.

"Hodges—he said, I wasn't good enough—not tough enough—that you and Hank made a mistake choosing me—"

"Christ, he knows *that* too?"

Dingo's exclamation made Henry flinch, but he said, "He implied it, yes."

"That explains a bit."

Despite Dingo's frown, Henry couldn't help but enjoy the fact that Dingo had made no attempt to pull away, his arms still holding Henry close. Rather, Dingo's hips seemed be rotating against his in a most distracting way.

"What does it explain?"

"Why he's always right in my shadow since my dad stopped coming over here. He tried it first with Gordon, trying to get in his good books, but Gordon had already been warned about him by my dad. I always thought there was a bit more to it than his obsession with seeing Tassie exterminated. After all, the government has done its work all too well; it's harder to find a thylacine alive in order to make an end of them than—"

Dingo stopped and shook his head. At the same time they felt the motors below their feet shudder into a lull. "We have to get off this boat. It's my bet that Hodges will head straight for the zoo, expecting that I'll be taking you there. We have to meet Jarrah, and then it's off into the wilds for us, my lad."

Henry tried to pull himself out of Dingo's grasp and was disappointed when the other man released him instantly. Hating himself for how he knew this was going to sound, he asked, "Who is Jarrah?"

Dingo tossed him a grin as he bent to his own packing. "One of those fearsome Aborigines I was telling our fair Diana about. Of course, that's the only thing about him that anyone ever takes notice of. And before you get your knickers in a twist, he's a friend."

Henry caught the bitter undertone beneath his first couple of sentences and wondered just how much this Jarrah meant to Dingo. And if he were handsome. "What do we need Jarrah for?"

"We need someone to watch our backs, with Hodges on the trail. And nobody knows the bush as well as Jarrah," Dingo said. "Get a move on, Dash. We have to beat Hodges off the boat."

"I'm not the one holding us up," Henry snapped back. "Why don't we hang back and let Hodges think he missed us?"

"Because he'll likely search the boat, looking for us if he misses us on the gangplank," Dingo explained with a chuckle. "And we'll leave him a little clue to keep him busy. That way, we get away, meet with Jarrah—"

"And run straight off into the forest," Henry said gloomily.

Dingo crossed the short distance back to him, and Henry found himself back in his arms.

"No," Dingo said. "We'll have one night." Henry looked up. Dingo smiled. "We'll have one night, before we make a trek for it."

Wondering if Dingo meant what he thought and hoping it was so, Henry nodded and reluctantly let go of the man who now seemed to be his, in some way. "What sort of clue do you mean to leave for Hodges?" He congratulated himself on his steady voice. His hands were trembling at the thought of a whole night with Dingo, the anticipation of seeing Dingo naked, touching his skin.... He was surprised he was still on his feet rather than on his knees, thanking whatever savage deity who watched over queers for this chance.

"This." Dingo held up what looked like a cloudy, rough piece of glass.

"An uncut diamond?" Henry gasped.

"No, it's glass." Dingo smirked. "But it'll take him a bit of time to figure that out, and by then we should be ahead of him. I'm afraid it'll be a race to *stay* ahead of him. You're sure you're up to—"

"I'm sure," Henry said. He suddenly noticed the glazed intent look in Dingo's eyes and nodded again. "I'm sure."

Dingo seemed to turn away with an effort, his eyes sweeping over the cabin. He laughed and headed for his bed, which was bolted to the floor. A bit of the flooring was sticking up out of alignment with the other planks, and Dingo knelt to pry it up with his pocketknife, leaving a raw gouge near the end of the strip of wood.

"Are you sure he'll find it there?" Henry asked dubiously.

"He's so used to overestimating me, completely justifiably of course, that I shouldn't like to make it too easy for him," Dingo said, grinning. "Just difficult enough." He replaced the splinter to rest in the gouge and grunted with satisfaction as he rose to his feet. "And if he doesn't, we've lost nothing by trying. All set then?"

"Ready," Henry said. He could feel his mouth spread wide with an answering grin.

12. THE LAST COLONIAL OUTPOST, WHERE JARRAH IS MET

IT WAS all they could do to keep from bumping shoulders familiarly as they walked down the rickety gangplank and onto the pier. They had to pass through a large tin shed that was stifling despite the cold weather outside it, and Henry watched Dingo's long legs move quickly through the crowd. He wanted to see them bare again, as he had in Melbourne, because this time he could lay claim to them instead of merely fantasizing.

He must be dreaming. Lay claim to them? If he *were* dreaming, he didn't ever want to wake up. Because now he'd had a taste of this new reality along with the taste of Dingo's mouth, and nothing else would suffice.

Dingo turned briefly to catch Henry appreciating him. "Save it for later, Dash."

Henry realized that watching Dingo with unbridled lust could lead to trouble, but he was barely aware that they were leaving the shed and heading away from the water. Hobart definitely seemed a colonial town, much more so than Melbourne. It wasn't so surprising, as Hobart only had a fifth the population Melbourne did. Despite a recent building boom, there had also been a devastating bushfire, and the town was still getting back onto its feet. The port, however, gave it a bustling feel, and as they weaved between whalers, mariners, townspeople, trams, and dogs, Henry felt rather crowded but didn't mind being pressed against Dingo's back every now and again. These fleeting touches were a preview of what was to come.

Mariner Terrace led them to Trumpeter Street, where their lodgings were to be for the night. The Shipwrights Arms was a squat, rectangular building that had been built in the last century and looked as if it had seen better days, but Dingo assured him that Hodges wouldn't be caught dead in it.

"Oh, he might spy on us in it," he said off-handedly, "but there's no way he'd sleep in it. Tony wouldn't let him, anyway."

"Who is Tony?" Henry asked.

"A friend," Dingo replied vaguely, maddeningly. "He's got our back."

For the first time since they had kissed, Henry felt the return of his self-doubt. With all the mention of Dingo's many friends, he had to wonder if he would be spoken about in such a way in the future, perhaps to somebody else acting as another of Dingo's tagalongs? Would he be just another past conquest who still stayed loyal, perhaps hoping for another shot? "*Who's Dash?*" the new companion would ask as they arrived in London. "*Oh, just another friend,*" Dingo would reply. "*We can trust him.*"

Dingo seemed unaware of Henry's internal distress and led them through the side door rather than the main entrance. It was darker and dingier inside, but it didn't seem to deter the drinkers as they turned to eyeball the newcomers. A look of recognition passed over some faces, and a cheer went up. "Dingo!"

Oh, for God's sake, thought Henry.

Dingo passed around them, shaking hands, slapping backs, intermittently introducing Henry, and headed to the bar. Henry forgot most of the names as soon as he heard them and just kept an insipid smile on his face, nodding as he followed the other man.

"Dingo!" the barman said. "Long time between drinks."

"Nah, not that long. How are you, mate?"

"Can't complain."

"Any sign of my little friend?"

"No, not yet. I'll let you know if he shows up, but."

Dingo nodded toward Henry as he made it to the bar. "This here's Dash. Dash, Tony."

"Pleasure," Henry said briefly, and Tony nodded.

"He's English," Dingo said, as if that explained everything. And for Tony, it seemed to. "Anyway, is Jarrah about?"

Tony tipped his head. "In the back."

"Still?" Dingo looked disappointed. "Tony…."

"It's the law, Dingo."

"You know better."

"Still can't break the law, Dingo. Even for friends."

"It's a cruddy world, Tony, that won't let a man drink with his friends in the front bar."

It seemed like an old bone of contention, a sad one with a dull heat where neither side was happy either with the same repetitive arguments or the outcome. "C'mon, Dingo."

Dingo waved half-heartedly. "We'll be at the back. Can you get us a round?"

"*That* I can do," Tony replied, somewhat happier.

Dingo led Henry further into the building and out the back to the colorfully named "Beer Garden." It wasn't as picturesque as it sounded, merely being a collection of dilapidated wooden tables and chairs in a paved yard that was exposed to the elements.

"What was all that about?" Henry asked.

"Despite being born in this country," Dingo said gruffly, "and being citizens just like the rest of us, Jarrah and his ilk are not allowed to inhabit the same rooms as the rest of us."

Before Henry could even formulate a response, another voice dropped in. "Ah, get off your soapbox, Dingo. It's the way it is now, but it won't always be."

The only customer sitting in the beer garden turned around to face them.

"Jarrah!" Dingo laughed. The two men embraced heartily.

"What's up with you?" Jarrah exclaimed, stepping back and looking at his friend.

"What?" Dingo asked suspiciously.

"You look like the cat that got the—" Jarrah broke off and looked at Henry, and his grin grew exponentially. "I see."

"Don't you start," Dingo warned. "Jarrah, this is—"

Henry stepped forward, determined to introduce himself. "Henry. Henry Percival-Smythe."

"He's a live one, eh?" Jarrah asked of Dingo.

"Just call him Dash."

Henry was about to protest, but Jarrah took his hand and pumped it energetically. "Welcome to Tassie, Dash."

Henry was slightly embarrassed, both that due to his jealousy he wanted to dislike the man but ended up taking to him immediately and also that his preconceptions of a "native Australian" were challenged by Jarrah himself. Henry had been expecting someone like those he had seen in photographs in the archives, perhaps a tribal elder with a scarred chest and a spear, not this young man in a long jacket with coffee-colored skin and dark, limitless brown eyes. He wondered if Jarrah had ever been a past conquest of Dingo's but admonished himself. *You can't be thinking that every man you meet must share the same desires.*

"Thank you," he finally croaked. "Nice to meet you."

Jarrah nudged Dingo. "A Pom I could actually like."

"Don't mind him," Dingo told Henry. "The English almost wiped the Aborigines off the face of Tassie."

"Bet *that* wasn't in your history books in school," Jarrah said.

"Oh," Henry said, wide-eyed, as if he were somehow personally responsible. "I'm sorry."

Jarrah looked a bit taken aback, unused to an apology ever being issued to him. "Uh, sit down, won't you?"

Henry followed Dingo's lead, and the three men sat down at the table again; Dingo stretched out his long legs and swung them up onto another chair, stretching his hands behind his head. He grinned at his two companions. "So, here we are in another right old mess, Jarrah."

"I can always rely upon you to get me in trouble, old friend. But how did poor Dash get caught up in it?"

"Dash roped himself in it," Dingo teased. "Nothing to do with me."

Henry snorted. "You did a fair share of it."

Dingo shrugged. "He's an expert in the tiger, Jarrah. At least as much as an expert can be who hasn't seen one living and breathing. Gordon recommended him."

Jarrah sized Henry up with the respect Dingo afforded him. Henry leaned in closer and asked in a whisper, "Have you seen one?"

Jarrah winked at him. "I've seen many."

Henry was about to ask more, but Tony arrived with their drinks. The men immediately ceased their conversation. Henry observed that Tony still seemed a little colored from the criticism he had suffered from Dingo at the bar, and he served Jarrah with an apologetic smile while Dingo was frozen out a bit.

As soon as Tony left, Henry was about to ask about the tiger again when Dingo beat him to the punch with another conversation entirely. "Hodges was on the boat."

"I know," Jarrah replied, sipping at his beer. "I read the passenger list. He hasn't made a booking here, though."

"Too low-down for him," Henry said, trying to sound part of the gang. Jarrah nodded, and Dingo grinned at him affectionately.

"He'll be on our trail soon enough," Jarrah said.

"I left him a decoy," Dingo said.

Jarrah set his beer back down. "He won't fall for it, mate. He's too wily."

"Still, it might buy us some time."

"Does that mean you want to go now?" Jarrah asked. "Leave your booking as a false scent?"

Henry looked at Dingo, panicked, wanting their promised night together, even though he was eager to set off after the thylacine. Dingo calmly stretched again.

"Nah, we need a proper night's rest in a good bed. We were seasick all the way across."

Jarrah's eyes twinkled. "I see."

Henry flushed, but the man didn't say anything else to embarrass them. He was hoping that Jarrah didn't know what was being intended, but he seemed to know Dingo far too well.

Jarrah reached for his hat. "I better be off. Leave you two to… your *proper night's rest*. I'll be back at first light."

"Tooroo," Dingo said, as laid-back as ever.

Henry downed the last of his beer in one desperate gulp as he was left alone with Dingo again. The beer shot straight into his bloodstream, infecting him with nerve and vigor, and from there it seemed to directly travel to his groin.

Dingo scratched at his belly, an area of skin on show to Henry, who stared and wanted to put his hands on it. "So, shall we go and check out our room?"

13. FIRST NIGHT, FIRST LOVE

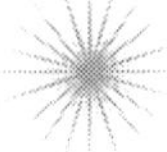

HENRY couldn't help but repeat it to himself as the door opened. *Our room.*

The fact that Dingo had taken one room in the tiny hotel seemed to signify that all Henry had hoped for was about to come to pass. But it wouldn't do to appear too eager. It might be simply that Dingo was being frugal, although that word was incongruous in the same sentence with Dingo. Or it might be that he felt it was safer for them to be together, and he would let Henry down easily after building his anticipation.

Henry resolved that when they locked the door behind them, shutting out the entire world, Dingo would have to be the one to make the first advance.

Therefore, it would be difficult to say which of them was more surprised when he pushed Dingo up against the door, forcing him to drop his bag at his feet as he staggered back unsteadily.

There were no words. Henry found Dingo's mouth with a sureness that surprised him, his tongue demanding entry, taking no prisoners in his quest to taste the flavor of the other man again. Fresh. Dingo tasted fresh, as if he lived outdoors all the time.

Dingo's response was equally explosive, as if after all the dancing around and the teasing, the obvious could no longer be denied.

His arms felt like bands of iron holding Henry against him. Henry thrust against the solid warmth of his body, his hands squeezing Dingo's biceps, keeping him in place. He whimpered in gratitude when he felt one of Dingo's hands between them, fumbling at groin level.

The shock of Dingo's hand on his erection made him sag, and he might have gone to his knees if Dingo hadn't kept a firm grip on him. And then he realized the blazing heat was Dingo's manhood rubbing against his, Dingo's hand wrapped around them both as they strained against each other, unable to wait another minute.

The first heated spurt of liquid made his cock slide within Dingo's grip, and Henry wrenched his mouth away to give a low guttural moan as he came, sagging against the other man. He could feel himself moving, riding on Dingo's heaving chest, the sweat trickling under his right arm, the rough stubble of Dingo's cheek against his, the huff of Dingo's breath in his ear.

A low chuckle made him raise his head, staring blearily at the other man, too close to focus his vision. "What?"

"Couldn't even make it to the bed," Dingo said hoarsely. "I would have liked the first time… but what can't be changed must be endured."

Henry started to laugh. "You make it sound like torture."

"It *has* been torture."

Henry was surprised at the sincerity in Dingo's voice and tilted his head back to bring his face into focus.

His voice gravelly with emotion, Dingo said, "I've been hungry for you since I met you, Henry."

Moved by hearing his proper name on Dingo's lips again after all this time, Henry didn't know quite how to respond. He yawned and then laughed. "If you only knew how I wanted you. But I never thought—"

Dingo waited, but Henry just shook his head. "Let's get washed up. And go to bed," Dingo said.

Henry nodded but gaped as he yawned again. "I want to, but I can't seem to keep my eyes open."

Dingo nodded understandingly. "It'll keep. We've got the whole night."

Henry shivered at the thought of it. "I want to make love to you," he said boldly.

"I want that too."

In the end, they barely managed to make it to the bed, falling onto the mattress together, curling into each other, as if now that they were welcome to touch, they couldn't bear not to. And then they were asleep.

HENRY awoke to find himself wrapped in a warm, masculine embrace. His few experiences had never ended like this, and he couldn't quite remember where he was. But Dingo's scent filled his nose, and he burrowed closer, wishing they had taken the time to undress. He wanted skin.

Moving gently, not wanting to wake Dingo until he'd had his sleep out, Henry managed to open his shirt, sliding his hand over the other man's chest. The light hair tickled his fingertips; so unlike his own smooth skin, while the solid muscle under his palm thrilled him, the fulfillment of inchoate desires that he never could have confided to anyone.

He felt the lift of Dingo's chest into his hand and a rumble as the other man spoke. "Should we get undressed this time?"

Henry only realized he was shaking when he heard the tremor in his voice. "Yes, please." He startled when he felt Dingo's fingers on his shirt buttons. No one had ever expressed any interest in undressing him before, and while he didn't know quite what to make of that, he was quite sure he wanted Dingo out of his clothing as quickly as possible.

But Dingo had other ideas, pressing warm lips against Henry's skin as soon as he exposed a bit of it, making Henry's stomach flutter with nervous excitement.

Boldly he rolled Dingo onto his back, sitting astride him, lowering himself to kiss him. He felt Dingo impatiently finish opening his shirt and push it off his shoulders, his hands lingering on his bare arms. As soon as his hands were free, Henry finished opening Dingo's shirt and flung it open with a cry of triumph.

Dingo's gasp echoed his own as Henry leaned closer for another kiss, and their bare chests brushed together for the first time. Henry could feel the strong thud of Dingo's heart against his own and felt the victory of another man's answering desire for him.

"Shoes," Dingo muttered.

Had they really gone to bed with their shoes on? Apparently they had. Dingo pushed off him gently and went to work ridding them both of their shoes and socks. Trousers still open, Dingo pushed his down while Henry did the same, sudden urgency robbing him of the desire for the slow exploration of the other man's body.

They rolled toward each other, coming together with a crash. Dingo's leg was between his, and Henry humped against it, desperate for friction even with the overload of all his senses. He had never been naked and pressed up against another completely naked person before, and the sensation almost overwhelmed him, but his overriding desire was to be inside the other man, to penetrate the mysteries of the beloved and as yet entirely unknown body that writhed beneath him.

"What do I do?" Henry gasped.

Dingo stretched and twisted under him, making him thrill again to the masculine strength of the body so like and yet so unlike his. Henry was filled with a sudden confidence that he would be able to satisfy Dingo, for after all, it was like holding up a mirror. He had explored his own body; he knew of certain secret pleasures that he had never shared with another, and now he burned to give that pleasure to Dingo.

The way the other man spread his legs, making room for Henry between his thighs made him feel that Dingo was as eager for this as he was.

He jumped and moaned as Dingo's slick fingers found his shaft and slid over his flesh, spreading the necessary lubrication on him.

"Can I—"

In answer, Dingo pressed the small metal tube into his hand; trembling a bit, Henry squeezed some of the lubricant onto his fingers, searching hesitantly between Dingo's legs, finding the root of his hard cock. He bent to lick at the head, tasting the salty bitter droplets at the tip, sliding his fingers over the rigid proof of Dingo's equal desire for him. He nuzzled at Dingo's balls, taking the low moans and sudden jerks of Dingo's hips as his due, although he knew he must be sadly lacking in experience. The musky scent of the other man nearly drove him wild.

His finger slid lower still, finding the dark valley he sought. One of Dingo's hands left his body, and Henry felt him spread his cheeks, offering himself, almost like in the dream.

Henry froze, uncertain of what to do, almost relieved when he felt Dingo's hands pull him up for a kiss.

"There's no hurry," Dingo murmured against his throat.

Henry moaned as he was rolled onto his back, lying pliant as Dingo started to kiss his way down his body. While he would have driven immediately into Dingo's body if he could, Dingo seemed to have all the time in the world.

And then Henry's brain shut down, and he could only feel as Dingo's mouth, hot and ardent, closed around one of his nipples and sucked. Never had he felt anything like that. He had never even touched himself there when he pleasured himself, unaware of all the nerve endings that came alive, making him thrash helplessly under the other man's assault.

It seemed that no matter where Dingo touched him, he set off a river of fire under his skin, one that roared down his spine and through his groin, making him achingly hard. By this time he was too lost in sensation to take control. Henry had never felt such unabashed desire, and he had no shame for the tiny cries of pleasure that Dingo managed to wring from him as he kissed his way to his groin.

The sweep of the tongue running along the furrow of his loins made Henry's hips leap into the air as he arched off the bed, feeling Dingo's hands upon him, moving his body where he wanted it. His own cries echoed loudly in his ears as Dingo's mouth captured his cock, enclosing him in wet heat. Henry no longer had words; he had ceased to think altogether as his essence spurted from him and his body convulsed in sinful rapture.

He lay shaking and limp as he heard a low triumphant laugh from the region of his groin.

"Ever had that before, Dash?"

Henry shook his head before he remembered that Dingo couldn't see him in the dim light, situated where he was. "Not like that," he said in a thread of a voice.

"Have you ever had a man take you?"

Henry felt the heat of his flush suffuse his body, grateful that at least Dingo couldn't see *that.* "Never."

"I'd like to be the first," Dingo murmured. "I'd like to show you how good it can be."

"Yes…." Henry breathed.

A sudden click and the light by the bed was turned on, hurting his eyes. Henry squinted at Dingo and laughed to see him squinting as well. And then he wasn't laughing when he saw the expression Dingo wore.

"I want to see your face," Dingo said.

He pushed Henry's legs back toward his chest, and Henry had never felt so exposed to anyone—and yet at the same time, so safe. The look on Dingo's face moved him. He knew now that he was not simply another man for Dingo to chalk up on his trophy stick. This meant something to Dingo, and knowing that made it all the more meaningful to Henry.

Fingers sliding in his cleft made his hips jerk when they found his entrance, but Dingo didn't push inside.

"I have to open you up to take me," Dingo said in a low voice. "I don't want to hurt you."

Henry nodded, holding onto his thighs to keep himself open. The feeling of Dingo's fingers massaging the sensitive skin of his opening made him aware of how intimate an act they were sharing already. He couldn't take his gaze off Dingo's, and they stared at each other until Henry closed his eyes and groaned at the feeling of being breached, of having some part of another man within him at last.

And yet it hurt. The burning stretch made him conscious again of the burn on his wrist, but he pushed the thought away. He didn't like to think that Hodges had branded him first with pain when the welcome burn of Dingo entering him was yet to come. *This* would be the real claiming.

"No one can have you unless you give yourself to them," Henry muttered, forcing himself to relax around Dingo's finger.

"And are you? Are you giving yourself to me?"

Henry opened his eyes, feeling unexpectedly tender over the pained anxiety in Dingo's voice. "Yes."

He moaned as Dingo withdrew his finger, missing the fullness until two were pushed inside. Dingo worked his fingers in the tight channel gently, twisting them to find the hardness on the anterior wall, sending a ripple of unknown pleasure through Henry.

"My God," Henry muttered.

Dingo smiled, working his fingers until they slid in and out more easily. "Are you sure—do you want—"

"Yes!" Henry almost shouted, and then he lowered his voice. "Yes, take me."

Dingo pulled his fingers out slowly and positioned himself between Henry's thighs, lining his cock up with one hand, his weight resting on the other.

Henry felt the blunt hardness pushing at his entrance, and he felt afraid. Dingo felt so big, and he wondered how much it was going to hurt, but he wanted this badly. "Please," he whispered.

"Yes," Dingo agreed. He watched Henry's face carefully as he pressed inside, knowing the head would be the worst part.

Henry lifted his hips, trying to hasten the penetration, and cried out in surprise as Dingo surged inside. His muscles worked frantically around the intruder; Dingo's cock felt so unyielding and hard. It burned.

"Take it easy. Relax for me, if you can." Dingo kissed Henry's temple, holding himself scrupulously still until he felt the ripple of muscles adjusting to him, welcoming him. "Tell me when you're ready."

"Go on. I want it all," Henry gasped.

Dingo rocked his hips gently, pressing forward in slow increments until he could feel Henry relax around him and his hips were flush with Henry's arse. "You've taken me all now."

Henry couldn't speak. Sweat slid into his hairline as he felt the hardness of Dingo's manhood inside him. But it wasn't painful anymore. It was the rarest of pleasures.

Dingo started to move. Somehow Henry could tell how much Dingo wanted to please him; he was being very gentle, looking down at him with a tender, anxious expression. To reassure him, Henry raised his hips to meet each slow thrust, and Dingo fell into the rhythm intuitively known from the beginning of all time.

Henry thrilled to the feeling of Dingo moving inside him. His own cock was hard again and bouncing against his belly with every thrust as Dingo pushed into him. Physically it was the single most profound act Henry had ever shared with another person, but emotionally it just felt so right to have their bodies joined as one.

"Stroke yourself for me," Dingo ordered.

Henry reached for his cock, still slick with the lube that Dingo had applied, not regretting for an instant that it had turned out this way. The way it felt when Dingo brushed against that spot deep inside him was incredible. In all his imaginings, he had never dreamed it could feel like this.

His orgasm hit him like a freight train, and Henry arched up frantically under Dingo, wrapping his legs around the other man as if trying to draw him in deeper and closer.

He looked up, watching as Dingo's face contorted in ecstasy, and felt him thrust deeper, pushing hard inside him until Henry felt the sudden rush of hot liquid. Dingo froze in place for a long moment before he lowered himself onto Henry's quiescent body, gasping and sweating.

Henry wrapped his arms around Dingo, kissing his shoulder as the only spot he could reach, wondering if this was to be their only night. Perhaps Dingo had used that animal magnetism on *him,* to get what he wanted—

"Next time it's your turn," Dingo panted. He turned his face to kiss Henry.

Henry could have kicked himself, but he couldn't stop himself from blurting, "So this wasn't just a one-time thing?"

Dingo laughed wearily, and his voice was hoarse as he said, "I can't get enough of you, Dash. You're… intoxicating."

Henry smiled against Dingo's shoulder. "I hope not like that foul stuff you made me drink in Bangkok."

"No hangover, but a craving for more, yes," Dingo said as Henry felt him slip out of the haven of his body. "Let's get some rest. You're going to need it."

"Why am I going to need it particularly?" Henry asked on a yawn.

"If you're going to satisfy my unnatural lusts, you'll have to be well rested."

Dingo's voice sounded very far away, and Henry wondered just how tired he was. He wrapped his arms around the other man and snuggled closer, their legs falling naturally between each other, groins pressed together.

DINGO stirred and found Henry's mouth against his nipple.

"Dash," he groaned. "You're insatiable."

The darkness and the naked intimacy with Dingo gave Henry a bravery and a vulnerability he had never been able to expose of himself before. "I've never had it like this before, Dingo."

Dingo's hand strayed upward to stroke Henry's hair gently. "What way?"

"Well, the obvious," Henry admitted. "But before, it never got to this stage. Where we lay together afterwards, where I could wake up with the other person."

"It was always wham bam, now piss off?"

Henry turned his attention to the other nipple, and Dingo groaned again. Henry lifted his head, absorbed in the way the nipple had hardened beneath his tongue, becoming a stiff peak begging to be tasted again. This time he used his teeth gently and felt Dingo's cock jab against his hip insistently. He wondered if there was a nerve that ran directly between the cock and the nipple, for Dingo certainly seemed to like it when he touched him there. "Something like that," he finally admitted. "They never stuck around."

"I'm not going anywhere," Dingo told him.

Henry pulled away. "Don't say that. Please."

Dingo sat up. "What?"

"Just don't say something like that… unless you mean it."

"I don't say things I don't mean," Dingo said firmly. "You should at least know that about me by now."

"But who knows what happens from here?" Henry asked. "Maybe it's too soon—"

"You think too much; that's your trouble." Dingo reached for him and claimed a kiss. Henry relented, opening immediately so Dingo's tongue could touch his. He let himself fall against Dingo's chest, and when they stopped kissing, he rested his head against the broad, furry shoulder. It was the best pillow he had ever had.

"I'm sorry the other times weren't good for you," Dingo said softly. "They should have been."

"It doesn't matter now," Henry reassured him. "At least now I know how it can be."

"And how it will be from now on."

"Yeah?"

"Yeah. In case you haven't noticed, Dash, look at what you do to me." Dingo pointed down his body, to where his legs were twisted around the sheets but his cock was making a noticeable tent amongst the folds.

Henry gave a short laugh. "I can't believe I do that to you."

"Well, believe it. I've wanted you since that day in the office when you wanted nothing more than to chuck the git from the colonies out."

"I didn't think you were a git. I wanted you as well. I was just scared you would find out."

"Why?"

"Because I didn't know you were like me."

"What, queer?"

"Yes."

"Well, I think I just proved I am."

Henry laughed again. "I suppose so. I think I have your father to thank for this."

"How?"

"He tried to hint on the docks, when we left, about you."

"They knew I was fixed on you, but I told them not to interfere. You know what parents can be like, though."

"Actually," Henry admitted. "I don't."

"Your parents don't know about you?"

"Of course not!"

Dingo whistled. "I know it's not exactly something you can shout from the rooftops if you want to survive, but your parents at least should know."

"My parents aren't like yours, Dingo. They wouldn't accept me like yours do."

"Then they're bloody idiots."

"At least I can hide behind the great English tradition of eccentric bachelor uncles. It helps if you wear glasses and work in the academic field. No one asks awkward questions."

"They might come around. Mine took a while."

"*Your* parents?" Henry asked in surprise.

"Time helps. It's not exactly the kind of thing you wish for your kids, is it? Not exactly an easy life."

"You make it look easy." Truth be told, Henry was a little jealous of that fact.

"No sense making it hard on yourself." Dingo ran his hand along Henry's body and rested it against his backside. "All I know is this feels good and it feels right. Don't you feel it?"

"Yes," Henry replied in all truth.

He had never been happier. Or more eager for his chance to love Dingo in return. Trying not to dislodge Dingo's hand from his bum, Henry thrust his tongue into Dingo's mouth, delighted when the other man submitted eagerly to the ravishment.

The first time they'd touched each other against the wall barely counted, and when Dingo had taken him, Henry hadn't had time to explore his body first or even to savor his own physical sensations; it had seemed so fleeting to him. He was determined to take his time and embarked on an exploration of Dingo's body, so desirable and yet still unknown despite the intimacy they had shared.

Dingo responded most favorably to the kisses and licks Henry bestowed in his slow progress down his torso, moaning without shame for more. Henry circled his hand loosely around Dingo's erection, feeling the hard flesh slide against his palm as he kissed his way along the defined ridges of Dingo's abdomen, feeling the muscles flex under his lips.

He lifted his head, smiling at the expression of blissful ecstasy on Dingo's face. There was no doubting that Dingo wanted this too; his body undulated in search of Henry's touch, and his cock stood erect from his loins.

"So eager for me, aren't you?"

Dingo opened his eyes a slit and stared at Henry with an intensity that shook him to the core. "I want to feel you inside me. I want *you*."

Just to hear that from another man made Henry tremble with the profound meaning of this moment. He laid a hand on Dingo's lean hip, feeling the strong muscle moving under the skin with restless need. He wanted to give back to Dingo what the man had given him, some sense of the sureness of their coupling, the need to join with him so that there was no separation between them.

Instead of dragging Henry from his exalted mood, the mechanics of preparing Dingo to take him seemed to heighten the experience, lifting it to a sacred ritual of sorts; the slippery feeling of the oil, the intimacy of touching the other man in the most secret of places, the way Dingo moved instinctively to accommodate Henry's wishes. That moment when Dingo bent his knees, inviting him in, and Henry lined up his cock, pausing, wanting to make sure he wasn't doing anything the wrong way, and Dingo's imploring cry for him to hurry.

Dingo cried out again as the head breached him, and Henry stopped in alarm, but Dingo grabbed him by the hips and motioned him to continue. The intense silken heat that enclosed him as he slid into Dingo's body, the hardness of Dingo's shaft trapped between their bellies as he moved, and the lift of Dingo's hips as he met each thrust all ignited Henry's ardent desire into a flame that burned like the heat rising off the pliant body beneath him.

A hand cupped his head and drew Henry down so that Dingo could kiss him before crying out as his orgasm began. Henry's arms trembled when Dingo's muscles clenched around him, drawing his climax from him. As he spilled his essence inside Dingo's body, Henry lost himself in rapture, unable for once to think; he could only feel, and it felt so right. And then he was falling into darkness, anchored only by Dingo's arms and legs wrapped securely about him.

"THE best pillow ever…" Henry mumbled, aware that it was warm, sweaty, and somewhat hairy. His pillow began to shake, and he heard the familiar rumble of Dingo's laughter transmitted through the solidity of his chest.

"At least you've found some use for me."

Henry reared up to protest but ended up kissing those tempting, smiling lips instead, chuckling himself at the absurdity of it. "You're a most satisfactory pillow."

"I'd hoped for bed partner at the least," Dingo said with a comical pout.

Henry snuggled closer, enjoying how Dingo's fingers dug possessively into his flesh. "You know damn well that you're that."

"Well, I don't," Dingo said. "One can't tell if one's satisfying one's partner unless he *says* something about it."

"You were very satisfactory in that department," Henry said primly. He yelped as Dingo slapped his backside. "Hey!"

"Give up the reserved British understatement, Dash, and tell me if it was good for you."

Touched at the note of uncertainty in Dingo's voice, Henry opened his eyes again. "You know perfectly well it was the most extraordinary experience of my life, Dingo Chambers. How can you even wonder—"

"Not everyone likes the same things," Dingo said. "Now that you've tried it, you might say, that was pleasant but not for me, thanks very much, old fellow. Pip, pip and all that, now piss off."

"It's far more extraordinary to me how a man like you could even look twice at me," Henry declared indignantly. Dingo seemed to be so eminently desirable to him that he couldn't imagine how every person who met him wouldn't vie to have him.

"A man like what?" Dingo sounded truly incredulous so Henry decided he needed to spell it out.

"Handsome, muscular, courageous, gay, cheerful, exciting, bigger than life—"

Dingo took Henry's face between his hands. "Don't underestimate yourself. You are an incredibly beautiful man, Henry. I wanted you the instant I saw you." Dingo ran a hand down Henry's flank, the shiver of response rousing his own desire once again.

"But I'm skinny, and I wear glasses—"

"You're not skinny; you're slim and lithe, with a swimmer's build. I'd never have guessed you sat behind a desk all day."

Gratified, Henry said, "I try to keep fit."

"Besides, a timid man wouldn't have jumped at the chance to come to an unknown country, facing unknown odds to find and save an unknown animal."

"With an unknown companion," Henry said, smiling.

"Let me introduce myself again," Dingo said, lowering his head to kiss Henry. "I'm Dingo Chambers."

Pausing for breath between heated kisses, Henry murmured, "Pleasure to meet you. I'm Henry Percival-Smythe."

Dingo chuckled. "Still not willing to claim your name, Dash?"

Henry smiled but concentrated on Dingo's body before him. He would never have thought that he could become aroused again in so short a time, but Dingo was more than happy to prove him wrong on that score.

DESPITE the excitement of getting closer to the thylacine at some point that day, it was a disappointment for Henry to look at the made-up bed the next morning as they began preparing to leave.

He didn't know when he and Dingo would be able to share each other again, especially out in the middle of the forest and with another man in tow. Which reminded him….

"So is Jarrah...." Henry hesitated, unsure whether it was sporting to ask about Jarrah's preference when it came to bed partners.

"He's going to point us to the most likely area, where the tiger has been spotted by his people," Dingo said, shoving a shirt into his bag. "He'll stay back here, just in case."

Henry didn't want to ask in case of what. "That's not what I meant."

"What did you mean then?" Dingo looked at Henry and came to him quickly. "We were never lovers."

"Then how does he know about you? When he first saw you, he said you were like a cat who'd gotten into the milk."

Dingo shouted with laughter. "More like the cat who got all the cream." He cackled at his own ribald wit and sobered slightly when Henry only smiled politely. "We're alike, you see. Scorned by the general population. But he wears his difference on his skin, where all can see it. Ours isn't so easy to spot. Makes us a bit safer."

Bitterly, Henry said, "It's hard to say which 'normal' men hate more, men of color or queers."

"Doesn't make a bit of difference when you're at the end of a rope," Dingo agreed. "He stays safe by playing the darkie, and we don our camouflage before we go out the door." He released Henry and stepped away from him. "Just remember, I may not be able to touch you out there, but I *want* to."

"Thank you for that," Henry said. He hoisted his bag. "What are we waiting for?"

"Dammit! Only one night." Dingo's face crumpled a bit, but then he put on a bright smile. "Well, let's get moving. We've a tiger to find."

14. THE SEARCH FOR THE TIGER TRULY BEGINS

HENRY was surprised that when they went down the stairs, Dingo skirted the bar room and headed directly to the kitchen. Another Aboriginal man was there, cooking at the large stove. He didn't look up when they entered the kitchen but jerked his head slightly toward a tiny table covered in oilskin, tucked behind a refrigerator. Two covered plates were on the table, as well as a steaming coffeepot and two mugs.

Henry and Dingo ate swiftly in silence. Dingo slipped a bill under one of the plates and rose without a word. The dark-skinned man kicked a box as he crossed the kitchen with a laden tray. Dingo waited until he had passed through the swinging door to lift the box, revealing a wrapped package, which he stowed in his pack.

"Food. Ready then?" he asked softly.

Henry nodded and followed Dingo out through the beer garden and thence into a narrow alley.

As Dingo had said, the town was crude and small, particularly in the back alleys that they walked through to get under the cover of the trees. With one glance around, Dingo stepped suddenly from the path into the underbrush, disappearing where Henry would have thought there was no ingress. He followed without giving himself time to think. The shock of the green dimness under the trees after the dazzling sunlight blinded him for a moment, but then his eyes adjusted, and he followed Dingo, trying to step where he did, perceiving that the other man chose a path on fallen leaves, skirting dead twigs likely to snap underfoot.

Dingo obviously had spent much time in the forest, for he moved soundlessly, and Henry was cross with himself for clumsily brushing against the leaves. He could hear the rustle they made against his clothing, but he couldn't move with the same care and still match Dingo's pace.

He nearly plowed into Dingo when the man came to a sudden halt at the edge of a small clearing. Dingo pursed his lips and gave a soft whistle, which sounded like some birdcall unknown to Henry. He knew enough at least to know that it was a birdcall.

Another bird obligingly called back, and Dingo edged around the clearing, staying in the underbrush, until Henry could see a dark shadow within the bushes. He wasn't surprised to see that it was Jarrah.

Jarrah gave them a brilliant smile but said nothing, merely turning and leading the way deeper into the forest. Henry took notice of the sun's position from the brief dazzling glimpses vouchsafed by the canopy overhead. The care the other two men were taking made the hairs on the back of his neck stand up. He didn't want to put words to it, but he thought he had better take note of the trail just in case he might have to find his way back on his own. He looked round for landmarks, but the forest seemed one giant green shadow to him.

The sun was directly overhead before Jarrah stopped. "Might as well eat here," he said in a perfectly ordinary voice.

So sudden was the change from all the ornate caution that Henry wanted to laugh. He bit his lip to keep it down, but the amusement was a welcome relief.

"Where is Hodges?" Dingo asked.

He seemed remote to Henry, a man fixated on his job rather than on *him*. Furiously Henry shook his head. Now was not the time to start acting like a lovelorn girl whose object of desire paid attention to some other girl.

Jarrah chuckled. "He hired a guide. A white man. Chances are you'll never see him because he'll be off chasing shadows."

Dingo smiled but said, "I'm learning not to underestimate Hodges. He may be a rat, but he's a clever rat with an eye on the main chance. He seems to be able to smell me, the way he's been glued to my heels."

Henry didn't blame Hodges; Dingo smelled incredibly wonderful to him, and he could imagine following him a fair distance just to get a whiff.

"He's still got his own weaknesses, though." Jarrah shrugged as he started digging around in his pack to produce a pot for billy tea. "He hates us darkies. If he was truly serious about tracking, he would've hired a native."

"That sounds like one thing that may work in our favor, then," Henry said brightly.

Jarrah gave him a strange look. "Yeah, that's the bright spot in it."

Henry flushed. Obviously he kept putting his foot in his mouth, even though he didn't mean to. Dingo winked at him, and even though it ordinarily would have made him feel a hundred times better, Henry still felt a jab of remorse in his gut.

The silence remained as they continued drinking their tea and letting the sounds of the bush wash over them.

Jarrah threw the remains of his tea into the fire, quenching the flames. "Let's get a move on, boys."

They packed in a comfortable silence, and Henry was embarrassed when his stomach rumbled despite his rather large breakfast. The two other men looked at him and laughed.

"Oh, I'm so sorry, Mr. Percival-Smythe," Jarrah said with a bow. "Having tea probably made your stomach want elevenses."

Rather than smart at being the punch line of a joke, Henry haughtily put his nose in the air. "I at least thought there would have been a biscuit on offer."

Jarrah laughed, rummaged in his swag, and produced a packet of plain biscuits. "You can have two, no more. We're on rations."

Henry opened the packet and divided a share out for everybody before carefully wrapping them back up and handing them to Jarrah. "Thank you, good sir."

"I don't know why I let myself get talked into this," Jarrah muttered, although good-naturedly, and hoisted his swag again.

Dingo winked at Henry and then leaned in and took a huge bite out of the other man's biscuit.

"Hey!" Henry protested. He was ignored as Dingo began following Jarrah into the bush. But Henry was pleased to notice that Dingo's bite mark fit perfectly into his own, and he smiled to himself with this discovery.

Jarrah took them on a circuitous route through the forest until they reached a small clearing. A rusted Ford truck that had seen better days was parked under a large tree. Dingo and Jarrah immediately threw their bags into the tray, and Henry carefully placed his case. He was glad they weren't going to be walking all the way, but he wasn't going to be admitting *that* to his companions.

Jarrah pulled a long tarpaulin over the tray until it dangled down to the ground, where a series of rips at the edge created a fringe. He caught Henry inspecting it with an unspoken question on his lips. "If Hodges somehow managed to follow us this far, this will throw him off our scent."

Henry wasn't sure how, but didn't ask. They all climbed into the cab of the truck. Once again Henry found himself in the middle; Dingo was obviously a window person who didn't like being hemmed in. But Henry didn't mind so much when the truck set off, and Dingo casually laid his arm across the back of the seat. Every now and again his hand would dip down and scratch affectionately at the nape of Henry's neck, and he would find his body reacting in uncomfortably obvious ways. Henry had to shift slightly, but he also craned his neck to fit into Dingo's hand more fully. A satisfied smirk appeared on Dingo's face, and Jarrah played the good friend by pretending not to notice.

Henry realized the ingenuity of the tarpaulin's design when he looked in the rear view mirror. The fringe was acting as a brush, helping to cover up the tracks of their tires as they sped through the bush. Hodges and his guide would have a hell of a time even finding where they began their journey in the truck.

"Genius," he murmured with appreciation.

"That's a Jarrah original," the man said proudly. "Your man here never would have thought up something like that."

Dingo doffed his hat to his friend, and Henry warmed at the words. *Your man.*

It seemed far too early for such ownership to be claimed. But the words seemed right, and Dingo certainly wasn't protesting their use. Henry decided to allow them to remain in being and accept them himself.

"So where are we going?" he asked instead.

"Have a stop-off to make first," Jarrah said. "My house. You can meet my missus."

The academic anthropologist in Henry was excited at the thought. True native living! Oh, the things he was seeing! And they weren't even on the true trail of the thylacine yet!

SECRETLY, Henry was a bit disappointed to find that Jarrah lived in a house much like any other. A bit smaller and shabbier that some in the town, perhaps, but there was no tent ornamented with colorful glyphs; no burrow with a hole in the ceiling for the smoke to escape from the continuously burning campfire. Instead, it was your typical Australian, three-bedroom, weatherboard house.

He was starting to believe anthropology was a science of stereotypes.

Jarrah's wife and two children seemed inordinately pleased to see Dingo, judging from the shrieks of delight with which they set upon him. The children, that was, not Mary. She merely kissed Dingo on both cheeks and told him to come in with an easy comfort from years of friendship.

She looked at Henry with a scrutinizing eye, as if *she* were the anthropologist. "Hello, I'm Mary."

"Henry," he said, offering his hand. "Henry Percival-Smythe. Pleased to meet you."

"Call him Dash," Jarrah said, swooping in to give his wife another kiss. "That's what Dingo calls him."

"Really," Mary said with a smirk, now turning her all-knowing eye on Dingo. "Well, come on in, Dash. Don't mind the kids."

Dingo and Jarrah, however, had more packing to do. While they moved about the house from room to room, adding to a pile they were forming in the middle of the kitchen, Henry asked, "What do we need all this for?"

Dingo threw a spare rucksack at him. "You can't scamper through the forest carrying a suitcase, can you? Might be a bit posh."

"It's just a bag," Henry said, although he could see the wisdom of having one's hands free to deal with whatever eventuality arose.

"Tell me," Dingo said curiously, "how precisely were you planning to convey a full-grown mating pair back to England with that one bag? I mean, it's big, but not *that* big."

Jarrah snorted at the unintended double entendre, and Mary slapped him for it before continuing to make tea.

Henry sniggered at the remark and was surprised at himself. "That might be a bit obvious when I tried to get back on the boat, wouldn't you think?" He quickly left the kitchen and was back just as quickly, carrying his luggage. He sat back down at the table, opened the case and pulled the meager pile of clothing out, setting it on the table. A smaller black case then followed like a set of nesting dolls, which when opened produced a clanking mess of metal.

"I brought two collapsible cages," Henry explained. "I thought if we put the tigers into one they might fight."

Dingo's lips twitched, but he very considerately didn't laugh. "And how did you plan to get the tigers into the frame of mind where they just trotted into the cage? Or keep them hanging about while you set it up?"

Henry's face fell. "Uh, well, now that you mention it…."

Dingo gave him a slap on the shoulder but softened the blow by turning it into a rub. "That's what we're here for." He looked toward Jarrah. "Nice to know we're still good for something, eh?"

"I dunno," Jarrah said, with a cheeky grin. "I'm sure Dash here could find some other use for you."

Intuition formed through years of marriage managed to help him avoid Mary's dishtowel as she threw it at him. "Leave those boys alone," she instructed him.

Thankfully, Henry observed, Jarrah listened to her.

Henry jumped when Dingo handed him a pistol. "What are you doing?"

"Do you know how to fire a gun?" Dingo asked.

"Yes, of course," Henry said.

"Well, you might have a need for it," Dingo said grimly.

"Why?" Henry protested.

Jarrah and Mary looked at each other and in silent unison left the two men alone.

"The forest is a dangerous place, Dash," Dingo said. "Best to be prepared but hope you don't have to use it." He pressed it into Henry's hand.

Henry hated the weight of it, both physically and morally. Even the smell of it revolted him, metallic with a lingering sense of some sort of powdered chemical.

"I can tell I'm going to have to give you lessons. We'll start with the rifle," Dingo frowned. He stood and yelled into the other room. "Jarrah! How're you fixed for ammo?"

Henry was left alone to wonder just what dangers Dingo anticipated that made him decide that weaponry was a necessity.

"Okay, kids," Dingo announced. "Scram."

The two boys didn't take offense at his light tone and obeyed as they ran off laughing.

"Why are you making them leave?" Henry asked.

Dingo looked at him quizzically. "You want kids to get ideas by being around guns?"

Henry nodded and realized that he was still getting to know this man who he was beginning to suspect he was developing genuine feelings for. His offhand nature about the gun in the kitchen had led Henry to believe Dingo would be equally casual about it elsewhere; Dingo, however, surprised him every time.

"Come along then," Jarrah said, poking his head into the doorway.

Henry and Dingo followed him to a small clearing that backed up to a hill that Jarrah clearly used as a safety bunker to stop the bullets. Henry could see a number of empty tin cans littered about, most with holes in them. A plank lay across two tree stumps, and Jarrah placed the rifle on the ground on a bit of sacking before he went to set up a pyramid of the cans on his makeshift firing range. Henry appreciated his frugality in reusing them until they were too riddled with holes to be considered a viable target any more, suspecting that Jarrah really couldn't afford a proper target.

Jarrah's first shot nicked the top can and sent it toppling to the ground. He missed the second, although not by much, and with the third took out the bottom can on the right hand side.

"Slipping, Jarrah?" Dingo teased. He held the gun pointed at the ground until Jarrah had set up another pyramid.

"No one can match your prowess, oh mighty white hunter." Jarrah delivered the jibe as if they had a long-standing routine of rivalry.

Dingo took up his stance. He hit the top edge of the first can and put bullets cleanly through the other two, sending them to the ground. He reloaded the gun while Henry watched and Jarrah rebuilt his little pyramid.

"Let's see what you can do with it, Professor."

Henry hadn't planned on showing off or even shooting the gun, but the hated nickname delivered so casually brought to mind certain other unpleasant occasions where he'd been teased for wearing glasses or being "bookish."

Carefully he brought the gun up and braced the butt against his shoulder, sighting down the barrel before squeezing the trigger.

His first shot kicked up one of the bottom cans, sending the other two flying up into the air. In quick succession, he squeezed off two more shots, tracing the arc of each can, making them spin in midair before they fell to the earth.

The silence that followed felt respectful to Henry, and he almost smiled as he lowered the rifle.

"That wasn't a happy accident, was it?" Jarrah asked.

"You know how to shoot!" Dingo accused him.

Henry shrugged. "One learns, living in the country."

"You bloody Pom!"

Henry winced as Dingo buffeted his shoulder in glee.

"You've been holding out on me, mate! Did you see that, Jarrah? The boy can shoot!"

"I'm not blind, Dingo." Jarrah went forward and stacked up another set of cans. "That wasn't a fluke then, Henry?"

"It's not often I miss," Henry muttered.

"Did your Dad take you hunting then? How much did you bag?" Dingo asked curiously.

"I've never shot anything… living."

Dingo gave a short nod. Henry almost laughed; his seeming approval was so different from his own father's disappointment in Henry's failure in this arena.

"Let's see it again."

Henry broke open the breech and reloaded. This time around, he sent each can into the air with one shot, nailing it with a second shot before it fell.

"Jarrah, toss a can up into the air," Dingo suggested.

Patiently Henry shot each can at the top of its arc as Jarrah sent them flying. "Satisfied?"

"Well done, Dash. Can you shoot a pistol as well?"

Henry nodded. "Of course."

"Brilliant. That's a load off."

The tone of respect in Dingo's voice was almost enough reward to erase the memory of the long summer afternoons spent shooting with his father grimly standing over him. But it was best not to dwell upon that. Far better to bask in the glow of Dingo's smile and think about how he might be rewarded later on.

Henry blushed, wondering if it was the Australian air that was making him have such an abundance of lascivious thoughts, but as Dingo bent over the front seat of the truck to retrieve something, Henry realized that it all had to do with the man who had dragged him halfway around the world.

Once again, he had to stop the self-doubt from sinking in, of what would happen once their adventure was over. It was all too easy to think it could go on forever, but as all things did, it would surely end. And Dingo lived on the opposite end of the earth.

"What are you thinking about?" Dingo asked.

"You," Henry said, forgetting to self-censor.

He could have almost sworn he saw Dingo blush, or at least start to. It gave him a boost of esteem, to see what he often felt himself displayed upon his paramour's face.

"You do go on sometimes, Dash," Dingo said, but when he lifted his face again he was grinning happily.

The thylacine was temporarily forgotten again as Henry thought of their night in the hotel together. He would almost give up the whole expedition to lock himself away with Dingo again, but he believed there would be more nights like that again. He had to now focus on what had fascinated him for long years: this almost-mythical creature in the wilds of a wilder land.

Dingo disappeared around the side of the house in search of Jarrah. Henry cleaned the pistol he had been given, readying it for the next time he might have to use it. He stressed the *might* in his own thoughts—they were not hunters going in search of prey; they were going out there to save them. It sounded a bit gormless, really, but he much preferred thinking that way about them.

He almost jumped out of his skin when Mary approached him from behind and tapped him on the shoulder.

"Mary! You gave me a start!"

She laughed, her teeth a contrast against her dark skin. It made her smile all the brighter. "You ready to go?"

Henry nodded. "Just waiting for the others, I assume."

Mary tossed her head. "That Dingo, he's probably looking for the beer."

"I think Dingo would feel it most un-Australian to spend time without beer," Henry suggested.

"You know him well." She peered at him for confirmation.

Henry turned away, certain his face could be read more easily than any book. And he was right, because Mary laughed again. It was more tender this time, though.

"Are you Dingo's fella, then?"

Once again, the fact that *everybody* seemed to know about Dingo astounded Henry. He wasn't sure whether he was astounded that so many people were cognizant of this usually most-secret information, or more importantly, that nobody seemed to care. But these *were* Dingo's friends.

Mary stood patiently, awaiting his response.

"Uh-well," he stuttered, "I guess, when you look at it—"

"I haven't got all day," Mary said impatiently. "I asked Jarrah, and he got all funny too. Said it was none of our business, and Dingo would tell us when he wanted to."

Henry frowned. "Dingo didn't tell you?"

"He never tells us. Most of the time, we have to get it out of the other fella."

"The… other fella?" Henry replied weakly.

Mary seemed to recognize that she had committed a major faux pas. "Well… not that there have been that many—"

Henry thought of all the other men whom he had met that shared such an easy familiarity with Dingo. Was he to believe that this man he was falling for might have fucked his way across the globe? It was a horrible thought, to think that he was just one in a long line of many, when for him Dingo had been in a queue that could be counted on one hand.

"Mary."

It was a new voice. Henry peered over Mary's shoulder as she turned to find Dingo standing behind them with another bag in his hand.

"Yes, Dingo?"

"Dash here *is* my fella."

Satisfied and happy with the outcome, Mary turned back to Henry. "You must be special. Like I said, he *never* tells us."

"Are you happy now, Mary?" Dingo said good-naturedly as she passed him on her way back to the house.

"Mmm hmm," she hummed wickedly, giving him a swat on the bum. Dingo postured as if to chase her, and she sprinted away, laughing all the while.

"So—" Dingo threw the bag into the back of the truck.

"I'm your fella, then?" Henry asked.

Dingo peered at him beneath the brim of his hat. "I normally say there's no such thing as stupid questions. But that's a bloody stupid question."

Henry's air supply was cut off as Dingo locked lips upon his. He could taste the beads of sweat above his mouth—so tangy, so irrepressibly masculine, and all Dingo—that he was afraid his bodily impulses would lead to them shaming themselves out in the open if they took control.

Jarrah interrupted them as he pushed past them to load a final set of bags upon the truck bed. "Hope you two aren't going to be like this the whole bloody trip."

Their lips parted, but their bodies remained pressed against each other. Dingo had to twist Henry slightly in order to face his friend. "Afraid you're going to be lonely? You could bring Mary."

The woman in question appeared with her children in tow. Henry tried to move away from Dingo, but Dingo was having none of it. The children seemed interested in what Dingo was doing with the man they had been introduced to this morning, but only for the fact that they had never seen their uncle like that before.

"He's your uncle Dingo's fella," Mary said matter-of-factly, as if it was the most natural thing in the world.

The children nodded solemnly and then proceeded to jump wildly into and upon the truck bed.

"I'm not going where there's no privy or tap," Mary told the men. "My bush days are over."

"You're my queen," Jarrah said, love-struck.

She nuzzled into him. "Right." Then another side of the queen was displayed as she drew herself up regally and bellowed, "Boys! Off the truck *right now*!" They scampered down and raced obediently to her side.

Dingo finally allowed Henry his private space again and moved to kiss Mary. "Bye, love."

"Take care of yourselves. And Dingo?"

He turned back. "Yeah?"

"You make sure Jarrah comes home safe. Or else I'll cut off your balls and wear them as a necklace."

Henry could tell this was no idle threat, even though it seemed to have been made many times and probably with the same level of ferocity.

"Righty-O," Dingo told her, with a bow of his hat.

Henry also offered his goodbyes, which Mary returned with a far less threatening attitude than she had afforded Dingo. The two men leapt into the truck to give husband and wife some semblance of privacy in their farewell, although Henry couldn't resist sneaking a look through the side mirror and catching them in a passionate kiss. Guilty, he looked down to see Dingo's hand coming down and resting upon his knee.

He placed his own over it.

15. INTO THE WILDERNESS

ON THE outskirts of a small town called Tyenna, they quickly disappeared into the wild as if they had never been a part of civilization at all. The forest became denser the farther they drove into it. Mouth agog, Henry stared out the window as the landscape moved past slowly. When he had researched Tasmania before leaving England, he had assumed based on the descriptions that the forests would be akin to those he had seen back home, but these trees were an entirely different thing altogether. Bunched together they formed a canopy above their heads, and the sky could only be seen in brief snatches between the foliage. Giant tree ferns pursued a tortuously twisted path between the eucalyptus trees, draped with other plants that seemed to enjoy a parasitical existence upon the fleshy stems. The meager amount of sunlight that reached the brush underneath meant that the plants had grown lush and tall in order to reach a share of it; the lack of sunlight resulted in a change of temperature that made Henry shiver slightly.

"I thought," Henry said, having to clear his throat as it had been a long time since he last spoken, "that the last tiger killed in the wild was a few years ago at Mawbanna."

"You know your stuff," Jarrah said.

Dingo grinned at Henry. "Mawbanna's near Burnie."

"Oh!" Henry said, his eyes lighting up in recognition. "That's why you made Hodges think we were going there!"

Dingo tapped the side of his nose. "Exactly."

"Do you really think he's gullible enough to go there?" Henry asked hesitantly.

"Why?"

"It's just that… if that was where the last tiger was caught, you would think there may have been more sightings from that region. And that's not where the reports are coming from."

"We're hoping Hodges doesn't know that."

"Hoping?" Henry's tone suggested that it wasn't exactly the best strategy to base your whole expedition upon.

"As far as we know, he just knows we're up to something. So he's following us and relying upon *our* information."

Henry knew that Dingo had the most experience with Hodges, but he was also aware that Dingo tended to underestimate his nemesis. He self-consciously touched the burn scar on his wrist; he was only too aware of just how ruthless Hodges could be.

How could Dingo be so nonchalant about it? He sensed there was more to their history together, and somehow Hank was all tied into it. Henry wasn't sure if he would ever be told the full story, no matter how much he thought about it.

So he let his criticism fall away and noticed that Jarrah was watching Dingo with interest to see how he would take the questioning of his methods. Dingo's jaw was set; he was restraining himself from saying something. Henry looked back out the window, hoping that it would soon blow over.

The small dirt path upon which the truck was riding was obviously only kept clear by the infrequent drivers that came along it. The branches and plants that clung to the fleshy tree ferns were rapidly trying to reclaim it for Mother Nature, every now and again they were so close that they temporarily pushed through the window and whacked either him or Jarrah. Dingo, who had most likely given up his usual window seat for this reason, remained relatively safe from their predatory intentions.

The branches and leaves were wet with rain that couldn't dry as the sun wasn't reaching them. After a few minutes in the thick of it, Henry was uncomfortably damp.

Dingo took pity on him. "You know, you *can* close the window."

Of course he could, but with the damp there was also humidity. If he shut the window, they would begin to boil. "It's all right." Henry shrugged.

Dingo's knee jolted against his as they hit a rut in the track. Once again, his arm rested behind Henry's neck, and Henry took comfort from it.

"You know," Henry said in awe, "I don't think you could find enough space in England to fit this whole forest."

"There are parts of this wilderness where no white man has ever stepped," Jarrah said, grimacing. "And I hope they never do."

"Why not?" Henry asked. "Think of what could be discovered!"

"Think of what could be destroyed," Dingo murmured. He looked at Jarrah, and they exchanged a gaze of shared pain.

Henry thought of his mother country and what she had done in the name of colonization. It all seemed so noble on their end; Henry had never actually met anybody who had to deal with their way of life being changed and affected by how their country had eventually ceased to be their own.

And he knew that he couldn't justify it, not to Jarrah, or Mary. Probably not even to Dingo, even though at some point his own ancestors would have also been part of those who came over from England in big boats with big dreams, no matter what the cost.

The thylacine was just one of a very long list. And the list grew exponentially as you took into account all of England's history and its role on other soil around the world.

"I guess that is one of the drawbacks of discovery," he said finally.

"That's a nice way of putting it," Jarrah said.

Henry wisely kept his mouth shut. There was an untouched record here he wasn't fully aware of, and he didn't think he could give voice enough to defend or to apologize. He felt ashamed of his silence but didn't know how to proceed.

They drove in silence the rest of the way.

16. Bush Magic

HENRY was glad of the fire; once the sun had gone down, the humidity lost the heat of the day, and the damp was merely cold. He lay propped on one elbow, staring into the flames that Jarrah kept to a modest size, rarely feeding in a stick when it relapsed into embers. He glanced around to find Jarrah and Dingo sitting away from the fire and staring into the darkened jungle.

Dingo caught his movement and said, "Best not to stare into the fire, Dash."

Henry nodded. His eyes had taken a moment to adjust to the darkness when he looked away from the bright light, and he realized what a handicap it was. He shifted so that he was sitting closer to Dingo, also looking outward.

"This is the last night you can build a fire," Jarrah commented. The embers collapsed with a shower of sparks, and he did not add another stick. "Once you're out there, it's too easy to spot, if anyone should be following."

"What'll we do for tea?" Henry asked, although he was thinking more of the tiny circle of warmth at the center of the vast chill that surrounded them. Already, just a few feet further away from the campfire, he had begun to shiver.

"Guess we'll just have to huddle for warmth instead," Dingo teased, chuckling at the quick look Henry threw at Jarrah.

Henry didn't deign to answer, but an inner heat seemed to spread through him at Dingo's words. Besides, Jarrah didn't seem to be paying attention to them anyway. "Shouldn't we get some sleep?"

"I'll take first watch," Jarrah said.

Henry shifted his ground cloth a bit closer to Dingo's, but he didn't have the nerve to actually touch him. He lay down and peered up at the canopy but could see nothing, not leaf, nor cloud, nor star. It was like being inside a building and yet completely different.

A low crooning lulled him to sleep as he wondered groggily what Jarrah was singing about.

When he awoke to the eerie green light that penetrated the jungle by dawn, Jarrah was still sitting by the blackened rocks where they had made the fire, his eyes dreamy and distant as if he were in a trance.

Dingo stepped quietly from behind a screen of foliage, holding three dripping canteens in his hands, apparently having gone to refill them. He smiled at Henry but put a finger before his lips when Henry would have spoken.

Henry sat up and rubbed his chin, wishing he could have some hot water to shave and to make some tea. He felt helpless in the face of Jarrah's abstraction and Dingo's unwonted silence. He had no idea how to make himself useful or even what they were waiting for. He reached for his pack, meaning to retrieve a few biscuits for breakfast, but when Dingo shook his head, Henry's hand dropped to his lap, and he just sat listening.

The song of unseen birds filtered through the stillness, and Henry suddenly became aware of a feeling of peace and oneness, as if he were a part of this land and the jungle around him.

Jarrah opened his eyes and looked directly at him. "You dream the knowledge."

Henry opened his mouth but didn't speak. He nodded slowly. He could never have put words to what he was feeling, but he knew just what Jarrah was talking about.

Jarrah smiled, his eyes still unearthly and his movements slow and deliberate as he picked up a piece of soft charcoal from the cold fire. With a few quick strokes on a flat grey rock, he brought the outline of the thylacine to life, lean, wolf-like, with its head raised and tail pointed. He drew fifteen stripes along the body. "This is not for everyone to see."

Henry was aware that Dingo remained motionless, as he had been since Jarrah first moved.

Jarrah started to chant, and Henry caught the repetition of the word "*kannunah*" several times, but the rest was in some unfamiliar language. A glance at Dingo's respectful face told him that he didn't understand much more, although he seemed to know what Jarrah was doing.

Jarrah leaned forward and took Henry's hand, placing it palm down on the drawing he had made of the tiger, pressing his hand to the smooth flatness of the rock. When he let go, Henry looked at his palm, where the faint lines of the stripes were transferred onto his skin.

Jarrah fell silent and gave a great sigh. He held out his hand to Dingo. "Hand me some of that water, mate."

Henry expected him to drink, but Jarrah carefully poured the water over his exquisite drawing, obliterating it.

"Don't—" Henry exclaimed, stretching out his marked hand.

Jarrah ignored him, washing the rock thoroughly 'til nothing remained. Then he looked up. "This is not for everyone to see. The ancestors permitted me to create a dream painting for you only, Dash Henry Percival-Smythe."

"But why? And why couldn't you save it? It was beautiful."

"They allowed me to call to the animal's spirit, and he chose to come to you. My people have walked this land side by side with the tiger for many years, many lifetimes. We did not hunt them; they did not hunt us; and yet we are both hunters. This dream painting is *andjamun*, sacred and dangerous. The *kannunah* would not come to you lightly. He has touched your spirit, and you have touched his. Let this knowledge live in your body. The creation ancestors who gave shape to this land and all who dwell here may give you dreams."

Jarrah gave a little shiver and picked up the stone, hiding it under some dead leaves and other debris at the foot of one of the tree ferns. Then he proceeded to conceal all traces of the fire they had made, scattering the ash and blackened stones so cleverly that Henry couldn't find them after he turned his head away and then looked back.

Jarrah stood up and stretched. "Right, mates. Well, I wish you good hunting. Here's where we part company. I'll be back here in twenty-eight days to pick you up. Don't fucking get killed." He stepped closer to Dingo and gave him a hug, showing no reluctance to embrace him tightly. Then he did the same for Henry, causing another powerful rush of emotion to rise up within him. "Take care."

He bent to pick up his canteen and vanished into the brush. After a few minutes, Henry heard the roar of his truck coming to life and then it faded in the distance.

Dingo glanced at him curiously but didn't speak, merely shouldering his rucksack and the one Jarrah had carried.

"What did that mean?" Henry asked.

"What did it feel like it meant?"

Henry struggled to settle his pack on his back and keep up with Dingo's energetic stride. "It felt like… something spiritual."

Dingo gave him a sidelong look and then smiled. "Nailed it in one, Dash, very good. It means you'll see Tassie this trip."

An explosion of excitement threatened to burst out of Henry's chest. "What, you mean that mumbo jumbo of his actually meant something?"

Dingo stopped so short that Henry plowed into him. "Don't do that. It was real, and you know it."

Ashamed, Henry nodded, lowering his eyes. "It's just—"

"I know, stiff upper lip and all that, and it's frightfully ill-bred to believe that a dark-skinned native might actually know something we don't, and faith is for the civilized on Sunday in church, after a good breakfast, but we don't trot it out any other day of the week."

His savage tone made Henry feel even more ashamed. "Look I didn't mean to… to disrespect him, it's just…."

Dingo started walking again, following some dim trail invisible to Henry. "Don't brush up against that grass; it'll cut you. For centuries before Europeans came here, the Aborigines managed not to kill off any species of animal, bird, or bug. They lived in harmony with the land. We can't do that; we seem to need to impose our will on it, wrest every last bit of value from the earth in triumph. In one short century, we've managed to almost finish the tiger, and that's not the only animal we're trying to wipe out."

"But I'm trying to save them!"

Dingo looked a bit milder as he glanced behind him. "I know. Jarrah knows that too, or he wouldn't have asked his ancestors to let you see that."

"I'll try to be worthy of it," Henry said humbly. "But what *was* that?"

"Ancient people tried to become one with the spirit of the land and the animals who roamed there. In Tasmania, Aborigines didn't hunt the tiger, so it's very rare that they left any images that they painted lying around. They believed you could call an animal to you by painting its image. That's why there are so many rock paintings of kangaroos because they hunted them for food. With the *kannunah,* it's different. They respected the tiger and wished it well. To paint its image as part of the ceremony was one thing; at the end they always erased it, so as not to harm the creature. Understand?"

"Not exactly," Henry muttered.

"Jarrah learned from the old people. He is one of the holders of magic knowledge. He must have liked you because he created that painting to ensure that you'll see Tassie this trip."

"So we'll be successful in our mission?" Henry was overjoyed, already imagining the triumph of his return with the specimens he sought, cute little tiger cubs tumbling about in his imagination as the desired mating at the zoo succeeded.

"You'll see the tigers," Dingo repeated.

"There's a catch."

"Isn't there always?"

"Well, what is it?" Henry felt a little belligerent; wanting guarantees that what he had dreamed of so often would come to pass.

"If you could see the tiger, but it meant that Hodges was right there next to you seeing it also, what would you want?"

Henry nodded slowly. "I would forego the chance to get a sight of them." He sighed deeply, hoping that he would not be forced to make that choice.

Dingo laughed. "Don't worry, Gloomy Gus, you've won Jarrah's stamp of approval. I'm sure you've only to sit down, and you'll have Tassie tumbling into your lap, wanting to lick your face."

Henry smiled at the thought, even though it meant all those teeth would be near his face. "I thought you said the full-blooded Aborigines had died out in 1878? So how is Jarrah a holder of magic knowledge?"

Dingo gave Henry another cryptic smirk. "I didn't say that; you did. If you wanted to take the land of the people who lived there, wouldn't it be a hell of a lot easier to pretend they didn't exist anymore?"

"You mean Jarrah—"

"Is a full-blooded Aborigine. Mary, however, isn't, so neither are their kids. When she was a girl, Mary got shipped off to one of those schools where they tried to make natives white and failed dismally. Aborigines still walk amongst us; we just don't acknowledge them as such."

"Somewhat like the tiger." Henry looked down at his hand and smiled. He could still see the faint stripes of Jarrah's painting on his skin.

Dingo caught him looking and seemed pleased. "You got it."

Henry wasn't sure what to make of Dingo's enigmatic smile, and as they started hiking farther into the forest it quickly vanished from his mind.

17. ALONE IN THE WILD

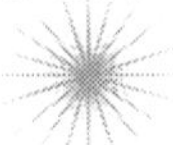

HE WASN'T athletic enough to withstand this kind of torture. Henry tried to wheeze as quietly as he could as he followed Dingo through the heavy shrub with his head down. The branches drew glistening stripes across him as he passed through, darkening his already damp shirt. The rain had stopped falling, for now, at least, but there wasn't enough sunlight to dry out the forest. He was cold, and wet, and tired. And most unhappy.

He remembered what Jarrah had said about the fire—and he worried about how he was meant to dry the clothes overnight if they were unable to build one. He glowered at Dingo's back as the other man moved easily before him. It was all right for him. He was used to this kind of life.

Maybe adventuring wasn't everything he had made it out to be.

Henry's muscles screamed with relief when the sun began to set and Dingo said they would make camp for the night. Henry was too tired to even ask about the tigers, and he worked in silence as he helped Dingo unpack the makeshift tent they would be sleeping in.

"You're quiet," Dingo said.

"Too tired to talk," Henry said shortly.

Dingo nodded, deciding to leave whatever he was going to say. He did the majority of the work in assembling their shelter, doing the work in half the time that Henry would have taken.

"You rest for a minute," Dingo said. "I'll go and fetch us some fresh water."

"I can help," Henry said defensively.

"I know you can," Dingo said casually. "But I don't need help getting water, do I?"

Henry shrugged and crawled underneath the shelter of the canvas, which was spread over a number of branches and tied down to the roots of giant trees where they arched up from the ground. He listened to Dingo move off and wondered irritably how they could get warm during the night when the wind seemed to cut through the material like a knife.

He knew he was being difficult, and he tried to will himself into thinking more positively. It was only natural that it would start getting to him at some point; after all, this whole life was something new to him.

And then, Henry grew angry, but with himself. He had *wanted* this. More than anything. And not only had he been given the very thing he had been wishing for, but along with it came a beautiful man who seemed to see something in him Henry had never believed about himself. He was an idiot to be acting in such a way, like a churlish, ungrateful child bored with a new toy.

His palm burned, and Henry sat up to examine it. There wasn't much of Jarrah's drawing left upon his skin, but what there was stood out in stark contrast to his natural coloring. He closed his eyes and remembered the rush of natural power that had seemed to course throughout his veins when the thylacine had first been marked upon him. It came back with such a strength that he almost jumped to his feet, and a moan escaped from his lips.

The surge dissipated, but the feeling remained. Shakily, Henry stood. Fingers trembling, he undid the buttons of his shirt and laid the damp cloth across the top of the tent. He knew as he stripped down to nothing that he should be cold, but he felt warm.

He waited for Dingo to return.

DINGO had to restrain himself from whistling a greeting as he stepped out of the shrub and almost stumbled into their camp. Straightaway he could see Henry's wet clothing strung out across the top of the tent. He knew it wouldn't dry at all, not even by morning, but he could understand why the other man would want to change. Perhaps they could break early tomorrow at daylight when smoke wouldn't be as discernible to build a fire and get them more comfortable.

"Haroo," he called softly. "Dash, you there?"

An arm emerged from within the tent, and Dingo's jaw dropped open when Henry stepped out. Completely naked, his skin had a greenish cast from the weak light that managed to infiltrate the canopy of the forest. It made him look ethereal, and if Dingo had been a more superstitious soul he would have thought that he had stepped through to another time with another being entirely.

Henry's skin looked even creamier, more delectable. His arms hung loosely by his sides; the dark bush below his navel threw a shadow to conceal what lay between his legs. He took another step forward, and the lines of his beautiful cock could now be seen.

Dingo swallowed heavily. "Well, you know how to keep a man on his toes."

Henry smiled. "Undress," he commanded softly.

Dingo didn't need to be told twice. His hands were steady and confident as he unbuttoned his shirt and threw it on top of Henry's, up on the tent. He was already hard as he stepped out of his trousers, and although he was tempted, he didn't touch himself as he wanted Henry's body against his to be the first thing he felt.

Henry walked toward him soundlessly and pulled Dingo closer to him by the scruff of his neck. Although the passion between them was as extreme as before, his kiss was gentle, yearning, slow. Dingo was already straining, but he let Henry take the lead. Entwined, they moved over to lean against a tree. Dingo worried that the bark would be digging into his back, and it should have been uncomfortable, but Henry didn't seem to feel it. Dingo concentrated on the feeling of Henry writhing in his arms, the silky hardness of their cocks as they rubbed against each other, and the hairs on Henry's thighs sliding and catching against his own.

Dingo wanted to speak, but if this was a spell they were under, he didn't want to break it.

IT WAS Henry who cut through the silence, moaning his name as he twisted within Dingo's embrace to face the tree, presenting himself. His chest rubbed against the wood, making his already-sensitive nipples tingle with pleasure. Dingo's chest was tight against his back; he could feel Dingo's cock rubbing against the valley of his arse. His eyes flew open as he remembered the use of the oil in the hotel room, but he didn't want to stop. Didn't want this moment to be interrupted.

Dingo was obviously thinking the same thing. "Dash, give me a minute—"

"No," Henry said fervently. "Don't stop."

"I'll hurt you," Dingo told him.

"I trust you." Emboldened, Henry pressed himself back against Dingo, practically trapping him. He clenched his cheeks, feeling the blunt head tantalizingly close to his entrance.

Dingo cursed under his breath.

"Take me," Henry muttered, squeezing again. He smiled to himself as he felt Dingo's hand run along his hip. He heard him spit into his palm and moaned again as a damp finger slid over his opening.

"You're still going to feel it," Dingo warned.

"I want to."

"You're one mad bugger, Dash, but I can't resist you."

Henry loved that. He had never felt like he was irresistible before… and to have it come from someone like Dingo, who seemed to have everybody in the palm of his hand whenever he interacted with them? He gasped as Dingo entered him with one hand on the small of his back to help keep him steady as he tried to push himself in with as little pain as possible.

"Should I stop?" Dingo asked anxiously.

"Don't you dare," Henry said through gritted teeth, afraid he would pull out.

Dingo's fingers were now pressing on both of his hips as he drove deeper into Henry. Buried to the hilt, he kissed Henry's shoulder. Impatient, Henry pushed back against him. Dingo took that as a sign for continuance and began to pump himself fully against his lover.

Henry grunted, his face pressed against the bark of the tree. He slapped his palm above his head, using it to balance himself as Dingo continued to rock against him. It *was* more painful without the oil, but Henry wouldn't have wanted it any other way at that point in time. It surprised him how forward he had been in seeking this out, how insistent he had been to have Dingo right at this very moment, without hesitation. Fanciful thoughts made him wonder if somehow being in the thick of nature was having some sort of primordial effect upon him, making him remember the call of the wild that humans had gradually become immune to over the years as they retreated into civilization. Had he awakened the beast within himself?

He couldn't believe that it was impossible to switch off his mind, even when being buggered senseless against a tree in the colonies. But then Dingo shifted a little, his angle changed, and Henry's thoughts ceased as eruptions of pleasure fanned through his body and straight into his brain. All he was aware of was Dingo's body against his, the satisfying fullness within him, and the feeling that shot through his heart when Dingo's arm flung over his and their hands gripped. They rode together, hands joined—bodies joined. Henry felt enveloped body and soul by Dingo as his other arm snaked around his waist and took him in hand, stroking Henry in unison with his thrusts.

Henry burst through the gaps in Dingo's fingers and couldn't stop from crying out as his lover mercilessly continued to pump him. It was too much, too much pleasure, his knees were giving out, the only things keeping him upright were the tree and the weight of Dingo behind him….

Dingo cried out hoarsely, and Henry felt a new warmth spread within him. Dingo sagged against his back, murmuring his name. They couldn't move. Sweating, shuddering, and gasping, they remained locked within each other.

"Dingo—"

"Dash." It was a statement to a query that had been incomplete.

But Henry knew he had been answered. His legs screamed for relief, so he didn't mind when Dingo pulled away.

"This is foolhardy," Dingo said, standing naked and glistening with sweat in the small clearing they had made. "I can't keep my hands off you, and we've probably scared Tassie away with all the hullabaloo."

Henry nodded. "We have a job to do."

"Still," Dingo said, and he broke into a grin, "nobody says we can't have a little fun every now and again."

"All work and no play," Henry agreed solemnly.

"Let's get some shuteye," Dingo said, clapping his hands together. "And mind you don't seduce me during the night again, Dash."

Henry nodded, trying not to smile back. "I promise."

"Besides," Dingo said. "It's my turn next."

As he turned to walk off into the tent, Henry could have sworn he was almost ready to start again.

THAT night they slept naked in each other's arms.

"Keeps the body warmer than in wet clothes," Dingo explained. As if they needed an excuse.

Henry was as warm as he could have hoped to be even though, as he had suspected, the wind easily penetrated the scant shelter of their makeshift tent.

His dreams were confused, a tangle of striped fur and gaping jaws and Dingo's sturdy arms wrapped tightly around him. He was so tired and sore; he thought it was a dream when his hips started moving. He couldn't pry his eyes open to determine whether he was still dreaming, but he knew it was no dream when he felt the gush of hot come between them.

"Sorry," he murmured, without opening his eyes.

"For what?"

"I promised not to seduce you in the night."

Dingo's body shook against his. "Ah, but I didn't make the same promise, and besides, the sun is up and so should we be."

"I thought we were. What we just did doesn't count?"

"It counted."

Dingo's voice made Henry finally open his eyes, squinting at the other man to find him staring at him with an intense expression that made his heart beat a little quicker. Henry nodded, unable to trust himself to speak.

Dingo kissed him softly and sighed with regret. "It must be the irony of the gods that if you get what you've been yearning for, you don't get the time to appreciate it." He pushed Henry away gently and crawled out, giving him a magnificent view of his backside before sticking his head back inside to say, "Come on, lazybones, or you won't be in time for breakfast."

Henry stretched, hoping to relieve the stiffness in his muscles from yesterday's trek, feeling a pleasurable reminder of their coupling the night before. He crawled out and stood up, scratching his hand idly over his stomach where the remnants of the morning's pleasure remained. "I suppose there's no hot water for shaving."

"We'll take a break after we move on. I hope you can hike on an empty stomach," Dingo said.

Henry made a face to see Dingo dress in his damp clothes from the top of the tent. He'd hoped that perhaps some miracle of nature might have occurred and they would be dry. He caught his own clothes as Dingo threw them at him and hurried to dress so he could help Dingo fold the tent cloth and remove the ropes that had held it.

"We'll move on about five miles and then have a small fire," Dingo said quietly.

Henry became aware that compared to Dingo, he sounded like a herd of elephants stampeding through. He lowered his voice. "I thought Jarrah said we couldn't have a fire." Dingo was already hoisting his rucksack to his shoulders, and Henry hastened to follow suit.

"At night, even with the dense foliage, a fire would stand out like a beacon, but during the day, if we take precautions, we can have a small one." Dingo grinned. "Besides, you won't need it to get warm. Today we're really going to march."

Henry was secretly dismayed to hear that apparently Dingo considered yesterday's hike to be a mere stroll. "Where are we going?"

"Into the heart of Tasmania, where the tiger has been driven to find sanctuary. Where there are no names attached to the land and the rivers run wild."

"How deep? And how will we cross them without a boat?" Henry asked, wondering if Dingo was going to pull an inflatable rubber raft out of his pack when they needed it.

"We'll cross that bridge when we get to it," Dingo said cheerfully.

Given what he'd seen of Dingo's resourcefulness, Henry felt sure that somehow they would, and yet he asked inanely, "There are bridges?"

"Of course not, you nong."

"So we'll have to swim for it."

"You might. I've never learned to swim." Dingo didn't sound as if he regretted it all that much. "My dad was never one for the beaches. He preferred to trek inland."

Henry was heartened just a bit to know there was at least one thing he could do that Dingo couldn't. He almost began to wish for an opportunity to show off his prowess and earn some admiration from the other man. "Well, perhaps it won't prove to be a barrier."

"It all depends on Tassie, doesn't it, mate? But you might say this whole territory is a barrier." Dingo looked back over his shoulder. "You're still game, aren't you?"

"Of course!" Henry said stoutly. "So have any men—any white men—been where you're taking me?"

"Well, yeah. My dad, my brothers, and me," Dingo said offhandedly. "Jarrah knows this place like the back of his hand."

Henry wondered, if that were the case, why Jarrah hadn't accompanied them, but he didn't like to ask. Besides, Jarrah had his wife and kids depending on him. Suddenly Henry felt a bit sad to realize that if he did go missing in the wilds, the only one who might truly mourn his loss was the man he was trailing after. He imagined his mother shedding a decorous tear at his memorial service while his father sat grim and unmoved beside her, irritated at Henry's carelessness by way of supplying suitable remains to be interred in the ancestral mausoleum. His father would be further outraged that Henry had underperformed professionally as well, leaving no tasty epitaph to sum up his worthiness to bear the name of Percival-Smythe. At least his nephew might think of him fondly even as his memory faded in time.

Before he could begin to feel too sorry for himself, Henry shook his head at his morose fancies and smiled. He dug a biscuit out of his pocket and started to munch on it. It might be quite a while until Dingo found a spot he deemed suitable to make a fire.

EVEN though there was no visible sun through the trees to help Henry guess the time of day, Dingo seemed to be on top of it at all times. He knew when to break for elevenses—"Gotta let you have some of your traditions," he told Henry with an affectionate smirk—and when to stop for lunch.

It would probably have been late afternoon when they reached their first watery obstacle, and Henry was so exhausted he was as irritable as a child.

"We should cross now," Dingo said, surveying the swift moving water dubiously.

"In the morning!" Henry snapped. There wasn't even a word for how tired he was, and besides, he was weary of Dingo always making all the decisions. Wasn't this meant to be a partnership? His feet hurt, and he suspected that Dingo knew it and thought he was the best joke going.

"My dad said never to leave food on your plate because you don't know if you'll get another meal tomorrow," Dingo insisted.

"Fine, that's good to know. No doubt he also said a stitch in time saves nine, but I'm not crossing that river tonight." Henry sat down and started to unlace his boots.

"Aw, Dash, you're no fun when you're a cranky pants," Dingo observed with his annoyingly cheerful grin. He put his rucksack down and started rooting in the food bag for his metal kit. Henry almost smiled to see it; that was where Dingo kept the matches, so possibly it meant that now they could have a fire. "My *mum* was in charge of teaching me to sew. What me dad *meant* by that—" He stopped short when he was interrupted by a dull roaring sound. "Oh fuck."

Moving faster than Henry would have thought such a big man could, Dingo grabbed for Henry's boots and tossed them away from the river. "Move your arse! It's a flash flood!"

Henry threw his jacket where the boots had landed and snatched at his rucksack. It was heavy, but he swung it by one of the straps and managed a fair toss. He grabbed for Dingo's pack, seeing the other man was still fumbling for something.

"My compass!"

"Dingo! No!"

The wall of water was upon them so quickly that Henry barely had time to jump clear with Dingo's pack. The compression of the walls of rock upstream released just as the river reached their clearing, so the water surged past them at breakneck speed.

Dingo made a snatch for the heavy bag, overbalanced, and fell into the angry river, disappearing into the yellowish dirty foam.

"You fucking thrill seeker," Henry growled. He took off his glasses and folded the temple pieces, hanging them carefully on a branch of a nearby tree, before he threw himself into the racing water without hesitation, kicking strongly for where he saw the blur of Dingo's sandy head bobbing.

He managed to grab Dingo's collar and held his head above the water. The current was so powerful he knew he would never be able to swim for shore with Dingo's weight dragging him down. He just hoped that the surge of water would subside and they would eventually wash up somewhere—as long as they weren't slammed into a rock first.

Henry thought he heard something and realized that the crazy Aussie was singing! Something dirty by the sound of it, but the roar of the water snatched the words away from him.

The current slowed at a bend in the river, and Henry desperately kicked for the shoreline. His arm and shoulder ached from holding onto Dingo, and with his last ounce of strength, he shoved the other man toward the sand.

Henry managed to grab onto to a rock and crawled out himself, panting for breath. When he could speak, he observed in a calm manner, "You're a fucking idiot, Dingo; you can't swim."

"Who says I can't swim, mate?" Dingo looked a bit like a drowned rat, with wet tufts of hair sticking up on his head, but his grin was as cheerful as ever. The water had almost torn the shirt off his back, and Henry noticed that this time his hands trembled as he buttoned it up. It was one of the first times his cockiness was betrayed by his body. He bent over suddenly and threw up water onto the sand. "Sorry," he apologized politely, brushing his hand over his mouth.

"*You* said you couldn't swim," Henry fumed. "Why the fuck did you jump in?"

"My fire-starter kit," Dingo said, holding up the battered box. "I've got my compass in there. We'd be lost without it."

"We'd be dead if that water was a little higher," Henry snapped.

"If we get lost in here, we'll be dead as well," Dingo said grimly. Then he collected himself and gave a rakish wink. "Besides, you couldn't bear to let me drown."

Henry wanted to smack that ever-so-charming smile off Dingo's face. "How do we get back to our stuff? We've got your fucking important box, but no food."

"See, that's why I was saying we should cross the river before nightfall," Dingo said.

"Don't blame me for this! You didn't say *that*; you said I needed to eat my vegetables or some such."

"You're cute when you're angry, you know that?"

That goddamn smile once more. Refusing to allow himself to be seduced by it yet again, Henry took a look at the roiling water. "I don't fancy another swim in that. I'm not sure I could make it across."

"Tired out already?"

Dingo's eyes were bright with mirth, and Henry had to clench his fists by his sides to control his temper. Maybe the only way to get rid of that insouciant expression was to kiss it off, a thought that had the power to cheer him insensibly. "Oh, I could make it by myself, but I don't think I could haul your worthless carcass across again."

"No worries," Dingo said. "Follow me."

"To the nearest ferry? Or are you going to build a bridge?" Henry got to his feet wearily, reflecting that while in the water, boots might have been a hindrance, but on land there was an argument to be made for them. And without his glasses, he was practically blind, reduced to following along behind Dingo like a puppy.

AFTER crashing through the brush for over an hour and sitting down to extract a thorn from his foot, Henry was hot, sweaty, and disgruntled. But he wasn't stupid, and he knew just what Dingo had in mind. They didn't dare wander away from the river to find an easier path; if they were going to retrieve their possessions, they had to get back across.

"We could just sleep on this side tonight and cross in the morning," he muttered.

"Because the gods have promised the water will recede by morning and we can just wade across?"

"Always have to have the last word," Henry grumbled.

"You're kind of the same yourself, Dash," Dingo said.

"That's not my name." He wasn't sure why he was dragging up that old argument again, but he felt like he wanted to take something away from Dingo, as the man always seemed to have some unnatural power over him.

It might have worked at that. For a moment, Dingo looked away. His face was expressionless, but it reset to normal when he looked back.

Henry swallowed, hating that he might have hurt him, but looked longingly at their packs on the opposite shore. "The water's still running too fast to swim across hauling dead weight."

"That's why we're not going to try," Dingo announced. "Keep going."

"My feet hurt."

"You said that earlier."

"I just had blisters then. I wish I had my boots. Then it wouldn't matter that I can't see where I'm stepping."

"Want me to carry you, Dash?"

"No!" But he wondered what Dingo would do if he had answered yes.

He probably would have, just to prove a point.

"Right then, keep moving."

Feeling contrary, Henry wanted to remind Dingo again that his name wasn't Dash, but it just didn't seem worth the effort, particularly as Dingo and everybody else in this blasted country went right on calling him Dash anyway.

He plodded on behind Dingo, grateful that the other man seemed alert, because if the famed Tasmanian Tiger emerged from the brush right then, intent upon making him its next meal, Henry thought he might just have laid right down and sacrificed himself. After he got over the excitement of seeing one alive, that is.

"Right, here we are," Dingo said.

"Where?" Henry lifted his head, just in time, for Dingo pushed him into the river and jumped in himself.

"Swim for the other side," Dingo managed before his head slipped under the water.

Henry reached for him, grabbing his hair. Dingo had been clever in choosing where to enter the river again. The current shot them around a curve and directly to the bank on the other side. When he was ten yards from shore, Henry knew he'd be able to make it, even while dragging Dingo along with him.

To his surprise, Dingo shook himself free and swam easily to shore on his own. He hauled himself out and turned to give Henry a hand.

"You lied!"

"About what?"

"You said you couldn't swim!"

"Well, I couldn't when I first went in, but after watching you, it didn't seem like such a difficult task." Dingo grinned. "I'm a quick study."

"I'll bet," Henry muttered, but this time he didn't want to hit Dingo for his insufferable ways. He wanted just to rest against him, hearing his heartbeat beneath his ear. But all he said was, "I'm starving."

"I'll cook." Dingo struck his battered tin box. "Got my matches."

"They're probably wet," Henry said, glad to be contrary about *something*.

"No worries, I've got my Aussie-bow just in case," Dingo said, in no way discomposed. He went into the brush and came back with a few dry branches and some leaves. "Help me drag that deadfall over here."

"We don't have any way to chop it up," Henry countered.

"What a bloody sad-sack you're being! We don't have to, we'll just feed one end into the fire," Dingo said. "By the way, present for you!"

He pressed something into Henry's hand, who breathed with relief at the familiar form of his glasses. He put them on, relieved to be able to see his surroundings once again.

"Now you can see my pretty mug again," Dingo winked at him.

"See it to give it a black eye," Henry muttered.

"What, and wreck this handsome face? Oh, Dash, you wouldn't want to do that."

Silently, Henry stamped on his boots and went to help the man who was still laughing at his own humor.

Dingo's matches did prove to be dry, thanks to the rubber gasket fitted to his precious box, and he coaxed the twigs to catch fire. Branches were added, and once they were crackling and snapping, Dingo artfully laid the end of the young deadfall onto the fire.

Then he stood up and started stripping off unconcernedly. Henry reflexively looked away out of long-standing habit but couldn't help sneaking a glance. Dingo in motion seemed to be made of pure muscle, moving with a masculine grace as he hung his wet clothes on bushes to dry. Henry once again took notice that his skin was a beautiful bronze all over with no tan lines, except for faint ones by his feet. He wondered if Dingo ran around naked often. Probably had since birth, a real bush baby. He ducked his head to hide his grin, amused at the thought of Dingo as a little feral child of nature, raised by tigers and devils.

"You better get them wet duds off, Dash."

"I'm perfectly fine, thank you."

"You'll mildew if you stay wet, and you're something of a damp squib already. Besides I want a look at that foot of yours."

Henry hadn't even thought that Dingo had noticed when he picked up the thorn. He undressed, following Dingo's lead in using the bushes as an impromptu dry line, and went to dig in his pack for his other pair of trousers.

"Don't bother putting on your tux for me, old boy," Dingo said in perfect, haughty society tones.

Henry had to laugh; Dingo sounded so like his pompous uncle Ferdy. "We're dining informally tonight?"

"From the tin, as it were." Dingo held up a tin of beans. "But first, your foot. You can't hike if it gets infected, and I'll leave you behind if you can't walk."

"Sure you will." Feeling a bit self-conscious but oddly free without his clothing, Henry sat on a convenient rock, sighing as he took his weight off his foot.

Dingo squatted on his haunches and lifted the injured foot with gentle hands. Henry wanted to cross his legs, but Dingo had one of them in his firm grip.

"There's a tip of the thorn still in there," he said. "I'm going to have to cut it out."

"Go on," Henry said.

"Right."

From his tin box, Dingo extracted a knife, smaller than the one he carried on his belt. "This is going to hurt a bit."

"Good thing we're lost in the bush, so no one will hear my screams."

"I'll never tell." Dingo grinned. "Shriek all you like."

"Too right you'll never tell, I'll just murder you and throw your body into the river," Henry countered.

He grabbed onto Dingo's shoulder when the other man turned his back, lifting Henry's foot and throwing him off balance. Dingo tucked Henry's leg between his arm and his body to hold him still. "Right then."

"Go on." Henry liked the flex of muscle under his hand. He tried to avert his gaze, but the swell of curved buttocks was right in his view, and it was a tempting sight. He didn't even gasp as the blade probed his foot, he was too busy suppressing his desire to reach out and grab—

Finally Henry could no longer resist. He leaned forward and bit into the round cheek being so temptingly displayed to him.

"Oi!" Dingo yipped, sounding like his father when demonstrating the tiger's call. "What was that for?"

"Because your backside is so beautiful," Henry said. He rubbed a hand over the firm behind. "And so conveniently close."

"So I'm standing here all innocent, trying to dig this thorn out of your foot, and you take a bite out of me?" Dingo sounded more amused than anything.

"I couldn't resist the forbidden apple." Henry snickered at his own sly allusion.

"So you regard my bum as the fruit of knowledge in the Garden of Eden?"

"Absolutely. At least for me…."

Dingo succeeded in extracting the thorn at last. "Don't put your foot down just yet until I get something on it." He went to his rucksack and dug around, giving Henry an excellent chance to ogle the portion of his anatomy in question. When he came back, his face was serious. "You know what happened when Adam and Eve ate of the fruit, don't you?"

"They were kicked out."

"It wasn't the sin, it was the knowledge of the sin," Dingo said. "Perhaps I've ruined it for you. Now that you know, you'll never be the same, out there."

"I'd rather know," Henry said softly.

"Spoken like an academic. Sometimes knowledge carries a heavy burden."

Henry had the feeling they weren't just talking about being queer, that somehow this connected to the tiger. "You think it's better to live in ignorant bliss?"

Dingo gave him a twisted smile. "I guess it depends whether ignorance makes you happy."

"It doesn't. Are you going to put that stuff on or stand there holding it?"

Dingo held the bottle out to him. "You put it on. I'll get a bandage. Rub it on the blisters as well."

Henry felt the sting of the liquid as he poured it onto the gash, and a rich earthy scent made him a little dizzy.

"I'll bind it up so you don't get sand in it. Keep it off the ground," Dingo instructed.

Henry did as he was told, feeling very exposed with his bits hanging out. His cock felt heavy, and he wanted to cover himself, uneasily remembering his wanton behavior of the night before.

He looked at Dingo's face, surprised when the other man stood before him. He was half hard as well.

Dingo merely grinned and kneeled to bind a strip of fabric around Henry's foot. "There. Put on some socks and your boots and don't step onto any more thorn bushes tonight."

"I wouldn't have stepped on one at all if you hadn't fallen into the river in the first place!"

"I didn't fall. I jumped!"

"Fell! I had to rescue you."

"Did you now?" Dingo gave him an odd look. "Well, let's eat."

After a quick meal of beans heated in the tin, Henry limped down to the water's edge, using the tin to scoop water for a quick bath of sorts. As he sluiced the sweat off his skin, he turned to find Dingo watching him, his eyes bright.

"Want a bath?" Henry dropped the tin in his confusion and bent to rescue it from the stream before it could be swept away.

"Careful with that," Dingo warned. He came forward to take it from Henry, his fingers warm as his hand closed over Henry's. "It's the only one we've got."

"One tin?" Henry demanded. "What do you mean, *one* tin?"

"Yeah," Dingo scratched his head ashamedly. "I hate to tell you this, Dash, but one of our bags must have got washed away."

Henry deflated visibly. "Let me guess. It had most of the provisions in it?"

"You got it in one," Dingo said, sounding more chipper than he actually was.

"Fantastic." Henry grimaced. "And what exactly are we supposed to eat for the rest of the expedition?"

"Hey, look on the bright side," Dingo said. "I don't fancy carrying a smelting mill's worth of metal with me. This tin will come in handy for things like washing and getting water. We have dried fruit and vegetables in your pack to eat. And I have a little bit of flour and some staples. Besides, we can forage off the land. Plenty of good eating if you don't mind snake."

"Snake?" Henry wrinkled his nose at the thought of it. "Things just keep getting better."

Dingo took pity on him. “River’s full of lobster and fish. There’s honey, roots, tubers, berries. There’s a bread plant and onions. We won’t go hungry. Anyway, you signed up for adventure, remember?”

“I didn’t sign up for starvation.”

Dingo laughed and quickly rinsed off. Henry eyed his gleaming skin, watching the rivulets of water bead and slide down Dingo’s trim flanks and rounded arse. He only realized that Dingo was finished with his bath when his eyes traveled up to see Dingo staring at him hungrily.

“My turn tonight, remember?” Dingo held out his hand, and Henry took it, his heart threatening to pound its way out of his chest.

Together, they spread a ground sheet and tied off the tarp to make a rude tent. The sound of the water rushing nearby made a soothing backdrop as they crawled under the shelter.

Henry leaned over Dingo to kiss him, and all his antagonisms of the day melted away with the beads of sweat starting to form along his forehead. There was no mistaking that the hunger in Dingo’s eyes was real and all for him. He stroked over Dingo’s chest covered with golden hairs that gleamed in the half-light of dusk, over his stomach and down to trail his fingers in the furrow that defined the divide between torso and thigh. Dingo moaned and spread his legs as Henry took him in hand, wrapping his arms around Henry and pulling him closer.

As they moved together, Henry lost himself in the shining reflections of Dingo’s eyes as he was buried within him, the blue of the Australian skies overlaid with the green of the verdant jungle, and when they cried out at the peak of their pleasure, the triumphant sound seemed to be part of the primal wilderness in which they lay.

18. CREATURES OF THE NIGHT

HENRY looked at the messy thatch of sandy hair resting on his shoulder, waiting for Dingo to wake. For once, he had awakened first, a fact he meant to thoroughly impress upon Dingo as insurance against being called a slug-a-bed in future.

Dingo stretched and made a contented sound, tightening his arms around Henry without opening his eyes. "Good morning."

"Dingo."

"Yeah?"

"Where are all the animals?"

"They're all around us, Dash."

"We've been trekking two days, and I've heard birds in the distance and rustling in the bushes, but I haven't seen a single animal."

Dingo chuckled. "That's because most of the denizens of Tasmania are nocturnal."

"Then why aren't we watching for them at night instead of keeping to daylight hours?"

Dingo sat up and gave Henry a quick kiss. "Because we're not there yet. And if you want to get caught up in the jungle, tripping and staggering over things you can't see at night, well, I don't."

"Where?"

"Where we're going."

"Where *are* we going?" Henry didn't quite like to mention it, but he was completely dependent upon Dingo for their whereabouts. Nothing *would* happen to either one of them, but if by chance something did, he wasn't sure he would be able to make it out of the jungle by himself. Even with the upside down, backward, down-under compass that Dingo had gone to such lengths to save.

"Further into the woods. It's not like saying meet me at the Parliament House, is it? Besides, I didn't think you'd be too keen on that tiger snake we walked past yesterday so I didn't bother to point him out."

"I didn't see any snake," Henry said suspiciously.

"Just as well. I don't think he saw us either. They're poisonous, you know. Wait, don't get dressed yet," Dingo said.

Henry paused by the bush that held his clothing. They were still a bit damp anyway. And he didn't even want to contemplate hiking in his wet boots. If he thought his blisters from yesterday were painful, it could only be worse today. "Why can't I get dressed?" he demanded crossly. He felt foolish and suspected Dingo of ogling his bum. Not that he objected, if that proved to be the case.

Dingo had dug the bottle of clearish liquid out of his pack and was now searching for something amongst the grasses by the stream. "River's gone down. We can wade across today." He stood up holding what looked like a hollow reed.

"Pity we didn't get here later then, before you jumped in," Henry grumped.

"Close your eyes and cover your ears," Dingo instructed.

"Why—"

Hurriedly Henry obeyed when Dingo sucked some of the liquid through the straw and sprayed it at him. He stood motionless while Dingo circled him, feeling the misting spray on his skin. His nose wrinkled as the camphorated scent drifted up to him. Clenching his teeth and barely moving his lips, he asked, "What *is* that?"

"Tea tree oil, made from native plants," Dingo said. "Another reason we haven't seen any wildlife is our scent. Did you know that a devil can smell a carcass from up to a mile away? The tiger has an even more sensitive nose."

"Well, I hardly think I smell like a carcass," Henry muttered.

"Here, be a sport and make me smell pretty," Dingo said, thrusting the bottle and straw into Henry's hands. He shuffled in a slow circle to make it easier, and Henry enjoyed the view without hindrance, as Dingo had squeezed his eyes shut. "Now you can get dressed."

Henry squeaked as Dingo took the opportunity to pinch one of his nether cheeks. "Lecher."

"Too right," Dingo agreed, unperturbed. "Let's go."

They were soon dressed, with their few possessions once more packed securely into their rucksacks. As Henry had anticipated, his boots squished with every step he took. The leaves of the trees standing next to what today was a sleepy stream glittered white in the sunlight, nearly blinding him and making him feel dazed. He was about to plunge into the streambed to cross it when Dingo grabbed his arm.

"Natural bridge," he said, nodding at a dead log that yesterday's torrent had deposited across the water.

"Where are we anyway?"

Dingo turned to face Henry, a teasing glint in his eyes. "You are about to cross the River Styx."

"Very funny."

"Really, that's the name of the river."

Henry gaped at him and then laughed uncertainly. "You almost drowned in it yesterday."

"But I didn't. And now that we've had a dip in it, we'll be invulnerable to danger. Like Achilles, except better because we went all the way in."

Henry suspected Dingo of trying to bolster his confidence but played along. "So, you're playing Charon for me?"

"After you," Dingo said, sweeping a low bow and waving his hand at the log.

"Thanks."

Henry led the way across, grateful that he didn't have to walk through the water with it filling his boots. Today the placid stream was clear, and he could see pebbles at the bottom through the amber-tinted water. The welcome shade of the forest closed around them once again, and he revived a bit, now that shimmering reflections of the water were behind them. His ruminations about the mythology of the Styx and how it might relate to the ultimate fate of the thylacines were cut short when he caught sight of some movement in the bushes.

"Dingo," he whispered. "I think the oil is working. Look over there."

Dingo looked where Henry was pointing. "Excellent spotting, Dash. It's a native hen. Not that tasty, but the devils like it. Dead or alive."

The hen scuttled off through the underbrush, and Henry watched it vanish, leaving only a swaying branch behind to mark its passage. "Where are the signs of all this nightly carnage? And how come we've never heard any of this going on?"

"Speak for yourself, mate. Didn't you hear the screaming last night?"

Henry shivered, remembering the descriptions that he had read in the books. Sounds so bloodcurdling that the first European settlers cowered in their beds at night, sure that the denizens of hell were making themselves known. Maybe it wasn't that bad not to have heard it. "Afraid not."

"You must have slept well." Dingo gave him a lecherous smile.

"I was the one doing all the work, if I recall," Henry replied tartly, although it wasn't as if what he had been doing to Dingo was a chore.

"Your turn. I'm surprised you didn't hear it, though. The devils were fighting over something, yowling and cursing like the little demons they are," Dingo said with relish, as if he admired them more than anything. "They don't leave much behind. Crunch right through the bones with their heavy jaws. Usually you only find bits of bone and teeth the next day."

"Charming."

"Useful. They're the housekeepers and undertakers of Tasmania."

Henry decided that Dingo was altogether too cheerful about this. "Would they eat a man?"

"They're actually rather timid around humans. We rather tower over them. But if you were to be incapacitated or they found you injured and unable to get away, they'd take care of you all right, and leave little evidence behind."

Henry shivered. "What about the tiger?"

"They're even more skittish about being near us. But there haven't been authenticated reports of one attacking a human being." Dingo's mouth was set in a grim line. "I'm not entirely certain that they really have eaten any sheep either. There are plenty of predators to share the blame. Quolls, devils, feral dogs, even feral cats."

Henry wouldn't have been surprised to hear that the government had heaped their transgressions upon the tiger as well in its quest to stamp them out. He blinked in surprise when he stepped out into what looked like a snug pasture transplanted from England in the midst of the trees. "Does somebody live here?"

"It's a kangaroo plantation; they keep the grass cropped like this," Dingo said. He held out his arm, stopping Henry from stepping into the grassy pasture. "We'll skirt around it. If we trample the grass, it'd be like leaving a signboard for Hodges. 'Dash and Dingo went this way!'"

"What if he has as good a tracker as Jarrah?" Henry asked.

Dingo didn't even hesitate in his answer. "There's nobody as good as Jarrah."

Henry found Dingo's loyalty to his friend admirable, but there was a little niggling voice in his mind whispering that Dingo still seemed to underestimate Hodges and what he was capable of. Henry hoped that Dingo was right; after all, he did know Hodges and had for a long time. But Henry brought a fresh perspective to their history, and his brief encounters with Dingo's nemesis would not allow him to subscribe to the lackadaisical analysis of the man that Dingo was trying to sell.

"THIS looks like a fine spot."

Henry came out of his fugue state with a longing expression on his face. "We're here?"

"We're here."

The climb up the mountain had been arduous; Henry had overcome his pride and asked for frequent rest breaks along the way. Dingo had been attentive but firm. They had to get to what would become their base by early afternoon.

"You rest," Dingo said. "I'll pitch the tent."

Henry shook his head. "I'll do my share."

"How are the feet?"

Henry tested them with a quizzical expression. "Better actually." What he didn't mention was that the rest of him more than made up for that.

Dingo gave him a nod of approval. Henry was glad that he was at least proving some kind of mettle on this expedition. Perhaps Hodges had been right and Dingo hadn't been expecting as much from him, given the look on his face. And maybe now certain affections had been revealed, Dingo might have been tempted to make things easier for his new lover, make allowances he wouldn't have done for anybody else. Henry didn't want to be given such liberties. He wanted to be worthy of Dingo's merit; even though there were many things Dingo was better at than he, Henry knew there were other things he could bring to their partnership as adventurers.

But he was relieved when the tent was up, and Dingo crawled within to lie down.

"Are we resting already?" Henry teased from where he was sitting outside.

"Get in here, Dash," Dingo said. "I want to feel your bones."

Henry didn't need any further persuasion. He thankfully crawled in beside Dingo, who immediately took him in his arms.

"Now the hard work begins," Dingo murmured.

Henry blanched. Their days of trekking hadn't been the hard work? He shuddered to think what could come next. "What next?"

"Sleep," Dingo said. "Tonight we start our watch for the tigers."

"We're in tiger country," Henry said, enthused.

"In the thick of it. Where they have been driven out and where only a handful of people know. To everybody else they're as good as dead."

Henry couldn't think of anything worse than a belief in total extinction, except there could be one thing even more horrifying—the numb acceptance of, or lack of caring about, the eradication of a species. "I can't believe I'm here."

"Believe it," Dingo said kindly. "You belong here, Dash."

Emboldened by both their physical closeness and the new emotional bond that was deepening between them, Henry said, "And I can't believe I'm here with you."

"Really?"

Henry struggled to convey the depth of what he was feeling. "It's as if two dreams have collided. And I don't know…."

"Don't know what?"

But this was the one thing Henry couldn't say. Going back to England would be like waking from this dream. He didn't know what would happen once this quest was over nor what lay in the future for him and Dingo. If he didn't speak of it, then maybe he would never have to think about the logistics of it and how everything seemed stacked against their favor.

Finally, he said, "Just, it's too good to be true."

Dingo nuzzled against his cheek, his breath warm against his skin. "Doesn't mean it can't stay like that."

It was a nice thought, but Henry knew both of them were realists. The wilds of Tasmania were a different world altogether; they could hardly live in total abandon the way they had the past few days among the cobblestones of Melbourne or London.

Time to change the subject, although Henry thought Dingo was doing the same thing in the way he was sliding his hand below Henry's shirt and lazily tracing the circle of his nipple.

Henry thought that it would have been impossible for him to be ready to sleep so early in the day, but the strenuous climb and now lying supine against the delicious warmth of Dingo, he could feel himself slowly drifting away.

"Dingo," he said sleepily.

"Yeah?"

"Tell me about the first time you saw Tassie."

Dingo chuckled to himself. "You want a bedtime story, Dash?"

"Yes, a story about young Dingo in the wild."

"You wouldn't have liked me back then. I was a cocky bastard."

Henry smiled. "Well, I like you now, and believe me, it sounds like nothing has changed."

"Too right," Dingo admitted.

Henry closed his eyes. "I'm listening. Talk to me."

Dingo rested his head against Henry's shoulder and let his hand remain under his shirt so he could maintain the touch of Henry's skin and the steady thump of his heartbeat on the right side of his palm. "I was just a snip of a kid, having just turned ten. I'd had to watch my dad take my brothers along for years, but Mum wouldn't let me go. She said I was too young."

"You're her baby," Henry murmured. "It's nice."

"Not when you're ten and you think you're a man already. But she finally relented. My dad packed us all up, and we went in search of Tassie. It was far away from here; back then the tiger hadn't been driven so far inland. We camped out, and I remember one night I slept through, and my brothers claimed they had seen a family of tigers while I snored my fool head off. I was so mad that I hit Johnno right in the kisser and was about to start in on Baz when my dad stepped in. They wouldn't speak to me for the rest of the day, Johnno especially, because I was so much younger than him and managed to best him. It was luck, really."

Henry laughed, and Dingo snuggled closer.

"Anyway, that night I was determined not to sleep in case the tigers were seen again. My brothers and I weren't talking, and my dad was mad at all of us for not talking, so he wasn't talking to any of us either. Dad let me have my first taste of beer—"

"At ten?" Henry asked, horrified.

"Relax, Dash, he watered it down. Just enough to taste it. But I tell you, it made me piss like a horse all night."

Henry chuckled again, imagining Dingo telling this story at his parents' dinner table. *His* parents would probably both faint into their soup, but he was sure that Helen and Hank were made of stronger stuff. Probably Dingo actually *had* told the story at some point, and more than once!

"On about my fifth trip into the bush, we had set aside for our dunny, that was when it happened. I was in the middle of going when in a small patch of moonlight just ahead of me, Tassie stepped into it as if she were about to go on stage and that was her spotlight."

Henry's eyes fluttered open, although sleep wanted to will them shut again. "What did you do?"

"Pissed all over myself, for starters, I was that excited. Oh, Dash, she was the most beautiful thing I had ever seen. Present company excluded, of course."

Henry shook his head but was pleased by the compliment, even though he didn't think anything could rival the strange and alien beauty of the thylacine.

"Her coat was this rich caramel color, and the stripes were vibrant against it. She looked straight at me, the moon reflecting off her black eyes, and she allowed me to see the width of her jaw as she opened it in a yawn. Like she was putting on a show. Then, just as quick as she appeared, she was gone."

"What happened then?" Henry asked breathlessly.

"I started screaming like a loon. My brothers and my dad rushed over to find me, my dick still hanging out for all to see, while I was pointing at an empty bit of bush."

"Did they believe you?"

"Johnno and Baz didn't want to, just to keep me going, but Dad made them stop. They could all tell by the look in my eyes that I hadn't imagined it. That I was now under its spell."

Henry knew the spell, that singular passion that the thylacine had aroused in him as well.

As if reading his mind, Dingo said, "You've got the look as well. That's why I wanted you to come. Besides the fact that I was hoping you'd let me have my way with you."

"Dingo," Henry groaned, but then he paused and asked in all seriousness, "How can I have the look? I haven't seen Tassie."

"Not in its natural element," Dingo agreed. "Or alive. But you've seen its legacy and its mystery. That's why you're hooked, just like the rest of us. It's why you had to come."

Henry closed his eyes again, happy. "That was a good story, Dingo."

And with that, his lips parted and a small snore issued forth between them.

Dingo pressed his lips against his lover's forehead. "Sweet dreams, Dash."

19. A CRY IN THE DARK!

HENRY awoke suddenly. All the hairs on his body were standing on end, and he didn't know why. He wasn't cold; the heat pouring off Dingo's body combined with the blanket should have had him sweating. He knew he hadn't been having a nightmare; the last remnants of his dream that he could remember were basically a replay of their session in the forest the night before. It was why his cock was now uncomfortably hard, but sex was the last thing on his mind.

"Dingo," he said urgently, shaking the man next to him.

Dingo smacked his lips but didn't open his eyes. "Let a man sleep, Dash."

"Dingo, wake up!"

This time, the tone of his voice seemed to permeate into Dingo's brain. He sat up straight away. "What is it?" He peered outside the flap of the tent. "Christ, Dash, how long have we been sleeping? We should have been up ages ago!"

Interested in spite of the strange feeling that remained with him, Henry asked, "How can you tell what time it is? By how many stars are out?"

"Magic," Dingo said. Then he held up his wrist. "It's called a watch, love."

Both of them froze at the word that had escaped unknowingly and unfiltered from him. Even in the blu-ish hue of the moonlight, Henry could see Dingo's face darken. Was that a blush? He had never seen Dingo blush; he wouldn't have even thought his skin capable of such a reaction.

"Of course," Henry said. "Silly me." But he leaned forward and pulled Dingo against him, crushing their lips together. Dingo responded fiercely, so fast and so strong that they toppled over, Henry on his back and Dingo against his chest. Henry shifted himself so that his still-hard cock thrust against Dingo's. Dingo's breath was hot in his mouth and his tongue insistent on playing with his own. Scarcely able to breathe, Henry pulled at the back of Dingo's trousers, just wanting him off for a moment so he could recapture his breath. But as his palm touched the band of Dingo's trousers and the exposed skin from where Dingo's shirt had pulled away, it began to itch and then burn.

The same palm Jarrah had drawn the picture of the thylacine upon.

Dingo was fumbling at their trousers, his cock now poking between the fly. He was working upon Henry's, unaware that the other man had stopped moving beneath him.

Henry stared at his palm, as if the drawing had come back. The skin appeared smooth and unblemished.

But then a strange noise penetrated the night.

Yip. Yip yip. Yip.

And now Dingo froze. "Just like I'm ten again, and my dick out once more."

"Shhh," Henry admonished him. "And get off me."

Dingo chuckled and did as he was told, pushing himself back within his trousers.

Henry pulled open the flap and scrambled out a short distance on his stomach. "Is that it, Dingo? Is it really the tiger?"

Dingo scuttled beside him. "We found them quicker than I thought. Jarrah was right, Dash. They want to see you."

Henry stared at the scrub before them. Would it be like the first time Dingo saw one? Would it just step out and parade before them? He could barely remember to breathe; he was anticipating the appearance of a tiger any second.

Yip yip.

"That was to our left," Henry whispered.

Yip yip yip.

"An answering call," Dingo said. "To our right. It isn't alone."

"*Two* of them?" Henry said, enraptured. It was too good to be true.

They could hear the rustling in the scrub, and they froze, their mouths open, their bodies taut.

Please, Henry thought. *Please, please, please, show yourself. Let me see you.*

But the rustling seemed to fade, and they heard the call again—*yip yip*—except now it was further away.

"They're going!" Henry cried, forgetting he was meant to be quiet. He started to shuffle clumsily to his feet, as if to give chase, but Dingo yanked him back down. "Dingo!"

"They know we're here," he spoke into Henry's ear. "And they chose to come this close. If we go floundering after them now, they'll be scared off. Patience, Dash. It's the way we have to do it."

"I want to see them," Henry said, aware that he sounded childish. His needy tone, its desperate whining, annoyed him, but he couldn't take it back.

Dingo's lips grazed along his cheek. "I know. And you will."

Henry allowed himself to be pulled back the short distance into the tent. This time he used Dingo as a pillow, his hand resting against Dingo's chest as they both lay awake, unable to go back to sleep just yet.

His palm no longer burned. Henry wished it would start again.

HENRY'S nose wrinkled as some delicious scent wafted in through the tent on a slight breeze. He stretched out and lazily opened his eyes.

"You didn't wake me," he called out.

"Thought you needed some sleep," Dingo replied.

He was sitting by a small fire he had built, watching the flames and what lay within them. Henry crawled out of the tent to join him and observed that it was the tin that had a million uses, one of the few items Dingo had permitted them to carry. Something was baking in it, and Henry's stomach rumbled. It smelled like fresh bread.

"What is that?" he asked, practically salivating.

"I thought we deserved a bit of damper." Dingo shrugged.

"Damper?"

"Bush bread, mate. You'll love it."

Henry didn't doubt it; it would be the first warm thing they had eaten in what seemed like forever. "How long has it been baking for?"

"About an hour."

"You've been up that long?"

"I've been up longer than *that*."

"You should have woken me."

"You looked too bloody cute to wake. I was lying there for ages watching you, but I figured somebody better get the grub on."

Henry stretched his hands out toward the fire, enjoying the warmth. Dingo had now turned his attention to two flat stones and was reaching within his jacket pocket. Henry's mouth watered again when berries were produced.

"Have you been out picking as well?"

Dingo nodded. "You can almost pretend you're back home at Ealing, having tea with scones and jam. And I'll be Hill. Pip pip and ole tosh, good Master Henry."

Henry snorted. "Hill would *never* be that obsequious. He felt unlucky to be stuck with me and the other drones in the basement. He would have preferred to have a Dean to wait upon."

Dingo laughed to himself as he placed a number of the berries on one stone and began mashing them with the other. "I bet you he's missing you right now, the way you used to babble at him."

"I did not *babble*," Henry said defensively, and then he paused. "Okay, maybe a little. But Hill would be used to it. Academics are meant to be eccentric."

Dingo smirked and pulled his knife out of his boot. Using a stick, he fished the tin out of the flames. He ran the knife around the rim of the tin and lifted the damper out. "Eat it while it's hot," he instructed Henry as he sliced it into thick pieces.

Henry longed for some butter but took the "jam" instead—and found that he didn't miss the butter at all. After a lackluster diet during the past few days, the wholesome and filling taste of the bread along with the natural sweetness of the berries made him a happy man indeed. Dingo washed out the tin and prepared tea for Dash and coffee for himself while he ate, and soon the breakfast was complete.

"We've got a bit of a hike ahead of us today," Dingo said, brushing crumbs off his upper lip. "So I thought we should have something a bit more substantial for brekkie."

"We're moving again?" Henry asked. "But the tigers are right in this area—"

Dingo shook his head. “They were moving off. You heard their calls to each other fading away, right?”

“It doesn’t mean they went *that* far away.”

“I told you; I’ve been up for hours. I studied their tracks. They’re on their way up the mountain.”

Henry bolted down the rest of his tea and stood. “Then up the mountain we go!”

HIS enthusiasm quickly flagged.

“Temperate, my arse,” Henry muttered, swiping at his sticky face with the back of his hand. Then he scratched at his palm absently.

“Told you the weather was changeable, Dash,” Dingo called back cheerily. “And this *is* a rain forest.”

Henry had hoped that Dingo hadn’t overheard, but he seemed to have ears like a bat. Not that they were perky and sat atop his head, just that he always caught whatever testy comment Henry would have preferred overlooked. In fact, Dingo had very nice ears; they sat flat against his head, and the lobes were tempting to nibble on….

A flicker of movement in his peripheral vision recalled him to the present, and Henry turned to look. Nothing was moving, save some grasses swaying slightly in a breeze that was insufficient to cool him off. In fact, he didn’t even feel it. He was hot, sweaty, and miserable, whilst Dingo gave the impression that if not for Henry, he would be loping up the side of this bleeding mountain.

“Bit of a break-off here,” Dingo called back over his shoulder. “Be careful.”

Henry opened his mouth to fire back that he could see it, thank you very much, when he stumbled over a rock in his path. He looked up sheepishly, hoping Dingo hadn’t seen him. Thankfully, he was plowing on without any apparent knowledge of Henry’s clumsiness.

“Lucky you have some redeeming features,” Henry grumbled, fixing his eyes upon the round firmness of Dingo’s arse as a lure to motivate him to keep moving.

Dingo was too far ahead of him and turned away, so Henry couldn't hear what his answer was. The flicker of movement caught his attention again, and he stopped, standing very still and not turning his head, just waiting to see if he could catch a glimpse of whatever it was in his peripheral vision. His palm started to throb when he saw what looked like stripes melting into the shadows.

He laughed tentatively; it couldn't have been. He turned to study the underbrush, noting how the tall grasses cast dark stripes over the leaves behind them. The tiger was nocturnal; everyone knew that. He was just seeing things because he wanted to so badly.

Dingo was out of sight when Henry turned to locate him. He started to trot to catch up, still uneasily aware of how disoriented he was to their location. The trails were so obscure that he might have to navigate by the position of the sun if he had to make it out of here alone. He looked back to see if he could pick out some recognizable landmark by which to steer.

Henry's thoughts on their time in the forest were mixed. He and Dingo were living a blessed existence together, and as much as Henry felt he should be enjoying every moment of it—because he had never believed that he would find this sort of passion and easygoing happiness with another man—the fact was they had come here for a reason. The tigers. And with each new day, it seemed that this other dream was slipping through his fingers.

Was it so selfish to want more than one dream? He wanted Dingo more than anything. And he seemed to have him, just as Dingo had him body and soul in return. But he was aching to see the tiger as well. He took those moments with Dingo with pleasure and tried to alleviate the guilt he felt about wanting it all.

Dingo had commented that Tassie was leading them on a merry chase.

"Like a woman," he said. "Wants to make you work for it before they give you a bit of the attention you want."

Henry had stiffened when he said that. What *was* Dingo's experience with women? He seemed to flirt with both sexes freely, although Henry had never heard him talk about past girlfriends, but he had seen the different men Dingo seemed to leave behind in every port.

But that wasn't fair either. He had no evidence to one way or the other.

So maybe he *wasn't* in the best of moods at the moment.

Distraction cost him again.

He felt, rather than saw, the slippery gravel under his feet. He had wandered too close to the edge Dingo had warned him about earlier. The sun blinded him when he turned around to face a gap in the bushes around the bend.

Henry lost his footing in the loose rubble and began to slide down the hill. He scrambled to catch himself, but the more his feet slid, the more the pebbles dislodged underfoot, showering into the creek bed below. With the weight of the rucksack on his shoulders and nothing to grab onto, Henry flung himself desperately at the edge of the cliff. The dirt crumbled under his hands, and he realized that a swift, ignominious descent was inevitable.

How come Dingo never has this happen to him? was his first thought as he slid the first ten feet on his tummy. He could feel pebbles working their way under his clothing and scraping the skin beneath.

As his center of gravity shifted and he found himself skidding downhill head first for a change, Henry thought, *He'd better not laugh if he knows what's good for him.*

He landed half-submerged in the shallow creek, gasping with the shock of the cold bath. Pulling his head out of the water and gasping for breath, Henry was only grateful that it was all over and Dingo was far enough ahead that he hadn't seen the entire thing. And for the fact that his glasses had remained intact and perched on his nose.

Groaning softly, he lifted his head and froze.

It can't be.

Blinking owlishly through the water on his glasses that rendered everything into indistinct masses, Henry felt that he wasn't alone.

And then his palm began to burn!

20. FIRST CONTACT

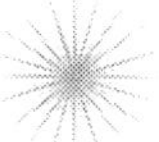

HENRY shivered, and it wasn't just because of the temperature of the water. An orange blob moved ahead of him.

Carefully, oh so carefully, Henry removed his glasses and wiped them on the leg of his trousers, which luckily hadn't joined him in the dip in the creek. Now the world was a complete blur, but it shifted into focus again when he pushed his glasses back on his nose, his palm itching all the while.

On a rock overhanging the creek, directly in front of him, approximately fifteen yards away, stood a Tasmanian Tiger.

The sun filtered through the leaves, lighting the caramel-colored fur but providing enough shade to perfectly camouflage the striped animal.

It shouldn't be there, not at this time, but there it was. And it wasn't spooked by him. It was almost as if it had been waiting there for Henry to make his inelegant descent down the slope into this small valley so that they could greet each other properly. The animal Henry had been dreaming about for so long, one he secretly had feared he would never get a glimpse of, alive and free, standing within its own territory and....

Laughing at him through gently grinning jaws!

And its huge grin was disturbingly reminiscent of Dingo's!

His heart started to pound with excitement, and Henry pushed himself up slowly, sliding his glance away from the animal, remembering that dogs took a direct stare as a challenge. And yes, the thylacine wasn't a dog, but most predatory animals shared that same trait. Above all else, he didn't want to do anything that might cause the tiger to disappear into the underbrush.

"You're a fair champion swimmer, if you can do a stroke in that bit of a bathtub," Dingo mocked gently from above.

Henry raised one hand, not even looking behind him, making a dismissive waving motion. If Dingo scared it away....

Dingo's laughter died abruptly as he followed Henry's sightline to where the tiger stood. Moving slowly, Dingo climbed down into the shallow ravine. "Don't make any sudden moves, Dash."

Henry nodded, resisting the temptation to roll his eyes. Hadn't that been what his dismissive hand gesture said before?

The thylacine sat down on its haunches with its tongue hanging out, watching the two men with interest, as if such entertainment had not often come its way and it planned to enjoy it to the fullest, having time on its hands.

"Sit up very carefully," Dingo instructed.

Henry did so, realizing that his top half was completely soaked and most likely everything he carried in his rucksack as well, but it was worth any discomfort to be in the presence of such a noble animal.

"Back up to me."

Henry moved to Dingo in a crouch, relieved to be out of the water. "What do we do now?"

"Watch her. She must have a litter nearby."

"How can you tell?"

"The pouch—it's stretched out but empty. She must be suckling." Dingo grinned with pleasure. "Dad'll be so pleased to hear that they're actually breeding. Her mate is probably with the cubs while she hunts."

Henry could tell from the exalted expression upon Dingo's face that he was experiencing the same joy in beholding the thylacine, even though he must have seen the tigers many times before. It was one of the things that made him feel closer to Dingo, this shared wonder over an animal whose fate was so uncertain.

"Should we—should we—follow her?" It was funny how now that they had found them, a new uncertainty had developed within him. Everything before had been a pipe dream; the reality seemed so alien.

"Maybe. We'll see." Dingo reached into Henry's pack for the waterproof camera, carefully snapping several shots of the tiger. "If the cubs aren't weaned, we can't separate them, you know."

"Dingo," Henry said urgently. "We might have found our breeding pair! We have to locate their den."

"Slow down, Dash. We'll see what we shall see. Then we'll decide." Dingo lowered the camera. "Clever of you to spot her, although you might have come down to investigate a bit more quietly."

"I fell on my arse, and you know it." Henry grinned when he said it, no longer worried that Dingo thought him incompetent. "I doubt I could have spotted her from above."

"Are you hurt?" Dingo asked gently.

Henry lifted his shirt, and Dingo winced at the raw grazes that now patterned his stomach.

"It's okay," Henry reassured him. He turned to look back at the thylacine. "It's okay."

The tiger cocked its head, as if hearing some far-off call, and within an instant it was back on its feet and had melted away into the brush, as if it weren't part of this earth.

Henry shivered again, although he wasn't sure if it was from the wet or the fact that his palm no longer burned. What had Jarrah done to him?

"There's still a little bit of daylight left," Dingo told him. "We'll set up camp in a clearing a little way from here, and then you can get out of those wet clothes, and I'll build you a fire. It may be a long night."

He stood and offered Henry his hand. He took it gratefully and stood up. The two men followed the track of the tiger deeper into the forest.

THE farther up the mountain they trekked, the colder it got. Henry was stuck with the uncomfortable realization that even though he was sweating from the humidity and the exertion of climbing, he was also cold. Damp, sweaty clothing wasn't helping with that either. The high he held from his contact with the tiger was only just beginning to dissipate, and the scrapes on his side were raw from the rubbing of his shirt.

He had seen a thylacine in its natural habitat. How long had he stroked the pelts in the archives back in England, trying to imagine the creature alive, wondering how it moved? It seemed like his memory of their meeting was already fading, and he couldn't distinguish between what he had actually seen and what he was now filling in with imagination or supposition. He wished he could record his memory like a motion picture, something to be committed into concrete reality forever.

Next time he saw the thylacine, he would be more observant and less dumbstruck. He snorted to himself. *Next* time? There was no guarantee of a next time.

But he *had* seen it. If that were all he came away with, wasn't it enough? Wasn't it worth it?

Of course it was. But the heart of the true adventurer always craves more. Once you succeeded at one goal, you just moved on to the next one. Otherwise you would stop moving, and what else would there be?

How can I go back home, after everything I've seen?

He silenced that thought.

"You're being quiet," Dingo called over his shoulder.

"I'm thinking."

"You're always thinking."

"Is that a bad thing?"

"No," Dingo said, surprised. "It's a good thing. Some people don't think enough. So there have to be people like you to take up the slack."

Henry grinned. How was it that Dingo always knew the right thing to say? "You're a thinker, yourself."

"Sure I am."

Dingo's brain was always ticking over. In fact, Henry could tell that even now he was deep in thought about something. "What is it?"

Dingo stared ahead of them into the forest. "Weather's worsening," he said. "And the dark is coming in earlier than yesterday. We should make camp."

"Already?"

"Yep. Don't like the look of it, to tell you the truth. We may be in for a rough night."

Henry shivered. "Great."

"The bad thing is it means the animals will probably stay in as well."

Henry swallowed his disappointment. "You never know. We could get lucky."

Dingo seemed disappointed as well as he didn't even fall for the obvious double entendre he could take from that. "I think we're going to get mist as well." Then he grinned. "Don't worry, Dash. I'll keep you warm."

Shivering a bit in his clammy clothes, Henry hoped he would.

AS THEY were pitching the tent, the mist started to roll in. It was like a living thing, blanketing all that lay in its path.

"Told you it would be a bad night. We'll not be able to see much in this pea soup," Dingo said, sounding pleased he could read the weather correctly and yet doom their surveillance all at the same time.

Henry was beginning to appreciate how Dingo's expertise enabled him to size up the terrain and position the tent where it blended best into the site, so that one had to be almost on top of it to even know it was there. Dingo cleverly used existing rocks and tree roots to tie off to; a quick yank and the slipknots could be released and the tent bundled away without one realizing it had ever been there.

The tent was being made differently tonight, the space within being smaller so that the canvas could be wrapped around to provide both groundcover and flaps. "Trying to conserve the heat," Dingo told Henry.

"You know," Henry said, trying to sound nonchalant, "you told me before that there is one way to conserve body heat."

Even though he already knew, Dingo wanted to hear him say it. "And what would that be, Dash?"

"Sleeping naked," Henry now said boldly.

"I like the way you think," Dingo said, bending down and hiding his face so that Henry wouldn't see his smile. "For purely scientific reasons, yeah?"

"Of course," Henry replied.

Dingo's head shot up. "Oh?"

"But it's fortunate that it will also have… pleasurable side-effects in this instance… for us to study," Henry concluded.

And it did. Later that night when Henry came back to the tent after relieving himself, Dingo was already under the blankets waiting for him.

"Now, you strip for me," Dingo commanded.

It must be being out in the wild that does it, Henry thought fleetingly as he started undressing without shame. He felt like there were no boundaries out here, and with Dingo he felt more alive than he had ever been. He even felt his worth as a sexual being. So he turned his disrobing into a slow tease for Dingo, who made his appreciation known with a slow whistle.

However, there was no way a man could strip off while on his knees due to the size of the tent they were in and manage to pull off his boots and still look alluring. Trying to kick one off, he lost his balance and collapsed upon Dingo, who gave an undignified *ooomph* as the breath was expelled from him.

"Need a hand?" Dingo grunted.

"Maybe," Henry said. "I still seem to be wearing clothes."

"I'll be glad to help you with that," Dingo smirked. His bare bum rose into the air as he came out from under the blankets and rolled his thumbs under the waistband of Henry's drawers. Without warning, he yanked them down, and Henry was fully exposed.

"Well, what have we here," Dingo said.

"Get my boots off, first," Henry protested.

Dingo laughed and struggled to wrestle them off. Henry only had to watch him to start getting hard.

"Is this exciting for you, Dash?" Dingo teased.

"Anything you do is," Henry admitted.

"What about this?"

Henry didn't even have time to reply, as all that came out was a strangled moan as Dingo threw aside the boots and took him into his mouth. He allowed himself to be played like an instrument as he ran his hands along Dingo's arching back. Dingo ran a finger tantalizingly behind his balls and along his crack, and Henry began thrusting upwards with wanton abandon. As he began to feel himself race to release, Dingo pulled free.

"I want to see you," he said. He picked up Henry's hand and guided it to his prick.

Henry couldn't stop himself from gasping; this was an all-new level of intimacy, for Dingo to watch him pleasure himself. "You too," he whispered.

Dingo nodded and scooted back slightly. His cock bobbed along with him, and he confidently took himself in hand. "Come on, Dash."

Their eyes glued to each other, they began stroking. Slowly, teasingly, displaying themselves for their lover.

Henry came first, Dingo's name upon his lips. He closed his eyes briefly, involuntarily, but then they flew back open so he wouldn't miss Dingo doing the same.

Dingo began to pump himself more furiously, the tip of his tongue showing between his lips and guttural cries sounding. Even though he was slightly sore, Henry continued to stroke his softening cock, excited still as he watched Dingo come in furious spurts while crying his name. Sweating, Dingo fell back, his knees in the air. Henry pulled them down and climbed on top of him, Dingo's half-hard cock resting against his arse. They kissed slowly as their bodies cooled rapidly in the night air.

With their mouths still touching, Dingo reached into his pack with one hand, somehow finding the bottle of tea-tree oil. He began to massage a bit onto the scrapes that adorned Henry's torso.

Henry sighed with immediate relief.

"It has an antiseptic quality," Dingo murmured.

"Any number of uses then."

Dingo nodded. "No room to pack a variety of medicines and remedies."

Henry felt a bit guilty, thinking that Dingo probably had no need of medicines or remedies except that he, a greenhorn—

A scream rent the silence of the forest, and Henry jerked away from Dingo.

"Shh," Dingo whispered. "It's just the devils. We probably woke them up with our own call of the wild."

Henry chuckled and kissed Dingo's chest. "Who would have thought such a sound could exist in an animal?"

"Are you talking about us or the devils?"

Henry considered this for a moment and answered, "Both."

Remembering that he was here to observe all that he could, Henry reluctantly crawled away from Dingo's warmth, and, bare-arsed, he positioned himself by the flap of the tent so that he could peer out.

"See anything?" Dingo yawned, reaching for the blankets.

"Nothing," Henry said, disappointed.

He felt the blankets being draped over him and then Dingo crawling beneath them and beside him.

The unnatural-sounding screams continued, and Henry was glad that Dingo was with him. Even though he never would have admitted the devils won their name justly, as they brought every childhood fear of the dark back to him.

It moved so fast it was almost a blur, but a small dark creature streaked past the front of their tent, its teeth a brief glint in the moonlight.

"You just saw your first devil," Dingo said.

"It was so small," Henry breathed. "How could something so small sound like that?"

"All the creatures here are miracles," Dingo said sleepily. "Even the scary ones."

Henry let the flap of the tent fall down.

"Better get dressed. It's nippy tonight," Dingo said.

Henry did so reluctantly, watching as Dingo did the same and regretting the necessity, but it did seem much colder than it had been so far.

Dingo had already closed his eyes when Henry wrapped the blankets around them like a cocoon and snuggled closer.

21. THE CALM BEFORE THE STORM

MORNING came quickly, and rain had been falling all through the night. Heavily. Dingo wasn't next to him. Henry rubbed at his face blearily and pulled open the tent flap.

Dingo was standing in the rain, naked. Water coursed over his skin, down the back of his neck, and broke off into branched rivulets over the slight hair on his buttocks and the thicker hair of his legs. He bent over, and Henry realized that he was soaping himself up and treating the rain as a natural shower.

Henry sniffed himself and knew immediately he could use a clean as well.

Dingo turned, lazily rubbing a bar of soap across his chest. "Morning, Dash. Not sure how long this will last, so you might want to hurry up." Without a hint of self-consciousness he began to soap up the dark bush of hair between his legs, and his cock perked up slightly.

Henry swallowed heavily, unable to tear his eyes away from the sight.

"Come on, Dash," Dingo implored. "You can do my back, and then I'll do yours." He smiled, stroking himself gently, but his smile faded as he took in the lust etched on Henry's face.

Henry stood up and deliberately took off his glasses, hooking them over one of the ropes. With the same deliberation he slowly peeled off his shirt and tossed it to the ground.

Dingo licked his lips nervously when Henry's hands dropped to his belt, unbuckling it with excruciating slowness. And yet Henry was not doing it to tease Dingo; there was no self-conscious smirk on his face as he stripped his trousers down his long legs and stepped out of them.

Henry started toward him, his sex swaying as if to some internal beat as he walked. Dingo stood there watching, his hand motionless on his dick, powerless to move until Henry was practically touching him. Dingo opened his arms to feel his lover against him.

His hands circled Henry's waist, still clutching the soap in one of them.

Henry started singing in time to the drumbeat of the rain, his mouth near Dingo's ear so the other man could hear him. It was a song popular right then, especially in the queer clubs, and Dingo seemed taken by surprise that Henry knew it.

We walk like tigers in the night
Staying hidden undercover,
Silent dancing by starlight
We claim our secret lover.

The lather made their skin slip sensually as Henry started them swaying to the tune.

"Come along, sing with me," he said softly.

Dingo cleared his throat and said hoarsely, "I can't sing." He ran the soap over Henry's back, sliding it lazily over each vertebrae as his hand went lower.

"It doesn't matter," Henry said. "Audience of one. Be a sport."

Stripes melting into shadow
Where the tigers go at night
And only we can follow
Slinking out of sight…

Dingo joined in, his voice cracking and wandering off tune. He slid his hands down to cup the creamy skin of Henry's arse, dropping the soap without thinking, pulling him tightly to him. Henry was surprised to realize he didn't feel self-conscious at all, listening to his voice muted by the rain, swaying as if they were dancing together in some swanky club. It felt natural to dance with his lover in the rain in the depths of the forest. And instead, Dingo seemed to be the one who felt a need to hide himself, keeping his face buried in Henry's neck.

No one else must know
The yearning we're concealing

The feelings we can't show
Staying hidden in plain sight
Burning eyes can't help revealing
That we are tigers in the night
Tigers in the night.

Dingo's voice cracked and died away, and he pressed his cheek against Henry's. The coolness of the rain contrasted with the heat of Dingo's skin where their bodies touched. Henry could feel Dingo's hard cock rubbing against his, and the desire that had been smoldering between them burst into the blazing need to satisfy.

"Let's go inside."

Henry leaned his head back and shook his head, smiling enticingly and squinting against the rain. "Let's do it here."

"It's muddy," Dingo said, pointing out the obvious.

"So we'll be dirty." Henry chuckled. "Very dirty. 'Burning eyes can't help revealing…'"

"I won't hurt you again," Dingo said. "Wait here."

Henry's gently mocking laughter followed him on his dash to the tent. "Where else am I going to go?"

Dingo came back with the tube of lubricant clutched in his trembling hand. Henry attacked his mouth, plunging his tongue teasingly between his lips, plundering the depths until Dingo submitted eagerly to him taking the lead.

Henry sank down onto the ground, dragging Dingo with him. Dingo grunted as he landed on top of his lover, bracing his weight so as not to crush him, but Henry wrapped his legs around his waist, keeping him prisoner as they kissed passionately.

Dingo shielded Henry from the rain with his own body, sliding a finger over his anus, using the lube to open him. Henry spread his legs wide, arching up as he was breached, not breaking the kiss, one hand cupping the back of Dingo's head, the other firmly holding him in place by the arse.

Henry yearned to feel the burning heat of Dingo's cock enter him, but Dingo continued to caress the inner passage, stretching the muscle to handle his girth until Henry bucked impatiently beneath him.

"Come on, then," Henry urged.

Recovering a bit of his usual bravado, Dingo grinned, lifting Henry's legs and draping them over his shoulders. He pressed forward with his cock gently until Henry relaxed enough to take him. Groaning, he pushed his way inside, entering his lover tenderly. His hands cupped Henry's cheeks, curling his body and pushing his arse up.

Henry stared up at him, blinking in the rain, his eyes full of trust and yearning. Dingo slid his cock home, leaning down to kiss him. Henry melted under the tender assault, almost wishing he had decided to take Dingo instead, but there was really no difference when their bodies were one. He felt as if they were truly as close as any two people could be.

Staying hidden undercover,
Silent dancing by starlight
We claim our secret lover.

The words to their song still played in his head, and it matched the rhythm of his hips as he began to move, meeting each of Dingo's slow thrusts, feeling the hardness of him to his depths. Dingo seemed to want to take his time, fucking Henry tenderly until their bodies caught fire and burning need overcame him. Soon he was riding Henry, their wet flesh slapping together, his groin pounding against Henry's arse.

With a sudden gasp, Henry arched his back, straining up against Dingo, his eyes closed in ecstasy, his hand urgently stroking his cock. Dingo watched the spurts of come land on Henry's chest with the righteous joy of a man who had pleased his lover.

And then Dingo was lost in his own climax, slamming into him with a force that pleased Henry, as a measure of his passion. He thrust until he was drained and panting, letting his full weight come to rest upon Henry.

Dingo pushed himself to the side with a shaky laugh. The mud felt silky and cool against his skin.

Henry reached up to brush his cheek. "You'll have to wash again."

"You too," Dingo said.

Henry couldn't bear to let Dingo pull out, and so they lay locked together. When it became inevitable, Dingo put his hand on Henry's side to push himself away as he slipped out. Henry looked down to see that Dingo's fingers had left stripes of mud on his pale skin that melted away slowly with the rain.

"Don't go," Henry said. "What is it?"

Dingo simply shook his head, as if he couldn't speak.

"Tell me," Henry urged.

Staring at Henry, Dingo muttered, "You do something to me, Dash. I've got you under my skin."

Henry smiled but looked puzzled. "Surely you've done this with lots of men before. Not in the mud, perhaps, but you've loads of experience—"

Dingo dropped his face against Henry's chest. "I've been with other men before, yes. I've taken them, and some I've even let take me. It was fun while it lasted. But with you, each time I feel it's not enough. I want you more than—"

"More than what?"

Henry ran his fingers delicately through Dingo's wet hair.

"More than I should. More than I can say." Dingo sighed and shivered.

After a short silence, Henry said, "You're cold. We should get cleaned up."

"Yes. We should." Dingo pushed himself onto his hands and knees, bending to kiss Henry, before getting to his feet and stretching out his hand. "I owe you that back wash."

Henry laughed exultantly as they stood together, their cocks half hard again, crossing like swords in front of them. "I'll take you up on that offer."

Gently Dingo turned Henry to face away from him, and Henry felt that for some reason Dingo wanted to avoid his gaze, but it didn't make him feel uneasy. Instead he felt almost triumphant at the way he had been able to arouse passion between them.

Dingo cleared his throat. "Anytime, Dash. And perhaps we'd better just rinse through our clothes as well. Or we'll stink as much as we did before."

He bent to retrieve the soap, and Henry could hear him humming the song under his breath.

22. HENRY FEELS THEY ARE NOT ALONE

THE air was full of mist, or drizzle, or both. It didn't really matter much, Henry thought, the end result was that after their *al fresco* bath, they were both slightly damp and doomed to remain so unless they stayed inside the tent all day. Of course, that would have been against Dingo's nature. Henry resignedly wiped his glasses against his shirt for the umpteenth time, although it resulted in smeared lenses rather than ones with droplets, and trudged after Dingo. His feet kept getting harder to lift as mud caked onto his boots with every step.

Still, the chance that they might get to see the thylacine again kept him moving.

Dingo stopped short and waved his hand behind him. Henry stiffened and peered through the grey mist, barely able to make out the ghost-like form standing on an outcropping of rock before them while his palm started to itch like mad. The dim light combined with the incessant rain to drain the color from the thylacine, but there was no mistaking it for any other animal Henry had ever seen. Even here in Tasmania, the land of bizarrely original creatures, the tiger stood alone, lean, muscular, elegantly shaped. Every other animal, predator or prey, had been roughly pear-shaped, tubby, and lower to the ground.

His fingers trembled as he lifted the camera, shielding the lens under the brim of his rakish hat, grateful now that he'd worn it despite Dingo's amused look. The tiger almost seemed to be aware of Henry's intentions, standing in profile, its nose in the air, tail outstretched and alert, as if offering the ideal pose.

The silhouette of the thylacine seemed almost to fade into the misty backdrop of the forest. The image he captured aroused all the poignantly protective emotion within Henry; it seemed so symbolic of the possible fate of the animal, especially when the tiger lowered its nose and vanished suddenly.

"Is it always like that?" Henry asked in a hushed tone.

Dingo turned to search his eyes. “The first sight of them and my heart beats faster. It’s always a phenomenon.”

Even Henry couldn’t mistake the glow in Dingo’s eyes. “Only for the tiger?” he murmured, stepping closer so their chests were touching.

“You know it’s not,” Dingo whispered, sliding an arm around Henry to pull him closer.

Henry could feel the beat of Dingo’s heart against his, both of them racing. Dingo was warm in his arms, but the rest of him was cold from the rain and damp. Reluctantly he let Dingo go.

“Should we follow him?”

Dingo cocked his head and looked up, although the sky and even the canopy of leaves overhead were hidden from view. “We can try.”

“I thought you could track a snake over a rock,” Henry teased.

“No, that’s Jarrah. I need a few more hints, but I’ll do my best.”

Following behind Dingo, Henry wondered at the obsession that drove them both. Part of him wanted nothing more than to drag Dingo back to their tent, tear his clothing off, and make love to him, but another part was desperate to *see* the tiger, not just enticing glimpses when the animal suddenly appeared as if on stage, only to disappear moments later, but to really *see* how they lived, what they ate, how the pair interacted with each other. There was so much that had to be learned!

DINGO was sleeping when Henry decided he wanted to take a walk and soak up the surroundings. So much of it had gone by in a blur when they were trekking that he felt like he hadn’t taken in any of it properly and was failing his job as an archivist.

He grabbed his journal, which he had neglected ever since arriving in Tasmania, and headed deeper into the woods. He knew not to stray too far, as he had no sense of direction or his surroundings, and being in a strange land with nothing familiar to landmark in his head to find his way back, he knew not to dice with getting lost and never being found again.

There was so much to take in. He collected various leaves and flowers, doing thorough sketches before laying them carefully between the thick pages so they would dry and survive the long trip back home. He would ask Dingo and Jarrah to help him identify them, just in case he could add anything else new or of value in his report to Lardarse.

Lardarse. His charcoal pencil scraped across the page as he smiled. He was really starting to think like Dingo, now. It wasn't that bad, though, to have a view of the world like Dingo's. He was a man who saw the wonder in everything but also had a healthy contempt for those who didn't.

Henry knew he loved Dingo, more than he had ever loved anybody in the world. He had fallen fast, and that was what made the future seem so scary and impossible.

Looking down at the page, Henry realized that his mind had wandered, and instead of drawing the leaf resting upon the opposite page, he had drawn Dingo's face in profile. It wasn't the most faithful of renditions, as Henry's talent ran more to still life than human subjects, but he had captured the smirk perfectly, the one that could infuriate him and excite him all at once. He imagined Dingo lying back in their tent, probably still naked beneath the blankets. He wanted to go back immediately and crawl back in with him, lying against his body in sleep. It was a beautiful thought.

But he had work to do. He turned the pages of his journal until he found a blank sheet and made another attempt at sketching the leaf in case it got damaged in transit. He was drawing the first fine line of the stem when, behind him and to the left, he heard a twig snap under a heavy foot.

Too heavy for an animal.

Henry turned slowly, hoping to make it look natural. He couldn't see anyone approaching him. He didn't know why he was suddenly so nervous; after all, it could be Dingo coming to find him.

"Dingo?" he called out softly.

There was no answer, no friendly "Haroo!" sung out.

Another sound of footfalls, this time, to his right.

Henry jumped up and stashed his journal into his pocket. "Who's there?"

It was strange just how definitely he knew it was a *who*, not a *what*. After all, it could have been some heavy animal he hadn't seen yet. But the animals in this patch of forest were quiet now, in daylight, so it wasn't another animal moving through. It was a predator.

"Show yourself!" he yelled, making sure his voice, at least, sounded sure of himself.

Out of the corner of his eyes, he saw brush move. He felt a trickle of sweat run down his back. The brush was heavy, and he couldn't see anything through it. But something—*someone*—was moving.

They kept well hidden, toying with him. Like a cat with a mouse.

He couldn't help himself. Henry turned and ran.

He could hear footsteps following him, but when he looked back, he couldn't see anybody. They were keeping under the cover of the brush.

Concentrating on what was happening behind him, he tripped on a tree root and went flying. His journal went skipping across the muddy ground. He leaped to his feet, grabbed the journal, and started running again.

Whoever was following him was getting closer. Henry just hoped he was running in the right direction back to camp. He thought a tree ahead looked slightly familiar; there was a knot in the trunk that he remembered looked like a doorknob.

As he circled it, he collided with Dingo. They both fell, sprawling together on the ground.

"Dash, what's the hurry?" Dingo asked, winded and amused.

"Someone's... out there...." Henry panted, holding his stomach where Dingo had got him with his elbow.

Dingo was up on his feet and running in the direction Henry had come from before he could even get another word out.

Henry managed to stand up, still catching his breath. "Dingo!"

There was no answer. The forest was silent again.

"Dingo!"

He began cautiously retracing his steps. There was no sign of Dingo up ahead, but the brush to his left started shaking. Henry looked around him, hoping for a fallen branch to use as some odd weapon, but he barely had time to even see if there were any when Dingo burst through, his arms scratched and bleeding.

"What happened?" Henry asked.

"Didn't see anyone," Dingo panted. "Those branches tore me up pretty good, though."

"No one?"

"Not a soul."

"There was somebody there."

Dingo nodded, but Henry thought he could detect a note of skepticism in his eyes.

"I'm not making it up!"

"I didn't think you were," Dingo assured him.

"Then stop looking at me like I'm some greenhorn who got spooked by a cat."

Dingo smiled. "There are no cats out this far. Feral dogs, yeah."

"It *wasn't* a feral dog. A dog would have growled or attacked me. This was somebody wanting to scare me."

"Well, they're gone now," Dingo said, trying to calm him.

"They're still out there," Henry argued. "Do you think it was Hodges?"

Dingo hesitated.

"Dingo—"

Dingo sighed. "Maybe. He's most likely scoping us out. Wanting to put the wind up us. We can't let him do that."

Henry stared off into the distance, then nodded, and looked down at Dingo's arms. "Let's go back to camp. We need to get some of that tea-tree oil on you."

"You're going to look after me?" Dingo grinned.

Henry knew he was being humored, but he let Dingo take him by the arm, and they began walking back to camp.

Dingo graciously allowed him to daub his scratches with the oil but sat with his head cocked, as if listening for any suspicious sound. "Feel better now?" he asked, reaching for his shirt and pulling it on.

Henry smiled. "I'm supposed to ask you that."

"Pack your things." Dingo did the same, tossing the few items he had taken out into his bag.

Henry had barely crawled out from under the tent when Dingo yanked on the ties, collapsing the fabric. Until now, Henry had always helped him fold the canvas, but Dingo had it halved and quartered before Henry was on his feet. He rolled it up and used the ties to lash it to Henry's pack.

Dingo lifted the ferns behind their now barren camp and ducked under, holding them up until Henry had followed suit. With his eyes lit with excitement and his skin green from the light that reflected off the leaves, Dingo looked like some overgrown, gleeful forest sprite as he held a finger to his lips.

Henry rolled his eyes in annoyance. He felt like telling Dingo sarcastically that he had grasped that they were moving on, thank you very much, as soon as Dingo had ordered him to pack. He followed Dingo, trying to tread lightly, glancing back frequently to see whether he could spot anyone following them.

They were moving upward again, and Henry felt his breath come shorter as the oxygen thinned. Suddenly Dingo stepped into the bed of a small creek. Henry sighed. It seemed they were always either too hot or too cold, too dry or too wet. Apparently today it was going to be wet. His boots filled instantly when he stepped into the stream, but he actually felt somewhat refreshed until the chilly water made his feet go numb.

Dingo led the way downstream about two hundred yards. Henry wondered if they were going to be wading all the way down the mountain in this wet thoroughfare, but apparently Dingo had been looking for a specific spot to leave the stream. He stepped out onto a rock covered with a lush coat of moss. When Henry followed him, he felt the moss cushion compress beneath his feet, but when he looked back, it had sprung up again, leaving no sign of their passing.

"That should slow them down," Dingo said with satisfaction.

"How did you know that was there?"

"I didn't. But one can expect to find that sort of moss alongside streams at this altitude." Dingo sounded smug and pleased with himself, which irritated Henry, but he had to respect his knowledge of the terrain.

"Then how do you know where we're going?"

"There are signs. The stars at night—"

"When you can see them," Henry grumbled.

"Moss really *does* grow on the north side of trees. And even in deep shade, you can still tell which direction the sun comes up."

"I feel like when I was ten, walking through the maze at Blenheim and the hedge was over my head, and I thought I'd never find the way out," Henry admitted ruefully.

"How did you get out?" Dingo demanded.

Henry laughed. Trust Dingo to hare off after a side topic that interested him even while escaping unknown pursuers. He swung around quickly to check behind them, but nothing was moving. "My brother James memorized the key, and eventually he took pity on me and led me out."

"That was nice of him."

"It cost me two weeks' pocket money," Henry said.

"Nice. Baz and Johnno probably would have nicked a whole month of mine."

For some reason, that made Henry feel better, as if it weren't just him, but that all older brothers were cut from the same cloth. Although, it was difficult to believe that Dingo, who had belted Johnno on the nose at ten, would have stood still for that sort of extortion. "So what if there isn't any moss and it's raining?"

"There's my compass." Dingo hefted his pack and turned back to say, "Look behind you."

Henry whirled, suspecting that his erstwhile chaser had come up behind them.

"What do you see?"

"Nothing!" Henry was ashamed to hear the rising panic in his voice.

"Sure you do." Dingo pointed. "See that tree, that one that has a hole about ten feet up?"

Henry nodded, starting to calm himself.

"There wasn't a hole on the other side. You have to look back at things when you're hiking. They appear different coming and going. A tree may look like nothing on one side, but on the opposite side there may be a spot where lightning struck and took off a branch. That makes it a landmark."

Henry nodded again, seeing just what Dingo was saying. And what he was leaving unsaid: how to get out of the jungle if something happened to him. "I thought you were looking at me whenever you turned around."

"You do tend to improve the landscape," Dingo said with that smile that made flutters start up in Henry's stomach, but then he was back to business. "All water flows downhill, heading for the sea. If you follow it, you'll come out *somewhere* and be able to find a town or village. Look here."

Dingo picked up a stick and shoved the litter of dead leaves aside with his boot, starting to draw a crude map in the dirt. "That's the River Styx—"

"Where you fell in."

"Jumped. We traveled northwest from Hobart to cross it. *That's* Maydena, another town where there were stories of a tiger sighting. Where we hoped Hodges was going." He drew another squiggly line that arced closer to the line representing the Styx. "This is the Tenna River. I suspect that Hodges and his guide may have come up that way."

"And in the middle?" Henry pointed at the blank area between the two rivers.

"Nameless, unexplored country. No farms, no towns. Only forest and water and animals," Dingo explained.

It made Henry feel a little thrill to know that he could climb a hill and know that no one else had ever walked there before—at least not a white man. "But Jarrah knows this area."

"Even Jarrah doesn't usually come this far," Dingo said. "Not that it matters. He's at home in the forest like no other man I know."

"Then—how did Hodges get this far? If his guides don't know the area?"

Dingo shrugged and for the first time Henry sensed his uneasiness.

"Probably using a compass, like we are. Maybe he's offered them a lot of money. Times are tough right now, not much work in Tasmania."

"*We're* not using the compass; you are."

"I'll show you how when we get there."

"Where's there?" Henry asked, feeling a bit of déjà vu.

"We'll know when we get there," Dingo said. Carefully he scraped over the map he had drawn in the earth with a leafy branch until it was gone. He scooped up a handful of loose loam from the base of a tree and let it sift between his fingers, and then he carefully arranged dead leaves to look as if nothing had been disturbed. He thrust the branch he'd used deep into the brambles and surveyed the scene before he turned to lead the way.

For the first time Henry felt Dingo did believe him about them being followed. He just wished it made him feel better than it did.

Henry settled in for the hike.

IT FELT like hours, but it was actually only two when Dingo slipped behind a thorny bush, threading through a thick maze of brush and stood gazing around. "This is a good spot," he announced.

Henry opened his mouth to ask why, but instead he looked around, trying to see what Dingo saw. It was an unlikely spot for a campsite. They had left any discernible path behind and pushed through the densest patches of brush to reach this spot. A semi-circle of four tall gum trees enclosed a tiny patch of ground, barely large enough for them to pitch their tent. He could hear the low sound of a stream nearby. Peering at the underbrush, he couldn't see out, which meant no one could see in either.

Even better, Dingo discovered a similar way out on the opposite side, so that they would not be trapped there if someone did discover their whereabouts. Henry let his pack slide off his shoulders and pulled the canvas free. Together, they pitched the tent in the compact spot.

"I'll get water," Dingo said. "No fires here, sorry."

"I'll live," Henry said, and then he shivered as if the words were some sort of talisman to ward off danger.

Dingo looked a little pale too, Henry thought.

"Too right. Back soon."

Henry tried to make the tent more comfortable by spreading out the blanket even though he left all his other belongings in his pack. The speed with which they'd abandoned their previous camp made him chary of unpacking and moving in for the duration. He was still on his knees when he felt a hand cup his bum and rub it comfortingly.

"That's a sight a man likes to come home to," Dingo teased.

Henry turned and lunged for him with a desperation that surprised even him. All his life, he'd felt that everything that made it worth living was passing him by. Now, on the most glorious adventure beyond what he could have dreamed, the scare of being tracked down in the forest made him feel that this was all too fragile. It could all be taken away too easily, and he hadn't had enough of Dingo yet. Possibly he would never have enough.

But Dingo was here and available, and Henry wanted him with all his heart. He pulled Dingo down on top of him, kissing him madly, feeling like he wanted to devour him. Dingo tasted fresh and pure to him, like water did to a man who'd been lost in some vast desert and stumbled across an oasis by chance.

Henry rolled over, pinning Dingo beneath him, biting at his throat while he unbuttoned his shirt. A yelp from Dingo made Henry realize he was being a bit rough and he raised his head. "Sorry…."

"Don't be. I like it when the tiger in you comes out," Dingo gasped, his hands holding Henry in place when he would have moved off.

Henry liked the way Dingo was looking at him. He ducked his head to kiss the spot he'd bitten in silent apology. He kissed his way down Dingo's chest as he unbuttoned each button, enjoying the way Dingo caught his breath when he licked over a nipple, gently scraping his teeth against the hard nub.

Dingo moaned in response, his body undulating slowly under Henry.

Henry cupped the hardness straining at Dingo's trousers while kissing his way down that feast of golden skin. Every muscle tensed with eagerness, showing off the perfectly defined abdomen when Henry rested a hand on Dingo's belt and paused. The intoxicating scent of him made Henry's fingers clumsy as he undid his trousers to catch a glimpse of the tip of Dingo's erection protruding from the waistband.

"Oh God," Henry said softly.

"What… what is it?" Dingo managed.

Henry shook his head slightly, the emotion welling up within him too profound for him to be able to express. He couldn't believe that this beautiful man was so aroused and hard, and it was all for him. And yet the evidence was right there. Henry pushed at the trousers, and Dingo obligingly lifted his hips, settling back with his cock resting on his stomach, a little glistening pool gathering under the tip.

With a confidence that amazed him, Henry bent to lick over the head, savoring the taste of the clear drops. Dingo moaned and reached down to cup the back of Henry's head in encouragement.

Dingo's cock was warm and hard, although the silky skin against Henry's tongue had a surprisingly delicate softness. The head filled his mouth, the weight satisfying on his tongue. Henry closed his eyes and inhaled, swirling his tongue around the shaft. Fingers tightening in his hair told him that Dingo liked what he was doing, and Henry gave himself over to the experience. Dingo's balls felt full and tight in his hand as he fondled them. He moved off Dingo's cock to lick them, nuzzling the tender skin of his inner thigh as Dingo spread his legs.

Henry opened his mouth to take the head again, wanting some part of Dingo inside him. He flicked his tongue over the thick ridge and as far down the shaft as he could reach, pleased with the way Dingo's cock filled his mouth. With his back arched, Dingo bucked his hips involuntarily. Henry put his hand flat onto his stomach to keep him still, looking up to catch the look of ecstasy upon Dingo's unguarded face. Henry marveled that the other man could be so trusting, even more so when Dingo opened his eyes and stared at him, letting him see the emotion reflected there.

Tremors shook Dingo's body and in turn made Henry shiver with desire. Then Dingo closed his eyes and threw one arm over his face as if the sight were too much for him. The movement of his hips quickened, and Henry sucked harder, breathing heavily through his nose, not wanting to break Dingo's rhythm. The thrusts grew shorter, quicker, until Dingo went rigid, smothering a low cry by biting his forearm.

Watching Dingo, feeling the pulse of him in his mouth, tasting the quick spurt of salty come pushed Henry close to the edge.

He opened his eyes when he felt Dingo's hand stroking his jaw. His glasses were askew, and Dingo gently took them off his nose, folding them and placing them to one side. "Come up here," he said in a low breathy voice.

Henry obeyed, feeling like he was floating rather than using any muscles to move. Dingo kissed him, his tongue gentle but demanding, taking possession of Henry's senses yet again.

"Let me return the favor," Dingo said, his hands busy at Henry's belt.

Henry clung to Dingo, aching with his need to be touched. When Dingo took hold of him, his hand warm and firm, his orgasm finally and quickly rushed over him, and Henry convulsed against Dingo's leg, rubbing frantically before he lay gasping for breath.

A low chuckle made Henry feel almost embarrassed, but he was too busy feeling blissfully content to really take umbrage. Besides, he knew that Dingo was pleased with his own prowess. He himself was feeling a bit set up to have gotten Dingo off for the first time with his mouth.

"You don't know… it was… very exciting to… to…." Henry tried to explain the completeness he felt when held in Dingo's arms, how very exciting it was to make love to him. He slipped his tongue into Dingo's mouth, trying to convey that way the emotion he felt.

And it seemed as if Dingo understood after all. He let Henry's tongue slide between his parted lips, kissing him back lazily as he pulled Henry closer.

"That was nice," Dingo said. He stared into Henry's eyes as if searching for confirmation of something.

Henry felt at a disadvantage without his glasses and reached for them. Dingo's hand covered his, fingers entwining with Henry's as he pulled him back.

"You don't need them this close."

"Yes, I do," Henry said nervously.

"You hide behind them sometimes. You don't need to with me."

Henry thought Dingo sounded curiously insistent. "I don't use them to hide; I use them to see."

"Look at me then. Tell me what you see."

Henry grinned, suddenly confident again. "Dingo Chambers, King of the Jungle."

"If only," Dingo said, but he smiled too. "Sounds like a comic book."

"Maybe you should star in your own." Henry didn't like to suggest that usually the heroes in the comics returned triumphant from their adventures, for what if they should fail to secure the thylacines for which they'd come? What if whoever was after them managed to prevent them… in some way. But it was bad luck to vocalize such a negative thought, and he didn't want to be the one to say it anyway.

And besides, it was too late. Dingo had fallen asleep, his lips slack as he drew long, slow breaths.

Henry lay still, running a hand over the solid curves of Dingo's chest. He felt too happy to sleep. There wasn't enough light to see very well, but Dingo's body was relaxed, and he was warm and slightly furry to the touch. Henry ran his hand down his stomach, scraping lightly at the remains of the spunk drying on his stomach with his nails.

Absently he scratched his hand, listening to the night sounds that always intrigued him. He was thinking he'd give anything to see which animal was making the sound when he heard a low whine. It didn't *sound* as if the animal was in distress, and he could tell it was an animal, not a human…. Henry scratched at his palm again and then held his hand inches from his face. He sat bolt upright, staring out into the darkness.

It was Tassie. It *had* to be.

Henry fastened his trousers and buttoned his shirt, remembering how the brush scratched Dingo's arms earlier. Thankful that he still had his boots on, he shook Dingo.

"Dingo! They're out there! It's the tigers!" Henry whispered, giving Dingo a sharp poke in the ribs. Dingo grunted and rolled onto his side.

"Dingo!" Henry tried one last, futile shake and gave it up. Dingo would kick himself later when he found out what he'd missed, but Henry wasn't going to worry about that now. This was his chance.

He cursed himself for a clumsy fool as he scrambled out of the tent, making enough noise to wake anyone but a post-orgasmic Dingo. The burning of his palm seemed to spread through his entire body, making his nerves tingle with excitement. The whine sounded faintly again, and Henry pushed his way through the bushes at the back of their hideout.

A soft rustle caught his attention, and a branch swayed in front of him. Without even thinking of the chase earlier where *he* was the prey, Henry pushed forward, realizing that whatever he was following was leading him uphill. A dim and silvery light ahead frosted the leaves blue. He stepped out from under the cover of the trees to find himself facing a steep drop-off with ghostly, moonlit trees crowding the valley below as far as he could see. He could make out a shimmery thread of water as a creek wound in and out through the leaves.

He barely caught the movement in his peripheral vision and turned in time to see the familiar silhouette of a thylacine. It gave an awesome yawn, stretching its jaws wider than he could have imagined, showing rows of gleaming sharp teeth and ending on a little squeak. Then it trotted off.

Henry followed. His entire body was buzzing with excitement now; he had no thought to spare to question the wisdom of this lonely midnight expedition. He forgot Dingo's careful instructions and never looked behind him. He wasn't worried about getting back; he was only determined that the tiger not shake him off this time.

The tiger led him across bare stretches of rock and under the canopy of trees once more. Henry could have sworn that the animal looked back at him, as though to say, "*Hurry up, I don't have all night*." The thylacine seemed almost to be bowing, and when it straightened up again, Henry could see something limp dangling from its jaws.

The tiger led him into an area of dense bushes, and Henry wished he could just slip under them the way the animal did. He pushed his way through, desperate to stay with it, although at times only the faint rustling sound kept him moving forward. When the sound stopped, he did too, in order to listen. Soft whining sounds told him he was close. He dropped to his knees to be closer to the animal's level and peered through the lower branches of the bush.

If the moon hadn't been as bright, he might have missed it, but enough light filtered through the canopy of trees for him to see the tiger drop his prize when a smaller, daintier thylacine approached him. They touched noses, exchanging affectionate caresses. He remembered Dingo telling him that the tiger, for all it resembled a dog so closely in shape, couldn't wag its tail. Both tails rose straight up as the two animals acknowledged each other. The male then pushed forward the dead animal he had been carrying. The female nodded her head, as if accepting the prize.

Shrill cries interrupted the adults. Henry was thrilled to see tiny, furry tiger cubs stagger into the light. They were so unsteady on their feet, falling and rolling about, he couldn't tell how many there were, but they showed definite interest in the dead animal. The parents started ripping the fur off and holding out shreds of meat to the squalling youngsters, who were quickly silenced as they chewed.

Henry was so wrapped up in the wonder of watching the family that he never heard a sound to warn him. The first thing he felt was a warm hand landing on his shoulder. He jerked around to find Dingo bending to peer through the gap in the bushes.

"Good work, Dash. I'd say you just found their lair."

23. VISITORS IN THE NIGHT

THE excitement of finding the lair ended up draining them, and once the tigers had finished their meal, Dash and Dingo left them in peace in order to return to their own camp and catch up on some sleep.

As they cuddled under the blankets, Dingo said, "Now that we know the position of their den, half the work's done."

"We just have to let them get used to us," Henry replied. "Hopefully before Hodges pulls anything else."

"We'll have to keep moving," Dingo murmured, sleep starting to drag him under. "That'll make Hodges think that we're just as much in the dark about where the tigers are. If he's watching us."

"He is," Henry said firmly.

Dingo sighed, his breath warm against Henry's back.

"Once they trust us," Henry said, "it'll make everything easier."

"Make what easier?"

"Preparing them. For London."

There was a long pause. Finally Dingo said, "I guess. Go to sleep, Dash."

Henry did so and was unaware that Dingo remained awake for a long time afterwards.

"DASH," Dingo said, struggling through the thick vestiges of sleep, "wake up."

Henry stirred against him. "What?"

"You're not going to want to miss this."

Henry opened one eye and would have scrambled to his feet so fast he would have scared them away, but Dingo held him down.

"Slowly, Dash." Dingo grinned at the wide-eyed wonder on Henry's face as he looked through the brush that surrounded their tent and saw the tigers to their left. There were two of them, both adult, and they were staring at the humans who were in their territory.

Without fear. As if they knew they were to be trusted.

Henry scratched his palm against his thigh and slowly sat up. "How long have they been there?"

"Dunno. They were just there when I woke up."

"Waiting for us," Henry breathed.

"Maybe," Dingo said. "Maybe it's presumptuous of us to think that."

Henry's palm disagreed, but he didn't say so. "I want to touch them."

"I don't think they'd let you."

They both froze as one of the tigers looked behind where it was standing, and suddenly, pushing itself between its legs was one of the cubs.

Henry couldn't restrain himself any longer. "Dingo—"

"Wait, Dash."

There was a series of *yips* as the cub was joined by its siblings. All three of them had come along on the journey with their parents.

"They did, Dingo. They came to us." It was beyond perfect. It was fate, as Jarrah had predicted. Henry had never been as sure of anything as he had been right at this moment.

Dingo was shifting behind him, pulling on his trousers.

"What are you doing?"

"Approaching them. Quietly. You stay here for a minute."

Henry wanted to protest; the little boy within him was screaming that it wasn't fair, he wanted to play with them as well. But he knew he had to trust Dingo's judgment.

As Dingo began crawling closer to the tigers, trying to appear as small and therefore as unintimidating as possible, Henry began to dress. He could see the muscles in Dingo's bare back stretch and knot as he continued making his way over to the tigers. The adults watched him carefully, and the cubs were just as wary, but Henry could see they were itching to sniff the stranger and see if he would be another playmate.

He remembered his camera, and cursing at how easily he had forgotten its existence, Henry reached behind himself and dragged it out of his bag. His fingers were trembling slightly as he removed the lens cap and focused on Dash approaching the animals.

They all looked up at the click of the release but after a moment dismissed it and focused back on Dingo. He was only a couple of body lengths away now, and he stopped, resting back on his heels. Henry guessed that he was now waiting for the tigers to approach him. If he had gone much closer, they might have run.

Henry continued to snap pictures but was transfixed even as he watched through the finder. He almost cried out with joy as one of the pups broke rank and bounded toward Dingo. Quick as a flash, one of the parents leaped forward and grabbed it gently but firmly by the tail with its teeth. The pup squealed, even though it was just a warning nip, and Henry laughed.

"Wrong Way Corrigan," he whispered softly.

Dingo snorted. "We can call him Corry," he murmured as the cub started off into the brush with renewed determination.

"Maybe his parents call him Dingo," Henry teased.

"So the other two can be Johnno and Baz."

The parent nudged the pup back to its siblings and turned back to face Dingo.

Dingo remained silent and still, and the tiger approached him. Henry continued snapping photos as the tiger sniffed around Dingo and finally sat next to him. Dingo kept his hands to himself, not wanting to startle it, but the tiger finally nudged his hip, and Dingo offered the back of his hand for it to sniff if it wanted to do so. Like a dog sizing up friend or foe, the tiger sniffed him gingerly, its nostrils flaring briefly at the end of its long snout. It snorted, and Dingo was rewarded with a thin stream of thylacine mucus. He didn't flinch, however, but looked back to see if Henry had caught it on film.

Henry grinned from behind the camera to let him know he had.

Dingo tilted his head slightly and jerked it back, indicating that Henry should join him.

Flush with excitement, Henry carefully placed the camera down on the blankets and tried to replicate Dingo's careful and steady movements as he crawled over to join him. The tiger that had adopted Dingo as a member of the family backed away slightly, and Henry's heart sank. But once he settled in closer to Dingo, the tiger decided to approach them again.

Dingo took Henry's hand and laid it over his own. Together, they offered their hands to the tiger once more. Henry's eyes widened as the tiger's wet nose snuffled against his skin, and he looked up at Dingo with a wide grin.

The other tigers remained at a short distance, but all of a sudden the ears of the adults pricked, and they began pushing their pups back through the brush.

Henry wanted to call out after them to stop, but he knew it would be foolish. He and Dingo remained silent until the brush stopped swaying and they knew that they were alone again.

"That was… unbelievable," Henry breathed, at a loss for words to signify just how wondrous the experience had been for him. All those hours with the pelts back at his college, he had never thought he would one day have a real live tiger sit next to him and leave a mark upon his skin.

Dingo merely nodded, lost in thought.

"There were three of them," Henry whispered. "The cubs, I mean. Excellent."

"It is. That's about the limit for what a pair can raise," Dingo agreed, sounding a bit short.

"No, I meant for breeding. If we can get near enough to sex them, we can take a male and female for breeding in the zoo."

"You can't!" Dingo practically spat at him.

Henry felt as if Dingo had raised his hand and struck him. Lost for words, he could only stare at Dingo, wanting to know where this sudden explosion had come from. Dingo had approached him at the college… they were meant to be after the same thing….

Dingo stared at his feet.

"What do you mean?" Henry finally asked.

Dingo looked at him, and Henry could see that he was struggling with the right words as well.

But Henry was losing patience. "What is it?" he demanded irritably.

"You can't take the cubs, Dash." Dingo's expression was both stern and sad, which just irked Henry all the more.

"What do you mean I can't take them?"

"You know that inbreeding usually yields a more weakly strain. Even if you could get them to breed, the offspring could be deformed or ill."

"Fine. You may have a point. Then we'll find another litter and take one from each," Henry said.

"How many other litters do you think are just lying about waiting for you to stroll up and raid them?" Dingo demanded angrily. "They're almost extinct. There aren't enough! We're damn lucky we even found this family!"

"That's not the real reason you're fighting me about this. Come on, out with it." Henry waited, his arms crossed defiantly.

"You want the real reason? It's simple," Dingo told him. "It's not *right* to take the cubs."

Henry felt everything he had achieved slipping through his fingers. "You said that if taken when young, they're easier to work with, almost growing up like pets."

"Well, but they're not meant to *be* pets, are they?" Dingo met Henry's glare steadily.

It was all so clear now. "You never meant to help me bring out the tigers," Henry said.

"Don't be mad, Dash," Dingo said earnestly. "I wasn't going to prevent you. I just hoped that you would see—"

"What good does it do to lead me on such an expedition and come back empty-handed?" Henry felt like he might be the one to explode now. "I want to save the species, and instead—"

Dingo reached out to touch Henry's arm, but he pulled away. "If you go back with evidence of their sanctuary, a busload of people will come out here looking for the tiger like they're some bloody circus animal to be gawked at. But don't you see? The more expeditions that return empty-handed, the more convinced the government and the world will be that the thylacine are extinct. It might be the chance they need to actually start rebuilding their numbers again."

Henry stared at him. "You think this is a better way of saving them? Leaving them here against all odds to take their chances?" he asked flatly.

"Better to leave them wild and free than to condemn them to a miserable existence in a zoo," Dingo declared hotly. "When you see them in a cage, you'll understand. It's not the life they were meant for."

"What I understand is that you dragged me out here under false pretenses." Henry took a few steps away and stopped to pick up his camera, putting the lens cap on carefully, although his hands shook with anger. "Perhaps I've made a poor choice of a guide. Maybe I've made a lot of poor choices on this whole trip." Henry whirled and plunged into the shadows, away from their camp, ignoring Dingo calling his name.

DINGO shivered and poked around in the tent to find his shirt. His imagination haunted him with images of Henry wandering around in the forest, getting lost. Maybe even worse. He followed Henry, listening to ascertain whether his movements would be carried back in the still of the night. But the sound that was carried to his ears came from the wrong direction.

And what was even more disturbing, the sounds were definitely human. Leaves brushing against fabric. A sound that stopped a moment or two after he stopped. A sound he wished he hadn't heard.

They *weren't* alone in the jungle any longer. Henry was right.

Dingo cursed himself for only half-believing Henry when he'd said he felt they were being watched. Henry had accused him of always underestimating Hodges, and Dingo had brushed it off because he hadn't wanted to alarm the other man. In truth, he'd been watching their back trail ever since they left Jarrah, and he *should* have spotted that someone was following them.

Instantly he made up his mind and started moving again. He didn't know precisely what Hodges's game was, but damned if he'd stand there like a stupid hen and get potted in the head. The best thing he could do now was to lead Hodges in a different direction from the way Henry was heading. His brain was frantic with schemes as he thought them through and discarded options. He decided that once he'd gotten Hodges and his guide headed in a different direction, he would slip into the trees and get behind them.

Damn Henry anyway! If he hadn't gotten all starry-eyed over Henry, he would have been more alert, more suspicious. More like himself. Now he would do what he had to in order to make sure that Henry made it out of Tasmania alive, even if the man he cherished ceased to be his lover. Protective feelings threatened to overwhelm him, and Dingo had to recall himself to business when he realized he was seething with anger at the idea of Hodges hurting Henry again.

Dawn was beginning to break through the branches above him as Dingo hiked faster to the bend in the trail.

When he turned he risked a quick sidelong glance behind him, smiling in grim satisfaction as he stepped behind an outcropping of rock. He dropped to his knees and scuttled soundlessly under the cover of some ferns to watch Hodges and his guide proceed past him in the bluish light. He thought the guide looked uneasy, but Hodges's thin lips were curled into a triumphant smile.

When they were out of sight, Dingo stood up and melted into the shadows, backtracking the trail but keeping undercover as much as he could.

He had to find Henry!

24. A STEP INTO DARKNESS

AFTER plunging blindly between the trees, Henry's steps slowed, and he stopped, his head hanging down. His mind was spinning. Dingo had been fooling him all along! And most likely the entire seduction was designed only to distract him from his quest. So he'd never meant anything to Dingo after all. Well, he'd known deep down that it was too good to be true, but he'd thought they were in this together.

At least he knew that Dingo's passion for the thylacine was genuine; there was no faking the fanatical light in his eyes when he was watching them, but he had *agreed*....

Henry paused. Had Dingo ever truly agreed that it was a good idea to bring the tiger out of its natural habitat to breed in a zoo? He couldn't actually remember Dingo *actually* saying anything of the sort. Henry began to feel rather ashamed of himself, and he suspected that emotion might be the source of his outburst against Dingo. He had a sneaking feeling that Dingo might be right after all. *Could* the tiger really be happy caged and confined? After all, many zoos had paid dearly for specimens of the thylacine, some even had made attempts at breeding them with a resounding lack of success, but perhaps if the animal were too depressed to breed away from the land and surroundings they knew, they might just refuse to cooperate, no matter how beneficent their gaolers.

Shrugging the tension from his neck and shoulders, Henry started walking again. He fully intended to return to their camp, pack up his rucksack, and go back to the lair where the tigers had left their cubs. He had come here to obtain a breeding pair, and dammit, he wasn't leaving without them! No matter what Dingo said!

His steps flagged once again as inconvenient questions started to rise up tauntingly. Of the two, he was less prepared to live off the land while feeding and caring for two immature predators. So was he to take what little food they had left and leave Dingo to survive on his own? And to feed the cubs, he would need to kill some other animal and probably butcher it as well. They didn't look old enough to cope with a carcass on their own. Another doubt assailed him: were the cubs even of age to survive without their mother's milk?

The thought of the female thylacine's reaction when she returned to find her cubs spirited away caused him yet another qualm, and Henry's steps slowed to the point where he was barely moving. He sat down on a convenient rock to think things out.

From the mother tiger's possible reaction, it was a short leap to what Dingo would think when he found out that Henry had taken the cubs against his desires, along with the food. To how Dingo would feel to know that Henry had started back on his own, after all Dingo had done for him. After all they had shared.

He had never shared his body fully with another man before Dingo. He had never shared *himself* with anyone before. Henry shook his head, finding it hard to believe that he was the same man who only two nights ago had been rendered speechless over the wonder of his two dreams colliding and becoming one. And now everything seemed to be turning into a nightmare.

Whether they ended up taking the cubs—Henry knew they could fight that out, but they would do it fairly and aboveboard. He didn't know if Dingo felt the same way about him now that everything was out in the open, but he couldn't allow this disagreement to drive a wedge between them. He hadn't yet had enough of living his dream. And besides, it wasn't honorable in his book to force the issue this way.

Henry stood up. He had to find Dingo.

He turned to backtrack his steps. If he knew Dingo, the man would be following him to ensure he didn't get lost. Perhaps they could discuss it away from the tigers' lair or shelve the discussion until later so they could follow the tigers and see….

DINGO froze as a haunting shriek of despair slashed through the usual background of jungle noises, silencing all of them. The strangled howl echoed again. For one heart-stopping moment, he thought it might have been Henry, screaming in pain, having stumbled somehow into Hodges's clutches. Then he realized just what it was.

"Tassie!" Dingo exclaimed, barely remembering the need to keep his voice down. He turned and started racing through the jungle toward the lair of the thylacines, leaping over fallen logs and sliding between the trees with the sureness of a man with long experience in the wild.

He caught a flash of white in the distance and hoped that it was Henry running as well, although the other man wouldn't be as quick, not having developed the same level of sure-footedness in the forest.

Without caution Dingo charged into the small clearing where the thylacines had nurtured their cubs in a shallow cave. The two adult thylacines had to be about somewhere but were well hidden as another mournful cry split the air only to break off into ominous silence.

Dingo lifted his head and emitted a howl of rage and despair at the sight that greeted him, the tiny body of one of the cubs swinging at the end of a rope wrapped around its neck, its body quivering with the last desperate attempt to breathe.

He sprang forward, catching the body of the cub and supporting it so he could free it. Frantically he worked the rope loose, but it was too late. The body was still warm in his hands, the eyes half-closed and dull, its teeth bared in a final grimace. It didn't move. Dingo massaged the tiny chest, trying to get it to breathe, but there was no response.

In despair, Dingo sat heavily on the ground, cradling the furry body in his hands.

A PRIMITIVE shriek shook Henry from his thoughts. Without thinking, he found himself running through the trees back to the clearing. His foot caught in a branch, and he crashed to the ground, lying there stunned for a moment.

The thought that Dingo could be hurt—after he had felt that they were being watched—Henry picked himself up and started to run in the direction of the screams. The third one choked off suddenly, but there was a quality to the cry that reassured him that it wasn't Dingo making those horrific sounds. That small comfort was dashed as Henry realized if it weren't Dingo, it had to be the thylacines. Dread gave swiftness to his efforts, and he sprinted for the clearing, stumbling to a halt when he saw Dingo slumped on the ground.

Another step brought him close enough to see that Dingo wasn't hurt himself but was cradling a small, striped body in his two hands.

"Dingo—" Henry managed to croak, his chest heaving with exertion and emotion. "Is it—is it—dead?"

Dingo looked up, and Henry took in a shuddering gasp of air. Dingo's face was wet with tears and his eyes were blind. Henry had never imagined that Dingo, his cheerful, optimistic, courageous Dingo, could seem so desolate, so beaten.

"He killed it." Dingo's voice cracked with emotion.

Henry went to his knees and crawled closer, stretching out one trembling hand to stroke the caramel fur. "Who—how did it die?"

"Hodges. You were right. Somehow he got close enough—he must have seen us," Dingo said. "I was too distracted—I should have—but I didn't—"

Henry put his arms around Dingo's shoulders, holding him tightly. Looking down at the lifeless body lying so still, he felt the hot spill of tears trickle down his cheeks. A cub that he had watched tumbling awkwardly with its siblings little more than an hour ago.... This was ridiculous. It wasn't as if he'd had a personal relationship with the animal, like a pet dog. Blinking fast, he realized the cub was the one they'd been calling Corry, short for Wrong-Way Corrigan, because of its tendency to wander away from its parents. And now it was dead.

"It's not your fault," Henry murmured.

Dingo shook his head hopelessly. "If it's not mine, then whose would it be? No, I've failed, and another of these miraculous creatures is dead because of me."

Henry swallowed hard. "Then I'm as much to blame."

Dingo looked up at Henry as if seeing him for the first time. "Yes."

Oddly, it relieved Henry to be permitted to share some of this burden of guilt. His impulse to apologize and explain would have to be shelved for another time, however. "Dingo, if Hodges is nearby, we can't stay here. We have to lead him away from the thylacines. They must have carried at least one of the other cubs to safety—"

"Two, there were two others," Dingo insisted.

"Two, then. But if we stay here, Hodges might find the parents and the other cubs. Let's not make it easy for him, right, mate?"

Dingo nodded dully, still holding the cub's body as if he could not bear to let it go.

"Dingo, its mother will come for it, don't you think? Put it down," Henry instructed, beginning to feel alarmed by Dingo's continued lassitude.

"She won't let the devils eat it," Dingo confirmed. "She'll nose at it, trying to wake it. They'll—they won't know—why it won't respond—"

"Come along then. We'll put it there, under those bushes, where she can get at it without having to show herself. We have to deal with Hodges," Henry urged, careful not to snatch the body from Dingo even though the need to do something about Hodges was becoming more urgent.

Dingo wiped his cheeks on his sleeve and rose effortlessly from his cross-legged position. He stooped to place the small body where Henry had indicated and stood up, squaring his shoulders. "When I heard the first cry—I thought Hodges had you—"

Henry's heart soared with joy; even if they were both culpable in the murder of the cub, at least Dingo still cared despite their argument. "*I* thought he had *you*. I've never run so fast in my life."

Dingo nodded. His smile was but a tragic echo of his usual cocky grin. "So you came rushing to the rescue again, Dash, eh?"

"Yes." Henry smiled, wondering if he looked as shaken as Dingo. "I was already coming back, though you needn't believe that. I wanted to tell you I was wrong."

"I may have been wrong too." Dingo sighed regretfully. "We had better move, and quick. It's possible that Hodges may have located our camp, in which case, we'll have to rough it. And I want a squint at that guide of his. I can't understand how they managed to track us."

"Can we—can we say a few words first?" Henry asked, hoping that Dingo wouldn't laugh at him.

"I'd like that," Dingo said quietly.

Henry groped in memory for some Psalm that was fitting. "'Be glad, earth and sky! Roar, sea, and every creature in you; be glad, fields, and everything in you! The trees in the woods will shout for joy….'"

The lump in his throat made it impossible for him to go on. He took a deep breath and looked up at the canopy of trees above them, tears shining in his eyes.

"Sleep well, little tiger," Dingo murmured. "Come on, Dash, we'd better go."

Henry swallowed. "Right. Lead the way, Dingo."

As they walked away, Henry heard a soft rustling in the bushes, but he did not look back.

"DINGO."

"Yeah?" Dingo didn't stop walking, slipping silently through the trees.

"We can't just stroll back into our camp as if nothing had happened." As he spoke, Henry realized that they were heading in the opposite direction from their camp. He almost wanted to congratulate himself for recognizing it but felt that he should have caught on quicker.

"We're not."

Henry opened his mouth and shut it again resentfully. Once again, Dingo hadn't shared his plan, so here he was trailing along uselessly behind him, feeling like a clumsy lout because he couldn't manage to move soundlessly like Dingo and because apparently his opinion of what they ought to be doing next made no difference whatsoever as it had not been solicited.

Too busy brooding to pay attention, Henry walked into Dingo when the other man stopped. Dingo reached back to steady him, giving his arm a squeeze, which made Henry feel a bit better.

"Hear anything?" Dingo whispered.

Henry listened. "All I hear are the usual noises."

Speaking quietly, Dingo said, "Might as well take a load off. It's getting dark."

"I realize I don't move as quietly in the dark as you do—" Henry started huffily.

"Dash, we're going to stay here for the night. Even *I* can't prowl around in the dark if I can't see where I'm going. If Hodges weren't about, I'd take the chance perhaps, but as it stands, we rest up for morning."

Dingo started for a huge gum tree and circled it with Henry following him.

"I know I said I thought someone was watching us—"

"I saw him following you *away* from the tigers when you took off," Dingo said. "I tried to draw him off and double back after you. Hodges is out there, but he's behaving oddly. He could easily have shot all the tigers and been done with it. I think he was sending me a message." He found a split in the bark and stooped to peer inside. "I hope you don't mind a few bugs."

"Bugs? What kind?" Henry shuddered. He wasn't particularly fond of bugs at the best of times.

Dingo crawled inside the cavity and turned to stick his head out. "They won't bite. Us, anyway."

"Right." Henry squared his shoulders and crawled in after Dingo, surprised to find such a hollow inside the tree. It felt warm, almost humid compared to the chilly night air outside. "Who made this?"

"Nobody, it happens naturally as the tree ages," Dingo explained. "At least we'll be out of sight, and we can both get some rest."

Henry's eyes adjusted to the gloom, and he could just make out that Dingo was holding his arms out invitingly.

"Get over here, you nong."

Gratefully Henry nestled into Dingo's embrace and slid his arms around Dingo's waist. He was quite certain that he needed the comfort of the other man's arms tonight, and the way Dingo was holding him, he suspected that Dingo might as well.

"What do you suppose Hodges is trying to tell you?" Henry asked after racking his brain in vain.

"If I knew that...."

Henry could feel the movement as Dingo shrugged. Apparently either Dingo really didn't know or he wasn't going to say. They sat curled together in silence. Henry was convinced that Hodges had killed the cub to draw them out, to find out where they were. And perhaps now *they* had become his prey, rather than the tigers. If so, he had to be toying with them, the way they'd raced through the woods making all kinds of noise. Or perhaps whatever he had planned couldn't be done in front of witnesses.

When the haunting calls of the adult tigers began again, he could easily picture the pair of thylacines, sitting on their haunches, gazing at their dead cub, pushing at it with their muzzles to rouse it. They had to know it was dead; they were predators.

He recognized their voices; even his brief acquaintance enabled him to tell their calls apart. The male made little noise; it was mostly the female who mourned. The jungle was silent, save for the unearthly cries, as if all stopped to respect the tigers' grief.

He'd come here to save the tigers and instead, one was dead. Guilt consumed him; if he hadn't insisted on coming here, would that have saved the life of the murdered cub? Hodges would most likely have stayed out of the jungle if he hadn't been following them. The thought that he might be unwittingly to blame crushed Henry.

The only thing that would be worse was if Dingo—cold fingers of fear squeezed Henry's heart. Hodges was still out there.

HENRY woke early, glad to remain in the circle of Dingo's arms until he awoke as well. Dawn filtered uncertainly into the center of the tree, and Henry could see daylight where there were a few holes. Finally Dingo gave a snort and sat up suddenly, wrenching himself out of Henry's hold.

"Morning," Dingo said gruffly, and Henry was reminded of his father's observation that he was not a morning person 'til he'd had his coffee. Resolutely he pushed the thought of coffee and food away, trying to ignore the gnawing pit of his stomach.

"What do we do now?"

"We have to keep Hodges away from the tigers." Henry's question seemed to have the effect of sharpening Dingo's wits, although not his stomach, which grumbled ominously. "And we need some food."

Henry nodded. "Should we circle back to our camp?"

"Probably not the best plan. I doubt Hodges could find it on his own, but for him to have followed us this deep and high onto the mountain, his guide has to have some skill."

Henry could barely see Dingo's face, but he could hear the grim tone in his voice. "So we're dodging two men out there."

"Maybe more, but first things first. We need some breakfast."

Dingo moved to block the light coming from the entrance, presenting Henry with a splendid view of his arse, if it hadn't been to dark to see or if Henry had been in the mood. Right now, food was more of a priority. He didn't question Dingo; their journey had given him plenty of reason to trust the other man's resourcefulness.

As he followed Dingo out of the tree, Henry suppressed a moan and stretched to his full height, his muscles sore and cramped from spending the night in tight quarters.

"Wait for me here."

"Where are you going?" Henry demanded, his voice rising in fear. What if Dingo took it into his head to go after Hodges alone? He was fully capable of it, and Henry wasn't going to be left behind and protected like that.

"I'll be back in a tick," Dingo said. "Don't worry."

Henry had to admit that he still couldn't move like Dingo as he watched the other man slip through the trees. He listened for any sound that might indicate that they were not alone.

A twig snapped behind him, and Henry jerked around to find Dingo emerging from the brush, his hands cupped as if he were carrying something. "Dig in."

Henry reached for the pink berries immediately, finding them tart and sweet. "What's that lump?"

"Better you don't ask. It's called bush bread." Dingo took a bite and chewed.

Henry steeled himself to try it. "It really does taste like bread. What is it?"

"A fungus." Dingo grinned at the grimace on Henry's face.

The two men ate quickly, and then Dingo led the way to a rock with water dripping from it. When they'd drunk their fill, Henry asked, "What do we do now?"

"We have to split up," Dingo said. "Hodges seems to be more interested in what we're doing than the tigers. If we can lead him further into the forest, maybe we can… discourage him."

Assimilating the dire implications of that statement, Henry asked, "And what about his guide?"

"Maybe we can reason with him."

"Get rid of him too?" Henry growled.

Dingo sniggered at Henry's bloodthirstiness. "Bribe him to keep his mouth shut. After all, he's probably only in it for the bounty."

"It seems like Hodges has anything *but* the bounty on his mind. The tigers aren't that plentiful any more, and they're well away from the farms up here," Henry argued. "Hodges has gone to a great deal of trouble to keep tabs on us."

Dingo looked away. "Let's just say I've known him a long time."

Henry didn't want to think that this meant what he thought. "You mean you two…."

Dingo looked at him kindly. "You have to stop doing that, Dash. I really don't have quite the checkered past you're imagining for me. It's nothing like that."

"We'd better get going," Henry said, feeling the heat color his face.

"I'm going to head for our camp. I need a gun and my compass. You head northwest, that way, toward the Tenna River. There's a good chance that after he chased the rumored tiger sightings to Maydena he followed the river inland. He always pitches his camp too close to the water. Maybe you can nip back ahead of him to warn me if you find him heading back this way."

"Right," Henry said confidently, remembering the map Dingo had sketched in the dirt for him the day before, but then he hesitated. "Then what do I do if I find him? I mean, should I confront him?"

"No, of course not, it's too dangerous. Wait for me. I'll find you. We'll face him down together." Dingo gave Henry a wink and started to walk away.

Henry watched him go instead of striking out on his own, and he was glad he did, because Dingo turned and came back, enveloping Henry in a tight hug.

"Stay safe," Dingo instructed.

"You too." Henry didn't want to let him go, but he felt a bit better. This time he turned and headed toward the Tenna River instead of watching Dingo walk away from him, trying not to think that it might be for the last time.

HIS slow progress frustrated him, but Henry tried to imitate Dingo as he moved toward the river. He stayed under the cover of the ferns, avoiding dried sticks or leaves that might give away his position. He paused frequently to listen. That eerie feeling of being watched hadn't returned, but he was taking no stupid chances. While he walked, Henry couldn't help thinking about how the goals of this expedition changed hourly. The main goal to locate the living animals had been achieved, although it seemed that not only circumstances but Dingo himself stood in the way of bringing the animals out of the forest.

Now it was all about staying alive and keeping Dingo alive as well. Henry couldn't allow himself to even contemplate the fact that they had become lovers; the dread of losing Dingo pierced his heart with a pain more intense than he had ever felt in his life. Resolutely he pushed the thought away. If they were to survive, he would have to stay focused on the task at hand, although if Hodges had by some chance decided to retreat by the river, Henry wasn't exactly sure of what he could do to prevent it. Or if he should. At least he would know where Hodges was, though.

The sound of water became louder as he drew closer, rising from a hush in the distance to a more discernible rushing noise. It had the effect of blotting out the other noises in the forest, and Henry paused more frequently, stepping carefully through the brush so as not to fall into a trap. Nonetheless, he continued on his way, walking as quietly as he could.

He pushed his way through a dense group of ferns and realized he had come to the edge of a small crevice, much like the one he'd fallen down when he first came face-to-face with the thylacine.

Henry dropped to his knees and backed into the ferns, lying on his stomach to survey the bank of the river that lay on ground some ten feet lower than his position. He had, against all expectation, found Hodges's camp, although it was more due to luck than skill.

The camp bore no relation to Dingo's, with his discreet habit of tucking his tent between trees. Hodges apparently enjoyed traveling in style; his tent was easily four times the size of theirs. Brush and foliage had been cleared away, and blackened rocks were placed in a circle around a pile of ash. There was even a folding camp chair set up by the big tent. A smaller tent was set up a fair distance from the river, close by the trees. And the river was much bigger and faster than the Styx, although the water was the same amber color, like tea.

Henry realized that although he was hidden from the camp where he was, he might be spotted by anyone coming up on the camp from behind him. He briefly considered climbing a tree, but the thought of being trapped up there with nowhere else to go, especially considering Hodges carried a gun, shot that idea down. He tried to think of what Dingo would do and gazed about him for inspiration, only then recognizing that he was actually quite well hidden. The ferns were dense and camouflaged him well. If necessary he could always make a run for it.

He settled in to wait, for it appeared the camp was empty. He must have nodded off briefly, because he found himself jerking awake in time to watch three men return to the camp. *Three!* Henry almost bobbed up in his surprise but remembered to keep still. Hodges didn't look around, but the other two men seemed much more aware of their surroundings.

Hodges wore his habitual expression of disdain and handed his rifle to one of the men, immediately sitting down in the lone camp chair. The other two men wore sullen expressions, but they got to work at once, building a fire, fetching water, and starting to prepare a meal.

From where he lay, Henry couldn't hear their quiet exchange, but he suspected that the two men were probably local guides, not government agents. Unlike Hodges who was clean-shaven, their jaws were dark with several days' growth of beard and their clothing was poor.

Hodges accepted a plate of food and a smoking tin mug from the stouter man, not bothering to thank him.

Henry's stomach growled as he watched Hodges eat his fill in silence. Then Hodges stood up and retrieved his rifle. "Stay here," he commanded loudly.

"Here, Hodges, where you going? It's not safe to wander about alone in the forest," the thin guide said ingratiatingly.

"It's *Mr.* Hodges to you, and it's none of your business. Stay here and guard the camp in case Chambers happens upon it," Hodges barked.

"Yes, sir, *Mr.* Hodges, if you say so."

"I do say so, and as I'm paying you quite handsomely, you'll do as I say." He paused to ascertain the two men's compliance before striding out of the camp.

Henry moved restlessly, wondering if he dared follow Hodges or whether the two men would notice him if he moved.

"I don't like this, Ev," the thin guide said.

"Shh, Larry. He might hear you."

Larry shook his head. "There's something bleeding wrong here. He asks us to lead him to the tigers, but after we kill that first old bugger, we walk right past three more of them 'til he spots them other two fellers. We're spending more time slipping about on their trail than looking for the sodding tigers. I'm beginning to wonder if our man is really a government agent at all."

"I came up here for the bounty," Ev grumbled. "A pound a head those tigers are worth. He didn't say nothing about other fellers competing with us."

"They're not. They ain't doing no shooting, except with their bleeding camera. And if you were to ask me, I'd say *Mr.* Hodges is after them. And all that screeching today! What was that about?"

"Didn't seem like he shot anything, did it?" Ev asked uneasily.

"I didn't hear a shot. So why did he make us stand there facing the other way?" Larry poked viciously at the fire. "I don't like this. Not one bit. Whatever *Mr*. Hodges is up to, he'll have to do it without me."

"What're you doing?"

Larry got up and went into the small tent without answering, coming out in a few minutes with his pack. He slung it onto his back and asked, "Coming, Ev?"

"He's only paid us half yet."

"I got a bad feeling about this, and I got a family. Half'll feed them better than none and me gone missing to boot." Larry pulled on his hat. "I'm going. *Mr.* Hodges can maybe get those other two to guide him back."

"Wait for me." Ev went into the small tent and presently threw out his pack. Crawling out, he stooped to enter Hodges's tent, emerging with the skin of an adult thylacine, stuffing it into his pack.

Henry gasped in dismay at the sight of the empty pelt.

"Let's go then."

"You're not taking it—"

Ev glared defiantly at his friend. "I come up here to hunt tigers for the bounty. I'm not leaving without this one. I found him fair and square, for all Hodges was the one to put a bullet in him."

"Hodges ain't going to like that," Larry said.

"He ain't here to speak his piece, is he?"

"You have a point."

A small part of Henry pitied Hodges for being abandoned. But another part of him was grateful when the guides disappeared from his view, slipping into the forest. At least now he could get away from here. He had to find Dingo. He had to warn him.

For the first time, he wished he were armed with a gun rather than a camera.

DINGO felt relieved that he'd convinced Henry to go to the river. He'd done what he could to protect the other man without letting on, and if the worst happened, Henry could simply follow the river downstream to make it back to civilization.

Firmly he told himself that they would get back safely *together.* He wasn't going to leave Henry to try to survive on his own. Although he himself could live off the land indefinitely, he cursed himself for rushing after Henry so impulsively that he hadn't given a thought to grabbing his pistol. That and ammunition would be a necessity, and a canteen and food would be handy. Ground sheet, blanket, and extra clothing could all be left behind, even though he grinned to think how rank they would both smell if they made it out. *When* they made it out.

Pure determination kept him going, and it was slow, careful work to hike to the spot where they'd left their things. Dingo spied out the camp from every angle before deciding upon his approach, cursing himself for having been so careless as to simply leave their things in plain sight although their camp was difficult to find. *Make it easy for Hodges, why don't you, you idiot?* he taunted himself.

Nothing had been moved. And there was no way he could reach what he needed without coming out from under the cover of the brush. He would have to take the chance.

He stooped by his pack, reaching for the box of ammunition, when suddenly a crushing blow hammered his wrist. He caught the gleam of the barrel of a rifle, but despite the pain flooding his senses, Dingo dropped and rolled into the bushes, regretted it instantly when his movement sent new pain shooting through his wrist.

A mocking laugh emanated from behind the tree. "Where's your pretty little Pom now, Dingo?"

25. HODGES LOSES COMPOSURE; DASH AND DINGO DO NOT

DINGO started to crawl, knowing that Hodges couldn't see him, but froze when he heard a soft rustling in the brush. If Henry blundered in upon this scene, he wouldn't have only himself to rescue, and Dingo would bloody murder Hodges before he'd see him hurt his lover.

Adrenaline surged throughout his body, but he remained motionless, unable to do anything to save the man he cared so deeply for. He decided he had to take a gamble and distract Hodges.

"Fuck off, Hodges; you'll have to make do with me. I sent him back, and he's gone down river. You'll never catch him."

After he spoke, Dingo moved quietly to a different spot so that Hodges couldn't locate him by sound, getting to his feet behind a large tree.

"Tsk, tsk, had a lover's quarrel?"

Dingo watched through the leaves as Hodges raised his gun and put a bullet into the bushes where Dingo had been.

"I'd quite hoped to find the two of you together. Be that as it may—" Hodges took a step to his right, trying to locate Dingo through the leaves.

"It was a cub—a baby!" Dingo moved as soon as the words were out of his mouth, crouching behind a rock for cover.

"Oh, dear, you're breaking my heart." Hodges raised the rifle to his shoulder, firing at the spot where Dingo's voice had last come from. "Wild takes to wild, doesn't it, Dingo? You were always a sucker for those ugly, useless beasts. At any rate, I need to—" Hodges spun on his heel and put two shots on either side of the rock where Dingo was hiding. "You know you won't get away this time, not with a broken arm."

HENRY heard shots in the distance and started to run, his heart thundering in his chest. At first he thought that perhaps Dingo had fired the shots to bring him to his side, but then he shook his head. Dingo wouldn't do that, not unless he was in real trouble. He heard voices near their camp and slowed down to reconnoiter. One of the voices he recognized as Dingo's; the other had to be Hodges.

Picking his way cautiously, Henry snuck up on the clearing, suppressing a gasp of dismay at the sight of Hodges turned away from him, holding a rifle pointed into the underbrush.

A chill ran down Henry's spine. He crouched lower and bit his lip savagely to keep from making a sound at the sight of a bit of striped fur hanging from Hodges's backpack, imagining that the man had circled back and filched the dead cub from its parents, brutally stuffing the dead body unceremoniously inside. Or had Hodges managed to kill yet *another* tiger?

Henry caught the echo of Dingo's voice and then heard Hodges casually taunting Dingo about a broken arm before shooting wildly into the trees. The rage boiling within him fueled his energy as he rose up from his crouch and ran forward, flinging himself bodily at Hodges, hitting him squarely across the back, hoping desperately that his gun was not aimed at Dingo.

His momentum carried him off Hodges's body when they both fell and made him roll away into the brush. He managed to spot Hodges vanishing into the forest and heard Dingo yell, "Run for it, Dash! Save yourself!"

Henry leaped up and plunged after Dingo. The close press of the bushes slowed his progress, and he struggled through them without heeding the long thorns tearing at his shirt and piercing his skin. Both Dingo and Hodges were instantly obscured from his view, but he realized that they were heading northwest toward the Tenna River. At least he knew where *that* was. He forced his way out of the bushes and started after them, knowing that eventually they would come out at the edge of the river. Hodges couldn't afford to allow them to stumble upon the two guides he'd left behind, though he did not know that they'd deserted him.

With Dingo's last words echoing in his ears, Henry tried to move quietly through the jungle, finding it nearly impossible in the thick underbrush, especially while distracted at the thought of Dingo trying to outrun Hodges with an injured arm.

Henry started to run once again, sharp twigs whipping his cheek. He flinched and reached out to brace himself against a tree, only to find his hand plunging through the bark to the rotten core. Off balance, he fell and started to roll down a short incline, coming to rest against a rock rather suddenly.

Cautiously, Henry listened to discover whether his noisy, crashing descent had attracted any attention.

Apparently not. Henry picked himself up, groaning from a new collection of bruises, but this wasn't the time to complain. He had to find Dingo. What if Hodges had—Henry bit his lip, reminding himself that Dingo had a knife as well as a gun, provided he'd managed to retrieve it, and was incredibly resourceful besides. Now all he had to do was find Dingo without allowing Hodges to find *him*.

He stopped to orient himself. It would do him no good to panic and get lost. His stomach growled loudly, and he put his hand over it as if he could placate it that way. He didn't have Dingo's expertise in finding food in the forest, and besides, the light was beginning to fail. Henry found it hard to believe that after an entire day the only thing they *had* succeeded at was keeping Hodges away from the tigers… but at what cost?

At this point, Henry didn't even know where the thylacines were. For the first time, he was grateful that he could no longer feel their nearness. His palm felt like it always did before he came to Tasmania, and he feared he might never feel that subtle buzz that alerted him to their presence again. He didn't really deserve to. But it was a price he was willing to pay for their safety.

He stretched his hands out before him; he could no longer see where he was going. Cautiously, he slid one foot at a time along the ground, worried that he might tumble down yet another ravine in the darkness. A step, and then another on solid ground. His foot hit the edge, and he sensed the openness of a drop beneath it. Henry went to his knees, feeling along the ground, even while cringing at the possibility of bugs and poisonous snakes. He had found the ledge that looked out over the Tenna River. Remembering what Dingo had said the night before about crashing around in the dark, he knew that he could go no further tonight.

He backed himself up against a tree and tucked his hands into his armpits. It was cold, especially without the warmth of Dingo's body against his. He'd become so accustomed to the comfort of sleeping next to Dingo; he wondered how he'd manage when he got back to civilization. *If* he got back to civilization. He tried not to think about Dingo wandering around out there with a broken arm and Hodges on his trail and settled in to wait for dawn, hoping that Dingo had managed to get away.

DAYLIGHT brought some small comfort to Henry. He was stiff and cold from huddling all night in one position, but once it was light he spied some pink berries that looked familiar to him. He got up and stretched before trying one. It was sour but edible. He stripped the few that were too high for animals to reach and ate them, thinking about his plan of attack.

He'd heard nothing during the night to indicate that Hodges had found Dingo. And he had enormous faith in his partner; somehow Dingo would manage to keep a step ahead of the agent. Henry knew he could simply head for the river and follow it downstream, but he wasn't going to abandon Dingo. Especially if Dingo needed help.

He knew where Hodges's camp lay, but Dingo didn't. Dingo's stated plan was to keep Hodges away from the tigers. The one place he might expect to find Henry would be where they last camped, therefore that was where Henry had to go.

Of course, he would be careful. He couldn't walk blindly into a trap. Hodges knew where their camp was as well and might be waiting for them. Henry knew how to get from their camp to Hodges's, and he could hear the river, so he decided to go to Hodges's camp and backtrack from there.

Going slowly, he managed to follow the edge of the ravine, although Dingo would have laughed at his pace. He recognized a rock and a tree that he'd passed yesterday and knew he was getting closer.

The sound of the river blotted out the other noises in the forest, and Henry paused often, stepping carefully through the brush so as not to walk into a trap. Nonetheless, he made progress, even going slowly.

When he first saw it, he recoiled in shock, falling to his knees. For one horrible, gut-wrenching moment, he thought the body was Dingo's. He had almost run into it, coming out from behind a tree to be suddenly confronted with the corpse, lashed to a tree. It was the guide Ev, his face purple with pooled blood and set in a contorted grimace of pain. He had nearly bitten through the gag that bound his mouth. A stream of ants marched steadily up the trunk of the tree and swarmed his shirt.

Henry could see why; lashed to the tree, Ev's body had been torn by the teeth of wild animals; his feet were gone and the flesh of his legs was shredded. A knife was still embedded in his neck, and Henry suspected that *someone* had chosen this horrible method of murder, using the man's own blood as a lure for the predators that lived on dead flesh. And there was only one person who could be that someone.

Ev's pack lay open on the ground, his meager belongings strewn about, but the pelt of the thylacine he had stolen was gone. If Hodges had decided to murder him simply for taking one pelt worth a pound at most, he couldn't possibly allow Henry and Dingo to leave the forest alive. He would have to ensure that all witnesses to his crime could tell no tales, and he wasn't worrying about the killing of the tigers; after all, he did that with the good will of the government.

If this was the way Hodges's brain worked, then he and Dingo were in even greater danger than they had suspected. Henry stood motionless, feeling that he should do something, search the man for identification for his next of kin, release the body so it could be buried. Then he shook himself from his abstraction.

The other guide, Larry, was still unaccounted for, although perhaps Hodges also had him strung up somewhere to another tree. And of course, Hodges himself was also out there somewhere.

Perhaps now Dingo would realize how he'd underestimated the man.

For the first time since they had split up, Henry lost his head and began to run. The grade leading up to where they'd camped took its toll on his breathing, and he started to gasp, staggering as he ran. The forest seemed alive with menace, crackling noises coming from behind every tree and bush. Fear magnified the sounds until Henry thought he could hear Dingo moaning in pain as he neared their camp.

He stared into the thick brush, hoping he wouldn't confront the sight of Dingo lashed to a tree the way Ev had been, but it proved to be a tactical mistake as he became entangled in what he thought to be the strap of his camera. He brought both hands up to his throat, gasping for air as the strap tightened around his neck, only then recognizing from the rough texture under his fingers that this was a rope.

Henry staggered back, slammed against the trunk of a tree, choking as he tried to lift the loop of rope over his head, but it was pulled taut around his neck until finally he stopped struggling, his fingers still clawing at the rope. He tested it, but the rope had been bound tightly around the tree. If only he'd had a knife, he might have been able to slash through the rope and make his escape.

He waited with a sinking feeling for Hodges to make his presence known. Henry knew well enough by now that Hodges wouldn't simply put a bullet in him from under cover, he would need to gloat over his triumph first. Henry swallowed hard against the rope, so tight around his neck that he feared that Hodges meant to strangle him with it, inch by torturous inch, the better to enjoy his slow death.

"Well, we meet again, Mr. Dash Chambers Henry Percival-Smythe. In search of supplies? Or perhaps you're just wondering where Dingo has got off to." Hodges spoke from a position slightly behind Henry and to his right. "So Dingo was wrong about your little sortie down river. Did you know, somehow I suspected he might have been lying to me?"

Henry tried to turn his head, but the rope was tight against his neck, and it burned when he tried to move.

"Nothing to say to me? No greeting? That's not very polite. I thought the British had better manners than we crude 'colonials'." Clarence Hodges stepped within range of Henry's peripheral vision.

His eyes ached with the strain of staring sideways, trying to see what Hodges was holding in his hands.

"I thought this might come in useful to you," Hodges said with a supercilious smile, his fingers caressing the handle of a knife that Henry recognized as Dingo's.

Henry closed his eyes in anguish for a moment. If Hodges had managed to get that knife out of Dingo's boot, it meant he had to be injured badly—or worse. "Where is he?" Henry demanded hoarsely.

Hodges moved in front of Henry, standing at a safe distance. "Your *cousin* Dingo was very reluctant to give this up to me, until I pointed out that I had you trapped. He seemed fond of you. *Unnaturally* fond of you."

Noticing the use of past tense in referring to Dingo, Henry lunged against the restraint, grunting when the rope dug into his windpipe, stretching his hands uselessly toward the man who held him captive. "If you hurt Dingo—!"

"You'll what? Rend that rope into shreds with your bare hands and come over here to teach me a lesson?" Hodges laughed. It was a chilling sound, echoing unpleasantly in the little clearing.

"If I have to," Henry croaked. He squirmed ferociously against the rope. It burned as it scraped his skin, but he felt a tiny bit of give. If he could keep Hodges talking, maybe he could actually earn some play in the rope and slip out from under it. "Why are you chasing us anyway?"

"I could give you the larger philosophical answer, the lecture about the rights of landowners and the interests of the government in the future development of the country. The Aborigines were bad enough, demanding that their ancestral lands be left alone, but thank goodness we've got past that roadblock."

"What's that got to do with us? Or the tigers?" Henry sputtered, appalled with the man's callousness.

"The tigers are just a detail that needs to be finished off."

"But you're from here! Don't you have any appreciation of the natural wonders—"

"Boring! You academics are all the same, thinking you know all the answers." Hodges's eyes narrowed, and he held the knife up, running his fingers over the shiny blade. "Which leaves the question, what am I to do with you?"

Henry's gaze dropped to the gun in the holster that Hodges wore tight around his waist, and he licked his lips nervously.

"That would be too quick. It wasn't quick with Dingo, and I see no reason you should have an easier time of it." Hodges mirrored Henry's gesture, licking his own lips and baring his slightly pointed teeth. "Besides, here we are in the great outdoors, far from civilization, where the pulse of nature beats raw and wild."

He took a step closer, his eyes raking over Henry's body. Henry became too self-consciously aware of the tear in his shirt as Hodges's gaze lingered there. He squirmed, wishing he could hide himself from the lascivious inspection. Hodges was staring openly at his groin now, and Henry felt a low growl start at the back of his throat.

"I saw you with Dingo, you know. I'd wondered what he saw in you, why he chose you to...." Hodges murmured. "The, ah... *stories* I could tell about you should make you see the wisdom of cooperation. I could use a man like you, intelligent, clever, and completely under my thumb. You never know, you might like... working for me." His voice was throaty, purring with power.

Henry had a moment of madness when he considered acquiescing, if only to get free from the rope around his neck, knowing that he could overpower the other man if only he could get close enough. He stared, mesmerized as Hodges came closer and reached out with a hand curved as if to cup his groin.

Without conscious thought, Henry swept his foot up, trying to nail Hodges in the crotch. Hodges jumped back and turned, catching the kick on his thigh and yelping. He bent over, pressing his hands to his leg, letting the knife fall unheeded to the jungle floor. "You'll pay for that, Smythe! I might have expected that sort of stupidity from Dingo, not you. No one does that to Hodges!"

Henry wondered if referring to oneself in the third person was a sign of either madness or egomania. He didn't like the look that glittered in Hodges's cold eyes when the man finally straightened up.

"Yes, Hodges is going to make you pay dearly for that." Hodges smirked at him, savoring the fact that he had Henry in his power. "Countless expeditions have been lost in this jungle. It's a pity when it happens, but here in the savage wilderness, far away from other people, there are so many… *interesting* ways to die."

"You'll never get away with it," Henry said hoarsely. He plucked at the rope with both hands.

Hodges watched his futile struggle with amusement. "Surely you don't think anyone is going to come looking for you? It will be one more tragic accident, and every time another tourist goes missing, it just convinces other foolhardy souls that it's not worth the trouble trying to chart the unknown."

"You're in the same boat as I am. Your guides are dead, by your own hand! Neither of us will be able to get back without Dingo. We both lost!" Henry said recklessly. He blinked against the unbidden tears that stung his eyes when he hoped that Dingo had met with a quick death, maybe a bullet rather than suffering at the hands of this madman.

"Do you think Dingo is the only man who can find his way in this godforsaken forest? How little you know me."

The angry glint in Hodges's eyes warned Henry that the worst was yet to come. Hodges did not like the implication that Dingo was the better man at *all.* And he was fully capable of venting that fury upon Henry, especially if Dingo had passed beyond his grasp to torment.

Henry had come here, knowing that there was a chance of dying in the jungle; his father had been helpful enough to point that out to him before he'd ever left England. But he'd had such high hopes for this mission when all he'd wanted was to give the thylacine another chance at existence; then he had found Dingo, and it was as if an entirely new world had opened up to him, full of wonder, adventure, and a sense of *belonging*….

The one thing he regretted most of all was that he'd never told Dingo that he loved him. And now it was too late. The thought of that gave him the fortitude to say, "Do your worst."

"Oh, I don't think you'd like that much. My worst is beyond what you could imagine," Hodges said. He sat down on a fallen log and rubbed his bruised thigh absently. "Shooting you would be far too quick. I could just leave you here tied to the tree for the animals. But that would rob Hodges of the pleasure of watching you die. It might take several days, and the thought of your screams... delicious...."

Henry shivered at the slow, cruel smile that spread over Hodges's face, wishing that he hadn't stumbled upon the body of the guide in the forest. He had a good idea that he would enjoy the experience of it even less. A rebellious part of him wanted to point out that Hodges was more than likely to die here with no one to help him get back, but the reality of his plight kept him from doing so. The instability of Hodges's mind was also becoming more and more obvious—had he forgotten that he had already killed Ev the same way? Or had he enjoyed it so much he wanted an encore of the performance? And this time, there was no Dingo to sweep in at the last moment to effect a rescue. Henry was helpless in this man's hands.

He resolved, no matter what Hodges did to him, he wouldn't gratify him by screaming. He gulped in trepidation, hoping he could keep that resolution.

"I expect you're thirsty, after all this running," Hodges said conversationally. "And alas, I've only sufficient water in my canteen to get back to my camp, so I shan't be sharing it with you. Besides, you can't be trusted not to kick me so I mustn't get too close."

Henry wondered where this was going.

"There's a convenient stream nearby, and I'm sure you'd suggest that after I let you drink, I simply refill my canteen and be on my way." Hodges jerked his head in the direction of the water. "But alas. You might be able to work your way free, and although no one would believe your word against mine, I can't have you planting any seeds of doubt about my absolute devotion to the interests of the government."

"That would never do," Henry said mockingly.

"I like your spirit. I suppose I can't persuade you to change your mind about joining up with me," Hodges said thoughtfully.

"I'm afraid not," Henry snarled.

"You should be afraid." Hodges smirked. "As you grow weak from lack of food and water, you won't be able to do much to ward the animals off. I suppose that Dingo told you all about the entertaining way that the devils eat the carrion they find? They like to start at the anus and tear their way into the carcass."

Henry swallowed. "I don't suppose it matters much once one is dead."

"Perhaps he didn't tell you that devils are not terribly persnickety about the state in which they find their meal. Unlike the vivisectionist, they don't require a death certificate before ripping into a body. I've always enjoyed watching them at their food; greedy and savage little beasts, I assure you. I've always wanted to watch them up close. And now you are going to help me realize that ambition."

"You're going to just leave me here?"

"Naturally I'll have to make it easier for them to find you. They can smell blood from over a half a mile away, you know." Hodges looked down at the knife, which lay close to Henry's feet.

Henry's eyes brightened at the sight. If Hodges came closer he would at least have a fighting chance at vanquishing the man.

"I imagine you'd enjoy another chance at kicking me." Hodges stood up and strolled out of Henry's sight, before reappearing with a dead branch in his hands, which he used to drag the knife closer to him. In one smooth movement, he bent to pick it up and threw it unerringly at Henry.

Henry only had time to catch the glint of the metal before the knife was embedded in his thigh. He gasped, just managing not to yelp at the sensation of the blow. It didn't hurt yet, it just felt odd. He looked down in horror as he felt something warm running down his leg.

Hodges seated himself again, his eyes riveted on the blood staining Henry's trousers as if fascinated by the sight of it. "This shouldn't take long. Devils will come out even in daylight if an easy meal is on the menu."

"You're seriously twisted, you know that?" Henry gritted his teeth as the pain finally began; a dull throb that started to pound the beat of his heart into his flesh.

"And those precious thylacines you're so in love with. You think that they would turn down a convenient buffet? Try telling them that you have their best interests at heart when those teeth are ripping your flesh, your blood running over their gaping maw…."

"If you admire them so much, why are you so intent upon killing them?" Henry taunted. "You seem have a lot in common with them." As he expected, the fact that he had discovered Hodges's crime seemed to enrage the man.

Hodges leaped to his feet, his hand on the sidearm in his holster. Henry smiled at Hodges, hoping to goad him into rash action. Perhaps the best he could hope for now was a bullet in the brain; at least it would end the sensation of his leg being on fire.

Hodges controlled himself with a great effort, forcing a smile of his own. "Very clever, Smythe, but all your cleverness will be a moot point once you are dead. After all, if I am the only one to return from the interior, who is going to question my word?"

A rustle from behind him made Henry turn his head. He swallowed hard. It was difficult not to picture his gruesome end, devils tearing chunks of his flesh away while he screamed in pain. There was no question of remaining silent in the face of that kind of agony, no matter what his pride dictated. And he knew that Hodges was correct about the tigers joining in; it truly was a jungle where survival of the fittest ruled.

He caught a slight movement and took in a deep breath. The bushes seemed to be alive with the sound of animals moving restlessly about. Henry couldn't decide whether it was better to just get it over with or if the cover of darkness would be preferable, when he would be unable to see the animals approach. Of course, Hodges most likely would light up the area with his torch for his own amusement. Even now his eyes were dancing with cruel excitement.

"You are a very sick man," Henry said in disgust.

Hodges took a quick step forward, his lips parted and his nostrils flared with rage. "You call *me* sick? After what I saw you and Dingo get up to—"

"Maybe you'd better not get too close. The devils might fancy you for dessert," Henry jibed.

"You're just like Dingo, perverse and unnatural. How his father can't see that in him—" Hodges broke off, beginning to breathe harder in anticipation. He took another step closer clenching his fists, but then he seemed to make a masterful effort to control himself. "I don't smell like blood, as you do. I'll be well away from here before they're through with you."

"Well, I came to Australia for adventure, even though I never meant to end as a meal for a devil," Henry said gallantly. He smiled. "At least it'll be different."

"Damn your impudence! We'll see how adventurous you feel when you're screaming in pain!" Hodges shouted. He started forward, and Henry strained against the rope, nearly strangling himself yet again as something flashed through the air and crashed into Hodges, sending him tumbling into the brush!

26. HODGES MEETS HIS MAKER; HENRY DOES WHAT IS NECESSARY

"DINGO!" Henry shouted, recognizing that sandy thatch of hair he loved so well. His heart was already beating like a trip hammer, but now it was with joy rather than fear.

The two other men had disappeared from his view. To Henry's relief, the rustling in the bushes stilled at the commotion. He could hear sounds of crashing and Hodges's voice shouting in the distance, but he couldn't make out the words. He held his breath, remembering Dingo's injury, hoping it wouldn't hinder him in the fight with Hodges and wondering how he had managed to swoop in like Tarzan.

He let out the breath with an explosive sigh when the underbrush parted and Dingo staggered into the clearing, looking slightly the worse for wear but still wearing his indomitable grin.

"Dingo!"

"Hey, Dash, why are you just hanging about?" Dingo asked casually, but Henry could see his left hand shaking as he cradled his injured wrist.

"I'm a little tied up at the moment," Henry answered, his voice trembling with laughter. "Where is Hodges?"

"Heading for the river, last I saw him," Dingo said, frowning. "He gave me the slip. Damned busted wing."

"Fuck. Think you can cut me loose before he comes back?"

"I lost my knife, mate," Dingo said apologetically.

"No worries." Henry grinned and looked down. "I found it for you."

"I'm going to kill him," Dingo said grimly when he saw the knife still buried in Henry's leg. "As soon as I've cut you loose, I'm going after him, and I'm going to bloody kill him." He plunged toward Henry and paused in front of him. "This is going to hurt."

"No! Is it really? Just get on with it. I'd feel a lot better if one of us were armed." Henry smiled reassuringly at Dingo. "Who's a big girl's blouse now?"

"I never called you a girl's blouse," Dingo protested. "Hold on." He pressed his injured arm against Henry's thigh to hold him still. "Brace yourself."

"Get on."

Before Henry was ready, Dingo had pulled the knife out in one swift, clean jerk. Henry gasped and bit his lip, feeling the surge of blood rush from the wound.

Dingo straightened up and sawed through the rope that bound Henry to the tree. "You'll have to stop the bleeding. I'll help all I can—"

"It's all right," Henry said soothingly. "I can handle it." He took the knife, shiny with his own blood, and sliced through the leg of his trousers above the wound. He twisted the cloth and wrapped it around his thigh as both bandage and tourniquet.

"We'd better get going," Dingo said regretfully. "No telling what Hodges will do next, and he has a gun. Once we're clear, I know some plants—"

"What do you think he'll do next?" Henry asked and took a step, staggering a bit when a sharp pain stabbed through his leg.

"He'll come after us. His obsession, whatever it is, amounts to a monomania, and he can't let us get back to Hobart to tell our tale. After all, he attacked us without provocation," Dingo said. "It would be two against one this time."

Henry stopped limping and put his arms around Dingo. "I thought he'd killed you."

"I'm a bit harder than that to knock off," Dingo boasted, but his eyes were filled with emotion.

Their lips met in a quiet kiss of reassurance and thankfulness that they were both alive and together again. Henry pulled away and rested his forehead against Dingo's. "What do we do now?"

"Come on, we need to fix you up first, you can't go romping through the forest bleeding like a stuck pig," Dingo said, putting his good arm around Henry's waist and pulling him away from the clearing.

"And you," Henry said. "Is there anything left of our camp?"

"Yes. I'll bet that's where Hodges is headed to wait for us to show up," Dingo said grimly. "But we have to risk it. We need a gun."

"I found Hodges's camp, and his guides… have decamped." Henry bit his lip. "Dingo, I think he killed one of them—maybe both—I came across the body—lashed to a tree—"

"Damn. He's gotten more reckless than I suspected." Dingo helped Henry limp along and waited for his partner to say something.

"Reckless?" Henry asked. "He should be in Bedlam." He noticed Dingo staring at him. "What is it?"

"Aren't you going to tell me you told me so?"

Henry chuckled painfully. "Do I have to?"

"No, you were right. I suppose I just got used to him."

"I don't think I can go much further," Henry said. He was suddenly feeling unutterably weary, but he chuckled with the sheer pleasure of seeing Dingo again, feeling his arm, warm and strong around him after believing him to be dead.

"Sorry, love, I should have thought—" Dingo led Henry to a fallen tree, helping him down to sit. "I have to get my hands on a gun. You stay here; I'll be right back."

"What if Hodges comes back and I'm sitting here like a rabbit blinded by headlights?"

"I don't think he'll suspect we would come here, but point well taken. We'll find you a hideout, where you *must* wait for me," Dingo said. He paused. "Could you shoot him if you saw him?"

Henry's face was troubled as he shook his head. "I don't think so."

"Well, it's probably a moot point anyway, seeing as we don't have a gun. He's probably licking his wounds and contemplating his next move. I did manage to get in one or two good punches. He squealed like a little girl before he gave me the slip," Dingo said. He gave Henry a hand up.

Henry couldn't prevent himself from dragging his leg a bit. The pain was made worse by the haunting dread that taking care of him could make Dingo vulnerable to Hodges. Henry didn't think the government agent had given up that easily. Dingo seemed to know Henry was flagging. He led the way into a clump of ferns that clustered at the base of a tall tree. "I'm sorry, this is the best I can do for now."

Henry peered through the green leaves. They were so dense he couldn't see past them. "I'll be fine here, Dingo."

"Look, we only have one knife between us. Have you ever thrown a knife before?" Dingo asked.

"No, have you?"

"Of course," Dingo said, as if it were a primary skill taught in Australian schools.

"It must be an Aussie thing. Hodges was pretty good with it," Henry said, grimacing as Dingo helped him slide down the tree to sit on the ground.

"Not as good as I am," Dingo bragged.

"How are you going to throw a knife with your left hand? I'm pretty sure you've a fracture at the least," Henry protested.

"I'll manage. Trust me. I'll be back soon. Just wait for me here. Stay put, I need to know where you are when I'm on the move."

"Go."

"I'll hurry."

Henry nodded wearily. The throbbing in his leg made him feel he couldn't take another step right now anyway, at least without the provocation of imminent danger. "I'll wait for you right here."

The flash of Dingo's grin showed he appreciated the faint humor, and he hurried off, making far less noise than the two of them had while struggling together. Henry allowed the tension to drain from his muscles. At least blood was no longer running down his leg, but he knew that before long, the carnivores of the jungle would scent the dried blood on his trousers, and he would become an object of intense interest. Much as he longed for another glimpse of the tiger, he vastly preferred to view the animal from other than the position of potential prey.

His head sagged and then jerked up at a sudden sound. Henry felt he owed it to Dingo not to nod off in comfort while the other man was doing all the work in what had become a struggle for their own survival. Suddenly, he wondered at the wisdom of simply giving up and sitting amongst these ferns to await Dingo's return. What if he didn't return? At this point Henry had little hope of getting out of the jungle on his own, without a compass or having to elude Hodges.

A sudden rush of adrenaline energized Henry. He stood up and looked around. The rustling noises that had ceased with their arrival were beginning to manifest again.

He realized that he'd been stupid to buy Dingo's story of going after the gun. It must have been the pain that clouded his head, for he knew now, as clearly as if Dingo had laid out his plan, that he had gone to track Hodges down, to put a stop to him.

With a surge of energy he'd thought was beyond him, Henry started away from his haven, keeping under the cover of the trees as much as he could, and headed toward their camp.

Fear for Dingo lent him strength, and he was barely limping in his effort to close the distance between them.

The murderous plan that would have horrified him only weeks ago seemed reasonable, if savage, considering the malign intent Hodges had revealed to him. A bullet to the brain seemed a clean end compared to what Hodges had designed for his own death, but Henry could not reconcile it with his conscience to force that solution onto Dingo. He must not bear the burden of this by himself; they were partners. And if Hodges had to die that they might live, Henry would shoulder his share of this burden.

He knew that he was going in the right direction. There was no trail he could see, but he had learned enough from Dingo that he'd begun to notice the different shapes of the trees. The forest was no longer an indecipherable green maze to him. He recognized the rock that looked like a kangaroo, and the gum tree with the dead branch hung up in it. Ahead of him lay the sheltered spot where they had made camp.

He peered through the dripping veil of foliage and saw Dingo bent over, searching through their scattered belongings. There was no sign of Hodges. He paused, listening, but there was no sound other than that of the birds and faint noises Dingo made as he picked up the pistol.

Henry stepped out from under the trees. "Dingo."

Dingo stood up, his face grey when he saw Henry. "What are you doing here?"

"I came to help you."

Their voices were barely above a whisper. "I don't need help," Dingo said. He hurried to Henry and forced his fingers around the butt of the gun.

"This isn't safe. You must come away," Henry insisted, unable to explain the source of his unease.

Dingo bent down again to pick up a box of cartridges. “I haven’t found the compass yet. We need it.”

“Not if we stick together—” Henry stopped speaking, listening to decipher whatever the sound had been, for it was not one he’d become attuned to during their expedition.

It was the click of metal on metal.

Dingo opened his mouth to argue, but Henry froze, sensing movement in the jungle beyond him, before snapping, “Get down!”

Instead of obeying, Dingo’s head whipped around, and he found himself staring into the end of a rifle barrel with Hodges’s grinning face behind it.

“I might have known I would find you two perverse lovebirds together.” Hodges licked his lips, looking at Henry. “I’ve been sitting here waiting for you. You’re late.”

Dingo leaped for him, and Hodges’s rifle blazed fire from the end of the barrel at the same time that Henry raised his gun and put a bullet unerringly between Hodges’s eyes, without thinking about anything other than saving Dingo’s life.

Henry stood there trembling, his arm straight out in front of him holding the smoking gun, unable to turn away from Hodges’s body, staring sightlessly at the sky with three eyes instead of two.

Dingo shakily got back onto his feet and came to him, gently prying the gun loose from his fingers. “You did what you had to, Henry. It was him or us.” He put his arm around Henry and turned him away. “Let’s get going. The devils will take care of him.”

Henry came to himself with a start. “He shot you!”

“He shot *at* me and missed. He was always a lousy shot,” Dingo said soothingly.

“Your wrist—”

“It’s fine, Dash.” Dingo grimaced at the weight of the gun, and Henry took it from him, putting it into his pocket.

“I’ll splint it for you.”

“Right. There are some dry sticks over this way.”

Henry realized Dingo was trying to get them moving away from Hodges’s body. Suddenly he felt he couldn’t put enough distance between them and the man who had hunted them so relentlessly. "All right, let's go." The burden of taking another man's life weighed upon him heavily, even though he knew he had to do it in order to save Dingo. That didn't make it any easier, though. He saw the hole appear in Hodges's forehead again and replayed the body falling soundlessly to the forest floor. Did he look like he had been surprised at being bettered in the end? Henry could barely see him, all he did was keep falling again and again.

"Come on, Dash," Dingo prodded him.

Henry shook his head clear, pushing away the vision although he wasn't sure how long he would be able to keep it at bay. He attempted not to limp, but all at once his wounded leg felt swollen and hot. He was grateful for the tourniquet but wondered how far they would make it in their battered state. "I found Hodges's camp. I can take you there."

"Blind leading the blind, eh?" Dingo grinned. "Might as well take advantage of the set-up Hodges left behind. We'll sleep in comfort tonight before the trek back."

Henry smiled but shook his head; sometimes it was still uncanny to him how Dingo seemed able to read his thoughts.

A sudden noise behind them and a blood-curdling shriek reminded Henry why they needed to keep moving, before full darkness fell.

"Devils found him," Dingo said matter-of-factly. "They'll take care of the evidence."

"If only every criminal had a clean-up crew like that."

"Henry, don't do that to yourself."

Henry repented at he looked at Dingo's haggard face. They had enough to contend with to ensure their own survival; he didn't need to berate himself right now. There would be plenty of time for penance later.

"He was camped by the river, like you said he would." Henry quickly described the general direction.

"Are you sure you can make it that far? I should have—" Dingo cut himself off.

Stealing a glance at his lover, Henry felt a glad little leap of his heart at Dingo's thundercloud expression. "I'm fine," he said. "Let's keep moving."

They hobbled through the underbrush, making more noise than they should have, but with both of them injured, it was tough going. Henry led Dingo to the Tenna River, and Dingo had to chuckle wearily when he saw the quantity of equipment Hodges had lugged along with him. Even with the guides, it had to have been hard going. "Too close to the water. Typical."

"There's one guide unaccounted for. He's likely to come back here, you know," Henry pointed out.

"Not if he witnessed what Hodges did to the other guide." Dingo shook his head and smiled, trying to distract Henry. "Hodges sure liked to travel in style. How do you fancy tinned corned beef for dinner?"

Henry hobbled to a folding camp chair that Hodges had left by the firepit and sank into it with a sigh. "I don't care. I could eat a—a roasted tarantula."

"Too bad, no tarantulas here, or I'd have a shot at catching one for you." Dingo bent to enter the tent, and Henry heard him grunt in satisfaction. He backed out, gingerly holding a loaded pistol in his injured hand and dragging a lumpy pack behind him. "Tins of food," he said briefly. "I'll make a fire."

"Let me take care of your wrist first," Henry said.

Dingo sighed wearily. "Yeah, I could use a sit down too." A flash of his old impudence showed momentarily as he grinned at Henry. "What'll it be? The other leg of your trousers or a sleeve from your shirt to bind me up? I'd like to see a bit more skin."

Henry snorted with laughter, wondering how he could laugh so soon after killing a man. "Well, seeing as I've already given up one leg, how about giving up a bit of *your* shirt?" He dragged himself to his feet, waving a hand hospitably at the stool.

"Done!" Dingo let himself down gingerly on the camp chair, holding his injured wrist. "At least the sleeve."

Henry found several straight branches and carried them back to where Dingo was sitting. Dingo reached up with his good arm and steadied Henry so he could sit in front of him, ignoring the pain from his wound for the moment. Henry stretched his wounded leg out in front of him and let out a sigh. Taking out the knife, he trimmed the branches of twigs and bark till he had smooth sticks to work with.

"All right, let's see to that wrist." Henry used the knife to cut off Dingo's sleeve, and tore it into strips.

Dingo held his arm out. "Just give it a yank, and the bones will go back into place."

"I know that's quicker, but if you can bear it, I can do it with less trauma to the surrounding tissue." Henry's slender fingers caressed Dingo's swollen wrist, probing gently to feel the fracture.

"Do what you must." Dingo set his teeth, determined not to cry out.

Henry massaged his wrist, manipulating the bone and gently pushing it back into place.

It hurt Dingo, but not like a brutal yank would have done. He worried his lower lip between his teeth as he watched Henry's face, totally absorbed in his task. "Where did you learn to do this?"

"My grandfather was a doctor," Henry replied. "Sometimes I used to help him."

"Really?"

"Well, I'm sure I wasn't that much help, but he would let me roll bandages and sterilize his instruments," Henry said, smiling. "He showed me a few things, though."

"He sounds like a kind man."

"He was. He was very kind to me."

"He liked having you around." Dingo smiled at the surprised expression on Henry's face as he looked up from his task. "Most men wouldn't take the time to show a boy how to do their job if they didn't like him."

"Thank you for that." Henry returned to his work, feeling when the ends of the bone were properly in place. "You're lucky Hodges fractured this cleanly, although I'm sure it wasn't his intention." He reached for his splints, holding them in place as he tied the strips of Dingo's sleeve around them.

"Your granddad doesn't sound like your father."

"He was my mother's father," Henry said. "A country doctor."

"I thought your father was titled."

"He is. My mother married well." Henry's smile was bitter. "She was ashamed of her father and didn't want us spending time with him. My brother didn't care about him much, but I loved him."

"You take after him," Dingo said.

That surprised Henry. "I'd never thought of that before, but I suppose that I do."

"A kind man," Dingo said pointedly.

Henry knew what he was about, and it touched him. He yawned. "How far must we go tonight?"

Dingo shook his head dismally. "I think we'd better tuck ourselves into a hole and get some rest. I'm no good for too much more. If we're going to make it out of here, we'll need to filch what's left of Hodges's supplies or some other tucker."

"At least there's water." Henry made a cup of bark and limped to where he heard a trickle of water, knowing he'd be unable to balance at the edge of the river to scoop water out. He bent to drink from the rill directly before filling the cup and bringing it back to Dingo.

"I should have gotten that. Your leg—"

"I'm no flipping pansy," Henry joked. "Are we going to stay here, then?"

"Might as well, for tonight."

Henry nodded. He was too tired to think about eating. Dingo seemed even wearier, and he wanted to take care of him.

Without speaking, they seemed to be of one mind that they would not sleep in the tent. Henry pulled out the ground cloth and spread it under an old gum tree where the roots seemed to form a cozy half circle that enveloped them in a welcome embrace.

Henry put his arm around Dingo and pulled him closer to rest his head against his chest. He stretched his throbbing leg out in front of him and leaned back against the tree.

He closed his eyes, wondering if he could sleep.

27. A REUNION BETWEEN FRIENDS AND FAMILY

MOVING softly through the jungle, Jarrah pointed between the trees. "There they are."

"Fuck," Hank said, for no other word would suffice. The sight of the two men sleeping, their clothing torn, their faces dirty and shadowed with stubble, and the bloody bandage on Henry's leg overrode the discomfort he felt he might otherwise have experienced actually *seeing* his son clasped in another man's arms. "What do you hear?"

"Normal sounds. If Hodges is in the jungle, he's not nearby," Jarrah said. He pushed through the scrim of leaves and went to the two men, kneeling before them to examine Henry's leg.

Hank followed him silently. He felt incredibly useless, but he was profoundly shaken by the drawn look of pain on Dingo's face. The thought that he might have lost his son— "Ants."

"Yeah, we're just in time." Jarrah brushed the insects away from the bandage.

The feather-light touch woke Henry from a deep sleep. He stared up at the two men and started to chuckle. "You'd better not prove to be a hallucination; I should be very disappointed in both of you."

Dingo woke up in response to an inadvertent dig in the ribs from Henry. "Oh, hello, Dad. Harroo, Jarrah."

"That's all you have to say to me? You'd better start explaining all this," Hank said belligerently.

Dingo smiled tolerantly at his father, knowing what was eating at him. "Hodges."

Jarrah unwound the bandage and was examining Henry's wound. "I'll gather some plants and make a poultice. You don't want to get an infection." He stood up and slipped away into the green dimness.

"Your wrist okay?" Hank inquired gruffly.

"Broken. Dash set it."

"Good man." Hank seated himself on the stool and looked down at the two men. "Jarrah said wherever Hodges is, he's not about here. I'm assuming he's responsible for—all this." He waved a hand to indicate their disheveled state. "So where is he? Don't say he managed to trap a tiger and made off with it?"

"Now would I let him do that?" Dingo demanded. "Settle down, old man."

"Then where is he?"

"I killed him," Henry said starkly. His eyes showed the whites skittishly.

"He deserved it," Hank growled, "whatever he did."

"He set up a snare and had Dash roped to a tree. Then he threw a knife into his leg to make him easier to handle. *My* knife!" Dingo snarled.

Henry stared at him for a moment before his lips trembled into a weak smile. "He tried to kill Dingo at our camp."

Hank put a hand on Henry's shoulder in silent sympathy. "You won't believe me now, but you did the right thing. You'll come to realize it."

He watched Henry open his mouth to protest and then close it after a glance at Dingo, who seemed too exhausted to intervene.

Jarrah returned with a handful of greenery and set about making a small fire. Hank took a pot from his pack, and Jarrah went to fill it with water. Henry and Dingo both drank their fill while Jarrah ground the leaves between two rocks. He started the water to heat up over the fire, dropping the leaves in and closing his eyes, muttering something in the foreign tongue he'd used when speaking his dreams.

When Jarrah opened his eyes, he smiled when he noticed the bark cup that Henry had made. "Not bad."

"Do you want an aspirin?" Hank asked Dingo.

"You brought aspirin into the jungle?" Dingo seemed to find that very funny; he started to laugh almost hysterically.

"You never know," Hank said. "Your wrist is swollen."

"I'll take one," Dingo said.

"None for you," Jarrah said to Henry. "Don't want to thin your blood."

Henry winced when Jarrah pressed the smoking mess of green mash against his leg but sighed as almost immediately the pain was lessened. The tingle made him feel better, as if the healing powers of the plants were insinuating themselves into his wound. "Thank you, Jarrah. I keep having to thank you."

"You have some sense." Jarrah flashed his beautiful white smile, and Henry felt as if he had been acknowledged as worthy in some way.

HENRY woke with a start and stared up at the canopy. He felt as if he'd lost hours somehow, but the security of knowing that Hank and Jarrah were looking after them had enabled him to sink into the sleep of exhaustion. The sound of Dingo's voice was comforting even if he couldn't make out the words. He sat up and looked over to where a fire crackled in the pit surrounded by rocks.

Jarrah was cooking something while Hank and Dingo sat close together. Dingo was waving his splinted arm as he explained something, but he looked over at Henry when he moved.

Henry found himself smiling back at the huge grin that came over Dingo's face.

"Haroo," Henry said.

Hank chuckled. "He's becoming a native."

"Hungry?" Jarrah asked.

"Starved."

"Good. You start to recover your strength."

Henry pushed himself up off his elbow and looked around for something to grab onto to get to his feet.

Jarrah nodded to his left. "Use that."

Henry saw that Jarrah had fashioned a rude cane from a branch that bent at a suitable height for a handle. Grateful that he didn't need assistance from one of the others, he got slowly to his feet. His leg felt heavy and numb, and the soreness seemed to make the cut flesh of his wound slide together disagreeably. Henry decided not to dwell on it.

"The devils rejoiced last night," Jarrah commented.

The events of the day before rushed back, overwhelming Henry. Jarrah put a hand up to steady him as he collapsed onto the camp stool without comment. He handed a plate to Henry.

Henry was ashamed of how he gobbled his food, but it felt as if he'd not eaten in days. In between mouthfuls, forgetful of proper etiquette and how he should swallow before speaking, he asked, "What made you come after us?"

"One of your bags was found by a ranger," Hank said. "A bag full of food, I might add, which raised some concern. Jarrah heard about it and contacted me."

"Lucky I have a sense about these things," Jarrah teased.

Hank refilled Henry's plate without him even having to ask. "Just go a bit easier this time, son."

Son. Funny how that sounded more affectionate coming from a man whom he had only just met than from his own father.

"I admit it," Hank said. "I was worried. And it's a good thing, because look at how we found the pair of you."

"We were fine," Dingo said, cheerily lying through his teeth. "Just taking a breather, that's all."

"You looked like you had dug yourselves a hole to die in," Jarrah observed.

"Quiet," Dingo muttered.

Jarrah grinned, indicating he would do no such thing. "Told you I'm the best tracker, didn't I, Dash?"

Henry nodded absentmindedly, still chewing.

"Now, perhaps one of you would like to explain how you let that numbskull sneak up and get the drop on you," Hank demanded.

"We found a tiger family. The mama had three cubs, and the parents decided to move them," Dingo started.

"No doubt because you poked your fat nose into their business," Hank complained. "How often have I told you not to go near them when they're breeding?"

"Hey, she found us!" Dingo protested.

Hank ignored Dingo's interjection. "And therefore you lost all common sense and forgot to look about behind you?"

Dingo looked sheepish, so Henry took up the tale. "The male had moved one cub, and the female set off with another. It was fascinating. I took pictures and we followed them… but we—" Henry broke off, unable to admit that their argument had been the cause of the entire mess. Now he had no doubt that Hodges had managed to locate them from their shouting and had been able to set up the entire trap because he'd lost his temper.

"We hadn't seen any sign of Hodges in a day or two," Dingo said.

"What did he do?" Hank demanded.

The color drained from his face when Dingo told him. "He killed the unprotected cub that was left behind."

Hank remained silent for long minutes. Henry feared further castigation for their carelessness in not guarding the one cub, but finally Dingo's father turned to him. "No court in the land would have condemned him to death, but you did the right thing in executing him. That was murder."

Henry hung his head. "I know," he said softly.

"Not what you did! What *he* did!" Hank exploded. "International zoos pay a king's ransom for the cubs! He could've at least—but he never would. The man was a beast!"

Henry shook his head morosely. It still couldn't be right.

Jarrah asked, "What did he do with the body?"

"We left it for the parents." Henry looked up, startled, and his eyes met Dingo's. "Wait a minute, Hodges had another skin in his pack. Did you find it?"

Dingo shook his head.

Hank said. "I'll bet he kept it to claim the bounty."

Jarrah stood up. "I'll go see."

Hank stood up as well. "Better make sure that soulless devil is truly dead," he growled.

"I'm coming along." Dingo stood up, cradling his injured arm.

"Then I'm going too." Henry struggled to his feet.

"You stay here," Dingo said soothingly. "Your leg—"

"I'm not staying behind again," Henry said. "Where's my camera?" He realized he missed the weight of the camera dragging on his neck.

Hank picked up the camera and handed it to Henry, who put the strap around his neck, caressing it. The films inside the camera might yet be the only proof of the miraculous animal he had seen. He had to have the pictures to prove the success of this journey, even if Larwood were the only one to see them.

Jarrah had not remained to mediate the argument between Henry and Dingo; he was already slipping through the jungle like a shadow. Henry felt that if only he had such prowess, much of what had happened might not have. Jarrah belonged here; he seemed to be part of the jungle, leading the way unerringly to the site of their abandoned camp.

Henry hobbled along behind the other men, trying to keep up. When he arrived at their old camp, Jarrah was surveying the ground, reading the signs of the struggle as Henry might read a book. He followed the tracks to where Hodges's body had fallen.

"Don't look, Dash," Dingo called out.

But Henry had already seen it; the mangled remains of what he identified as a torn human hand, still clutching a pistol, lying on the blood-soaked ground.

Jarrah nudged at the gory meat with his boot, dislodging the gun so that he could pick it up. He took the precaution of wiping off as much of the blood as he could on some grasses that were matted down by the devil's nocturnal feast and stuck the pistol in his belt. He kicked the disembodied hand away. "That'll make a meal for Tassie if he can nip in before the devils."

"Sort of poetic justice," Dingo said. "If Hodges had succeeded in killing us, I'm sure he would have picked off the tigers one by one as they came to feed on our carcasses."

Finding Hodges's rucksack some distance away where the skirmish of the devils feeding had pushed it, Jarrah opened it. He gave an audible sigh as he reverently removed the pelt of an adult tiger. "This one was not a cub, maybe too old to run."

Hank drew closer and put out a shaking hand to stroke the fur, but Jarrah held the furry skin away from him.

Henry watched, fascinated, at the silent confrontation between the two men, their eyes locked together. In that moment, Jarrah's face took on an ancient savagery, as if he wished he could slay Hank and all the white men who had caused the ruination of his land. Then his eyes softened, as if he remembered who Hank was, and he held the pelt toward him.

Hank stroked the lank fur twice, running his hand over the long tail. "He is yours, Jarrah. Thank you for letting me—" Hank turned away abruptly, and Henry caught the glint of tears in his eyes.

When Henry focused on Jarrah again, the tiger's skin had vanished, and Jarrah was fastening his own rucksack. Henry didn't ask, but he understood. The body of the thylacine did not belong to white men. Jarrah would not suffer it to be used as proof that the animal still existed and bred in its jungle home. The thought of the body being put on display as an object of wonder, fear, or loathing went against all Henry believed in, and he was content to leave its fate in the other man's hands. Jarrah would take care of it in his way, whatever that might be.

Henry actually wondered if in focusing solely on the thylacine, he weren't missing a bigger tragedy. Perhaps the Aboriginal people and their customs were equally in need of rescue. Somehow he knew that if he asked, Jarrah would say that the secrets of his people were of no value to the white conquerors and better they not pry into what did not interest them.

In that moment, Jarrah stood on one edge of a great divide, and he, Dingo, and Hank stood on the other, as huge a gap between them as if it were the deepest chasm, never to be bridged.

Helplessly, Henry held out a hand in apology. "I'm sorry, Jarrah."

Jarrah nodded with the innate dignity that always characterized him.

Then he turned back to his task, picking up a pair of bloody boots. Henry felt his gorge rise as Jarrah poked into them with a stick, dislodging the dismembered feet, still clad in socks. "Might as well let the devils have him all."

Unable to bear the grisly sight, Henry turned away to survey the remains of their belongings. In the state they were in, they were in no shape to carry everything out. "So much for leaving no trace of our presence."

"This wasn't precisely part of the plan," Dingo said with a grin. "Allowances can be made."

Silently Jarrah moved about the site, hiding a tattered shirt under rotting leaf debris, where Henry knew with the constant rains they would soon be unrecognizable. Jarrah looked Henry over thoughtfully before he rolled up a torn pair of trousers and put it in his pack.

"Will anyone be able to identify Hodges...." Henry's voice trailed off as he remembered the hand.

"They will not look very hard for him," Jarrah said calmly. "Foolhardy men who venture too far into the jungle disappear all the time. We are dust from the earth, and we return to dust."

"There's—there's another body to take care of," Henry said hesitantly. "Hodges murdered one of his guides and left him for the devils. Over that way."

Jarrah nodded. "Hodges started with two guides. If it makes you feel better, one of them is still alive, heading down river to Maydena. I doubt he will talk much about what happened in the forest, no matter what he saw."

Henry described as best he could where he'd found the man, and Jarrah nodded before disappearing into the trees.

He wasn't gone long. "I cut his body down. I knew him. Not a good man, but not a bad one. He had no family."

Henry nodded, understanding that Jarrah meant to let the man's fate remain a mystery. Ordinarily he might have objected, but he just felt numb, save for his leg.

"We have to get moving," Hank said. "You know the government boys will be hard on my heels. It's not often I come over here to Tassie, and they'll be curious as to why I did."

"Why *did* you come?" Dingo asked.

"Jarrah got a message across to me that you were in trouble," Hank said grimly. "If you *will* get yourself into such a fix, who else is going to come after your sorry arse?"

Dingo grinned. "Mum might."

Hank gave a short bark of laughter. "She might at that." A softer look came over his face. "It's been years since I heard the tiger yipping in the night. I wanted to hear it one more time."

Roughly, Dingo said, "You'll hear it many times more, old man."

Hank chuckled, and Henry was struck again by how alike father and son looked with that mischievous grin.

"At least on the walk back. Come along." Hank hovered close to Dingo as he herded him to the dim trail.

Jarrah helped Henry to his feet. "Put your arm over my shoulder."

Henry shook his head and lifted the cane. “I can make it.”

“You won’t make it very far with only that cane to lean on,” Jarrah said. “We need to move fast to keep Hank and Dingo safe.”

Henry hesitated. His leg was still giving him some pain, although Jarrah’s poultice had worked wonders.

“Sometimes the gift is to the giver,” Jarrah said.

“Very well.” Henry allowed Jarrah to pull him closer, circling his waist with his arm. “Thank you.”

“We thank each other, my brother.”

Sudden tears stung Henry’s eyes. He had not succeeded in bringing back a thylacine, but he felt he had succeeded beyond his wildest dreams in securing something so much more precious. It was holding onto it that could prove more difficult.

“STEADY on,” Jarrah murmured, tightening his hold around Henry’s waist.

Henry nodded miserably. Coming down the mountain had been torture for his injured leg, having to brace constantly against his weight being pitched forward. Henry stabbed the dirt ahead of him with his cane, knowing that if not for Jarrah’s support, he would have fallen a long time ago and simply rolled down the incline in Dingo’s wake.

Up ahead, Dingo seemed unusually quiet, walking behind his father with his arm in a sling. When he’d turned around once or twice to flash an encouraging grin at Henry, his face appeared white and drawn. Henry knew it would have gone hard with them if they’d had only each other to depend upon.

In addition to feeling like an added burden for Jarrah, Henry knew he had to be a particularly odiferous one; he was hot, and sweat was pouring off him. He was tired and his leg hurt.

Hank came to a halt, holding up one hand to warn them into silence. Even Dingo waited patiently while Hank scouted ahead.

“Come ahead. I found a campsite,” Hank announced when he returned. “We might as well make use of it.”

Henry sat down heavily when Jarrah lowered him to the ground. His leg was throbbing and yet numb to the point where he could no longer support his own weight. He watched dully as Hank built a fire using wood that had been left behind. Jarrah disappeared and returned quickly with water. Henry felt he was nothing short of useless, a tenderfoot who even at his best was of little use in the forest compared to the quick ease of the two men.

With a concerned glance, Jarrah set a pot of water to heat by the fire and came to Henry. "A watched pot never boils, Dash. Look away so I can have hot water to bathe your wound."

"My leg itches," Henry roused himself enough to say.

"Where?"

Henry pointed vaguely to the back of his calf.

Jarrah bent to look and made a displeased sound. "Land leech." He went to the fire and brought back a burning stick, holding it close enough that Henry could feel the heat, and smell the singeing of his leg hair. He watched Jarrah apathetically, too exhausted to even move his leg away from the red-hot stick.

Jarrah gave a satisfied nod. "That took care of it. My apologies, my friend. The leeches sense our body heat. With your trouser leg cut off…." He shrugged fatalistically.

Henry couldn't help at all. He simply sat lethargically, allowing Jarrah to unwind the soiled bandage, bathe his wound, apply the poultice, and bandage him again. He stared at the amount of blood Jarrah wiped from the back of his leg.

"The leech injects a poison that keeps the blood flowing," Jarrah explained. "It's not dangerous. It will stop soon."

Henry looked up to see Dingo watching, frustration on his face as Jarrah helped Henry out of his clothing. He mustered the energy to smile reassuringly at Dingo, relieved when the other man's expression lightened. Jarrah ripped his ruined trousers into rags, using them to rinse the dried sweat from Henry's body. He helped Henry into the torn trousers he'd rescued from their camp and replaced his socks and boots.

"I'll rinse the shirt." Jarrah rose gracefully and vanished with it, going to the source of water he'd located, Henry surmised.

He crossed his arms across his chest, made more self-conscious by the fact that Hank never lifted his head from his task of preparing food. Dingo gave him a sly wink, and Henry found himself smiling feebly.

The shirt was cold and damp when Jarrah helped him put it on, but the lower altitude was steamy with humidity, so it was a relief to Henry. A mug of warm broth was put into his hand, and he drank it without question, surprised at how filling it was.

He didn't remember falling asleep.

It was dark when he awoke, except for the dying embers of the fire. He could dimly see Dingo's sleeping face across the clearing, where he was lying near his father. A sudden yearning to feel Dingo's arms around him hit Henry so hard he gasped for breath. The ten feet that parted them could have been ten miles; with Hank and Jarrah there, the casual touches, the kisses, the nights spent curled together were now a thing of the past.

Suddenly Henry knew what Dingo had meant when he'd asked if it were better to know. Now Henry *did* know what it could feel like to be the forbidden lover of another man; once they were no longer alone, they were more alone than ever, confined to secret glances. Even though Dingo claimed that his parents accepted his homosexuality, Henry could sense Hank's discomfort with obvious demonstrations of affection, so gratitude and mere politeness dictated that they refrain.

While he pondered, Dingo's eyes opened, and he gave Henry a look of such longing, he knew he wasn't alone.

Henry whispered the lyrics of the song, *their* song, not knowing whether Dingo could hear him or make out the words from the movement of his lips, but it made him feel better.

No one else must know
The yearning we're concealing
The feelings we can't show
Staying hidden in plain sight
Burning eyes can't help revealing
That we are tigers—

His throat tightened at the last words, and he swallowed hard, unable to continue.

Dingo nodded at him and closed his eyes.

Henry stared into the embers for a long time before he fell asleep again.

DINGO was lying next to him when he opened his eyes. Jarrah and Hank were also asleep on the other side of the fire.

"Haroo, Dash," Dingo said, his voice little more than a croak.

"Haroo, Dingo," Henry replied, his own voice also strained.

"Dash, I'm so sorry," Dingo said, reaching across and entwining his fingers with Henry's. "I promised you adventure, but all I got you were lies and danger."

"I got more than that," Henry whispered. "I got you. And I got to see the tigers. That's worth everything."

"But you thought you were coming to start your career."

"I still could. I have the pictures."

"You can't use them, Dash. It would go against everything we've tried to set up here."

"What have you tried to set up?"

"There are plans in place. Gordon's been working them out for some time now. That's why the thylacines have been tracked. But for it to work, the tigers have to stay where they belong. Not in zoos. Especially not in London, where it's rainy and cold and they'd pine away longing for the Tassie wilderness. It may not be the answer you hoped it would be, but it's the best one."

"Maybe you're right, but it does no good for me and the people *I* have to answer to."

Dingo shook his head. "Always so self-deprecating, Dash. Why shouldn't it? You're backed by the college, and you have a reputation in certain circles, or didn't you know that?"

"What circles?" Henry cried out, exasperated.

"People who want to make sure the tiger lives free and in secrecy." Dingo laughed. "You thought *you* found Gordon Austin, but he was looking for someone like you. It was part of the plan, to find a man of good reputation, bring him here and prove that the tiger was extinct. That way the world would stay out of Tassie and give the thylacine a chance to live in peace."

"And that's all you wanted from me?" Henry asked coldly.

"Until I clapped my eyes on you. Dash, you have to know how I feel about you by now," Dingo said beseechingly. "If I didn't believe in your integrity and honor, I could have led you a merry dance in the forest, and you'd never have set eyes on the tiger. But once I met you and fell in love with you, I wanted to share this with you. There might never be another opportunity for you to see them. And I know you can keep a secret; you have it now, the sight of an animal so miraculous—what is it?"

"You love me?" Henry was smiling.

"Hadn't I mentioned that before?" Dingo started reddening, but he met Henry's gaze faithfully.

"Not really."

"You know, it's customary when one receives a declaration of love to, ahem, reciprocate in some way."

Henry took Dingo's face between his hands and stared into his eyes. "I love you, Dingo Chambers."

"And I love you both," came the voice of Jarrah through the flames. "But you both need to stop gabbing and let a man sleep."

Both Henry and Dingo laughed softly, and soon all three of them were asleep again.

HENRY clamped his jaws in misery. The only good thing was that his leg no longer itched from the leech, but he was tired, filthy, and there seemed no end to the forest. If Jarrah hadn't been helping him, Henry might have been tempted to simply lie down and become a meal for whatever wanted to eat him. He couldn't see that they were making any progress at all.

The other thing that kept him going was Dingo. If Dingo could keep moving, so could he.

He heard and smelled the river before he saw it. And if he wasn't imagining it, Jarrah got them moving a little faster, now that their goal was within reach.

"The River Styx," Henry murmured. It felt like a victory, to be alive, to pass to the other side of the river again.

Jarrah smiled at his words. "The boundary between Earth and the underworld."

Not surprised to hear a classical allusion from Jarrah's lips, Henry managed to grin back. "But which is which?"

"As long as the tigers stay on the other side, they may yet have a chance," Jarrah told him gently.

From there, it wasn't that far to Jarrah's truck, and soon enough they were leaving the natural world and all its wonders behind them.

28. A RETURN TO CIVILIZATION

IF HENRY hadn't been so unutterably exhausted, he might have felt embarrassed to be shown into the best hotel in Hobart in his battered state. His trousers were tattered and filthy, while his shirt was stained with sweat and torn by the branches of the jungle that now seemed loath to let him go.

If not for Jarrah's support, Henry wasn't sure he could have made it up the steps alone. Despite his weariness, he roused himself to mumble, "Jarrah, I can make it from here. Don't want you to…." His voice trailed off as his brain failed to come up with words to express the rudeness of the reality that a man native to this land, who had risked his life to help him, would not be permitted to pass through the front door of the hotel.

In a subservient voice completely at odds with his true character, Jarrah murmured soothingly, "Don't worry, sir. I'll have you to the doctor in no time."

Henry nodded wearily, understanding the cryptic message that Jarrah would be able to pass unmolested if seen to be in service to a white man.

The doctor talked to him all the while that he cleaned and dressed the wound, and Henry nodded blankly at intervals. He was aware of Hank and Jarrah answering questions and asking some of their own, but Dingo was uncharacteristically silent, sitting in a chair and holding his injured wrist.

When the doctor finished bandaging his leg and had said cheerily, "I think you'll do, Mr. Percival-Smythe. Next patient," Henry looked longingly at the chair that Dingo vacated to get onto the doctor's table, but Jarrah guided him from the room.

Henry didn't want to leave Dingo, but he was in no shape to protest, dreading the stairs. He was grateful to find that even in Hobart there was a lift in the hotel, which Jarrah put him into, helping him to lean against the wall before he stepped out.

Henry was wondering exactly what he was supposed to do when he arrived at the second floor, but Jarrah was there when the doors slid open. Apparently the hotel's beneficence only extended so far; once Henry had been patched up, it was decided that Jarrah could perfectly well use the back stairs.

The lift operator gave Henry a supporting hand so that he could totter toward Jarrah. The strong hand gripping his arm was a relief, especially as he had no idea where he was going.

"What room?" he managed.

"I've got the key, sir, don't you worry about anything," Jarrah said, steering him down the hall to a room at the end.

When the door was unlocked and closed behind them, Henry muttered, "Sorry, Jarrah."

"No worries."

Jarrah took Henry's rucksack and propped it against the wall on the far side of a dresser, where it could not be seen from the door. Then he started to undress Henry.

Henry murmured incoherently and tried to brush Jarrah's hands away from his shirt.

"Don't you want to be clean?" Jarrah asked, pausing in his ministrations.

Clean.

It felt ages since he'd been clean. Eyeing the pristine white sheets, Henry nodded. He wanted nothing more than to be clean and to fall asleep on a soft bed with crisp, freshly laundered sheets. Actually, there was one thing more that he wanted, but Dingo was still with the doctor, they were back in what passed for civilization, and who knew when Henry would feel Dingo's body against his again?

Too weary with pain to care if Jarrah didn't, Henry allowed the man to strip him and lead him into the bathroom. He submitted to the sponge bath, feeling nothing more than gentle care, watching dully as Jarrah's dark hands passed over his own fairer skin. It was just so nice to be clean again. Jarrah even rubbed a damp washcloth over his hair. Henry felt dimly that the hotel would still have cause to mourn their sheets after he slept on them, but at least it wasn't as bad as it might have been, had Jarrah not been there.

He startled when Jarrah helped him to his feet. Despite the clean bandage, his leg burned and throbbed, and Henry felt as if he couldn't take another step without falling to the floor and crying. But Jarrah managed it so that soon he was lying against the sheets he'd craved. Jarrah pulled the covers up and tucked him in as if he was a little boy, before stroking his hair. Henry never heard the door shut behind him.

HENRY awoke to find the room dark. It felt unfamiliar all at once to be inside a building after so many nights in the jungle. He missed the noises of the birds and animals that had become a familiar background to his conversations with Dingo.

He thought it had been some sound that had awakened him and listened intently. The soft sound of a latch being clicked carefully made him stiffen in bed, prepared for Hodges or another of his government cohorts to be invading his room, perhaps to search it. His first thought was for the camera, lodged in his rucksack.

Then he felt the mattress dip and the warmth of another body against his. Dingo's scent filled his nose, and he sighed with contentment.

He turned into Dingo's warmth slowly, cautious of his leg and the other man's arm.

Without words, their lips met in the darkness with unerring certainty. The light brush of Dingo's mouth against his made him start to get hard, and Henry chuckled to find he wasn't too tired for *that*. Then he sighed.

"What?"

It was a mere whisper of sound, as if Dingo thought that they might be overheard.

"I can't help but think I've failed."

"You haven't, Dash. Not in any way."

"I didn't do what I set out to; secure a mating pair and transport them back to London," Henry said miserably.

"That's not how I saw our goal," Dingo said. "We set out to save the tiger, right?"

"Right, and I haven't done a thing—"

"If we report that we saw no sign of the tiger, that we believe it's extinct, then people will stop coming after them."

"It goes against everything I've ever believed in the name of science," Henry said. "A cover up, a conspiracy."

"If it keeps Tassie safe, what does it matter?" Dingo cocked his head to one side. "You don't think my dad is really afraid of boats and the crossing, do you? It's well known how he feels about the tiger, and if he kept coming over here, a lot of people would assume he was coming to look after Tassie.

He stays away to keep them safe. That's why I can only come over every so often, and why Jarrah stays here."

Henry opened his mouth several times and shut it without speaking. If that were so, he wasn't sure he'd ever heard of such an enormous act of self-sacrifice before. The look on Hank's face when he'd seen that striped coat flashing through the bushes on their way back as if the tiger had let itself be seen to say goodbye to them— "Maybe you're right."

"Face it, Dash, I've been right about everything every step of the way," Dingo said smugly. "Besides, how did you ever think you were going to load two crates onto a boat labelled '*thylacinus cynocephalus*' and our government were just going to let you waltz on board and sail off into the sunset? They have their own interests at heart as well."

"The King—"

"Oh yeah, mention the King's name, and all Aussies bow down and kiss the ground immediately." Dingo gave a guffaw that reminded Henry that he was in a very foreign land.

"Maybe you have a point," he conceded.

"I do."

"Your father really is afraid of boats, you know." Henry couldn't resist taking a little wind out of Dingo's sails.

"He is *not!*" Dingo protested.

Henry grinned at him; he seemed so like a ten-year-old boy protesting that his father was too the strongest, bravest man in the world. "Right, that's why he closes his eyes when he gets near the dock."

"Stop talking about my father," Dingo murmured. "Especially when I'm doing this."

Henry closed his eyes as Dingo took him in hand. He immediately hardened, and Dingo stroked him gently. Henry reached down between them to provide the same pleasure to his lover, and they moved in concert, their kisses deepening into breath-stealing intensity.

Henry was mindful that they had to keep their voices down, unlike in the jungle, where their cries had melded with the freely expressed opinions of the animals along their journey.

A gasp and the bite of Dingo's fingers into his flesh heralded the other man's climax. Henry slid in the hot fluid spilled between them, finding his own orgasm a moment later, suppressing a groan of satisfaction and relief.

He could feel Dingo's chest heaving against his as his breathing calmed, and their essence begin to cool against their skin, but he didn't want to have to move. Finally it became uncomfortably sticky, and Henry started to roll away.

"I'll go," Dingo whispered.

Henry waited, hearing the sound of water running and then stopping. Dingo was merely a black shape in a dark room when he stood by the bed, gently wiping Henry's stomach with a washcloth.

He must have dozed off, because he started again when he felt Dingo's hand slide over his shoulder and down his arm. Slowly, creakily, the two men found a position tangled together that suited both their injuries and nestled under the blankets.

Henry heard the first drops against the glass. It was nice to be safely inside with Dingo pressed up against him while the rain fell outside. Henry smiled sardonically, knowing how ephemeral the feeling of safety truly was. Despite Hodges's death, or perhaps because of it, they would soon be the focus of interest to government officials. Even now they might be camped outside his door, only waiting for first light to break in.

And the mere fact of Dingo's presence in his bed spelled another kind of danger; if that were to become known, they might be the subjects of yet another kind of witch hunt. It would be safer by far if Dingo went back to his own bed, but Henry couldn't bear to let him go.

Who knew when they might be able to lay together again?

Despite the comfort of holding Dingo in his arms and feeling Dingo's good arm around him in the dark, when the wind started to rage, lashing drops of rain against the windows as if angered that it couldn't reach them, the sound seemed to mimic the desolate cries of the two tigers when they discovered the dead cub Hodges had murdered.

When Dingo's body started to shake, Henry wrapped his arms around him and held him in his grief.

THE next time Henry opened his eyes, he was alone again—a state he supposed he would now be forced to accustom himself to. His leg had stiffened up and threatened to collapse under him when he attempted to get to his feet. He flexed his knee several times and tried again, managing to limp into the bathroom.

There was a door on the far side of the bathroom, standing slightly ajar. Henry hadn't noticed it last night, but he peered through the crack to find Dingo heavily asleep in a darkened room. Henry shut the door quietly so as not to awaken him and ran the water in the sink, waiting for it to heat up.

He gave himself a good scrub, as well as he could considering the collection of bruises, scrapes, and wounds he bore. He still felt like he was carrying the forest with him, despite Jarrah's thorough cleaning of him the night before.

Returning to his room, he noticed clean clothing on the chair, presumably left for him by Hank or Jarrah. It was a relief to put on a clean shirt and whole trousers again, but there were no socks or boots for him. *I suppose they don't want to take a chance on me running away,* Henry mused with a chuckle. No chance of that, not with the man he loved lying asleep in the next room.

He tossed the filthy remains of his jungle clothes into the trash bin, thinking back to the night at his flat when he'd tried them on, full of naïve illusions about this journey. How differently it had all turned out—

The knock on the door was quiet but insistent. Thinking that perhaps Hank had sent a waiter up with breakfast, Henry limped to the door and opened it.

Two men pushed into the room, and he staggered back against the wall to avoid a painful collision. "Here, who are you?"

One of the men was taller than he and glowered at him silently. The second was more conciliatory, bringing out a folding case from his inner pocket and holding his identification so that Henry could read it.

"William Mortimer. My colleague, Walter Robbins. We're with the government."

"Which government, Mr. Mortimer? And what business do you have with me?" Henry crossed his arms and glared at the two men.

"We're with the Tasmanian government, from the Animal and Birds Protection Board," Mr. Mortimer explained.

"And what do you want with me?"

"We know you went looking for the thylacines, in the company of one Jack Chambers." Mr. Robbins pushed himself forward for the first time. "With intent to carry one of the animals out of the country."

Henry laughed. "And you think I've got one hidden under the bed right now?"

"We want to know where Chambers is. *And* his dad," Mr. Robbins insisted.

The door between their rooms swung open, and Dingo sauntered in, looking rakish and adventurous in his dirty clothes, making Henry feel almost unnaturally civilized even though his feet were bare.

"Dingo," Mr. Mortimer said, politely.

"What are you doing here, Will?" Dingo asked, as if he didn't already know.

Henry rolled his eyes. Again! Even the government agents who were after them seemed to be on first name basis with Dingo!

"Where's Hodges?" Mr. Robbins growled.

"He's not in my bag," Dingo said dryly. "You can search the closet and the priest's hole."

Henry wanted to laugh at the wildly startled look on Mr. Mortimer's face, although Dingo's repartee didn't deter the single-minded intensity of Mr. Robbins.

"Don't give us that. We've had no word from him. Yet here *you* are."

"It's a big fucking country. People can take a while to cross it."

"Tasmania isn't that big."

"He's always had his own agenda at heart. Perhaps he's gone exploring."

Mr. Robbins scoffed at this. Mr. Mortimer looked mildly interested and spoke this time. "Mr. Hodges wasn't the type to go off on his own without informing his superior as to his plans."

"Well, I don't know what to tell you boys. What I *do* know is that he isn't here. And neither is a tiger."

"Did you find any?"

Dingo laughed. "Like I would tell you."

Mr. Robbins resumed his visual inspection of the room, and Henry twitched when he saw the agent's eyes light upon his camera.

"What would be on the film here if we were to develop it?"

Henry spoke up. "Just some holiday snaps. To show my family what I've been up to."

"They're nosy buggers," said Dingo.

"Yes," Henry said, playing along. "Quite… nosy buggers. Can't do a thing about them."

Robbins looked over at the camera with interest. "Really."

"Feel free to develop it, but don't be disappointed with the results." Henry caught the flash of alarm on Dingo's face that vanished as quickly as it appeared. He limped to the chest where the camera lay, reaching it before Mr. Robbins, who was a step behind him.

Henry turned and staggered into Mr. Robbins, dropping the camera when they collided. "Damn you! You've ruined the camera!" He kept his eyes downturned to hide his dismay as film unspooled from the open camera; all the photos of the tigers, especially the shots of Dingo interacting with them, those exquisite moments of history, all lost. It was enough to break his heart.

"That was rather clumsy of you, Mr. Percival-Smythe," Mr. Robbins said grimly.

Defiantly Henry raised his head, alert to the fact that the man had used his proper name although he hadn't introduced himself. "Sorry. But there was really nothing on film that you would have found interesting."

"I'll buy you a new camera," Dingo said.

"Thanks."

Henry looked down at the film again, sighing heavily. Even though he had seen the tigers for himself, the tangible evidence that had now been destroyed made it seem like a mere dream—a fevered fantasy no more real than those he had dreamed up while still in the college archives.

"This isn't the end of it, Chambers," Mr. Robbins warned.

"You know they're working on a law now," Dingo told him. "Soon there will be official government protection for the tigers, and there'll be nothing else you can do against them."

"Well, that day isn't here yet. And when it comes, it'll be too late for them," Mr. Robbins said.

"Get the fuck out of here," Dingo hissed.

Mr. Robbins gave Dingo one last look and stalked out. To Henry's surprise, Mr. Mortimer quietly said, "Sorry about the camera, Mr. Percival-Smythe. Good to see you, Dingo." Then he followed his partner out.

Dingo kicked the door shut after them and turned to Henry.

"It's never going to be enough."

"Who were they?" Henry asked.

"They really do work for the Tasmanian government. Robbins is a crony of Hodges's. Will's actually not that bad; he does what he can."

Henry picked up the exposed film and ran it helplessly through his fingers.

"I'm really sorry about your camera, Dash."

"It's okay," Henry said, and he believed it was. "It's not like we really could have kept those photographs a secret. The tigers are better protected if there's no evidence."

"I guess you've decided then. I admire that you had the balls to do it." Dingo paused, but Henry didn't answer. "I'll get you another camera."

"I don't care about the camera, Dingo!" It came out more harshly than he intended, and he was immediately apologetic. "Sorry, I guess it's all catching up with me."

Dingo nodded. "C'mere, Dash."

Henry willingly stepped into his arms, and they stood holding each other until time once again became inconsequential.

AFTER a couple of days' much needed rest, they, along with Hank, moved back to the pub where their Tasmanian adventure had started from. Tony had seemed concerned by their bruised bodies and beaten demeanor and doted on them. Although they kept separate rooms for appearances, they still only lived in one.

For some reason, Hank seemed to be avoiding them, but Henry was too apathetic to ask Dingo why. And he never saw Jarrah.

They didn't speak about the extreme emotions that had played between them their final night in the hotel, because it was too painful. The memories of the tigers were raw, and they couldn't revisit them just yet.

"There'll be another time and a place for that," Dingo had said in the early hours of the morning. "Just hold me, Dash."

And Henry had.

Returning to the pub brought them some more unwelcome attention, however. After having lunch their first day back there, they had trudged back upstairs to find the door to Dingo's room slightly ajar. Dingo pressed his palm against Henry's stomach to stop him from walking in and motioned for him to be quiet.

And Dingo kicked the door with such force it almost flew off the frame.

Two men were going through the belongings they'd left behind, and although they had been caught in the act, they didn't even have the decency to look guilty at being caught in the act.

"Get the fuck out of here," Henry snarled.

Dingo glanced at him in surprise before turning back to the two men. "What are you doing?"

"Where's Hodges?"

The goon advanced on Dingo threateningly, but Dingo stood his ground.

Before he even knew he was doing it, Henry stepped between them. He took a deep breath. "He wasn't one of our party."

"So you weren't traveling with him. We knew *that.*" The man seemed at a loss of what to ask next, especially confronted with two men who showed no signs of backing down.

Henry wasn't in the mood to help him; he just stood there and waited. Dingo stepped up next to him and glared at the two men.

"We want to know where Hodges is."

"Have you ever thought maybe he's double-crossed you?" Dingo smirked at them. "Maybe he changed his mind about the tiger."

"As long as he was always on the opposite side of you, his interests and ours were one and the same," the goon growled.

"Well, we haven't seen him. Now beat it!" Dingo jerked a thumb at the door.

"We're keeping our eye on you, Chambers."

"That won't help you find him. I don't have him and I don't want him."

"He's missing."

Dingo smirked. "So go look for him."

The two men shuffled their feet uncertainly, not wanting to admit defeat. At last they circled around Henry and Dingo, leaving the room without closing the door.

"More government men?"

Dingo peered into the hallway and closed the door. "They work for the same group that hired Hodges."

"What kind of crooks—"

Dingo held up a finger to his lips and said quietly. "That's the shame of it. It's not a group of criminals or even the people who supply specimens to zoos. Just farmers and ranchers who want to protect their property."

Henry shook his head in disbelief, even though he had seen enough to realize it was probably true. "And where will they go now?"

"They'll probably go and search for him, but Jarrah will have covered his, and our, tracks completely."

"And where is Jarrah? And your father?"

Dingo shrugged. "Maybe it's better that we don't know. They'll be back."

THEY slept better that night, despite the run-in with the goons. But when Henry awoke in the morning, the space next to him in the bed was cold, long vacated. He gave himself a quick wash at the basin and made his way downstairs. Tony was behind the bar, and he jerked his head toward the back. Henry nodded and found Dingo sitting in the beer garden, a cup of cold coffee sitting before him.

"Morning," he murmured, sitting across from him.

Dingo looked at him, and then he glanced at his coffee cup and grimaced at the contents. "Morning. Shall I get you a coffee? I think I could use another."

"Sure," Henry said uncomfortably.

Fortunately, Tony had already beaten them to the punch and brought out a fresh pot just as Dingo was standing up. Alone again, they silently poured their cups, and Henry wondered how to breach the alien quiet that had started between them.

It was Dingo who spoke first. “I have to go back to Melbourne.”

“Oh?”

“Yeah. I’ll have to report back to… the interested parties. And let *them* know about Hodges and what happened to the cub.”

“How will they take it?”

Dingo twirled his cup on the saucer. “Not well. But at least we managed to save the parents and two of the cubs. Although their rationale would probably be if we hadn’t gone there in the first place, Hodges wouldn’t have followed us.”

“It’s my fault,” Henry said bitterly.

“No, Dash, it’s not.”

“It is! This only happened because I dredged it all up, from following it back home. *I* made people look and keep me informed. That’s how Gordon found me.”

“Hodges already knew we were looking, because of what we were doing here anyway. He knew we kept making tracking parties into the forest, trying to observe the numbers of the tigers. It would have happened with or without your involvement.”

“That doesn’t make me feel any better.”

“Dash—”

Henry stared down at the table.

“Dash, look at me.”

Henry looked up and met his gaze.

“Jarrah said you were meant to see the tiger. You were *meant to*. Sometimes things are set in motion, and we don’t know why. Maybe you were meant to come here, for your own reasons, but you were to come away with something else entirely.”

“Like what?”

“Maybe you were meant to become their protector. Like us.”

“How much protecting can I do from England?” Henry asked.

“You have your own report to hand in,” Dingo said. “It depends what you put in it.”

“You mean lie,” Henry pointed out.

"Or protect."

"And after that?"

The moment had come. The one Henry had been dreading. Farewells and cheerios, promises to meet again that would never be fulfilled. The last goodbye. "When I woke up this morning, and you were gone, I thought—"

"I don't want to leave you, Dash. Don't you know that?"

Henry felt his blood warm, although logic prevailed. "I don't want to leave either."

"Maybe," Dingo said carefully, "just maybe, you don't have to stay in England."

Henry felt the prickles of sweat develop against his hairline. "But my whole life is back home."

"And it sounds as if you weren't that happy there."

Henry didn't answer; he couldn't.

Dingo continued prodding him. "You could start over again here."

"It would mean giving up everything."

This time it was Dingo who remained silent.

"Sometimes…" Henry said hesitantly, "it's better to stick with what you know." He wasn't sure if he could fully articulate just what he meant. He had a job, a flat, a potential career back in England. If he were to give all that up, what guarantee would he have about a life in Australia? What kind of life could he have with Dingo?

Dingo downed the rest of his coffee. "I guess that's that, then."

Before he could stand and leave, there was the sound of footsteps behind them. Hank and Jarrah entered the beer garden; Hank looked tired, but Jarrah looked just as usual, with a placid good humor that spoke of a man satisfied with his work.

"Hey, old man. Haroo, Jarrah," Dingo said.

"Boys." Hank nodded, and they took a seat.

"What have you all been up to?" Dingo asked.

Jarrah bent to extract his pack from under the table. Carefully he pulled an object wrapped in cloth patterned with a striped pattern. Henry's palm began to tingle.

"You came a long way to go home empty-handed," Jarrah said. "A gift for one who loves the tiger as we do."

Henry took the object in both hands, surprised at its weight. He hesitated.

"Go ahead, open it," Jarrah said.

Henry unwrapped the cloth, stroking the soft cotton striped with caramel, orange and brown. He uncovered a piece of sandstone. It was tan and mostly smooth with a few sparkly bits of gunmetal grey, like some sort of ore. He looked up at Jarrah questioningly, even as the feeling in his palm intensified.

"Look at it closely."

Henry picked it up and tilted it. Excitement began to build as he caught the faint lines on the surface. He recognized the line of the spine, leading to the stiff tail, the wide-spread jaw, the stripes drawn over the haunches. "Tassie," he whispered joyfully.

"A rock painting," Dingo said in a reverent tone. "Does Mary—"

"She wants Dash to have it," Jarrah assured him. "This is very old. The ancestors painted it." He licked his thumb and swiped it over the surface of the rock.

Henry gasped and jerked, as if to pull it away, but for some reason, he let Jarrah do as he wished. If he had some good reason for destroying this one as he'd done with the first—

"It's over one thousand years old. Silica has leached out of the rock and covered the painting. It cannot be washed away, no matter how many tears are shed over the tiger," Jarrah said. "Take that with you, Dash, to remember that you saw the tiger alive and free."

"I'll never forget it," Henry said.

"I know." Jarrah stood up and held out his hand to Henry. "Good journey, my brother. And Mary said to tell you she will kick your arse if you don't come to see her again. For some strange reason, she took quite a liking to you."

Henry put his precious rock down carefully on the cloth wrapper and stood up, putting his arms around Jarrah and hugging him tight. "Thank you, Jarrah. You are a true brother." And it was true, for he felt more of a bond with this man than he ever had with James.

Jarrah's arms were around him, and he heard him whisper something but the words weren't in English. Then Jarrah released him and turned to Dingo.

The two men hugged and thumped each other's backs. "Toorroo," Jarrah said.

"Toorroo, Jarrah."

Henry sat down, watching as Jarrah slipped out of the back gate of the Beer Garden. He ran his fingers over the rock, unable to believe that Jarrah could bring himself to part with such a treasure.

Dingo cleared his throat and sat down, scraping the wooden chair over the uneven pavement. Ferociously, he turned on his father. "All right, old man, talk!"

To his surprise, Hank didn't reprove Dingo. Instead he nodded, looking uneasily from one of them to the other. "I owe both of you an apology."

"That's for damn sure. What drove Hodges mad like that? Did you know he was that close to the edge when you sent us out there?" Dingo demanded.

"I rather think that I'm to blame," Hank said with a sigh. "I don't know if you remember how Clarence always used to be hanging about when you were a lad—"

"Vaguely. I do remember he was older than me and I wanted to punch his snout in."

Henry laughed. He could easily imagine after his success with Johnno that Dingo would have wanted to test his prowess on all the older boys around.

Hank sighed again. "He seemed genuinely interested in the thylacine. And in those days, the government wasn't quite so gung-ho about decimating their numbers. I used to give lectures to some of the boys who were interested in the native animals of Australia and Tasmania, take them on hikes to show them how they lived. Clarence came to me, and he seemed quite a polite boy. Timid, almost. Had no father, only his mother."

With a flash of insight, Henry said, "You became a father figure to him."

"Got it in one, Dash. Wish that I'd seen it back then, but no, I was too obtuse to pick that up," Hank said regretfully. "Baz and Johnno never liked him. I thought it was jealousy, and it was, but not on their parts. He was a right little varmint when my back was turned, but Baz and Johnno were capable of looking after themselves."

"And Dingo?" Henry asked.

Dingo looked a bit embarrassed.

Hank laughed. "Dingo was never a retiring sort. He had no trouble handling Clarence. Until—"

"Until?" Dingo leaned forward, and Henry realized that Dingo was just as curious as he.

"Do you remember when you first saw Tassie on that trip we took when you were ten?" Hank asked.

Henry and Dingo exchanged a glance.

"Of course."

"Clarence had wanted to come along on that trip. I told him family only." Hank shook his head. "I didn't handle it well. I could tell he was upset. But after you saw the tiger, I *saw* the fire in you. I knew you were the one. The one of my boys who was going to carry on with my work…."

"And Clarence felt slighted," Henry said.

"Exactly."

"And *that's* why he's been on my arse for years?" Dingo asked. "What was his game? Did he think if he arranged for me not to come back, he could move in and take my place?"

"I don't know. And whatever pathetic fancy he conjured, I didn't realize he'd become so unbalanced as to come to the point of actually being willing to *kill* for it." Hank rubbed his hands over his face. "I suspect he didn't plan on either you or he coming back from this trip. Or Dash."

Dingo looked rather shocked, and Henry felt pretty much the same. After a moment, Dingo asked, "What makes you say that?"

"He killed his guide. And from what you've said—" Hank shook his head. "He didn't tell his cronies at the department of animal protection where he was going. He no longer cared about the fate of the tiger. It was you or him, in his eyes."

"He must have been mad!" Dingo exclaimed.

"Or sick," Henry said. He, at least, had a bit of understanding for the man. This was one thing Dingo might never understand, having always had the love of both his parents. He almost felt sorry for Clarence Hodges. He rubbed his leg absently, stroking over the wound.

"Poor Clarence," Hank said.

Henry reached for his painting, wrapping it carefully in the cloth, his palm throbbing. "Will those goons be back to try and steal this?"

Dingo gave a short bark of laughter, recalling the yip of the thylacine. "They're not interested in beauty. I think your rock is safe."

Glad that things seemed a little bit better between them, Henry leaned in closer to Dingo. "There's one last thing I want to do before I leave Hobart," he told him. "Will you come with me?"

Dingo didn't even ask what it was he wanted to do and nodded. Henry could tell he had already guessed.

29. IN WHICH WE MEET BENJAMIN

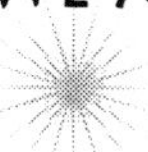

THE zoo was so still that it was almost like being out in the wilderness again. The animals were quiet and listless; they could not see any other visitors around, and even the wind seemed to be off for the day and visiting elsewhere.

Dingo miserably kicked a stone along the path. "What did you want to come here for, Dash?"

"I thought this would be the starting point of this adventure." Henry's fists were jammed deep into his pockets against the bitter cold. "It turns out it's the end of it. Like crossing the River Styx. Final. I guess I just wanted to see the last known thylacine." His tone took on a sharp edge toward the end of his sentence.

"It's depressing."

"I feel like I owe it… to them." Funny how his palm wasn't burning when he *knew* he was in the vicinity of a tiger. Henry wondered if it only worked in the wild, or if the magic had been leached out of his body along with his blood when Hodges had stabbed him.

Maybe it was a fruitless endeavor. Maybe Dingo was right, and it would bring him nothing but sorrow. But Henry felt he had to come here before he went home. To remind himself about what the journey had been for.

"Here," Dingo said, his voice full of reproach.

A small fenced-in area with dead grass, some dirt, and a tiny concrete hut. This was the home of the last Tasmanian Tiger. It burned Henry's heart to see such a pitiable enclosure when he had seen others in their natural habitat, to know that this would have been the result had he been able to fulfill his original plan.

"Bloody zoos," Dingo muttered. "Don't know what they offer, but suffering."

"That wasn't my plan," Henry said, turning to look at him. "I thought if I could get a pair, we could breed them in safety, get the numbers up again—"

"I know *you* had the best of intentions, Dash," Dingo said earnestly. "And maybe some of those other zoos did as well. But maybe some animals are better off in the wild. They just can't survive in captivity."

Henry had read enough research from around the world to know that attempts at breeding the tiger had hardly any results. Perhaps Dingo had a point. The small number of tigers still in the wilds of Tasmania might just have a chance if they were left alone.

"So where is she?" Henry asked.

The owners had christened the tiger Benjamin, and for such an animal of celebrity, her conditions were in no way relative to her worth.

Dingo pursed his lips together, and a familiar sound issued from them: *yip yip yip*.

Henry held his breath as he heard scuffling within the hut, and he was unashamed by the tears that formed in his eyes when the tiger stepped out from the gloom within. Its ears were cocked, and if Henry could be forgiven for giving the animal anthropomorphic features, it seemed to be looking around excitedly for the source of the noise—perhaps hoping for a reunion with its own kin.

Benjamin stood looking down at them, realizing that the humans were the only other animals around than the usual zoo inhabitants that it already knew by smell.

"Hello, beautiful," Dingo whispered.

The tiger yawned, showing its huge mouth, and just like that, Henry's palm began burning in his pocket. He drew it out and wrapped his fingers around the chain-link fence. Benjamin trotted over, stood on her massive hind legs, and sniffed at the two men who she now almost towered over. Henry looked into her black, bottomless eyes and seemed to see his whole adventure in Australia through them. He could see what he had been and what he had become. He could go back, but things would never be the same. He wasn't the same person anymore.

Benjamin dropped back down to all fours, and without even looking back, ran into her hut.

The spell broken, Henry stepped away from the fence, feeling dizzy.

"Dash, are you okay?"

He wanted to fling his arms around Dingo and kiss his sorrows away, but even though they seemed to be alone it couldn't be risked. He placed his hand on Dingo's arm, however. "I'm an idiot."

"What are you talking about?"

Henry looked back into the now-empty cage, his mind now filled with lines long forgotten. "'Tyger! Tyger! burning bright'," he murmured, as if he were far away.

Dingo looked as if he wanted to laugh maniacally. "You're quoting Blake at me?"

Henry looked at him in surprise. "You know Blake?"

"Every bugger who goes to school knows Blake," Dingo said scornfully. "Besides, it's my dad's favorite poem."

"Of course it would be." Henry stared back into the cage, wishing Benjamin would show herself again.

"'In the forests of the night,'," Dingo prodded.

Henry closed his eyes. "'What immortal hand or eye',"

"'Could frame thy fearful symmetry?'." They spoke the last line together.

Henry opened his eyes again and smiled at Dingo. "Do you remember the whole poem by heart?"

"Probably not all of it. I would have to call in Dad to do that."

"There's a stanza… 'When the stars threw down their spears, / and watered heaven with their tears, / Did he smile his work to see?'"

"'Did he who made the Lamb make thee?'" Dingo murmured, now remembering. "Everything's made for a purpose, Dash." He swallowed, hard. "Even us."

Henry nodded. "Even us. I think Blake got it wrong, though."

"What?"

"Well, in this case, the tiger is the lamb. Which makes the humans the tiger. We're the ones who should be feared."

"Not all of us," Dingo reminded him.

Henry shifted in closer to him, as close as he could dare. "It just makes me think. Because Jarrah's right. And you're right. I was brought here. To be one of their protectors."

Dingo waited for him to continue, not daring to interrupt.

"But I was also brought here for us, Dingo. Ever since we met, we've collided. Maybe all of this is mixed up together, I don't know. But here I am."

The look Dingo gave him was scorching, as if he yearned to scoop up Dash in his arms and holler his triumph to the heavens. But that could not be, here out in the open and in a public place. Instead, Dingo briefly closed his hand over Dash's. "Here you are."

There would be logistics to be sorted out later; Henry knew he still had to return home. But all that mattered for the moment was that the future now seemed to be open with all kinds of possibilities that had never been believed in before.

EPILOGUE

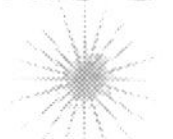

IT WAS as if nothing had changed, and yet everything had changed.

Henry sat in his office, watching the rain stream down the window, remembering the day four months ago that he'd sat there, letting his tea get cold, poring over the correspondence about the thylacine from Gordon Austin. He had dreaded meeting this colonial, Jack Chambers, whom Gordon had sent to guide him to locate his obsession.

Now he would have given anything for a sight of Dingo or to hear his cheery "Harroo, Dash!"

But he'd had to leave Dingo behind in Melbourne in order to return home and tie up all the loose ends of his adventures to the college board. They had parted without touching at the docks as Henry climbed the gangplank to the boat that would take him back to England; Dingo had been unable to secure him a plane ride. They had spent one last night in Dingo's bedroom at the Chamberses' house, and Helen and Hank had made sure to give them space. They had lain together one last time in Dingo's small bed, every inch of skin was committed to memory as their passion threatened to consume them and leave nothing behind to tell the tale. But all the way home, across the oceans, Henry had tried not to remember the look on Dingo's face as the boat pulled away from the dock and how rapidly his face had become an unrecognizable dot all too quickly thereafter.

No one had called him Dash since his return from Australia either. Once again, he had become dull, boring, academic Henry Percival-Smythe. Miss Winton, Professor Larwood's secretary, had ever so casually inquired where *that refreshing Mr. Chambers* was upon Henry's return, even while claiming that Professor Larwood was really rather busy today, Mr. Percival-Smythe, and he would surely see him tomorrow.

It had been all too easy to forget the fire that he felt within when he was in Tasmania or the burning on his palm where Jarrah had drawn the tiger. He wanted to hold onto that, but it was as if home was having a narcotic effect upon him and extinguishing all he had felt before. He missed Dingo. He missed the person he had been with Dingo—not Henry Percival-Smythe. Just Dash. He missed Dash.

Hill came in, bearing the mail on a tray with a pot of tea and a cup and saucer, setting it upon the desk just as he always had.

"Nothing's changed, Hill, has it?" Henry asked.

Hill shot him a reserved glance that Henry was at a loss to interpret. "No, sir. Will that be all, sir?"

Something was different. Something felt wrong. "Hill, what's been going on around here while I was gone?"

"I'm sure I couldn't say, sir. I just fetch the tea." Having put Henry satisfactorily into his place, Hill left the room, shutting the door quietly behind him.

Henry frowned and reached for the mail. As he did every day since returning, he hoped for a missive from Dingo. Once again, there was nothing from him. But there was a letter in a familiar hand, and he eagerly tore it open.

> March 22nd 1935
>
> Dear Henry,
>
> I know you have been back home for a while now. I have just returned from meeting with Hank and Dingo and finding out all the details of what occurred in Tasmania. I know you must want answers, and although Dingo supplied you with some of them I should give you my side of the affair.
>
> You most likely feel some sense of betrayal about how I sent you to Australia under the pretence of obtaining live thylacine specimens when all along I expected you to return home empty-handed. I do feel guilt over my deception, but you must realize, Henry, that I wanted you to become part of our team. Your interest in the thylacine was so passionate and pure that you served to remind me of myself, twenty or so years ago. I knew that once you saw the tiger for yourself, you would make the right decision on their behalf. Your addition to our ranks will only be of benefit to us and to the remaining tigers. In time we will divulge even more details, and what our future plans involve.
>
> But for now, my dear Henry, I need to make you know that I have absolute faith in you. Everything the Chambers men have told me only serves to accentuate

that. They spoke highly of you at every opportunity. You have lifelong friends in that family, and believe me, they are the best allies you could ever have in your life.

Write soon and tell me everything. I want to hear your own story in your own words. And hopefully one day soon we will meet in person.

Respectfully, your friend,

Gordon Austin

Henry sighed and folded the letter closed. He wondered whether he should destroy it, but it was a tangible link to Australia and to Dingo. He would take it home and find a safe place to hide it. There was a part of him that wanted to be angry with Gordon, but he remembered what it felt like to see a thylacine in its natural habitat and to know that in the end leaving it there was the best thing for it. So he couldn't be angry. It was a bittersweet feeling, however.

And now he sat here, waiting. Waiting for some response to the report he had turned in, some acknowledgement of the amazing adventure he had been on, even though he had returned to report failure. The extinction of the thylacine. Even though he had "proved" a negative, it was still an advance in the scientific understanding of the world they lived in, and Henry could not fathom why there had been so little response.

He got up and went to the window. He could barely see the grounds for the water streaming down the window, but a group of men, huddled under umbrellas, entering the main administrative building caught his attention.

If Dingo had done nothing else for him, he had at least taught Henry to pay attention to his instincts. Leaving the tea to get cold once more and disdaining the use of an umbrella or hat, Henry strode downstairs and out into the rain, limping only a little bit now.

He raised his face into the rain and smiled, remembering a certain occasion in Tasmania where he and Dingo had danced naked in the rain. A rush of heat suffused his body, and he hurriedly pushed the memory into the background. It was something to savor in private, definitely not a subject he wanted to be dwelling on in Lardarse's presence. *Larwood*, he reminded himself.

He took the stairs two at a time, opening the door to the anteroom without knocking. Miss Winton looked up in shock.

"Mr Percival-Smythe! You can't—you can't go in there!"

She circled her desk and took up a position in front of Professor Larwood's door, holding her arms out as if to prevent Henry's passage.

"Why, our goddess Diana. Anyone would think you weren't happy to see me!" Henry grinned as he put his hands 'round her waist and picked her up, moving her bodily out of his way, all the while wondering where he got the balls to do that. The temerity, he amended.

"Mr. Percival-Smythe!" Miss Winton gasped, patting her heaving bosom with one trembling hand.

Henry almost laughed to see the newly worshipful expression on her face, as if he had been transformed instantly into some manly hero, burst from between the covers of a romance novel to sweep her off her feet. Clearly Miss Winton had cast herself in the part of the damsel in distress and was enjoying her foray into the realms of fantasy. Suddenly he had an inkling of how Dingo must have reveled in his brash behavior. This was fun!

"Miss Winton." He acknowledged her politely. Carried along as if he had imbibed some of Dingo's intoxicating personality, he pulled open the door in time to see flashbulbs going off, and Professor Larwood standing behind his desk, holding the piece of rock for the reporters in white-gloved hands. *His* piece of rock.

Henry stood there for a moment, listening to what Professor Larwood was telling them.

"This rock is streaked with osmiridium, a very rare mineral, found in only a few places on earth. It's quite valuable, a natural alloy of osmium and iridium. Our geological department has tested the sample, and there are traces of other platinum group metals present as well. It is resistant to corrosion and useful in a number of manufacturing operations that require high-wear metals—"

"But that's not the most interesting thing about that piece of rock," Henry interrupted.

The reporters turned to look at him, sensing a scoop. One of them spoke up. "Kevin Haywood here, London Daily News. Who are you?"

"My name is Henry Percival-Smythe, with a dash," Henry said with a grin.

Professor Larwood was giving him a warning scowl, but he approached the desk in spite of it.

"May I?" Without waiting for Larwood to answer, Henry took the flat piece of stone from him, caressing it with his fingers.

"This is the truly fascinating discovery," Henry said, turning the stone around so the dully glittering minerals were hidden from view.

"I don't see anything," Mr. Haywood said, leaning closer to peer at the surface of the streaky stone.

"Keep looking," Henry advised.

The reporters gathered closer, and Henry turned the stone slightly so the light played off the surface.

"My word, what *is* that—that animal?" one of the photographers asked.

"It's a thylacine, a Tasmanian tiger, now sadly extinct. There is only one known to be alive yet, living caged in the Hobart Zoo in Tasmania," Henry explained.

"A pity about the animal, to be sure," Professor Larwood interjected, a ferocious scowl on his face. "But in the light of day, what possible use would keeping a predator like that alive, especially as it was known to worry sheep—"

Mr. Haywood ignored him. "What, in your opinion, Mr. Percival-Smythe, is the true importance of this stone, if not for the traces of a valuable mineral?"

"This is a dream painting on rock, executed by the native Aboriginal people, more than one thousand years ago," Henry said softly, struck once again by the sacrifice Jarrah had made in giving it to him. All for the tiger.

"How can you tell that?" Mr. Haywood asked skeptically. "Anyone might pick up a piece of charcoal and scratch out a crude drawing yesterday and claim it was thousands of years old."

Henry licked his thumb and swiped it over the painting, while the reporters gasped in shock. "A thin coating of silica seeped out over hundreds of years. It has protected the charcoal from the elements all these years, and now the painting is embedded in the stone, preserving it. Our geological department—" he bowed his head sardonically in Professor Larwood's direction, "—will surely be able to date this stone and give us a more precise estimate as to the true age of the painting."

Mr. Haywood seemed to be the self-appointed leader of the reporters; at least none of them challenged his dominance, merely scribbling notes as Henry spoke. "And where did you get this rock? Rumors have circulated that this college mounted an expedition to locate and secure a pair of the tigers and bring them back to the London zoo for breeding. If that was really your quest, it's fair to say that you failed, isn't it?"

Henry shook his head and laughed. “The goal of any institution of higher learning is the collection of information. My goal was to discover the truth about the existence of this creature.” His expression became dreamy as he remembered his first sight of the tiger. “Sadly, I’m afraid it’s too late for the thylacine; their day has come and gone. There is a remote possibility that in some of the more impassable areas of Tasmania some of the animals may still eke out an existence, but with development and farming, it would be astounding if the tiger stood a chance of survival. That knowledge alone is worth the price of the journey, as it should stand to enlighten us in our treatment of the fauna of any land of which we are the custodians.”

Henry continued. “The truth is that this piece of art was given to me by a full-blooded Aboriginal native, still living on the island in conditions of disgrace. Our empire has relegated these native peoples to a second-class existence in their own country!”

“Is it true they wear bones through their noses and practice cannibalism?” asked another reporter.

“That’s a fairytale. Thanks to our gracious government, the Aborigines are well educated and wear clothing just as you or I do. They purchase their food at the shops and showed no interest in getting a taste of any member of the expedition.” Henry’s lips curled sarcastically at the questions.

“Right. Well, back to the painting. What do you plan to do with it?” Mr. Haywood asked sharply.

“As the British people have such an interest in archaeological artifacts, I’d hoped that after suitable studies were carried out upon the specimen that the college would see fit to mount an exhibit open to the public. In our archives, we possess photographs, hides of the thylacine, bones and teeth. Little is known about how they live in their natural habitat. One of my contacts in Tasmania has provided me with a movie of the thylacine in captivity, which would surely interest the British people….”

As Henry continued to speak, he was aware of Larwood’s enraged flush slowly turning his face to purple. But he couldn’t stop now. He had gotten into the habit of asking himself what Dingo would do in this situation.

Granted, the answer almost always turned out to be that Dingo would throw caution to the winds and do whatever he thought would most provoke the nearest authority figure, but Henry loved playing this new role. And in some odd way, it made him feel just a little closer to Dingo.

Eventually the reporters’ curiosity was sated, even when Henry had to inform them that he couldn’t answer all their questions, simply saying that more research was needed, and they filed out. Henry shook each of their hands and collected the cards they pressed on him, promising to keep them apprised of his next expedition, whenever that should happen.

Finally, the room was empty, save for Henry and Professor Larwood. He turned to face his erstwhile mentor, mentally girding his loins in Dingo-inspired bravado.

"Mr. Percival-Smythe," Professor Larwood started icily. "The governing board of this college came to the decision that the ridiculous adventure that you set off on was not to be mentioned to the press, seeing what a lamentable end it came to. And yet, you have the audacity to burst uninvited into my office, intruding yourself into an appointment to which you were not included, disseminating information—"

"Professor Larwood," Henry interrupted boldly. "*I* am the person who went to Tasmania, and as such, *I* am the man in the best position to judge what information should be shared. Do you truly think it's in the best interests of that country to start a gold rush for an obscure mineral of dubious value? What do you think will happen to the land there? The animals? The people?"

"The resources of the British Empire are truly inexhaustible, and I see no reason why *you* should consider yourself to be the only reliable authority on how they should be used," Professor Larwood said coldly. "If the Crown should deem it to be desirable to exploit this find, that would be left up to Parliament and the King. I very much doubt that they would be calling upon *your* expertise to decide this matter."

"Well, they certainly won't be if they have no idea of my existence!"

"Considering the disgraceful spectacle you made of yourself and this college in the Australian press, I'm astonished that you had the temerity to show your face here again!" Larwood opened a drawer and drew forth a newspaper, slapping the folded paper with a force that amused Henry before tossing it onto his desk.

"I didn't reveal that the college had sent me to Tasmania," Henry reminded him.

"You didn't need to. A modicum of research would have revealed to any curious reporter that you were in our employ when you set out upon this foolhardy adventure. You managed to link the name of this fine place to a failure! A failure! Ealing College is not accustomed to failure! Especially in public!" Larwood shouted.

"I'm beginning think it was a bad idea that I turned this specimen over to you at all." Henry stretched his hand out to take up the painting.

"Don't touch that!" Larwood exclaimed. "It belongs to the college. However mistakenly, we funded your trip, and unless you repay all expenses related to your pointless… spree, you will be working to pay it back for a very long time, Mr. Percival-Smythe."

"What expenses?" Henry scoffed. "Dingo arranged for our journey to Australia so that the college was not put the expense of paying for my passage. And I paid for my trip back to England. I'll give you my personal check to replace the camera, gladly. I'm terribly sorry it was damaged, although by rights, the Australian government should be obliged to pay for that, as its agents are the ones who caused its destruction!"

"I'm certain that Sir Percival-Smythe will be most interested to hear how you've carried on here today, *Mr.* Percival-Smythe," Professor Larwood said with a malicious smile. Invoking the name of Henry's father had always worked to cow the young man into compliance in the past, and he took a perverse satisfaction in trotting out that well-worn scare tactic now.

Henry picked up his rock painting, wondering why he had always been so anxious to toe the line in the past. He knew precisely what he was doing, although it felt like taking a step out upon an uncertain precipice with a steep drop below. "Call me Dash. And tell him anything you please. After today, my behavior, good or bad, is of no concern to either of you."

He headed for the door, carrying his prize.

"What is that supposed to mean?"

Henry paused, his hand upon the knob. "It means that as of today, I no longer work for you, Professor Lardarse."

"Why—why—you—you can't—just up and leave—" Professor Larwood huffed. "You're fired!" he shrieked as Henry wrenched the door open.

Miss Winton fell into the room from where she'd been eavesdropping with her ear pressed against the door, her eyes agog.

"Pardon me, Miss Winton." Politely, Henry put a hand on her elbow to steady her. "Good day to you both. I shall vacate my office immediately."

Henry ran lightly down the stairs, barely feeling the wound in his thigh, buoyed along by the excitement of the scene. Damn it! Dingo might have something with his devil-may-care attitude after all. It was quite—*exhilarating* to tell the old so-and-so where to get off!

Henry stowed the rock painting under his jacket to protect it from the rain and made a dash for his own building. *Dash!* He laughed at the irony of it.

When he got there, Hill was standing guard in front of his door, holding a cardboard carton with a few of his books in it. “Begging your pardon, Mr. Percival-Smythe, but Professor Larwood says you’re not to return to your office. You’re to be escorted off the university premises immediately.”

Thanking his luck that he had kept the painting hidden under his jacket, Henry asked, “In that case, would you mind just fetching my raincoat out of the room, please, Hill? And my hat. Oh, and my umbrella.”

Struggling between his impulse to give Henry the cold shoulder and his natural inclination to be of service, Hill shifted from foot to foot. Finally he set the carton upon the ground. “I’ll only be a minute, sir.”

When Hill had vanished into his office, Henry swiftly bent down and concealed the painting under the pile of books in the carton. He stood up and held out his hands for his things. “Thank you, Hill.”

Hill held onto the coat and hat. “I’m sorry, sir, but Professor Larwood asked that I have you remove your coat first.”

Smirking, Henry did so, doing a slow turn for Hill’s benefit. “I assure you, the family silver is safe from me, Hill.”

“Thank you, sir,” Hill said gruffly. He held the raincoat so that Dash could slip it on, handing over the hat and umbrella.

Henry snapped the brim down, like Dingo always did, and pulled it low over his eyes. He took the umbrella and smiled at Hill. “Tell me, Hill, do I look the part of the dashing explorer?”

Hill seemed to feel safer washing his hands of the whole affair. “I’m sure I couldn’t say, sir.”

“No worries,” Henry said. He stooped and picked up the carton. “Cheerio.”

Walking down the hallway for the last time, and then down the stairs, Henry felt a moment of sadness, not so much for the place or the people, but for the relics of the tiger he left behind. He’d spent so much time with them, holding the pelt in his hands, stroking the fur, dreaming of an improbable animal in an improbable land. *That* would be what he missed most out of his mingy job.

But then he realized that the memories of actually seeing the tiger, smelling it, watching the family together in the wild, was an experience that could never be taken from him. The musty pelts could remain behind within the archives of the college. He had witnessed the tiger in person, something that, tragically, would most likely prove all too rare in the coming years.

The thought of what his father would say about all this didn't deter him at all. Henry felt that after today's adventure, his father's disapproval would never affect him quite the same way.

It was a good thing he was a frugal man, Henry thought, as he unlocked the door to his flat. It would be some months before he was forced to figure out what he was going to do next. He had always refused an allowance from his father, although his father had seemed to think that the modest way he lived was not at all suitable for a Percival-Smythe.

He locked the door behind him and turned on the fire before taking off his dripping hat and coat and hanging them in the hallway. He dug out the rock painting and settled into his chair, staring dreamily into the fire, holding the weight of the stone upon his lap, stroking over the stripes of the mythical animal.

He wondered what Dingo was doing now. And when he would ever see him again. The man had gotten into his blood, and Henry was suddenly stricken with a grief he'd been staving off ever since his return. Their lives had been inextricably bound together, not only by the sharing of their bodies, but by each owing the other his very life, several times over.

The surge of power that had carried him through the morning now deserted him, and Henry sagged in his chair, leaning his head against the cushioned back, feeling that he'd give anything to hear Dingo's voice once again.

Just then the phone rang, and Henry put his rock painting carefully onto the table by his elbow. He picked up the phone, expecting the worst: his father in a cold rage, his mother ready to induce guilt with her lachrymose reproaches, possibly Professor Larwood, threatening recriminations for making off with college property.

Instead, the line crackled with a voice with an Australian accent.

"Dash! How are you, old man?"

"Dingo!" Henry gasped. "Dingo!"

"Ready for another adventure?"

"Too right," said Dash.

CATT FORD lives in front of the computer monitor, in another world where her imaginary gay friends obey her every command. She likes cats, chocolate, swing dancing, sleeping, Monty Python, Aussie friends, being silly, spinning other realities with words, and sea glass. She dislikes caterpillars, cigarette smoke, and rude people who think the F-word (as in faggot, or bundle of sticks) is acceptable. A frustrated perfectionist, she comforts herself with the legend about the weavers of Persian rugs always including one mistake so as not to anger the gods, although she has no need to include a mistake on purpose. One always slips through. Writing fiction has filled a need for clever conversations, only possible when one is in control of both sides, and erotic romances, where everything for the most part turns out happily ever after.

Visit Catt's blog at http://catt-ford.livejournal.com/.

SEAN KENNEDY lives in the second-most isolated city in the world, so it's just as well he has his imagination for company when real-life friends are otherwise occupied. He has far too many ideas and wishes he had the power to feed them directly from his brain into the laptop so they won't get lost in the ether.

Visit Sean's web site at http://www.seankennedybooks.com/.

Dreamspinner Press
For more of the
best M/M romance,
visit
Dreamspinner Press
www.dreamspinnerpress.com

LaVergne, TN USA
20 January 2010
170569LV00009B/32/P